Charles Voysey

An examination of Canon Liddon's Bampton Lectures

Charles Voysey

An examination of Canon Liddon's Bampton Lectures

ISBN/EAN: 9783337260859

Printed in Europe, USA, Canada, Australia, Japan

Cover: Foto ©Andreas Hilbeck / pixelio.de

More available books at **www.hansebooks.com**

AN EXAMINATION

OF

Canon Liddon's

BAMPTON LECTURES

ON

THE DIVINITY OF OUR LORD AND SAVIOUR JESUS CHRIST.

BY

A CLERGYMAN OF THE CHURCH OF ENGLAND.

Prove all things; hold fast that which is good."—St Paul.

" The licence of affirmation about God and His proceedings, in which the religious world indulge, is more and more met by the demand for verification.

" Assertions in scientific language must stand the test of scientific examination."
—Matthew Arnold.

LONDON:
TRÜBNER & CO., 60 PATERNOSTER ROW.
1871.

PREFACE.

In theological controversy a disputant does not necessarily deny the *truth* of a tenet, by denying the tenet to be susceptible of a particular kind of proof. Different schools of reasoners may erect the same dogma on different bases, and the very men who refuse to admit the soundness of one basis, may resolutely cling to the dogma in connection with another. Methods of exposition are, moreover, to be assessed from the position occupied by the expositor. Protestants cannot, without grave fault, adopt a scheme of interpretation wherein the Church's subsequent definitions determine and amplify the meaning of the New Testament ; and the meaning of the New Testament, thus settled, throws significance into the Old. Avowed acceptance of such a scheme would be repudiation of Protestant principles, and application of it, without avowed acceptance, would betray either gross ignorance, or dishonesty ; but a Catholic can blamelessly follow the method from which Protestants are debarred. Father Newman, in a 'Letter' called forth by Dr Pusey's *Eirenicon*, declares even of the great St Athanasius,—" I am sure that he frequently adduces passages as proofs of points in controversy, which no one would see to be proofs, unless Apostolical tradition were taken into account, first as suggesting, then as authoritatively ruling, their meaning."

The question discussed in this volume is obviously one of primary importance, and has every claim to be treated with candid, searching fearlessness. And it is not a question merely for scholars and students in Theology ; it is also within the reach of every intelligent Christian who will honestly search the Scriptures, using the very accessible helps to the ascertainment of true Text and true translation, which now surround us.

No one acquainted with history and plain facts, will affirm that the formulated dogma of Christ's Deity has ever yet undergone the ordeal of free inquiry. However securely it may repose on the authority of a Church commissioned to reveal, it certainly has not acquired the unanswerable evidence which real, long-continued exposure to re-examination, modification, and disproof, furnishes. It has no pretensions to stand before the world as the pure net result of investigation freely applied throughout the Christian Ages. From the Fourth Century to the present hour, the dogma has been mainly upheld by modes of external force ; and though among Protestants this force is rapidly diminishing, it still exists, and exerts in Orthodox circles a very perceptible pressure.

In handling a fundamental topic, inseparable, within the Reformed Churches, from immediate and practical issues, I have taken no pains to be reserved and unreal. I shall therefore, doubtless, incur the censure of those stunted and stationary Protestants who, unhappily for their own peace of mind, cannot bar out reasonable interpretation, though they do approach the Bible with warily contrived and wholly unwarranted preliminary assumptions. But much of what I have written will probably gain the approval both of genuine Catholics and of progressive Protestants. And if I have not despicably failed in executing my purpose, my work will contribute to meet an existing need, and be welcome to students who deem love of truth a part of piety, and dread of inquiry a sure indication of faith's decay.

I expect to be credited with bad motives, but that, among Christians is a small matter. Our best intentions can never be wholly free from defects and demerits, but I possess the testimony of a good conscience, and know that I have written, and am now publishing, from motives which I can trustingly entreat our Father in Heaven to behold and bless.

The reasonings and expositions criticized are copiously, and, I believe, fairly exhibited, so that my "Examination" presents, to an unusual extent, arguments on both sides; but I wish to be read in company with the Bampton Lectures for 1866. Reading cannot always be extensive, but purely one-sided reading in controversies of vital interest, is always an evil; it can never make soundly instructed teachers of religion, and is not unlikely to mar good men.

Later editions of Mr Liddon's Lectures appear to be reprints from the second—the thoroughly revised, and presumedly final, shape of his work. I have used the third edition.

The Indexes of *Texts specially referred to : Quotations, &c.,* will, it is hoped, render reference easy.

CONTENTS.

CHAPTER I.

INTRODUCTORY.

The fault of Mr Liddon's position, and the point of view from which alone
this Examination of his Lectures is pursued.—The superiority of the
Catholic as compared with the Protestant basis for the maintenance
of Orthodoxy.—Progress of Anglican opinion regarding the Bible's
insufficiency.—Difficulty, alarm, and mischief engendered by the
attempt to ally Protestant principle with Orthodox faith.—The
doctrine Mr Liddon undertakes to defend, a crucial test of the worth
of this attempted alliance.—Defective Education in relation to the
doctrine, of both the Anglican Clergy and Orthodox Nonconforming
Ministers.—Some plausible evasions, &c., which are made to fill the
place of arguments, noticed.—Premature assertions of the spiritual
inefficiency of Christian Theism as compared with Protestant
Orthodoxy.—The obligation of the Clergy of the Established Church
to faith in Christ's Godhead, impaired by the Church's acceptance of
conflicting fundamental principles.—Excessive imposition of dogmatic propositions has resulted in sanctioned laxity of assent.—The
Anglican *Via Media* stated and criticized.—Appeal to Orthodox
Protestants, from the ground of fairness, facts, and policy.—Some
further remarks on characteristics of Mr Liddon's Lectures, and on
the aim, occasion, and method of this Examination.   .   Page 1

CHAPTER II.

Precise statement of the dogma maintained, and of some more genera
objections to which it is exposed.—Mr Liddon's theories respecting

the organic unity, perfect trustworthiness, and minute accuracy of
the Scripture records, not sustainable in the presence of free
inquiry.—His argument for the Apostolic authorship of the Fourth
Gospel considered, and some leading points of adverse evidence
stated.—On this topic, Orthodox preconceptions have the practical
advantage of forbidding intelligent criticism.—Though Mr Liddon's
method is critically unsound, and devised for the service of his
dogma, he may, nevertheless, be met upon his own assumptions, and
convicted of arbitrary and irrational interpretation of Scripture.   30

CHAPTER III.

Supposed intimations in the Old Testament, of the existence of a
Plurality of Persons within the One Divine Essence.—The plural
form of the Name of God (*Elohim*).—Significance of the Theophanies.
—Imagined Personality of the *Divine Wisdom* as depicted in the
Hebrew Canonical Books, and the Apocrypha.—The *Logos* of Philo,
Judæus, and the probable relation of Philo's speculations to the Fourth
Gospel.—Periods of Messianic Prophecy in the Jewish Canon.—
Supposed evidence for Christ's Deity in the *Psalms, Isaiah, Jeremiah,
Haggai, Zechariah,* and *Malachi,* examined.—Reckless and unwar-
ranted reference, on the part of Mr Liddon, to Rabbinical litera-
ture.   46

CHAPTER IV.

Brief criticism of the argument entitled, " Our Lord's work in the world
a witness to His Divinity."—Christ's authority and kingship.—Characteristic 'originality and audacity' of His teaching and plan.—Evidence
for the contemplated universality of His kingdom.—Difficulties attaching to the supposition that genuine words of Christ are recorded in
St Matt. xxviii. 19, 20.—Are the 'Synoptical accounts of our Lord's
Nativity in *essential* unison with the Christology of St John's Gospel?'
—The argument concerning the 'Doctrine of the Eternal Word in the
Prologue of St John's Gospel' examined.—Strong contrasts between
the accounts in the Synoptists, and in the last Gospel, of the time and
manner in which our Lord's Messiahship was freely made known.—
The reasonable conclusion from a general view of his Gospel is, that
the latest Evangelist did not intend in his Prologue to affirm the absolute Deity of the *Logos* or *Word.*   72

CHAPTER V.

Discussion of texts supposed 'expressly to assert the doctrine of Our Lord's Divinity;' viz., 1 John v. 20; Titus ii. 13 ; Romans ix. 5 ; Philippians ii. 6–11.—Examination of Mr Liddon's exposition of passages in the Epistles to the Colossians and Hebrews, and in the Apocalypse. 89

CHAPTER VI.

Illuminative action of the Holy Ghost, and presumed resulting unity of Apostolic doctrine.—The 'incidental expressions implying a high Christology in St James's Epistle,' considered.—Supposed evidence favouring the dogma of Christ's Godhead, in St Peter's Missionary Sermons.—Difficulty involved in the constant ascription of our Lord's Resurrection, to the power of the Almighty Father.—How far are John ii. 19 and x. 18 able to bear out the summary assertion, 'Christ raises Himself from the dead?'—Argument from the Missionary Sermons continued.—Argument from St Peter's General Epistles.—'St Jude's implications that Christ is God.'—Rational statement of the evidential purport of the documents referred to in this Chapter. . 125

CHAPTER VII.

Dissection of the reasoning by which Mr Liddon endeavours to show that 'Christ's Deity is bound up with St Paul's whole mind,' and is implicitly taught throughout his Epistles.—In reality the Bampton Lecturer refuses to take the point of view which St Paul's writings, and other New Testament Scriptures, incessantly present.—Doctrine of the Real Presence in the Holy Eucharist.—Mistaken deductions from the Epistles to the Ephesians and Colossians.—Some additional imaginary implications of a Christ, Divine in the sense maintained by the Lectures.—Adverse testimony of St Paul exhibited, and an appeal made from the ground of that testimony, to the honesty, intellectual conscientiousness, and common-sense of Orthodox Protestants.—Catholic Churchmen not liable to this appeal. . . . 149

CHAPTER VIII.

The title *Son* as expressive of relationship to God.—Supposed indications, in the Old Testament, of a Divine Sonship internal to the Being of God. —Synoptists' use of the title *Son of God.*—Mr Liddon's attempt to show that *the Son* is identical with *the Logos* or *Word*, and that the two descriptions complete and guard each other.—The expanded title, *Only-begotten Son.*—Weakness of Mr Liddon's position metaphysically. —His view of the bearing of the miracles upon the question of Christ's Person.—His deductions from the Self-assertion exhibited in the first or Ethical stage of our Lord's teaching.—Difficulties connected with our Lord's exposure to temptation, &c.—Mr Liddon's arbitrary evasive treatment of a troublesome saying reported by two Evangelists.— Inferences drawn from the authoritativeness of Christ's teaching.—Did He ratify the Pentateuch as a whole? 180

CHAPTER IX.

Mr Liddon's view of the second stage of our Lord's public teaching depends almost entirely on materials peculiar to the Fourth Gospel.— These materials discussed in detail, and shown neither to warrant Mr Liddon's deductions, nor to contain the presumed dogmatic revela· tions of Christ's Co-equality and Essential Oneness with the Father. —No consciousness of Eternal Being is unveiled in John viii. 58, and there is no justification for connecting that text with Exodus iii. 14. 200

CHAPTER X.

Supposed evidence that the Sanhedrim condemned Christ for claiming to be God.—The Title, *Son of God,* never in Jewish estimation equivalent to *God,* or more than a Messianic designation.—Force of the Exclama· tion attributed to the Apostle Thomas, when he was convinced of Christ's Resurrection.—The argument from certain sayings in the Synoptical Gospels assumed to be closely similar to sayings found in the 'Gospel according to John.'—Baseless, reprehensible, and irre- verent character of the dilemma : 'If Jesus Christ is not God, He is not morally good.'—Language ascribed to Christ Himself is, plainly and often, not rationally reconcileable with the Dogma of His God- head. 235

CHAPTER XI.

Examination of the Scripture testimony adduced in support of the proposition : "From the earliest age of Christianity, Jesus Christ has been adored as God."—The terms which precisely and definitely describe the worship and service due to the Supreme Being, are never connected with the Name of Christ.—Detailed investigation of the feeble and forced pretexts on which Mr Liddon relies.—Meaning of the expressions, *to call upon the Lord*, and, *upon the name of the Lord.*— Dying petitions of St Stephen.—Words of frequent use, and specific, restricted application, denoting prayers and vows to the Almighty, are never used of petitions addressed to Christ.—The prayer at the election of the Apostle Matthias, was offered to our God and Father, not to our Lord Jesus Christ.—Argument from the prayer of the disciple Ananias, and from the first prayers of St Paul, examined.— Supposed recognition in St Paul's Epistles, of prayer to Jesus Christ, including the Apostle's entreaty to be freed from the ' thorn in the flesh.'—Strained and erroneous constructions of passages in St John's First Epistle, and Apocalypse.—Brief summary of the evidence that Christ was *not* worshipped as God.—A glance at some arguments from the earlier Fathers.—Frequency of devotional addresses to our Lord Jesus Christ in the Anglican Book of Common Prayer.—Remarks on the action of the Clergy, and on the use of Family Prayers, and Hymns, wherein Jesus Christ is studiedly equalized with the Father, in the language of supplication and praise. 252

CHAPTER XII.

Texts which imply or assert Limitation of Knowledge in Christ.—There is nothing to prompt or justify Mr Liddon's forced explanations.—Asserted illuminative power of the dogma of Christ's Deity, in relation to the Atonement.—Examination of an attempt to meet the objection that the dogma detracts from the value of Christ's Life as an ethical model for Mankind.—The dogma cannot be shown to be morally fruitful in giving intensity to Christian virtues, and is not calculated to promote the devotion of the heart to God. 294

CHAPTER XIII.

The doctrine defended by Mr Liddon is, wholly and necessarily, outside the
sphere of reason.—Even the explicit statements of the Creeds cannot
be rationally harmonized, and are fitted for a blindly confiding rather
than a reflective and intelligent reception.—Utter insufficiency of the
supposed Scriptural testimony for Christ's Godhead ; and recapitula-
tion of the adverse testimony.—Mistaken impressions kept up by false
statements in Commentaries, Sermons, &c.—The Church's teaching
cannot be fairly appropriated without an acknowledgment of the
Church's paramount authority.—This fact appears to have been at times
forgotten, even by great Fathers in the Church.—Necessity for an
explicitly-speaking Supreme Tribunal.—The inevitable outcome of
Protestant principle.—Conclusion.   312

Supplementary Note.   331

INDEXES.

Texts specially referred to.   .   339
Quotations, and some principal Topics.   341

AN EXAMINATION

OF

doctrine Mr Liddon undertakes to defend, a crucial test of the worth of this attempted alliance.—Defective Education in relation to the doctrine, of both the Anglican Clergy and Orthodox Nonconforming Ministers.—Some plausible evasions, &c., which are made to fill the place of arguments, noticed.—Premature assertions of the spiritual inefficiency of Christian Theism as compared with Protestant Orthodoxy.—The obligation of the clergy of the Established Church to Faith in Christ's Godhead, impaired by the Church's acceptance of conflicting fundamental principles.—Excessive imposition of dogmatic propositions has resulted in sanctioned laxity of assent.—The Anglican *Via Media* stated and criticised.—Appeal to Orthodox Protestants, from the ground of fairness, facts, and policy.—Some further remarks on characteristics of Mr Liddon's Lectures, and on the aim, occasion, and method of this Examination.

ANY true doctrine would be imperilled if defended from ill-selected and untenable ground. Mr Liddon, with anxiously good intent, has done the dogma he maintains the disservice of exposing its weaker side, and presenting it on a basis which, in fact and logic, is utterly unsound. No transient popularity, and

A

AN EXAMINATION

OF

LIDDON'S BAMPTON LECTURES.

CHAPTER I.

INTRODUCTORY.

The fault of Mr Liddon's position, and the point of view from which alone this Examination of his Lectures is pursued.—The superiority of the Catholic as compared with the Protestant basis for the maintenance of Orthodoxy.—Progress of Anglican opinion regarding the Bible's insufficiency.—Difficulty, alarm, and mischief engendered by the attempt to ally Protestant principle with Orthodox faith.—The doctrine Mr Liddon undertakes to defend, a crucial test of the worth of this attempted alliance.—Defective Education in relation to the doctrine, of both the Anglican Clergy and Orthodox Nonconforming Ministers.—Some plausible evasions, &c., which are made to fill the place of arguments, noticed.—Premature assertions of the spiritual inefficiency of Christian Theism as compared with Protestant Orthodoxy.—The obligation of the clergy of the Established Church to Faith in Christ's Godhead, impaired by the Church's acceptance of conflicting fundamental principles.—Excessive imposition of dogmatic propositions has resulted in sanctioned laxity of assent.—The Anglican *Via Media* stated and criticised.—Appeal to Orthodox Protestants, from the ground of fairness, facts, and policy.—Some further remarks on characteristics of Mr Liddon's Lectures, and on the aim, occasion, and method of this Examination.

Any true doctrine would be imperilled if defended from ill-selected and untenable ground. Mr Liddon, with anxiously good intent, has done the dogma he maintains the disservice of exposing its weaker side, and presenting it on a basis which, in fact and logic, is utterly unsound. No transient popularity, and

A

no confirmation of disquieted but credulous waverers, can ultimately compensate for the damage he may thus inflict. He denies that the tenet of Christ's veritable Godhead was, in the natural sense of the word, a development. He will not even concede, it was "related to the teaching of the Apostles as an oak is related to an acorn." He pronounces its real relation to their teaching to have been "that of an exact and equivalent translation of the language of one intellectual period into the language of another. As a matter of fact the Nicene fathers only affirmed, in the philosophical language of the fourth century, what our Lord and the Apostles had taught in the popular dialects of the first. If, then, the Nicene Council developed, it was a development by explanation. It was a development which placed the intrinsically unchangeable dogma, committed to the guardianship of the Church, in its true relation to the new intellectual world that had grown up around Christians in the fourth century." (Pp. 428, 429.)

Now, these assertions unequivocally embody the proposition— the Divinity of Jesus Christ, as taught by the Church, is the probable, rational, and fairly provable sense of Holy Scripture. They exclude the ideas of progress, growth, and revelation, in the consciousness of the Church, and they refuse to recognise the Church's possession of unwritten Apostolic traditions which either supplemented the incompleteness, cleared the ambiguities, or shed necessary light on the concealments, of the written Word. However far Mr Liddon's phraseology may at times diverge from that of ordinary orthodox Protestants, he here proceeds upon distinctively Protestant principle, and proffers his dogma to be tested by the Bible thoroughly investigated and reasonably understood. To prove his confidence justified, and his conclusions sustained, by the Bible, is the one great end of his carefully-compiled, and, from his own side virtually exhaustive, pleadings. If he had not thus chosen to stand upon indefensible ground, I should not have ventured to criticise his Lectures. Against the evidence for the doctrine of our Lord's Deity regarded as a revelation through the Church, or, as resting on ecclesiastical authority, I have said nothing. The Christian Church is as grand a fact in the world's history as is the Bible, and, with reference to the doctrine under consideration, the mind of the Church Universal has long displayed a perspicuity, explicitness, and uniformity of expression, of which the Bible is conspicuously destitute.

If Orthodoxy is to be retained, some comprehensive preliminary assumption *must* be made, and the assumption that the Church is the divinely-appointed organ and vehicle of Christian revealment, the Bible being a subordinate factor in the Church's hands, seems to me incomparably more simple, expedient, and valid, than the assumption that the Bible is the one inspired and sufficient repertory of the dogmatic faith proclaimed by the *later* two of the three great Creeds. Each assumption has its own special difficulties, but the former is not like the latter, self-refuting, and rife with decomposing elements. If it should be urged, an inspired Book does not address the rational intelligence, and is not to be rationally interpreted—the Church is in effect brought back under the character of interpreter, with an authority hampered and obstructed in administration, but not really limited and controlled. Granting, for argument's sake, that inspired and authoritative Scriptures can be ascertained and assured without the Church's aid, still, the choice of Orthodoxy must lie between reasonable interpretations which challenge scrutiny, and decrees which demand assent; in other words, between the findings of free individual judgment and the ordinances of the organized body; or, putting the antithesis in its most condensed shape, between reason and the Church.

Into the question of the Church's title to authority, I have in no degree entered, and therefore should not have the right, if I had the desire, to impugn any Article of the Church's Creeds. My examination of Mr Liddon's representations is conducted entirely upon the hypothesis, that Protestant principle in relation to the sufficiency and sole supremacy of Scripture is true; and while confining myself to this hypothesis, I have been unable to escape the conclusion, that the dogma Mr Liddon advocates is false. The Catholic principle which acknowledges, within the human exterior of ecclesiastical organization, the secret infallible guidance of the Holy Ghost as an abiding source and guarantee of dogma, is disallowed by Mr Liddon, not controverted by me. Though Protestants may be demonstrably unable to hold, without inconsistency, the doctrine of our Lord's Divinity, yet, if Catholic principle is firm and sound, the doctrine has a sure foundation. The subject-matter about which the following chapters are employed, is not, therefore, the truth or falsehood of a doctrine, but the security or insecurity of a foundation on which a minority of Christians have attempted to erect that doctrine.

In debating the point which Mr Liddon's method raises, we go to the very heart of modern theological controversy. No intelligent observer can have failed to notice how, ever since the great Tractarian revival of Church sentiments, a conviction of the Bible's inadequacy as the rule and fountain of orthodox faith, has been spreading and deepening among the more thoughtful of the Anglican clergy. With more or less thoroughness and consistency, nearly every Anglican writer of note has sought to throw upon Church authority some portion of the vast burden which pure Protestantism throws upon the Canonical Scriptures. Indeed, we may safely affirm that, among the clergy of the Established Church, only the shrunken and intellectually bankrupt party, called Evangelical, now tries to combine Orthodoxy with strictly Protestant views of the nature and office of Scripture. Anglicans of every shade of Churchmanship, from Moderate to High, perceive Orthodoxy to demand something more than the Bible for its groundwork.* This perception is the mainspring and core of the High Churchmanship, which some unreflecting Protestants, who are loud-mouthed for orthodox beliefs, so incessantly misconceive and vilify.

An apprehension of the Bible's inadequacy is often incongruously qualified by a professed retention of the Bible as a standard of doctrine and court of appeal ; but inquiry easily elicits that the retention is peculiarly conditioned. The canonical standard must be applied, and the appeal in the court of Scripture must be prosecuted, by those who thoroughly believe the Church's dogmas—by those who bring to the handling of Scripture ecclesiastical enlightenment, assured information, and faith already systematised. To collect from the pages of the Bible the distinctive features of Orthodoxy, decided mental bias and prepossession are needed. The conclusion to be reached must be seen, and grasped, and cherished, before the investigation is begun. The Bible is explored for illustrations of the explorer's

---

* I had marked for quotation, in illustration of this fact, passages, from the fifth of Dr Jelf's Bampton Lectures for the year 1844 ; from Dean Goulbourn's "Farewell Counsels of a Pastor to his Flock" (Sermon VI.) ; and from the calmly effective volume, entitled, "The Bible and its Interpreters," by Dr Irons, recently Vicar of Holy Trinity, Brompton. But it seemed needless to support a statement which no moderately well-read man will be inclined to deny.

The delicate sensitiveness of the perception to which I refer, has been lately manifested in the intrepid protests of some Churchmen, and the deep murmurs of many, against the mingling of a few heretical scholars among the selected Revisers of the English Version. Learning and sincerity, without orthodox opinions, do not qualify a man to take part in translating the Church's Book. Minds not taught by an external authority the true sense of the Sacred Volume, may be expected to misunderstand, with pertinacious blindness, some of its most momentous dogmatic words.

faith, or to do the laudable service of ingeniously reconciling discrepancies between Biblical statements and the explorer's previously accepted opinions. It is only under conditions which make the invocation practically insincere, and the response settled beforehand, that the Bible is invoked on the dogmas of the Creeds respecting the Divine Nature. The felt, though not always confessed, necessity for such conditions is the root of the difficulties which thwart every plan of general elementary religious education. No sensible person denies the existence of great and most essential features in religion, about which all believers in a personal God and Father, and a life beyond the grave, are agreed. The duties of devotional and moral service, obviously comprised in the two great commandments—to love God, and to love our neighbour; the efficacy of prayer for spiritual blessings; the sense of sin; the expectation of entering in the next life upon a portion suited to the character we have formed in this; the broad belief that Jesus Christ is to us a Messenger, Instructor, Example, and Master, sent and inspired by God; surely, these things might be deduced from, and enforced by, the Sacred Writings—would cover all the morals and religion necessary for social purposes, and would lay an ample and a solid foundation for the reception in after years of any dogma not glaringly devoid of evidence and consonance with the religious sentiments.

But men who identify Christianity with the definitions of the Nicene and Athanasian symbols, are governed by a suspicion, tantamount to persuasion, that nothing short of training in explicit dogmatic faith from infant years will suffice to ensure orthodox conviction. They perceive in the saying of Jesus concerning little children—*of such is the kingdom of heaven*—a pointed reference to the receptiveness, and easy flexibility with which a child's mind learns to wear and revere the bandages of inexplicable doctrinal statements. By early habit, dint of repetition, and close pinioning of what is weak, to what is cogent and reasonable, the end must be achieved, towards which, developed intellect and devout feeling are worse than unequal means. The more minds not ecclesiastically indoctrinated in childhood, believed in One God and Father—the more they gave earnest heed to spiritual things, and appreciated practical Christian virtues, the less likely would they be to admit the Church's conception of a Trinity, and its dogmatic pendants. Their spiritual wants would be satisfied without a merely verbal analysis of the One God into three Persons, or a real division of the One Divine Nature into three Gods; and their reason, freely searching

Scripture, would be unable, by any defensible mode of interpretation, to extract from "the popular dialect employed by our Lord and His Apostles, the intrinsically unchangeable dogma which the Church has affirmed in the philosophical language of the fourth and subsequent centuries." Unsuccoured by the bent of early and heavily-impressed bias, the mature intelligence of a cultivated mind would be peculiarly unlikely to attain the proportions of ecclesiastical orthodoxy, or to comprehend how *person* can mean anything but a complete individual Being, and *three* anything but one thrice counted.

The truly Protestant view of scriptural interpretation, vividly stated in Professor Jowett's celebrated Essay, is very objectionable in the eyes of many who profess and call themselves Protestants.

"The office of the interpreter is not to add another interpretation, but to recover the original one; the meaning, that is, of the words as they struck on the ears or flashed before the eyes of those who first heard and read them. He has to transfer himself to another age; to imagine that he is a disciple of Christ or Paul; to disengage himself from all that follows. The history of Christendom is nothing to him; but only the scene at Galilee or Jerusalem, the handful of believers who gathered themselves together at Ephesus, or Corinth, or Rome. His eye is fixed on the form of one like the Son of Man, or of the Prophet who was girded with a garment of camel's hair, or of the Apostle who had a thorn in the flesh. The greatness of the Roman Empire is nothing to him; it is an inner not an outer world that he is striving to restore. All the after-thoughts of theology are nothing to him; they are not the true lights which light him in difficult places. His concern is with a book in which, as in other ancient writings, are some things of which we are ignorant; which defect of our knowledge cannot, however, be supplied by the conjectures of fathers or divines. The simple words of that book he tries to preserve absolutely pure from the refinements or distinctions of later times.

"The growth of ideas in the interval which separated the first century from the fourth or sixth, makes it impossible to apply the language of the one to the explanation of the other. Between Scripture and the Nicene or Athanasian Creed, a world of the understanding comes in—that world of abstractions and second notions; and mankind are no longer at the same point as when the whole of Christianity was contained in the words, 'Believe on the Lord Jesus Christ, and thou mayest be saved,' when the

Gospel centred in the attachment to a living or recently-departed friend and Lord."

Although, among nominal Protestants, there are increasing numbers who discern the moral and spiritual sovereignty of the Church, and see in her the depository, guardian, and living channel of truth revealed by God to man, yet a frank unconditional confession of what they discern is comparatively rare, and from the confession when made, an orthodox multitude vigorously dissents. The effect of this is, as might be surmised, very palpable, and full of injury to religion. Dependence upon the better foundation is not avowed, and discussion conducted upon the other foundation is avoided, in virtue of a logical insight truer and deeper than loudly-repeated professions.

The subject selected by Mr Liddon supplies the crucial test of Protestant principle in its relation to the Church's Creeds. If that principle is, in its results, compatible with the ecclesiastically prescribed faith of the fourth and more immediately succeeding centuries, on the topic of Christ's nature and attributes, then, the future of orthodox Protestantism may be anticipated without misgivings ; but if the principle is not commensurate with the Church's Creeds, orthodox Protestantism is drifting to complete and speedy wreck. Not only the clergy, and a growing section of the better-educated laity, in the Established Church, but the ministers of orthodox Nonconforming communities also, are beginning in various degrees to see or scent the danger. At present, however, there is little visible movement outside the Anglican body ; sensibility is roused, but intellect is repressed and passive. Orthodox men are too often ready to denounce and stigmatise those who unveil the obnoxious facts that must sooner or later be faced. They chafe at opposition, recoil from inquiry, and try in practice to make puny and contemptible individual *dicta* fill the place of the vast and venerable dogmatic authority which Protestant theory rejects. With respect to Christ's Deity, they seem to be wholly bereft of the tranquil reliance on truth's power and eventual triumph, which ought to flow from inward assurance that the doctrine is from Heaven, and has a verifiable, trustworthy foundation in the written Word of God. This sensitive and distrustful frame of mind can be traced in the exaggeration, and excited obliquity of vision, with which they meet the supposition that the Uncreated, Imperishable Essence comprises only a single Personality. Some of them would appear to be even incapable of conceiving faith in God, unless such faith embraces the notion of a Triad of coequal Beings within the Divine Nature, to each

of Whom all the attributes of Deity pertain. The denial of
Christ's Deity is, in their view, equivalent to Atheism.

Now, if this mental attitude is not the fruit of barely suppressed
involuntary scepticism, it is the fruit of gross ignorance. The
ingrained prejudgments of early education, and the defects of
ministerial training, suggest that, in the greater number of instances, ignorance is the malady under which the Protestant
clergy are labouring. Their theory enjoins the exercise of individual reason and conscience, but their habitual practice
neglects the means by which alone rational beings can test the
worth, and if need be, correct the leanings, of educational bias.
They have, and rather pride themselves on having, as regards the
central topic of controversy, only a knowledge which is in effect
the worst kind of ignorance—knowledge of one side. The majority of the men who now enter the ranks of the Anglican priesthood, study nothing in theology, beyond Butler's Analogy, Paley's
Evidences, the fifth Book of Hooker, and standard expositions of
the Thirty-nine Articles, and the Apostles' Creed. The Old and
New Testaments are, of course, read with the notes of approved
commentators, and with a view to mastering the arts of intrusion
and inference, the latest editings of the legacy of elaborately-con-
trived expository methods by which the junction between Holy
Scripture and traditional dogma is effected. Some knowledge of
Church history, also, is acquired from handbooks of trusted and
orthodox complexion. Coming after the deeply-instilled lessons
of childhood, and according with impressions interlaced with
every form of habitual devotion, this process has been, on the
whole, cheeringly successful in producing obstinate adherents, and
dogged defenders, for the foregone conclusions from which investigation has been warded off. Similar circumstances, and a similar
process, would create faithful ministers of religions which have
but a small fraction of the moral and spiritual beauty, the power
and self-luminous truth, which are enshrined in the undogmatic
precepts of the religion of Christ. The risk of free-thinking is
provided against, and the feelings attuned to repel, with fractious
irritation and disgust, the first approaches of reasoning against
predominant dogma. In the persons of the ordained teachers of
Christianity, the traditional faith is thus entrenched, so far as
human means permit. Some avoidless danger arises from the
presence, in the educated and more influential classes, of many
who have not been moulded by training after the clerical fashion,
and their breadth of view, added to the diffusion of a freely inquisitive and sceptical literature, tends to diminish the clerical

horror of inquiry, and occasionally so far breaks down the barriers of pre-engaged feeling, that even staunchly evangelical minds are betrayed into examination and its results.

Another, though perhaps lesser, source of jeopardy, is contained in those secular portions of every gentleman's education which develop and exercise the rational faculties, and encourage the pursuit of truth for its own sake. But this danger has been in a measure obviated by recruiting the clerical ranks from Theological Colleges, instead of from the Universities ; and, if Protestantism is to continue its unnatural alliance with the Church's tenets, the expediency of enlarging and multiplying such Colleges, and stocking them with students whose capacities for belief have been as little as possible affected by a liberal culture, becomes matter for serious consideration. The strengthening and enlightenment of the intellectual powers by the methods of secular education, have a marked tendency to indispose the mind for the compliant faith, which can cement into one composite rule, a supremely authoritative book addressing reason and conscience, and a traditional interpretation of that book, setting reason at defiance.

Even among the more scholarly and better-informed of the Anglican clergy, there are very few who have taken the one easy, and absolutely needful, step towards an intelligent, honest, and steadfast belief in Christ's Deity. Not one in a hundred has tested and consolidated his hereditary faith by a close study of the arguments which those who differ urge against it. What the majority know of the adversary's case, has been gleaned from controversial teachers on their own side.* The treatises of Bishop Bull, Waterland, Jackson, and Archbishop Magee, added to books already mentioned, are presumed to furnish the mind perfectly, whereas, in reality, when taken alone, they confirm preconceptions without enlarging knowledge. No man can arrive at a stable and enlightened conviction on a debated question, unless he reads, reflects upon, and mentally grapples with, the view opposed to his own, presented and enforced as an earnest competent opponent would present and enforce it. When our information comes exclusively through writers in one camp, we are very

---

* The excellent Dean of Chichester, whose historical work, "Lives of the Archbishops of Canterbury," is so admirable, appears, in his Introduction to "The Church and the Age," feelingly to deprecate investigation into inherited opinions on fundamental dogmas. What could have prompted him to expend his valuable time, and pleasant English, upon the shallow Essay entitled, "Anglican Principles?" "Soothing Syrup for Aged and Infant Anglicans," would have been a more appropriate title.

unlikely, whether our opinions are right or wrong, to understand
a contested point. Our persuasion, be it what it may, is not, in
relation to ourselves, morally and intellectually healthy and secure.
And this general maxim is especially true in regard to that not-
able doctrine which was eagerly fought over in the fourth century, and has never, since the sixteenth century, lacked keen-
witted and irrepressible assailants. Other doctrines have been
assailed by greater numbers, and with greater enthusiasm, but
no doctrine has summoned opponents so uniformly above average
in ability, cultivation, and fearless appeal to the plain rational
sense of Scripture. The conception of the Personal Unity, as
opposed to the Personal Plurality, of the Divine Nature, has,
since the Reformation, been asserted with a force of reasoning,
and an undaunted reliance upon Scripture, which ought to compel the attention of every theological student. The subject is
confessedly of no secondary moment, but of the primest importance. The Unitarian doctrine is no " paradoxical speculation
with which the public mind may from time to time be astonished
or amused," but is of a thoroughly fundamental, crucial character. Yet the mastery of one standard Unitarian book is no part
of prescribed clerical preparation in the Church of England, and
is an exceedingly rare accomplishment among her better-read
divines. How, then, can the truth be known, or the dogma that
Jesus is God, if true, be effectively maintained ?

And the choicer specimens of orthodox Nonconformist ministers, are in no better plight than ourselves. They study the
pages of Pye Smith, or Wardlaw, or Moses Stuart ; are familiar
with commentators of repute in their own community, and, perchance, with Church of England authors, but not one in a
hundred reads Wilson, or Yates, or Andrews Norton.* Their
students, like ours, are acquainted with the most formidable,
though not the most demonstrative of adversaries, only through
the writings and lectures of their own controversialists and professors ; in other words, they are not honestly and genuinely
acquainted with the adversary at all.

The deficient and discreditable state of theological training

* These are standard authors on the Unitarian side. With Professor
Norton's " Statement of Reasons," &c., I am well acquainted. It is, as
might be supposed, very able and suggestive, but not, I think, quite adapted
for general reading. Wilson's " Scripture Proofs and Illustrations of Unitarianism," I have recently looked into, but not closely examined. Its plan
seems good and exhaustive, and re-edited by a competent hand it would
leave little to be desired. Of Yates' " Vindication of Unitarianism," I know
nothing, except that it is very highly esteemed by members of his own communion, and has passed through several editions.

among adherents to Protestant principles, necessarily produces the results unhappily so common, namely; a dread of inquiry—a consciousness of insecurity—an aversion to apply the Bible as the sole and Divine Rule of Faith—a prompt uncharitableness, and rising venom, whenever the tenet of our Lord's Deity is referred to in any terms but those of vehement affirmation and ostentatious assent. There is, manifestly, some more deeply-seated feeling than mere dislike to disturbing but legitimate polemics; there is the logical distrust which attaches to suspected foundations and insufficient means of defence. And when controversy is ventured upon, plausible evasions, supercilious cant, and thinly-disguised insolence, are apt to take the place of reasoning.

The mysteriousness of the great ecclesiastical dogma is often pleaded on behalf of its reception without inquiry, but the plea is valid only in conjunction with the announcements of a living, explicitly speaking authority, and does not touch the question whether the sacred writers held and inculcated the dogma. If Jesus be indeed God, the mystery of His Being oppresses and baffles the understanding, but is no bar to definite and distinct statements of *the fact* of His Godhead. A mystery can be unambiguously preached, and clearly implied, without being explained. The point at issue is, not the intelligibility of the proposition, " the Son is equal to the Father as touching His Godhead," but the presence in Scripture of the proposition itself, or of testimony which warrants the proposition. The search is not for a solution of the mystery, which, if real, may well be insoluble, but for the existence of the mystery. To arrest examination by the cry of mysteriousness is, therefore, poor subterfuge. But when this subterfuge is not permitted, the ungracious cant of spiritual self-complacency too frequently crops up. Hearty acceptance of the dogma is said to pre-require a certain moral condition, the absence of which indicates defect in spiritual-mindedness, humility, and love of holiness. In this complacently ill-bred suggestion, however, two plain facts are overlooked: (1), That the question is an intellectual one, so far as it pertains merely to the existence of particular evidence; (2), That, so far as it pertains to the formal conception of the dogma for which evidence is presumed to exist, it belongs entirely to the domain of the speculative intellect, and not of the religious emotional sentiments. A want of healthful moral and religious interest—an undeveloped or perverted spiritual condition—may, doubtless, disincline men from faith in the primary supersensible realities

to which the religious components of our nature point, and which
reason does not contravene ; such as, the disembodied life of the
soul, and the existence, perfections, and moral government of an
Omnipotent Creator, Who is also the Helper and Father of His
creatures, and holds intercourse with their spirits. These realities,
together with the grand lines of our duty to God and to our
neighbour, are forms of truth which cannot be rightly apprehended without moral earnestness, but which cannot lose by
scrutiny, speculation, and experience. They have no need to
shun the light, and are commended and strengthened by re-
investigation. But the theory of Christ's Godhead stands quite
apart from realities of this class, and cannot be associated with
them otherwise than by an arbitrary and artificial junction. To
bind ecclesiastical dogmas upon primary religious truths, for the
purpose of making proofs of the latter bear the weight of the
former, may be an astute, but is not a very respectable device.
Before theologians, rendered irascible by scarcity of reasons,
resort to impertinent innuendoes about the moral condition of
their fellow-Christians who, having examined, cannot accept certain theories, they would do well to ponder seriously how far
their own moral condition may be disordered by educational
bias, excited feeling, and neglect of single-minded, painstaking
search. Protestant ministers are, in virtue of their own fundamental maxims, under strict obligations of intellectual duty
towards God and towards their brethren ; when they shall have
fulfilled these obligations, they will be better qualified to talk of
other men's " moral condition."

Conceding, as we must, freely and thankfully, the existence
and claims to recognition, of moral affections, predispositions,
and sentiments which favour, and lead up to, the acceptance of
some constituent features in Christianity, the question meets us,
What are these features ? are they the dogmatic definitions, or
the more general and deeper ethical and spiritual truths ?
The most traditionally-minded Protestant, if he be also a man of
ordinary truthfulness and acumen, will not contend that moral
intuitions and spiritual instincts, such as (taking a much-cited
class for example) conviction of sin, self-condemnation, doubt
of pardon, point to precise doctrines, but to undetailed though
actual relations between responsible creatures and their Creator.
All real instincts of our nature, whether spiritual or physical,
have corresponding truths and objects ; but for the rightful
apprehension of these truths and objects, the inquisitive and
constructive exercise of the intellect is needed. Mere sentiment

is a blind guide, and our best intuitions can but indicate directions for the excursions of thought. The sentiments belonging to an imperfect and slowly unfolding rational constitution, must be liable to every degree of suppression, deflection, and perversion ; and it is an observed fact, that deformities and distortions are, to a considerable extent, capable of hereditary transmission. Moral affections are also exposed to the influences of sympathetic contagion. In connection with the religious emotions, especially, particular forms of expression and manifestation strengthen and propagate themselves, during periods more or less prolonged, by the mere infection of existence, and in spite of demonstrable and even monstrous errors. Whenever, therefore, spiritual instincts, moral sentiments, and primary religious tendencies are appealed to in defence of concrete theological theories, the first inquiry must be, Have these underlying elements been fairly interpreted, or pervertingly handled ?

The class of feelings and intuitions to which I have, for the sake of illustration, referred, reminds us of attempts sometimes made, to engraft upon the sense of guilt the orthodox conception of the Atonement, a conception which makes the co-equally Divine *God the Son* take upon Him an apparel of flesh and blood, in order to satiate and satisfy, by obedience, sufferings, and death, the righteous judicial demands of *God the Father*. But may not every suggestion really wrapt up in the sense of guilt, be more genuinely met by the revelation of a Father who forgives *freely* the imploring penitent, and, through His own quickening presence in the soul, helps to generate and deepen the emotions of penitence, and the hunger after righteousness ? The upbraidings of conscience, the alarms of remorse, the cravings for assurances of release, are not the only instinctive witnesses to a Holy God, with which our souls are furnished, and are witnesses singularly susceptible of developments, partial, exaggerated, twisted, and false. Spiritual instincts as deep and real, but displaying other aspects, are not to be excluded ; they are, indeed, softening, consolatory, and corrective of the hard despair engendered by self-accusing remorse. Hope, trust, and love witness for a tender and helpful God, Who is not extreme to mark what is done amiss ; and there is, in the human heart, the capacity, encouraged and sustained by the intellect, for a strong faith that our heavenly Father has towards us, infinite stores of the forbearance and loving-kindness which He commands and enables us to cultivate towards each other.

The appeal to native moral predispositions, and primary

spiritual instincts, is quite legitimately made when we are examining the foundations of theological doctrine, but let it be made equitably, not in a partisan spirit, and with a view to create that muddled mental atmosphere, which favours the reception of orthodox mysteries, and the protracted substitution of current phrases in place of intelligible ideas. The moral condition of a man as regards his religious belief, is not blameworthy, unless ; (1), he wilfully rejects a sufficiently well-authenticated external revelation, or, while professing to accept it, refuses to search out and be guided by its meaning ; or unless ; (2), he captiously objects to tenets which are " commended to the mind as true in themselves, and are in harmony with other truths, and with those general principles of belief, which belong to the constitution of our rational nature." The moral condition of a Protestant who is unable to collect from the Bible satisfactory proofs of Christ's Godhead, is not, therefore, blameworthy.

The " moral condition of the recipient " argument, has some collateral accessories slightly less offensive than itself. One of these is, that our own better nature responds to the orthodox doctrine of Christ's Person. If this vague statement is not an insinuation aimed against the better nature of opponents, no more is really meant than that the doctrine, when its verbal expression has been carefully adjusted, may be restrained from collision with truths which correspond to instinctive religious susceptibilities and cravings. Response to our devotional nature is a plea which Protestants should handle with extreme caution. Catholics of the Roman Communion can show that the *cultus* of the Blessed Virgin meets wants of man's devotional nature, no less really than does the worship of Deity in a second personal Form incarnate in Jesus Christ.

A Continental theologian of pre-eminent learning and ability, traces the existence of an historical parallelism between the gradual exaltation of the Virgin Mary, and the Deification of her Son :—

" The history of the worship of Mary, offers one of the most instructive parallels to that of the dogma of the Deity of her Son. In our days, and notwithstanding the very powerful reasons which may be alleged from ancient Catholic Orthodoxy, the great majority of ardent Catholics have declared themselves in favour of the dogma of the Immaculate Conception, without exactly knowing what this may mean, and just because profound devotion to Mary finds more satisfaction in proclaiming this doctrine than in denying it. The gradual deification of Mary, though slower in its progress, follows, in the Romish Church, a course analogous to that which the Church of the first centuries followed, in elaborating the Deity of Jesus. With almost all the Catholic writers of our days, Mary is the universal mediatrix ; *all power has been given to her, in heaven, and upon earth.* Indeed, more than one serious attempt has been already made in the Ultramontane camp to unite Mary in some way to the Trinity ; and if Mariolatry lasts much longer, this will probably be accomplished in the end."—Réville : *History of the Dogma of the Deity of Jesus Christ* (p. 75).

Sometimes experience is cited, and Protestant champions proclaim loudly, "Take away belief in Christ's Deity, and you take away an element of mighty attractive and awakening power." But when scrutinised, their assertion is found to rest on an assumption of the belief's being in itself a spring of vital energy, rather than the eternal and generally acknowledged verities with which in concrete fact the belief is always joined. Moreover, in comparisons between the effectiveness of Christian Theism on the one hand, and the theories of the Sacerdotal and Evangelical schools on the other, the enormous force of sympathy and example attending widely prevalent and historically rooted opinion is systematically forgotten. But with the gregarious multitude, this force is equal to most potent evidence, and averts inquiry. The circumstance that a particular tenet has been for a long time, and pretty generally, maintained, suffices to draw the bulk of mankind into professions and acts for which they have never attempted to qualify themselves by cogitation and research. Except with the thinking few, devotional feeling and practical piety have unfolded themselves in association with implicit uninquisitive faith in orthodoxy. All living religion is, in the ideas of the vast majority of Christians, entangled with the acceptance of Nicene and Athanasian theologies. We should beware, therefore, of instituting comparisons for which no proper materials exist ; and it is very premature to talk of the failure of Christian Theism to reach the hearts of millions, and to produce the spiritual effects of the Gospel as presented in Evangelical and Catholic preachings. All introductions of new doctrines, and all reformations of old, are, in their earlier stages, unavoidably open to the charge of spiritual feebleness. They have to fight against heavy odds, and to win their way slowly. And if the swelling agitation of theological thought in this country, is fated to carry Protestantism to the natural issues of primary Protestant axioms, the progress at first will be among the educated, and not among the unreflecting masses, who, even with the Bible in their hands, are very slowly incited to the trouble of searching what the Bible is, what the Bible means, and, whether traditional, systematic theology is not composed as much of worthless husk as of precious kernel—as much of the inventions and mistaken inferences of men, as of the revealed and rationally verifiable messages of God.

Popular enthusiasm, and the surgings of excited religious emotions, are not likely to be at once allied with pure Monotheism, though Monotheism may include every ingredient needful to satisfy the intellect and quicken the heart. Fifteen centuries of inherited tradition, the assent of successive generations numbering hundreds of millions, and the admixture of unchanging, inestimable truths, are influences which, when they concur, break up tardily, and cannot break up at all, without lowering for a time the pulse of religious life. If their ecclesiastical progenitors have taught for doctrines the commandments of men, consistent Protestants must not fancy they can undo the error without suffering much obstruction, persistent misrepresentation, and the payment of a penalty in the temporary derangement of the very sentiments they prize most, and most ardently hope to expand and intensify.

But when impotence for the production of spiritual results is contrastingly laid to the charge of Theistic or undogmatic Christianity, the question may in all fairness be retorted, What marked spiritual results is Protestant Orthodoxy now capable of producing? Does it lay hold of, arouse, and satisfy cultivated minds? Do not educated men, in augmenting numbers, either fall away from it wholly, or yield to it no more worthy tribute than torpid acquiescence and timid conservatism? In minds disposed to investigate, it survives less and less through the conviction that it is true. Its remaining chance is with the bigoted, the ignorant, and the unthinking. In its missionary labours, it is powerless whenever it is called to confront cultured intellects trained in the more refined and spiritual forms of non-Christian faith. What has it ever been able to accomplish among Mohammedans, Jews, and educated Hindoos? What is it doing in any country of Europe to revive among the masses the old lively faith in its own distinctive tenets, or to raise and purify morals in the common relationships and transactions of life? If anything has been effected, the effect has assuredly not been in virtue of the dogma that God is Three Persons rather than One Father, but, in virtue of truths which are the property of Theism as much as of Ecclesiasticism. What orthodox Protestantism did achieve, in times differing in moral and mental atmosphere from our own, is fast disappearing now, because it built upon the emotional, without a proportionate regard to the intellectual, capacities of our nature. When it can manifest, either at home or abroad, some conquering might and vitality, it may excusably venture to decry the spiritual efficacy of Christian Theism, but not before. The Theists may justly reply :—" With your great possession of numbers, and your many prescriptive advantages, we should confidently expect to propagate our faith rapidly, and to make the One God and His commandments universally known and honoured."

When variations of moral character and religious opinion, in successive family generations, are ascribed to definite causes, conjecture almost necessarily adulterates deduction ; but Theists may, at the least, claim to be as successful as orthodox Protestants, in producing descendents of sound morality and settled convictions. The lapses of Evangelical offspring from the faith and morals of their fathers, are only too observable ; and its own intellectual deficiencies generally ensure the failure of Evangelicalism in the second educated generation. Broad facts, in the present day, prohibit Protestant Orthodoxy from boasting of superior moral and spiritual effectiveness.

And further ; when comparisons are instituted, Theists may justly complain against the identification of their faith in a God intelligibly One, with the peculiarities and somewhat arbitrary narrowness of Socinianism. The reformed communities which have continued rooted in the Trinitarian tradition, would probably not be gainers by an equitable historical comparison with the dryest and coldest formal Socinianism. Faults and deficiencies, almost equally grave, though very diverse, would be seen to exist on both sides. But the Socinianism of bygone times is not identical with that rectified faith in the One God and Father, which, as distinguished from faith in Three Persons, each of whom by Himself is God, is the chief element in the unorthodox Christianity now rising in its might to wrestle with Catholicism for the suffrages of spiritually-minded thinkers. And it would be vain to deny that progress has been made, and fruit of righteousness borne. The assaults on slavery, and other social evils in America, were led by Unitarianism ; and in the instance of slavery, undoubtedly, were long opposed by Orthodoxy. Of Theistic faith Réville's summary is strictly true :—

" It has spread with marvellous success in America. From

Boston, its principal centre, it has been diffused throughout New England, and amongst the other States. Such names as those of Ware, Channing, and Theodore Parker, are in themselves sufficient to shed lustre upon a religious communion of recent date. Even more than in England, has it extended in America beyond the Unitarian Churches, properly so called, and this chiefly amongst the Universalists and the Society of Friends. Without exaggeration we may say, that it is in fact the religion of the majority of enlightened men in the young Republic. From it have sprung the great movements in matters of philanthropy and social reform. The unity of God—Christ recognised as the great revealer and the model of the truly religious life—love as being the essential attribute of God, and constituting the essential quality of the Christian,—such are the invariable characteristics of this remarkable tendency."—*History of the Dogma of the Deity of Jesus Christ* (p. 139).

The desperate plea is sometimes advanced; " Unitarianism makes no progress among the poor." Theists, of course, reply by frankly admitting the passively obstructive power of ignorance, thoughtlessness, and intellectual dependence. The plea is, indeed, only another symptom of the tendency produced by theological prepossession, to build on the ground of mere habit and blind sentiment, when driven from the ground of intelligence. The doctrinal religion of uneducated men and women, consists usually of prevailing tenets unreflectingly absorbed, and held with an obstinacy proportioned to the lack of thought. The practical piety and conscientiousness of the poor are often bright and elevating, and their errors and superstitions are not the reprehensible consequences of neglected intellectual duty.

But it may be said; members of the Established Church, and more especially the clergy, are, in all honesty, debarred from Theism, being bound by solemn promises to continuance in the orthodox faith. The authoritative documents and formularies of the Church affirm the doctrine of Christ's Deity with such explicitness as to leave no room for doubt, no licence for discussion. The case may perhaps be so, and would without doubt be so, if the Church had not, in her sixth Article, pronounced Holy Scripture to be the sufficient rule and repertory of the Christian faith ; in her twentieth Article declared the sense of God's Word written, to be superior to, and restrictive of, the Church's decrees and expositions ; and, in her Services for the Ordination of Priests and Consecration of Bishops, exacted an engagement that the Sacred Scriptures shall be the fountain of doctrine, and the diligently-consulted standard and guide. These Articles and Services throw the clergy in the most emphatic way, not upon decisions of doctrine, which the Church has ruled, and not upon interpretations to which the Church witnesses, but, upon the Bible itself, as the source of sound doctrine and the bulwark against error. If their expressions are to be taken in the plain, unadulterated, legitimate meaning, the Bible is made supreme, and individual judgments are invited and enjoined to ponder its teaching, and follow its light. The rudimentary Protestant principle is taken for granted, and applied. The Holy Scriptures are constituted the sole visible, external, sovereign instrument, from which the revelations and precepts of God are to be sought and accepted. The Church rears no Article of the faith upon her own illumination and authority, but refers all to Scripture, and prescribes that all shall harmonise with, and bear to be tried by, Scripture. Between Holy Scripture and private judgment, no dominant mediator, no divinely-delegated instructor, is made to intervene. If there is not express affirmation that Scripture was written for the very purpose of teaching the faith to all the ages, there is the assumption that, in matter of fact, Scripture is the single, adequate, authoritative criterion and embodiment remaining to us of Apostolic doctrine.

On the other hand, it may be argued; the Church imposes on the minds and consciences of her clergy Thirty-nine Articles, and the general significance of copious Liturgical Formularies, thus making incumbent the acceptance of particular interpretations of Scripture, and forbidding the supposition of her either encouraging or allowing the exercise of private judgment in deductions from the Written Word. In particular, she has distinctly affirmed the doctrine of the Trinity, and unreservedly endorsed the three Creeds. Her appeal to Holy Writ is, therefore, merely a notification that therein she has found, and directs her clergy to find, such and such tenets. The conclusions to be arrived at, are in reality dictated, but, in exuberant confidence of their truth, investigation is solicited, and even enjoined. The one foundation on which the whole superstructure reposes, is the authority of the Church; but the authority is shown in expounding an original and a wealthy deposit, not in imparting a continuous revelation.

But disguise the fact how we will, there is a most real and confusing incongruity between declaring the Bible to be the one sufficient fountain and evidence of Christian doctrine, and imposing Articles and Creeds containing hundreds of propositions, not a few of which admit of no respectable scriptural proof. Reference to the Bible is nugatory when what we are to find in the Bible is prescribed with so much elaboration; and the royalty of the Church is reduced to a name when her proclamations are submitted to the test of Scripture, explored by individual judgment. The contrariety between Catholic and Protestant first principles is indestructible; though shackled together, and imprisoned within the legal fences of an Establishment, they are not reconciled, and can never be true yokefellows.

The practical effect of the position our Church occupies, is the enfeeblement among her clergy of the sense of moral obligation to believe her dogmas. By her unguarded appeal to the Bible she has granted so much freedom, and by her multitudinous propositions inflicted so much constraint, that her hold upon the conscience is loosened, and her moral rights abridged. When religious opinions are dictated, it is, before all things, necessary that the constitution and methods of the dictating authority should be clearly and concordantly defined. If discordant premises are avowed, and perplexing directions given, the claim to prescribe is forfeited, and the sense of obligation sapped. And the Church of England does appear to be justly exposed to the indictment of having attempted to amalgamate irreconcileable axioms, and to build upon two incongruous foundations. This may not have been suspected by her remodellers in the sixteenth century; they may have failed to perceive all that their own legislation of compromise involved; but the letter of their enactments, and not their ignorance or their intentions, is the law of the Church. Assumptions virtually at variance with each other, and methods which cannot be harmonised, are mutually counterpoising, and leave the mind unbound, to the full extent of their discrepancy. The fate of the sitter on two stools is proverbial, and nowhere more certain than in the imposition of Articles of theological belief.

And over and beyond the general deteriorating result of inconsistent primary principles, the doctrine of Christ's absolute Deity is surrounded with oppositions of thought and expression, which make the voice of unambiguously authoritative injunction doubly needful. The Articles begin with an announcement of the Divine Unity. " There is but one living and true God, the Maker and Preserver of all things." Now, if inquiry, reflection, and freedom of thought are not prohibited, this simple declaration will appear to most minds effectually to set aside, and render hopelessly unmeaning, the subsequent statements : " in the Unity of this Divine Nature there be three Persons of the same substance, power, and eternity ; " and, " the Son is very and eternal God of one substance with the Father." To ensure the reception of propositions so conflicting, a supreme revealing authority must be recognised in them. The Catholic Churchman does recognise such an authority, and, with the recognition and consequent submission of mind and conscience, his difficulties are ended, and his way is logically clear. But the orthodox Protestant, with his theories about the right and duty of private judgment,—his professed dependence on the Bible alone,—and his depreciation of the Church's revealing functions, is in the anomalous posture of inviting inquiry, while in practice, and by indirect reasonings, he with tremulous vigilance treats the dogma of Christ's Godhead as a point settled for ever, and on no account to be re-investigated or re-opened. In the insuperable difficulty of intelligible and consistent explanation, unorthodox men, of course, discern a demonstration that the dogma ought not to be made a term of communion. They refuse to believe that, in the good news from God, salvation is made to hang upon faith in exceedingly abstruse and enigmatical, not to say flatly contradictory, definitions respecting the Infinite, Uncreated Nature.

Arguing from the mysteriousness which no one is disposed to deny, they contend that, presuming the actual existence of a mystery beyond our knowledge, or our capacity for knowledge, we are not thereby justified in making the mystery a subject for minutely formal statements. If the intelligence of orthodox Protestants had not been terribly dulled and debased, under a system which, without bowing to a supreme infallible voice, scorns logic, thought, and history, there would be recognised in mysteriousness the most conclusive of all reasons against imposing definitions ; because the very idea of a mystery is, that which the mind cannot grasp and formulate. No man, or society of men, while abjuring the Church's authoritatively interpreting and revealing functions, is legitimately empowered to bind upon the conscience doctrines which have not reasonable evidence, and do not admit of reasonable detailed exhibition. To what have Sectarian attempts to state and impose dogmatic puzzles tended ? have they not plainly tended to weaken united witness in favour of simple spiritual truths, and to thwart united action for good ends ?

To these considerations might be added the admitted laxity engendered by the foolish, immoral, and as experience proves, inefficacious form of Clerical Subscription in the Established Church. The quantity of matter imposed is so excessive, that legislative interference has recently diluted the quality of the assent, and now, with a sanctioned reduction of meaning, candidates for Holy Orders gravely aver their agreement with a mass of propositions, the chief of which their Protestant theological preceptors devoutly hope they may never thoroughly examine. But the impolicy and worthlessness of Clerical Subscription, as now exacted, belongs only incidentally to my subject. It conspires, however, with other and more important considerations, to relieve consciences from that sense of obligation to faith in the Deity of Jesus, which declarations of assent to the doctrine contained in the Anglican Articles and Liturgy, might not unnaturally be expected to awaken.

Earnestness and conscientiousness, when joined to intelligence, afford no guarantee that a Protestant who has been caught in the meshes of Clerical Subscription will either rescind his vows, and cease from the exercise of his ministry, or try to frame his faith and teaching according to the notions and aims of the divines who compiled the Articles and Book of Common Prayer. In many, perhaps the majority of instances, devoted and upright men who are able to see, will disregard the pretensions of a system whose rudimentary principles nullify each other, and will shape their conduct simply by their perceptions of duty to God, and what they believe to be His truth. Ministrations within the Established Church, occupy the most advantageous position for the dissemination of precious spiritual truths, and for the promotion of moral improvement and practical piety. The duty of continuing to act from this advantageous position, is, to many morally keen and sensitive minds, the motive which determines their course, and emancipates them from all sense of bondage and uneasiness on account of past pledges to believe and inculcate a mass of propositions, which would still be wantonly burdensome, even if they did not jostle. They adhere to one fundamental base of the Church's teaching; and the quantity of inconsistent formally enjoined material, their adhesion causes them to cast away, does not, after the first pain of awaking to the perception of a difficult situation, disturb the serenity of conscience. This I take to be a true account of prevalent feeling among the consistently Protestant, or Broad Church, Anglican clergy. The retrograde and impracticable device of engrafting Protestantism on to Catholicity, they leave to men whose wisest and most dutiful aspirations are directed to the avoidance of unsettling inquiry, and the perpetuation of the motley doctrinal structure which satisfied the more eminent English Reformers.

There is, however, a modification of the device just named, not destitute of plausibility; a cautiously-adjusted middle way, which a few years since enlisted the suffrages of learned and able men; but it always exasperated hearty Protestants, and it is now seen to fall short of a tenable and coherent Catholicity. Put in its best form, the position known as the *Via Media*, may be thus stated:—The Primitive Church possessed an oral tradition setting forth *explicitly* doctrines which Scripture contained only *implicitly*. The growth and settlement of interpretation practically incorporated this tradition with Scripture, and in the dogmatic enunciations of the first four General Councils, the whole of the Church's inherited knowledge in its bearing on controversies of faith, was exhibited in due correlation to the Divine written Word, so that no more room was left for development and elucidation. The Bible presents obscurely and germinally, the Bible and the Creeds present perspicuously and definitively, the whole counsel of God, so far as that counsel need be compacted into Articles of a common faith. Further developments by definition are unnecessary, if not mistaken, and would certainly be spurious should they involve new articles of belief.

Now, this position is evidently an abandonment of Protestant principle, and the query inevitably occurs; What faculty passes judgment adverse to developments beyond the date of the fourth General Council, or beyond the enunciations of the Athanasian Creed? The answer must be, reason; and if reason is competent for that decision, why is reason to be precluded from examining whether the Creeds bring out, add to, or contravene the meaning of Scripture?

From the Catholic side, too, exception may be justly taken at limitation, which seems unwarranted and capricious. If the central verity of orthodox Christianity was, in effect, trusted to the knowledge, and formal unfolding, of the Church, it is certainly probable that points of minor importance were committed to the same instrumentality. Why should the three Creeds accepted by Anglicans, be supposed to exhaust the Church's stores of traditional enlightenment, and the corresponding Scriptural supply of minute dogmatic germs which elude the eye of rational research? Why are Papal supremacy, Masses for the dead, Purgatory, and Invocation of Saints, excluded? The ability to find, in the document of which she is the guardian and expositor, senses which none but herself can descry, is a standing manifestation of the Church's prerogatives and mission. It attests at once, her endowment with peculiar wisdom, and the wonderful adaptation to her office, of the Book whose mystic recesses she alone is able to penetrate. If it should be said, the Church, though orally inheriting Apostolic doctrine not explicitly contained in Holy Scripture, has been merely the witness and historical conduit for the descent of that doctrine, then, her teaching is surrendered to every customary method of rational investigation, and we are brought back again to the Protestant basis.

I know well, how irksome these statements will appear to men who, in the honest infatuation of prejudice and half-knowledge, are sure Protestantism brings no peril to the dogma of Christ's Deity. They eagerly re-echo—"the Bible does teach the dogma to rational and painstaking searchers,"—and they can perceive nothing illogical, and no forfeiture of moral claims, in offering the Bible to individual judgment, and, at the same time, dictating the most momentous conclusion to be reached. I can only entreat them, for the sake of the doctrine itself, as well as for their own sakes, to give themselves to the task of diligently searching the Scriptures, with the single view of ascertaining, from the indications those Scriptures furnish, what were the mind and meaning of the writers. Let them, at least, try to acquire that familiarity with Scripture, without which it is impossible to understand Scripture. If, in any other department of knowledge, they had to encounter opponents who differed from them about the sense of a document, they would righteously insist that the diverse interpretations should both be carefully studied, or, at all events, that the document itself should be read without predeterminations and bias. Let them accord to the Volume, for which they profess so deep a reverence, the fair treatment they would accord to any other document they sincerely desired to understand. Let the inquiry not be, what does the Church teach? or, what do the bequeathed and widely-accepted traditions of ages teach? but, what saith the Scripture?

No Protestant who is cognizant of the large variety of opinions entertained by men who start from the same fundamental maxim,—"Scripture alone is sufficient,"—needs to be reminded how easily errors harden into theories which are transmitted and buttressed through generations of blindly confiding and immovably obstinate adherents. Ecclesiastical history, as Protestants read it, is one continuous note of warning against human liability to falsehood and corruption, and human persistency in upholding false doctrines which have once gained a footing. If the Bible is, indeed, the sole sufficient rule and storehouse of doctrine, the reference to it should be incessant, free, and watchfully impartial. For the genuine Protestant, who would keep a good conscience towards God and towards his brethren, there is no other course. What would a Trinitarian Protestant think of some sturdy Mono-theist who should be abusively confident in his faith, without having weighed the Trinitarian scheme of interpretation, or endeavoured to look at the Bible from the Trinitarian point of view? Timidity, reserve, reluctance to study conflicting expo-sitions on prominent and presumedly vital points, are, in men who make the Bible their standard, suggestive of weak diffidence and moral cowardice, if not of culpable negligence and positive dishonesty.

The mere fact that a stream of traditionalism on the subject of Christ's Deity, has flowed on in Protestant communities from the time of the Reformation, is no proof the stream is the tide of truth. The Reformation in England accepted, and permitted to survive, most things not manifestly corrupt and mischievous. The removal of practical evils was far more aimed at than the purification of dogmatic theology. Wherever dogmas were struck, the blow was instigated by crying abuses with which they had become entwined. Whatever did not directly minister to the usurpations and vicious procedures of the priestly order was very generally retained, and, unquestionably, large sections of existing ecclesiastical exposition were, by tacit consent, preserved intact; and thus a potent directing impulse, not yet spent, was carried over into Protestant interpretation of Scripture. In the pathway of untrammelled, searching, and rational understanding of the Bible, this impulse has been a stubborn impediment, causing men to stop short with assuming the Canonical Writings to afford ample proofs of Christ's Godhead; of which, in reality, they afford no proof whatever, unless they are subordinated to the Church's light and supremacy. But reflecting Protestants in these days are ceasing to be satisfied with the assumption. They are beginning to act upon their distinctive axiom, and to feel they must either renounce that axiom, or abide by the con-sequences it entails.

No policy can really be worse for Protestantism than the policy of suppression and half-information, which is in vogue at theo-logical seminaries. The claims of the Church are repudiated, the claims of the Bible are, indeed, laid down in theory, but are neutralised in practice, by the weight of received, unsifted inter-pretations, and the opinions of selected commentators. No foundation is felt beneath the feet, no rudimentary principle or preliminary assumption is heartily grasped and fearlessly reasoned from. Theological students are not encouraged to be candid, unshrinking, and consistent in the application of any fundamental aphorism. The very aim of their education would seem to be the production (as varieties of individual material may determine) of unreasoning, tenacious bigots, and of apprehensive faint-hearted shufflers, unacquainted with the strength of their adversaries' position, and the details of their adversaries' tactics, and so, utterly unable effectively to repulse their adversaries' assaults. If fear, hatred, and contempt of heresy, can be instilled without any frank examination of heretical arguments, the grand end of orthodox Protestant theological training would appear to be achieved. That this state of things is not extremely perilous, no sensible man will imagine. The surface may for awhile be kept smooth, but the doctrines shielded and fostered by such false methods are being surely undermined and betrayed.

Even in theology, nothing but truth and straightforwardness can eventually prosper. And it is not truthful and straightforward proceeding to parade the Bible as far as the Bible will serve, and then, by sleight of hand and under cover of the Bible's name, to import ecclesiastical assumptions. If the notion that Holy Scripture, reasonably interpreted by its own light, is the sole and sufficient Rule of Christian faith, is mistaken, let it be resigned ; if it is correct, let it be boldly adhered to, acted upon, and admitted in all its logical results. Whether the notion is or is not compatible with Orthodoxy, cannot be tried by a better and more crucial test than the dogma for which Mr Liddon argues. If it fails with respect to this dogma, its failure in relation to Orthodoxy is complete and irreparable.

But whether it fails or not, every man set apart to the Clerical office, should be compelled by his theological education to subject it to severe scrutiny, and so, to estimate its real worth. Lack of knowledge of the Scriptural argument, as set forth by those who doubt or deny the co-essential Godhead of Jesus, is a real disqualification for the effectual discharge of Ministerial duty. The individual faith of the teacher is timorous and intellectually nerveless; he is tempted continually to cast his burden upon man, and to lean upon a *consensus* of great divines ; cogitation, search, reliance upon God, and " God's written Word," are, in practice, abjured, and the pages of fallible orthodox commentators are resorted to, for consoling and conclusive corroboration of prejudgments already backed by powerful incentives, and therefore needing, the more urgently, scrupulous inspection and testing. The faith of the taught unavoidably suffers, and is mentally too sickly to endure trial, because it stands upon deficient and delusive instruction. Intellectual defencelessness is not, indeed, immediately, though it is ultimately, a fatal flaw in religious belief. What has been remarked upon another subject, by a great leader of thinkers in our day, is especially applicable to faith in religious dogmas, and to none more than to Protestant faith in the Deity of our Master Jesus Christ.

" So long as an opinion is strongly rooted in the feelings, it gains rather than loses in stability by having a preponderating weight of argument against it. For if it were accepted as a result of argument, the refutation of the argument might shake the solidity of the conviction ; but when it rests solely on feeling, the worse it fares in argumentative contest, the more persuaded its adherents are that their feeling must have some deeper ground, which the arguments do not reach ; and while the feeling remains, it is always throwing up fresh entrenchments of argument to repair any breach made in the old."—(J. S. Mill.)

But, as regards a dogma so grave and aspiring, we ought not to rest satisfied with the unfixed, temporary tenure of blind but earnest feeling. Real lovers of truth will not be at ease in the habit of listening delightedly to reason in confirmation of long-descended theory, while reason is refused a hearing against that theory. Neither will they be content to call even their dearest prejudgments, their " highest religious feelings and instinctive perceptions," and they will hesitate to give themselves airs of profound philosophy, in " evolving from their own inner consciousness " a theological dogma which defies consistent exposition.

If, by a searching, and, I trust, thoroughly fair examination of Mr Liddon's appeal to Scripture, I can help others to see the true basis on which the Orthodox doctrine concerning Christ's Person must be placed, my object will have been gained. For a dozen years after my Ordination, I was as firmly convinced as any man who had read a good deal on one side of the question and nothing on the other, could be, that a reasonable exposition of Holy Scripture yielded the conclusion of Christ's Godhead. But a popular Evangelical book, in which Jesus was everywhere, and God our Father almost nowhere, provoked suspicions that Protestant orthodoxy was, in its central feature, out of Scriptural method and proportion, and repeated examinations (the last in company with Mr Liddon) have convinced me of the inability of unbiassed individual judgment, rationally exercised, to deduce from the Bible the doctrine of Christ's co-equal Deity. Assuming the doctrine to be from God, facts of the plainest character appear to compel the admission that He has seen fit to promulgate it, not through the Sacred Volume, but through the living voice of a divinely-organized and divinely-inspired Church. Men who esteem Orthodoxy a vitally precious possession, gain nothing, and risk the loss of everything, when they strive to put the doctrine on a basis different from that which the Almighty in His wisdom has chosen to provide.

For the matter of the following pages I have no apology to offer, and do not deprecate any just criticism, however stringent and severe. I only ask at the hands of Reviewers who may deem me worth their attention, "the same measure which I have meted." I have tried, with anxious care, to present Mr Liddon's case equitably, and to reproduce and dissect the whole strength and substance of his reasonings from Holy Scripture. His treatment of critical questions bearing upon the accuracy and authorship of the Sacred Books is extrinsic and incidental, and so, in consequence, is mine. For a full and adequate discussion of such questions, the theological reader must look elsewhere. The main, and more completely treated subject, is the meaning of the Canonical Scriptures, assuming them to be, in origin and authority, all that Mr Liddon imagines.

Whatever opinion may be formed of Mr Liddon's reasoning, his rhetoric cannot fail to be admired. No treatise so attractively eloquent as his, has been written upon the same subject. And, although his arguments are not always well selected, and his special ability evidently does not lie in the direction of vigorous thought and close disputation, yet his Lectures, taken as a whole, deserve the foremost place among books on his side of the controversy. If he has rehabilitated some pleadings palpably too inane and bad, he has, at the same time, omitted nothing pertinent and plausible. He brings forth every weighty argument arrayed in the best dress it can be made to wear.

My own book I must leave to speak for itself. Its faults will, doubtless, be even more obvious to other eyes than they are to mine. It is certainly not the book of a rhetorician, and in that aspect I gladly acknowledge the unapproachable superiority of Mr Liddon's volume. My heart's prayer and purpose have been wholly directed to the end of writing truthfully, calmly, and clearly. While I have never been forgetful of corrections and amendments in readings and renderings, I have shunned all

needless references to the Hebrew and Greek languages, and
have, I hope, written nothing which general readers, of good
English education, will not be quite sufficiently able to follow.
Writing anonymously, I have naturally preferred, at several
points, to strengthen my positions by quotations from authors
of undoubted eminence and scholarship. The course of Mr
Liddon's argument has, in all important features, determined the
course of mine, which is really a close running commentary; but
I have departed from his order of topics, and, in particular, have
made the examination of texts from the Epistles precede the
examination of sayings recorded in the Gospels. I may add,
that my criticisms were not written continuously, but at
intervals (sometimes wide intervals), as I could find leisure from
the requirements of parochial work.

In tracking the brilliant preacher's footsteps, and meditating
upon his methods, I have been increasingly impressed with the
justice and accuracy, from the Protestant point of view, of the
following sentences in that contribution by Professor Jowett,
which is the gem of the much-abused, but essentially Protestant volume, *Essays and Reviews.*

"All the resources of knowledge may be turned into a means,
not of discovering the true rendering, but of upholding a
received one. Grammar appears to start from an independent
point of view, yet inquiries into the use of the Article or the
Preposition have been observed to wind round into a defence of
sound doctrine. Rhetoric often magnifies its own want of taste
into the design of inspiration. Logic (that other mode of
rhetoric) is apt to lend itself to the illusion, by stating erroneous
explanations with a clearness which is mistaken for truth.
'Metaphysical aid' carries away the common understanding
into a region where it must blindly follow. Learning obscures
as well as illustrates; it heaps up chaff when there is no more
wheat. These are some of the ways in which the sense of
Scripture has become confused, by the help of tradition, in the
course of ages, under a load of commentators."

And again, an undeniable, but perpetually neglected truth, is
well presented in the words :—

"Many persons who have no difficulty in tracing the growth
of institutions, yet seem to fail in recognising the more subtle
progress of an idea. It is hard to imagine the absence of conceptions with which we are familiar; to go back to the germ of
what we know only in maturity; to give up what has grown to
us, and become a part of our minds."

CHAPTER II.

Precise statement of the dogma maintained, and of some more general
objections to which it is exposed.—Mr Liddon's theories respecting
the organic unity, perfect trustworthiness, and minute accuracy of
the Scriptural records, not sustainable in the presence of free inquiry.
— His argument for the Apostolic authorship of the Fourth Gospel
considered, and some leading points of adverse evidence stated.—On
this topic, Orthodox preconceptions have the practical advantage of
forbidding intelligent criticism.—Though Mr Liddon's method is
critically unsound, and devised for the service of his dogma, he may
nevertheless be met upon his own assumptions, and convicted of
arbitrary and irrational interpretation of Scripture.

In his first Lecture, Mr Liddon states briefly and clearly the
doctrine he asserts. After pointing out the insufficiency of moral
divinity resulting from any gift or infusion of the Divine presence
in man, he excludes all forms of Being, however ancient and exalted, which had in any sense a beginning and an author. Such
forms of Being are " parted from the Divine Essence by a fathomless chasm ; whereas the Christ of Catholic Christendom is internal to That Essence." He further informs us :

" This assertion of the Divinity of Jesus Christ depends on a
truth beyond itself. It postulates the existence in God of certain
real distinctions having their necessary basis in the Essence of
the Godhead. That Three such distinctions exist is a matter of
Revelation. In the common language of the Western Church,
these distinct Forms of Being are named Persons. Yet that
term cannot be employed to denote Them, without considerable
intellectual caution," and must be understood in a sense different
from that in which it is applied to men,—but, " we are not, therefore, to suppose nothing more to be intended by the revealed doctrine than three varying relations of God in His dealings with
the world. On the contrary, His Self-Revelation has for its basis
certain Eternal Distinctions in His Nature, which are themselves
utterly anterior to, and independent of, any relation to created
life. Apart from these distinctions, the Christian Revelation of
an Eternal Fatherhood, of a true Incarnation of God, and of a

real communication of His Spirit, is but the baseless fabric of a dream. These three distinct Subsistences, which we name Father, Son, and Spirit, while they enable us better to understand the mystery of the Self-sufficing and Blessed Life of God before He surrounded Himself with created beings, are also strictly compatible with the truth of the Divine Unity. And when we say that Jesus Christ is God, we mean that in the Man Christ Jesus, the Second of these Persons or Subsistences, One in Essence with the First and with the Third, vouchsafed to become Incarnate ;" *i.e.*, as explained in the next paragraph, "He robed His Higher Pre-existent Nature, according to which He is Very and Eternal God, with a Human Body and a Human Soul" (pp. 32-34).

These theories are supplemented in Lecture V. by more precise statements respecting Christ's incarnate Being. Mr Liddon insists that our Lord's Godhead is exclusively the seat of His personality.

"The Son of Mary is not a distinct human person mysteriously linked with the Divine Nature of the Eternal Word. The Person of the Son of Mary is Divine and Eternal. . . . . Christ's Manhood is not of Itself an individual being ; It is not a seat and centre of personality ; It has no conceivable existence apart from the act whereby the Eternal Word in becoming Incarnate, called It into being and made It His Own. It is a vesture which He has folded around His Person ; It is an instrument through which He places Himself in contact with men, and whereby He acts upon humanity. . . . His Manhood no more impaired the unity of His Person than each human body, with its various organs and capacities, impairs the unity of that personal principle which is the centre and pivot of each separate human existence, and which has its seat within the soul of each one of us. 'As the reasonable soul and flesh is one man, so God and man is one Christ.' As the personality of man resides in the soul, after death has severed soul and body, so the Person of Christ had Its eternal seat in His Godhead before His Incarnation" (pp. 259, 260).

From the foregoing extracts we gather that, in Mr Liddon's view, our Lord Jesus Christ has a necessary Being in the Self-existent Everlasting Deity—a Being not derived from, not originating in, and in no way whatever dependent on, the choice, or power, or action of the Father. He belongs to the necessary mode of the Self-existent Essence, and is bound up within It by the indissoluble bonds of inherent nature.

Now, although on the whole evidence of which Protestants can take cognizance, this doctrine is incredible, there might, on merely *a priori* ground, be no valid objection against it, if it were taught by a competent authority. Self-existence—which must be ascribed to the Almighty—is a property so utterly beyond the grasp of our intellect, that we are in no position to deny, either, that one Self-existent Substance may be distributed into two, three, or more individuals, the exact counterparts of each other, or, that there may be Self-existent Substances distinguished by differences from each other. But we do not approach the subject on purely abstract and *a priori* grounds. Reflection on our own nature and the works of creation which surround us, points to the conclusion, there is One Being, and One only, in Whom the mysterious attributes of Deity reside. And this conclusion, which commends itself to natural reason, the teaching of Scripture confirms with marked emphasis, and frequent repetitions. Mr Liddon's theory is, however, a virtual denial of the Divine Unity, because we are unable without dividing the Self-existent Substance, to recognise in That Substance two or more Forms, Subsistences, or Persons, each of Whom, having all the attributes of Godhead, is truly and properly God. Attributes or properties are inconceivable apart from a substance in which they have a connecting and supporting basis, and no specious refinements of phraseology can hide the fact that the possession of personal attributes implies the possession of distinct individual Being. If the Second and Third Persons in the Trinity have the attributes of Deity, they are second and third Gods. The supposition that they are of the same Self-existent Substance with the First Person, gives them no real numerical unity, but makes them exact counterparts and *fac-similes* of each other. If by person is meant anything more than a manifestation in action, or a mode, aspect, and relation, as conceived and contemplated by our minds, a threefold personality in one Divine Essence, is a division of that Essence into three separate Gods, and since ideas of quantity are inapplicable, these Gods are repetitions of each other, and Deity, according to the language which I have quoted, is the same Infinite Spirit three times repeated. If we are compelled to confess each Person to be, *by Himself* (*singillatim*), God and Lord ; clearly, not reason, but inspiration and infallibility alone, can prohibit us from believing and saying, there are three Gods. This obvious dilemma does not escape Mr Liddon's notice, and in a note to his first Lecture, he adduces the perfectly unintelligible patristic imagination of a mutual indwelling, or interhabitation, by which the three Forms, Subsistences, &c., in the

Divine Substance, having gone forth into plurality, recede into oneness, and sees in it "The safeguard and witness of the Divine Unity."* Elsewhere, in subsequent Lectures, mention is more than once made of our Lord's subordination, on the ground that the Father alone is "Unoriginate, the Fount of Deity in the Eternal Life of the Ever-blessed Trinity," and that "the Son is derived eternally from the Father." "Christ is the exact likeness of the Father, in all things except being the Father." But these verbal precautions are unavailing; they have no lucid ideas behind them, and do not in any degree shelter the doctrine of the Divine Unity, unless they are joined with the admission that the derivation of the Son was not from a necessity inherent in the Self-existent Substance, but from an act of the Father's choice, and power, and will. Mr Liddon, however, cannot admit the Being of the Son to result from any free and voluntary action on the part of the Father, because origination by the will of another is not distinguishable from creation, and implies inferiority and dependence. The statement of his doctrine is, therefore, incompatible with the truth of the Divine Unity, and also with the verbal requirements of ecclesiastical orthodoxy. He throws out clouds of subtle, eloquent, and bewildering words, but his language, if it is not quite empty of meaning, leads to one of two heresies—either the dividing of the Substance, or, the confounding of the Persons.

Mr Liddon's account of the manner of the Incarnation is as much open to criticism as his description of supposed structural economics in the inner regions of the "One Uncreated, Self-existent, Incorruptible Essence." He avows; our Lord "took human nature upon Him in its reality and completeness;" and then, afterwards, denies Christ had a human person, and declares; "His Manhood is not of Itself an individual being." Surely this is a contradiction in terms. What is a "real and complete" impersonal human nature? Our nature, in its completeness, is inconceivable, except as existing in persons. To enfold a Divine Person with the constituent elements of humanity, not combined into the living entity of a real human person, is not to take our nature, but to form a new nature, which is God *plus* what might in another combination have been man. The dwelling of God in

---

* John xiv. 11 ; 1 Cor. ii. 11, to which Mr Liddon refers, should be compared with John xiv. 20 ; xvii. 21, 23 ; 1 John iv. 15, 16 ; v. 20, and other texts which will occur to every thoughtful reader of the New Testament. Aspects of this profoundly mysterious Unity in Personal separation, are expressed by the terms, *immanence, emanence,* and *retrocession.*

man, is a thoroughly credible and ennobling truth, the conception of which pervades all religious history, and lies at the root of all spiritual aspiration and development; but the robing personal Deity with an impersonal manhood, is an operation which defies understanding, and, whatever else it may be, is certainly *not* taking " our nature in its reality and completeness." The reception of a personal manhood into God, is, in any case, a process the inversion of that to which reason and spiritual instinct point, but the clothing of God with " a manhood which is not of itself an individual being," is an eccentric fancy which Scripture never hints at, and reason refuses to entertain.   The futility of the illustrative proposition from the Athanasian Creed, —" as the reasonable soul and flesh is one man, so God and man is one Christ,"—is evident when we write; " so God and the reasonable soul and flesh is one Christ."   The fact of two constituents composing one Being, does not assist us to apprehend how the same two constituents, together with a Personal God, compose one Being.

In his attempts to prove the position taken in his Lectures, deducible from Scripture, Mr Liddon assumes the Bible to be, in a peculiar sense, a consistent organic whole, and that, in relation to moral and spiritual truths, and more especially in relation to the central truth which he seeks to enforce, the writers were guarded from error by the superintendence of a practically effective inspiration.   He uses the Gospels as perfectly trustworthy, and minutely accurate records of Christ's sayings ; and, in commenting on the Acts and Epistles, takes for granted he may ascribe to language which will bear more than one meaning, the precise significance, the extreme pregnancy, and the dogmatic definiteness, which the Creeds of later times demand.   This method is, no doubt, very convenient, perhaps indispensable, in orthodox Protestant exegesis; but after all, no adjustment of theory respecting the unity, continuity, and infallibility of the revealed written deposit, can establish the right to interpret that deposit unreasonably.   The difficulties of the Nicene and Athanasian theologies can never be materially lessened, so long as the sense of Scripture is supposed to lie open to the intellect and conscience of individuals.   And, measured by rational criticism, the assumptions to which Mr Liddon resorts are made in the face of facts too palpable to be ignored.   The origin of all the Gospels is wrapt in obscurity.   The New Testament Epistles, though they may betray reminiscences of sayings which the Evangelists have preserved, contain no quotations from the Gospels, and do not in any way assert or recognise their existence. While oral testimony was a fresh and living voice, they were not called for, and we have no pretence for fancying they appeared until the apostolic generation had nearly died out. And they were not at once exalted to the rank accorded to the earlier Scriptures. Though honourably distinguished from inferior and less truthful records, they did not reach otherwise than by a gradual progress, extending over at least a hundred years, the high place and authority which we find conceded to them in the third and following centuries. And if we had unimpeachable evidence of their genuineness, and could be sure they were originally written by the men whose names they bear, we should still have to consider the phenomena they present,—the patches of verbal identity in the first three; their want of connected and orderly arrangement; their superficial differences, resulting from omissions and slight variations, which are not incompatible with historical fidelity; and their marked discrepancies, which cannot be reconciled. We are not, moreover, able to deny the possibility and probability of changes, interpolations, and additions in the course of transcription and transmission; and we cannot be justified in assuming we have correct accounts of all events, and correct reports of all discourses.*

There was, unquestionably, an interval of transition from an oral and traditional, to a written Gospel, and the latter rose in estimation as the advantages of it were increasingly felt. At the most inauspicious time, therefore, a time of seething mental commotion, and ill-regulated enthusiasm, when writings misnamed Evangelical and Apostolic were produced, our Gospels were neither tested by the vigilant criticism, nor protected by the jealous custody, which subsequent veneration too tardily secured. Apart from the postulate of a supernatural guidance within the Church, in all that related to the faith, we have no

---

* "From the third century we have the confirming testimony of Origen respecting the *wilful* falsifications of Scripture. He writes that the difference of the text in the various copies of St Matthew's Gospel was caused 'either by the carelessness of copyists, or by the *malicious boldness* of the correcting writers, or of *those who have added or taken away.*' If Origen had written this about Luke's Gospel, he might possibly be supposed to refer to Marcion's counterfeit of the same. As it is, Origen admits that different versions of Matthew's Gospel were, even in the third century, in circulation, and that they originated partly in the activity of malicious gospel forgers. In the end of the fourth century, Jerome writes the same thing in other words about the Latin translation, and he adds, 'There are as many texts as manuscripts.'"—E. DE BUNSEN'S *Hidden Wisdom of Christ*, vol. ii., p. 109.

No extant manuscript of the New Testament can be dated earlier than the middle of the fourth century.

reason to think highly of the capacity for weighing evidence, possessed by Christians who lived between the middle of the second and the end of the third centuries. We should be careful not unduly to depreciate their acquirements, and their interest in truth; but, knowing from their writings something of their style of thought, their methods of illustration, and the extent to which they gave the rein to a credulous fancy, we cannot honestly say they were the men wisely to reduce swollen traditions, or rectify corrupted texts. Looking at the whole subject from the Protestant pathway of historical research, the utmost we can reasonably assert respecting the Synoptical Gospels, is; they are in the main trustworthy, and substantially true.

·In relation to the Fourth Gospel, there are peculiar and almost overwhelming difficulties to be encountered by the free investigator. Mr Liddon struggles to show, not I think with success, the existence of external evidence decisively favouring St John's authorship. He appears to forget that the Apostolic Fathers do *not* invoke the Logos doctrine to explain the nature of Christ. When he affirms; " In their writings there are large districts of thought and expression, of a type unmistakably Johannean" (p. 214), he uses the language of exaggeration, and also appeals to treatises of doubtful genuineness, and undoubtedly adulterated text. " St Ignatius' allusion to St John in his Letter to the Romans" (chap. 7), is, according to the Syriac version (which, if the Epistle is genuine, probably represents its original form more nearly than the Greek text): " I seek the bread of God which is the flesh of Jesus Christ; and I seek His blood, a drink which is love incorruptible." But the Ignatian Epistles, if authentic, would not help to sustain the doctrine of Christ's Deity, and their authenticity in any shape is exceedingly doubtful. A well-informed critic in the *Athenæum* (Jan. 19, 1867), writes :—" The discussions of Baur, Hilgenfield, Lipsius, Merx, Denzinger, Düsterdieck, &c., present the most recent arguments, the result of which is, that neither the Syriac nor the Greek Epistles are authentic."

" Justin's emphatic reference of the doctrine of the Logos to our Lord, not to mention his quotation of John the Baptist's reply to the messengers of the Jews" (the bare words, *I am not the Christ*), " and of our Saviour's language about the new birth," does *not* " make his knowledge of St John's Gospel much more than a probability." The matter of the Fourth Gospel stands aside from the common oral tradition, which was embodied in, and for a while survived, concurrently with, the other three;

and therefore a reason existed for mentioning St John by name, which did not exist for mentioning the other three Evangelists. The particular form of Justin's doctrine, also, supplied him with weighty motives for using the statements of the Fourth Gospel, and bringing forward, if he felt he could bring forward, the name and authority of the Apostle St John ; and, his omitting to do so, is made the more prominent by his express mention of "a certain man whose name was John, one of the Apostles of Christ," as the author of the Apocalypse.

The supposed citations in Justin, and other writers, are very inadequate vouchers that, before the middle of the second century, the Fourth Gospel was known and accepted as the work of an Apostle. It is the merest assumption to call verbal scraps quotations from St John, when St John is not named, and when it is notorious that, through the influence of the writings of Philo, the Logos doctrine was familiar to educated Jews, and also that, traditionary retentions and early records of Christ's life and sayings were in circulation, which were very likely to contain, and give currency to, some of the sentences wrought up into the Fourth Gospel. That Gospel preserves sayings worthy of the Christ of the Synoptists, and not fairly ascribable to mere invention. The better and more veracious of floating materials, whether documentary or oral, would naturally be selected by the Evangelist, and would in his narrative survive in a fixed and authoritative form. It would be no less unwise to argue—none of his distinctive matter has a good foundation in historical truth—than to argue, the whole must be accepted because portions commend themselves as authentic. But the extreme insufficiency of the indirect, fragmentary testimonies, which are imagined to reveal the presence of the Gospel in the former half of the second century, must strike every unprejudiced inquirer who examines them, even as they are exhibited by those who believe in their validity. A passage from the treatise of Hippolytus, *Refutation of all Heresies*, is often adduced to show that Basilides (about A.D. 125) used the " Gospel according to John." But exactness in allusions to the writings of his predecessors is not among the merits of Hippolytus, and it is very far from being clear whether the reference is to Basilides and his followers in a succeeding generation, or to Basilides alone. The language admits both constructions. The context rather favours the supposition, Hippolytus was thinking of the Basilidian school collectively, down to his own day ; and, as the case stands, nothing more decisive than the opinion of Mr Liddon and consentients,

as against that of equally good judges, is contained in the staunch
assertion ; "It is certain from St Hippolytus that Basilides appealed to texts of St John in favour of his system " (p. 216).*
The real evidence for the Apostolic authorship of the latest Gospel begins after A.D. 150.

With regard to Justin's "knowledge," very competent and impartial recent investigators, who approach the subject from different sides, concur in judging ; "There is no good proof that
Justin used the Gospel of John.   All that can be appealed to, is
the similarity of some of Justin's expressions to those of John "
(Donaldson's *Critical History of Christian Literature and Doctrine*, &c., Vol. ii., p. 331).   This conclusion of Dr Donaldson is
shared by the late Mr J. J. Tayler, in his work *On the Fourth
Gospel;* and also by Mr Ernest De Bunsen (*Hidden Wisdom,
&c.*, Vol. ii., p. 103), who holds that the Gospel in question had
its origin with St John, but "was not published till an advanced
period in the second century."   Dr Davidson, after closely reviewing the evidence, concludes : "The result of our inquiry into
Justin's writings is, that his use of the Fourth Gospel is not
proved " (*Introduction to New Testament*, Vol. ii., p. 387).   Mr
Westcott's individual persuasion, and the persuasion he is
anxious to impart, is, doubtless, that Justyn Martyr was acquainted with the four Canonical Gospels ; but his perception of
the force of evidence, saves him from the overweening confidence

---

* The passage on which Mr Liddon and others have built, is in the " Refuta-
tation of Heresies," vii. 22, and their inference turns on a presumed exactness
in the use of the singular verb $\phi\eta\sigma i$ (*he says*).   But Hippolytus often uses
$\phi\eta\sigma i$ to indicate an unnamed representative of the sect referred to, or, perhaps, the sect regarded as professing a particular opinion.   The late Mr J. J.
Tayler on "The Fourth Gospel" remarks : "In vii. 20, Hippolytus mentions
Basilides, and Isidore his son, and *the whole troop of these*, and then cites them
collectively through the whole of the following paragraph, by the word $\phi\eta\sigma i$.
Nor is this the only instance.   In vi. 29, speaking of Valentinus, Heracleon,
Ptolemy, *and all the school of these*, he quotes the opinion of the school, by the
singular verb $\phi\eta\sigma i$.   It is surprising that so great a scholar as Baron Bunsen
should have laid all this stress on so small a matter.   *It says* ($\phi\eta\sigma i$), is the
familiar mode of citing the doctrines of a particular school, whether represented by many writers or by one.   Scripture, notwithstanding its multifarious
contents and numerous authors, is constantly quoted by writers of the second
century in this form."   (See, also, to the same effect, Dr Davidson's "Introduction to New Testament," vol. ii., pp. 388–93.)

Mr David Rowland on "The Apostolic Origin of the Fourth Gospel" (Long-
mans), calls Mr Tayler's argument " a feeble objection," and exhibits it by citing
only some comparatively unimportant observations which introduce the sentences I have quoted.   Mr Rowland's Essay purports to submit the topic he
discusses " to an examination of the kind which courts of law employ in
investigating rights or titles to property dependent on ancient traditional and
documentary evidence."

indulged by Mr Liddon. In treating the precise question, "How far Justin witnesses to St John's Gospel?" he says : "His references to St John are uncertain ; but this follows from the character of the Fourth Gospel. It was unlikely that he should quote its peculiar teaching in apologetic writings addressed to Jews and heathens" (Westcott, *Canon of New Testament*, p. 201, 1st Ed.)

Mr Liddon appeals to a Catalogue of the books of the New Testament, purporting to belong to the latter half of the second century, and known as the Canon of Muratori, but he does not reproduce the information on which he builds. "At Rome, St John's Gospel was certainly received as being the work of that Apostle, in the year 170. This is clear from the so-termed Muratorian fragment" (p. 212). The fragment ascribes the Fourth Gospel to "John, one of the Disciples," and gives an account of the causes which led to its production. "At the entreaties of his fellow-disciples and bishops, John said, ' Fast with me three days from to-day, and whatever shall be revealed to each of us, whether it be favourable to my writing or not, let us relate it to one another.' On the same night it was revealed to Andrew, one of the Apostles, that John should—the rest revising (*recognoscentibus cunctis*)—relate all things in his own name. And so, although differing elements (*principia*) are taught in the several books of the Evangelists, yet there is no difference in the faith of believers, since in all the books, all things are set forth by one and the same directing Spirit." Now, this story has a suspiciously defensive and explanatory look. Its attempt to throw around the Gospel the special sanction of Divinely-suggested origin, rather implies, the Gospel's apostolicity was not a well-attested and accepted fact, but viewed with doubts and hesitancy.

In concluding his undaunted, but very one-sided, argument on the external witness which he supposes to prove "the Fourth Gospel certainly St John's," Mr Liddon jubilantly writes (p. 218) :—

"Ewald shall supply the words with which to close the foregoing considerations. ' Those who, since the first discussion of this question have been really conversant with it, never could have had, and never have had, a moment's doubt. As the attack on St John has become fiercer and fiercer, the truth during the last ten or twelve years has been more and more solidly established, error has been pursued into its last hiding-places ; and at this moment, the facts before us are such, that no man who does not will knowingly to choose error and to reject truth, can dare to say that the Fourth Gospel is not the work of the Apostle John.'" The fervour, modesty, and sweetness of this deliverance will have their reward in the applauding sympathy of orthodox Protestants. Ewald, however, has not, on many topics, the good fortune to coincide with Mr Liddon, and the latter complains (p. 15): "Ewald may see in Christ, the altogether human source of the highest spiritual life of humanity;" and again (Notes, p. 505): "Ewald's defence of St John's Gospel, and his deeper spirituality of tone, must command a religious interest, which would be of a high order if only this writer believed in our Lord's Godhead." But where the great German elucidator of the Old Testament does retain a morsel of orthodoxy, his dictum is triumphantly conclusive! Those who know his history will perhaps be disposed to wonder more at his having travelled so far in the paths of Rationalism, than at his having, in advanced age, stopped short of some conclusions which seem inevitable to younger men of his own school. If he is to be made a judge on questions connected with the New Testament, let his failure to discover Christ's true Deity in the Fourth Gospel be balanced against his success in convincing himself the Fourth Gospel is a work of St John.

But, as will be confessed on both sides, the controversy hangs more upon internal than upon external evidences. If the fourth did not differ from the earlier Gospels, more than they differ from each other, the external credentials might pass unchallenged, not because they would amount to proof, but because, in favour of probabilities, comparatively slight testimony is required. The differences between the Fourth Gospel and its predecessors are, however, differences of striking contrast and wide divergency. The most able English champion of traditional views concerning the New Testament Canon, assures us : " It is impossible to pass from the Synoptic Gospels to that of St John, without feeling that the transition involves the passage from one world of thought to another. No familiarity with the general teaching of the Gospels, no wide conception of the character of the Saviour, is sufficient to destroy the contrast which exists in form and spirit between the earlier and the later narratives ; and a full recognition of this contrast is the first requisite for the understanding of their essential harmony " (Westcott's *Introduction to the Study of the Gospels*, p. 231). The full recognition which Mr Westcott recommends, cannot be attempted here. It is enough to remark ; not only are the mysticism and obscurity which characterise many of the discourses in the Fourth Gospel, utterly unlike the general simplicity and clearness of the sayings recorded in the preceding three, but there are also, contradictions as to plain matters of fact,—contradictions which refuse to be reduced into superficial differences, or varieties of detail. " One form of narrative excludes the other. If the three first Gospels represent Christ's public ministry truly, the fourth cannot be accepted as simple reliable history. If we assume the truth of the fourth, we must reject, on some fundamental points, the evidence of the three first" (Tayler, *On the Fourth Gospel*, p. 7).*

Mr Liddon contends : " St John's Gospel is an historical supplement, and a polemical treatise addressed to an intellectual world widely different from that which had been before the minds of the earlier Evangelists." He also admits : " St John's translation of the actual words of Jesus may be coloured by a phraseology current in the school which he is addressing, sufficiently to make them popularly intelligible. But the peculiarities of his language have been greatly exaggerated by criticism, while they are naturally explained by the polemical and positively doctrinal objects which he had in view" (p. 223). The explanation is not to the purpose, and the admission is damaging. Two conflicting versions of the same events cannot both be truthful ; and, in relation to the discourses, the Evangelist is not supposed to be the composer, but the reporter. The explanation required is, that our Lord himself addressed widely different intellectual worlds, and, in consequence, employed totally distinct styles of thought and diction. Will Mr Liddon venture to offer this explanation ? The supplementary theory, and reasons drawn from the purpose of the Evangelist, do not relieve the difficulty involved in the fact of the Fourth Gospel's having so little in agreement—so much in contrast—with its predecessors. And the theory itself seriously disparages the credit of the Synoptists. Matthew, Mark, and Luke, may reasonably be presumed to have intended to proclaim the gospel in its connection with Christ's life and teaching, and to have given us what, in their judgment, was a true and sufficient presentation of Christ's words and works. But what must we think of their knowledge, memory,

---

* Similarly, Dr Schenkel :—"If the synoptic representation of the evangelical history be the correct one, then that of the Fourth Gospel is not correct, and *vice versa*."

Dr Davidson, *Theological Review*, July 1870, supplementing the discussion in the second volume of his "Introduction to the New Testament," exposes the worthlessness of Irenæus' testimony, and the decided untruth of the conjecture; "Irenæus attests the authenticity of the Gospel out of the tradition of Polycarp."

and spiritual discernment, when they could all omit such materials as the fourth Evangelist brings together? What was the character of their inspiration, and what share had they in the promise their successor records: "The Holy Ghost shall teach you all things, and bring all things to your remembrance, whatsoever I have said unto you?" Does Mr Liddon consider the New Testament narratives to furnish a complete Gospel, excluding what he believes to be the testimony of St John? Could he, without the Fourth Gospel, prove, even to his own satisfaction, that the doctrine his "Bampton Lectures" were written to maintain, has any foundation in our Lord's teaching? The supplementary theory, therefore, evidently impairs the credit of those who, while they proclaimed the gospel of Christ, could, singly and collectively, leave room and occasion for such a supplement. The hard pressure of facts, which Mr Liddon seems unable duly to appreciate, is keenly felt by a theologian who is in no qualification, except the graces of style, his inferior. Mr De Bunsen labours, with much thought and learning, to assign "a satisfactory reason for the mysterious fact, that the first three Evangelists have evidently agreed not to refer to any of those important sayings of Christ which have been recorded only by the Beloved Apostle" (*Hidden Wisdom*, Preface). But he does not withhold the confession: "Truly lamentable is the fact that the tradition of the Roman Church has not made known to the world under what circumstances the first and incomplete evangelic record of Matthew was written, and why it had to be followed, first by the Paulinic Gospel after Luke, then by the more compromising Gospel after Mark, and, finally, by the uncompromising Gospel after John. The Roman Church need not have dreaded the consequences of making known to the world that the gradual revelation of pure Christianity was a work of almost a century" (*Hidden Wisdom*, &c., Vol. ii., p. 113).

Mr De Bunsen must be allowed to have lightened some difficulties; but, after all his efforts, his conclusion has to be expressed in terms of compromise.

"We may therefore firmly believe that the Apostle John has recorded the secret and hidden sayings of Christ, and that during, or after, the Apostle's lifetime, one or more of John's personal friends faithfully embodied the apostolic record into the Gospel 'after' John, which the editors composed in the form we possess it, and not without especial reference to the state of the Church towards the end of the second century" (Vol. ii., p. 328).

The embarrassments, which an examination of the contents

of the latest Canonical Gospel throws in the way of its reception as a work of St John, are increased by the broad differences distinguishing its style and spirit from those of the Apocalypse. When the two documents are carefully compared, it is very hard indeed to avoid inferring, both have not the same author. It is also noteworthy that, in the Apocalypse, the writer frequently refers to himself by name, while in the Gospel there is no direct statement of authorship, except in the chapter which is generally admitted to be a subsequent addition. The 35th verse of chap. xix., so far from distinctly suggesting the writer was an Apostle, or an eye-witness of what he relates, rather indicates he was not himself an eye-witness, but relied on the testimony of one who was.

After a recognition of the peculiarities* in form and substance which put the Fourth Gospel so widely out of agreement with its predecessors, suspicion becomes almost inevitable, that the promise ascribed to Christ (xiv. 26) is an anticipatory explanation and apology for the production of matter so distinct from what the common oral tradition, and the existing written memoirs, embraced.

The spiritual depth and beauty which have been discerned in the Fourth Gospel, are sometimes thought to attest its truthfulness and apostolic origin ; but there can be no doubt our estimate of its contents is, in a very great degree, shaped and coloured by our foregone conclusions. Intellectual criticism and clear-sighted moral perception, are not possible while we are persuaded we have before our eyes the very words of God Himself, preserved in the narrative of an historian infallibly inspired. Reason may ingeniously expound and defend, but can never fairly investigate discourses and narratives which are believed to have such overwhelmingly awful sanctions. The preconception puts intelligence out of the field, for all but defensive and laudatory purposes. But if the controversy respecting the inspiration of Scripture, and the authorship of our latest Gospel, issues in disburdening men's minds from the supposition that St John, under the guidance of a plenary inspiration, has recorded with minute accuracy the very words of Christ, a widely different judgment will probably be arrived at as to some portions of the Fourth Gospel ; and passages from which it is next to impossible

---

* Peculiarities are, of course, not all or necessarily discrepancies ; but Mr Westcott adopts the calculation that, " If the total contents of the several Gospels be represented by 100, there are in St John's, 92 peculiarities and 8 concordances."—*Introduction*, &c., p. 177.

to elicit any clear consistent sense, will no longer be pronounced profoundly spiritual and full of beauty. Disturbance of rooted opinions on this subject is, as clerical inquirers learn from experience, peculiarly distressing, but, in the order of Divine Providence, abstinence from inquiry would appear to be the condition of Protestant continuance in the orthodox faith. Whatever the meaning of the fact may be, application of individual intellect and research does not bring peace and contentment to the holder of traditional dogmas. But, upon all questions touching the formation of the Canon, and the authorship and meaning of the Canonical Books, orthodox men may secure repose of mind, without immediate diminution of practical piety, by abnegation of reason, and by trust in the Church.

The considerations to which I have briefly drawn attention, will suffice to show that, in assuming the Gospels, and more especially the last of them, to furnish verbally correct accounts of Christ's sayings, Mr Liddon has followed a method whose radical unsoundness vitiates all his reasonings. With the essentially Protestant and rational criticism, by which time-honoured assumptions about the Bible have been besieged and curtailed, he makes only a semblance of grappling. He neither screens his conceptions of the Bible behind the paramount authority of the Church, nor vindicates them from the fundamental objections to which free inquiry gives rise. But if the faults of his method are not insisted upon, and the broader results of modern investigation and historical criticism are not urged against him, other ground remains on which his conclusions may be combated. The dogma for which he argues so impetuously is eminently a question of interpretation ; and if that dogma is really deducible from the Bible by individual judgment, it must be deducible by just and reasonable, and not by arbitrary and irrational, expositions. A review of the leading features in his argument will, I believe, prove pretty conclusively that Mr Liddon does not find his doctrine in Scripture, but puts it there, sometimes by contravening the clear sense, and more often by impregnating vague phrases, straining figurative expressions, and misunderstanding obscure texts. He cannot, I know, be charged with originating his expositions. But he rejoices to inherit, accept, and deliberately reiterate, a string of interpretations full of the worst faults with which any exegesis, not avowedly either irrational, or super-rational, can be laden. Brief and indecisive words are laboriously drawn upon ; explicitness is cleverly darkened with rapid and discolouring touches. Contextual settings, the scope of the particular Canonical document in hand, and the plain general teaching of the whole Bible, are treated as if they did not exist, or existed only to be curtly explained away. Barely possible senses of rare, difficult, and arbitrarily-detached expressions, are employed to override and transmute the abundant and perspicuous sentences which, by every rule of reason, determine the probable meaning of ambiguous texts. Writers and speakers are understood as though they had written and spoken in jerks, without mental continuity, or firm hold of the momentous conception assumed to have been presiding and influential; in a style, in short, which makes the pages of the New Testament swarm with psychological enigmas, and tempts us to conclude that inspiration involves, not the quickening and expansion, but the restraint and contraction of our intellectual powers.

CHAPTER III.

Supposed intimations in the Old Testament, of the existence of a Plurality of Persons within the One Divine Essence.—The plural form of the Name of God (*Elohim*).—Significance of the Theophanies.—Imagined Personality of the *Divine Wisdom*, as depicted in the Hebrew Canonical Books and the Apocrypha.—The *Logos* of Philo Judæus, and the probable relation of Philo's speculations to the Fourth Gospel.— Periods of Messianic Prophecy in the Jewish Canon.—Supposed evidence for Christ's Deity in the *Psalms, Isaiah, Jeremiah, Haggai, Zechariah*, and *Malachi*, examined.—Reckless and unwarranted reference, on the part of Mr Liddon, to Rabbinical literature.

IN the plural form of the name of God (*Elohim*), and in the use, a few times repeated in the earlier chapters of Genesis, of a plural verb, &c.,—*let Us make, &c.; like one of Us; let Us go down* (i. 26 ; iii. 22 ; xi. 7) ; together with Isa. vi. 8—*Whom shall I send, and who will go for Us ?*—Mr Liddon detects " intimations of the existence of a Plurality of Persons within the One Essence of God ;" intimations all the more significant because the Divine Unity was so fundamental an article in the Hebrew faith.

The answer, with respect to the noun *Elohim*, is, that it seems to have remained in the plural from remoter times, because the Deity was contemplated as the aggregate of manifold forces and powers, and as combining in Himself all the energies which polytheism had distributed among the " gods many " of the heathen world. " His internal resources were regarded as infinite and yet united. It is with reference to such *multiplicity* of the manifestations of Divine power, that the plural *Elohim* was employed by monotheism " (Davidson's *Introduction to the Old Testament*, Vol. i., p. 194).

" Whatever the names of the Elohim worshipped by the numerous clans of his race, Abraham saw that all the Elohim were meant for God, and thus Elohim, comprehending by one name everything that ever had been or could be called Divine, became the name with which the monotheistic age was rightly inaugurated,—a plural conceived and construed as a singular. Jehovah was all the Elohim, and therefore there could be no other God " (Max Muller; *Chips, &c. Essay on Semitic Monotheism*).

When *Elohim* is used in its plural sense to denote false gods, the verbs and adjectives with which it is joined are, of course, in grammatical concord, but the very great majority of the numerous instances in which the word is used to denote the Almighty, have the verbs in the singular, and there is an overwhelming probability on the side of the conclusion that the stringent monotheism of the Jews made the exceptional usage unmeaning, unless with relation to the Almighty's attributes, as compared with the conclusion that there was in it any hint of Personal Distinctions within the Being of God.* When Mr Liddon says of the passages in Genesis above referred to; "In such sayings it is clear that an equality of rank is distinctly assumed between the Speaker and Those Whom He is addressing," he promotes neither his cause nor his reputation. Any explanation of these forms of language is more admissible than an explanation which the Jews would have understood to contradict the grandly distinctive conception of their theology. Kings when speaking of themselves employ the plural pronoun, and the royal usage may have been transferred to the King of kings.

The fancies, that, the threefold repetition of the Divine Name in the priestly blessing prescribed in the Book of Numbers (vi. 23–26), and, the similar repetition of the word Holy in Isa. vi. 3, and, "the recurrence of a Threefold rhythm of prayer or praise in the Psalter," contain significant and preparative adumbrations of "the Most Holy Three, Who yet are One,"—are sufficiently refuted by being mentioned. †

From these subtle linguistic suggestions of Personal Distinctions within the Unity, Mr Liddon goes on "to consider that series of remarkable apparitions which are commonly known as the Theophanies, and which form so prominent a feature in the early history of the Old Testament Scriptures." In one of the three superhuman Beings who came to Abraham in human shape, and partook of his hospitality (Gen. xviii.), Mr Liddon, guided

---

* Fuerst (*Heb. Lex.*) says, that "after the earlier period, the construction with the plural was avoided as polytheistic." It is noticeable, also, that the Hebrew poets resuscitated the singular *Eloah*. The plural usage is, in none of its aspects, progressive, but the reverse, and therefore could have had no share in conveying a doctrine the foreshadowings of which are presumed to have become more frequent and definite as time went on.

† It must be confessed, however, in this species of interpretation Mr Liddon has been surpassed. "The threefold mention of the Divine names, and the plural number of the Word translated God (Deut. vi. 4), are thought by many to be a plain intimation of a Trinity of Persons, even in this express declaration of the unity of the Godhead."—*Religious Tract Society's Commentary*, compiled mainly from Henry and Scott.

by the plain meaning of the text, recognises Jehovah, and, with characteristic acuteness in the manipulation of words, adopts the observation that, "when we are told (xix. 24) that 'Jehovah rained upon Sodom and Gomorrah brimstone and fire from Jehovah out of heaven,' a sharp distinction is established between a visible and an Invisible Person, each bearing the Most Holy Name."* The mysterious Being who wrestled with Jacob; "the Angel of the Lord;" "the Angel of God's Presence;" "the Captain of the Lord's Host;" "the Angel of God who refuses to disclose to Manoah his Name, which is secret or wonderful;"—who appear in the Pentateuch and the books of Joshua and Judges, are, by a confiding literal acceptance of the Scripture phraseology, identified with special apparitions of Jehovah. "The Angel of God's Presence (Ex. xxxiii. 14, compare with Isa. lxiii. 9), fully represents God. God must in some way have been present in Him. No merely created being, speaking and acting in his own right, could have spoken to men, or have allowed men to act towards Himself, as did the Angel of the Lord" (p. 54). But in handling the precise question, "Who was this Angel?" Mr Liddon hesitates, though his opinion seems to incline towards that of "the earliest Fathers, who answer with general unanimity, that the Angel was the Word or Son of God himself." But an Arian abuse of the Theophanic interpretation prevalent in the Ante-Nicene Church, produced a more guarded explanation, in establishing which St Augustine took the lead. The Arian reasoning was: The Son was seen by the Patriarchs, the Father was not seen; an invisible and a visible nature are not one and the same.

"St Augustine boldly faced this difficulty by insisting upon the Scriptural truth of the Invisibility of God as God. The Son, therefore, as being truly God, was by nature as invisible as the Father. If the Son appeared to the Patriarchs, He appeared through the intermediate agency of a created being, who represented Him, and through whom He spoke and acted. If the Angel who represented Him spoke and acted with a Divine authority, and received Divine honours, we are referred to the force of the general law whereby, in things earthly and heavenly, an ambassador is temporarily put in the place of the Master who accredits him. . . . The general doctrine of this great teacher,

---

* In his admirable article on the "Jewish Messiah," (*Theological Review*, January 1870), Dr Davidson supplies the scholarly and common-sense elucidation : "*Jehovah rained from Jehovah*, is Hebraistic for *the Lord rained from Himself*, a noun being used for a pronoun."

that the Theophanies were not direct appearances of a Person in the Godhead, but Self-manifestations of God through a created being, had been hinted at by some earlier Fathers, and was insisted on by contemporary and later writers of the highest authority" (pp. 56–58).

Since Augustine's time this explanation has received the predominant, though by no means the exclusive, acceptance of the Church; and Mr Liddon, while remarking, "it is not unaccompanied by considerable difficulties when we apply it to the sacred text," confesses that, "it certainly seems to relieve us of greater embarrassments than any which it creates." The difficulties are, I think, very manifest when the explanation is applied to the accounts in the xviii. and xxxii. chapters of Genesis. The writer of those accounts does identify with Jehovah and Elohim, the mysterious visitant who ate and talked with Abraham, and wrestled with Jacob, and he gives no hint he imagined himself to be recording other than literal, veritable facts. Our intelligence, and our reverence for the Almighty and Infinite Spirit, would forbid us to think as the writer thought; but have intelligence and reverence any claim to be heard against the statements of a narrative divinely inspired, and dealing with the very topics around which the instructing light and controlling care of inspiration more especially move,—the miracles and manifestations of God?

But, whatever were the exact form and nature of the Old Testament Theophanies, they have, according to Mr Liddon, an important bearing on the doctrine of our Lord's Divinity.

"If they were not, as has been pretended, mythical legends, the natural product of the Jewish mind at a particular stage of its development, but actual matter-of-fact occurrences in the history of ancient Israel, must we not see in them a deep Providential meaning? Whether in them the Word or Son actually appeared, or whether God made a created angel the absolutely perfect exponent of His Thought and Will, do they not point, in either case, to a purpose in the Divine Mind, which would only be realised when man had been admitted to a nearer and more palpable contact with God than was possible under the Patriarchal or Jewish dispensations? Do they not suggest, as their natural climax and explanation, some Personal Self-unveiling of God before the eyes of His creatures? Would not God appear to have been training His people by this long and mysterious series of communications, at length to recognise and to worship Him when hidden under, and indissolubly one with a created

D

nature?   Apart from the specific circumstances which may seem
to have explained each Theophany at the time of its taking
place, and considering them as a series of phenomena, is there
any other account of them so much in harmony with the general
scope of Holy Scripture, as that they were successive lessons
addressed to the eye and to the ear of ancient piety, in anticipation of a coming Incarnation of God?" (p. 58).

Now this reasoning has hardly the merit of being even
superficially plausible.   If "the Word or Son" did not appear
in the manifestations referred to, they suggest nothing respecting
"Personal Self-unveilings of God," or, distinctions of Persons in
the Godhead.   The whole force of their meaning, in relation to
the doctrine under discussion, depends upon their having been,
what a Puritan author has called them, "prelibations of the
Incarnation of Deity."   How could the fact of the Almighty's
making a created being His representative, and the exponent of
His Will, foreshadow that, within His own Infinite Invisible
Essence, there was a Second Person Who would one day come
forth to clothe Himself permanently with a created nature?
How could passing manifestations of one kind be in any sense
lessons anticipatory of a grand enduring manifestation totally
different in kind?   Would a pious Jew, meditating on the
Theophanies, have been able, in his most devout and spiritual
moments, to catch a glimpse of the inference, that, because God
had made angels His authoritative messengers, therefore He
would at some future day—not make them so again—but,
substitute for manifestations and messages through them, a
permanent Incarnation of His own Essential Being, disclosing
the existence of a Second Person equal with Himself?   And if
the Theopanies were designed to be suggestive preludes to the
Incarnation, it is, to say the least, remarkable they were not
continued beyond the earlier, twilight periods of the Jewish
history.   They were a series broken off at a very early stage,
and the narratives which enshrined them do not hint at a
connecting principle, or an ulterior significance, but rather
present them as separate exceptional events, attached to special
cases and circumstances.

Another assessment of the Old Testament Theophanies is
stated in the learned Article on *The Jewish Messiah*, to which
I have already referred.   Dr Davidson writes : "Angels
belonged to the mythology of the Hebrews, who personified the
powers of nature.   Extraordinary operations, unusual phenomena, manifestations of God, were invested with personal

attributes. They were angels or messengers of Jehovah, and are identified with Himself, because they represent no distinctive being. Without independent existence, they are only the mode of His appearance, the invisible Deity unveiling Himself to mortal eyes. The word *Maleach* (Angel) favours this hypothesis, because its form is indefinite. It means *a sending :* not, one sent; and is, properly, an abstract noun. Almost all the appearances of angels in the Old Testament are to be explained in this manner. The *Angel of Jehovah's presence* is identical with Jehovah, because what is so termed, is only the manifestation of His presence at a certain time and place—a personified mode of His operation. The Old Testament itself, in identifying the Angel with the presence of Jehovah, and with Jehovah Himself, confirms the correctness of this explanation."

"The preparatory service rendered to the doctrine of our Lord's Divinity by the Theophanies in the world of sense," was, in Mr Liddon's view, "seconded by the upgrowth and development of a belief respecting the Divine Wisdom, in the region of inspired ideas." He considers the language put into the mouth of Wisdom, in the first section of the Book of Proverbs, to be more indicative of a real person than of a poetic personification, and insists that in chapter viii. 22, *possessed*, and not *created*, is the accurate translation. He appears to have overlooked the fact that possession by acquirement is, in the case of God, equivalent to production or creation. The Lexicons of Gesenius, Fuerst, and Lee, are in substantial agreement in the meaning they assign to the word in the passages to which Mr Liddon refers, and show that the sense, *to possess*, is unfolded from the more radical sense *to get* or *obtain*. Dr Davidson, in his remarks upon the text of Proverbs under consideration, says :—

"The verb never means *to possess* simply and solely, but always indicates *the act of coming into* possession. All good Hebrew scholars, together with the Septuagint, Targum, and Peshito, translate it *create*. . . . The whole passage (22-31 verses) has no relation to the doctrine of the Trinity. It contains nothing more than a bold personification of the antiquity, excellence, and dignity of wisdom. The feminine gender would not be employed to set forth the second Person in the Trinity, for the matter is more than one of mere grammatical form. Wisdom is represented as a female, *she :* showing a simple personification. In short, it may be confidently asserted that the passage contains nothing about the internal relations of the Godhead " (*Introduction, &c.*, Vol. ii., pp. 349, 350).

These remarks may be, in substance, transferred to the figurative language of the uncanonical and therefore technically uninspired books, Wisdom, Ecclesiasticus, and Baruch. In the former two especially, *Wisdom* is, after a mode of conception rare among us, except in poetry, described in language which, literally understood, implies real, personal existence. The *Logos* (Word or Reason) of God is also spoken off in a manner which intimates *Word* and *Wisdom* to have been only different expressions for ideas so nearly identical as to admit of interchange. This fact points to the conclusion that *Word* and *Wisdom* were not intended to stand for real personages, but were both expressions for manifestations of the Divine attributes —verbal equivalents for collective human notions of the pervasive, operative, quickening, and enlightening energy which is ever going forth from the Almighty Father "in Whom we live and move and have our being."

Mr Liddon, who finds everywhere significant traces of the mystery he has undertaken to defend, "seems to catch," in the Apocryphal books, "the accents of those weighty formulæ by which Apostles will presently define the pre-existent Glory of their Majestic Lord." He is most unwilling to admit personification even where personification is obvious; and distinctly metaphorical language is, to his mind, literal. Figurative descriptions, and the application of conceptions derived from the nature and actings of man, seem to him out of place in that region where to others they seem most allowable and inevitable —the Nature and actings of God.

The writings of the Jew Philo, who lived in the century before our Saviour's birth, abound in statements respecting the Logos of God; and of these Mr Liddon has given some well-selected specimens, though he has not been careful to inform his readers that the title *Logos* is given by Philo to Moses and Aaron, and in the plural applied to angels. It is needless, however, to discuss the controverted question whether the Word was to Philo's mind a real person, or, a name for attributes and qualities conceived to be inherent in, and in various ways exercised by, the Divine Being. The view which is really antagonistic to Mr Liddon's, is not that the Logos of the Fourth Gospel is a mere reproduction of Philo's Logos, but that it had its origin in the application to Christ's Personality, of ideas suggested by current speculations, of whose prior existence and diffusion we have evidence in Philo's writings, and also, less distinctly, in the ancient sacred books which lie without the precincts of the Hebrew Canon. The Logos doctrine is one which would almost of necessity undergo modifications in every mind through which it passed. Vague and shadowy, it could not escape subjective influences in transmission, and when applied to define the presence of God in Christ, it was, of course, moulded and coloured by contact with Christian facts, and combination with Christian ideas. There is no need to surmise that " Philo was St John's master," or that there is in the Fourth Gospel any close and premeditated adherence to speculative teachings found in Philo and the Apocrypha. Occasional coincidences of thought and language, and some similarity of phraseological forms, are not denied to exist, and these point to a common and suggestive intellectual atmosphere. No one disputes that the Gospel ascribed to St John contains elements to which Philo was a stranger, and to which his general views may even stand in a relation of moral discrepancy. Philo's idea of the Logos was certainly not conjoined with Messianic anticipations, and may well have been, as has been suggested, " to a great degree, a philosophical substitute for them." The question at issue has little or nothing to do with Philo's doctrine, taken as a whole, but concerns one elastic and pregnant speculation. Mr Liddon's reasoning on this point is needless labour. Philo, and the authors of the Apocryphal Jewish books, were not Christians, and the author of the Fourth Gospel was a Christian, and that circumstance at once entails large differences. But since a Logos doctrine is found neither in the three first and earlier written Gospels, nor in the writings of the Apostolic Fathers, does it not appear more probable the writer of the last Gospel adopted a widely diffused and attractive conception, than that he stated a peculiar and fundamental Christian dogma, which the writers of the preceding Gospels knew, but had held in reserve? It is conceded, " Philo could do much in preparing the soil of Alexandrian thought," and that, " among the ideas circulating in the intellectual world, the most instrumental in supplying a point of connection on which to base the doctrine of a God revealed in Christ, was the Logos of Alexandria, if not the exact Logos of Philo." On the *assumption* that the later Gospel is the work of an infallibly inspired Apostle, and throughout in real, though undiscernible harmony with its predecessors, these concessions are only recognitions of a Providential preparation carried on outside the circle of Revelation ; but on the ground of criticism and free inquiry, they suggest a departure from the primitive type of doctrine, and an accommodation of Christianity to external thought, by the infusion of a foreign, though easily assimilated ingredient. In another Book of the New Testament, the date of whose composition precedes that of the Fourth Gospel, the influence of the Alexandrian Jewish Theology is too manifest to be ignored, though I do not observe that Mr Liddon anywhere acknowledges the fact. Conybeare and Howson, in their *Life and Epistles of St Paul*, candidly avow: "The resemblance between the Epistle to the Hebrews and the writings of Philo is most striking. It extends not only to the general points before mentioned, but to particular doctrines and expressions ; the parallel passages are enumerated by Bleek."

The summary into which Dr Pye Smith (*Scripture Testimony to the Messiah*, Book ii., chap. vii.) compressed the results of his quotations from Philo, furnishes materials for a tolerably accurate judgment as to the relation of the Philonian ideas of the Logos, to portions of the New Testament Scriptures.

" In these extracts, I think that the sum of the doctrines of Philo, concerning the Word, may be found. To this Object he gives the epithets—the Son of God, the First-begotten Son, the Eldest Son, the Word, the Divine Word, the Eternal Word, the Eldest Word, the Most Sacred Word, the First-begotten Word, the Offspring of God as a stream from the fountain, the Beginning, the Name of God, the Shadow of God, the Image ($\epsilon i \kappa \grave{\omega} \nu$) of God, the Eternal Image, the Copied Image ($\dot{\alpha} \pi \epsilon \iota \kappa \acute{o} \nu \iota \sigma \mu \alpha$), the Express Image ($\chi \alpha \rho \alpha \kappa \tau \grave{\eta} \rho$) of the seal of God, the Branch or Rising Light ($\dot{\alpha} \nu \alpha \tau o \lambda \acute{\eta}$), the Angel, the Eldest Angel, the Archangel of many titles, the Inspector of Israel, the Interpreter of God, a Representative God, a Second God, a God to those creatures whose capacities or attainments are not adequate to the contemplation of the Supreme Father. . . . To this Word are ascribed intelligence, design, and active powers ; He is declared to have been the Instrument of the Deity in the creation, disposition, and government of the universe. . . . He is the instrument and medium of Divine communications, the High Priest and Mediator for the honour of God and the benefit of man, the Messenger of the Father, perfectly sinless Himself, the Beginning and Fountain of virtue to men, their Guide in the path of obedience, the Protector and Supporter of the virtuous, and the Punisher of the wicked. Yet the Word is also represented as being the same to the Supreme Intellect that speech is to the human ; and as being the conception, idea, or purpose of the Creator, existing in the Divine Mind previously to the actual formation of His works."

The anticipation of a better future, the instinct of expectation, without which, as a nation, Israel could not live, was, we are assured, provided for and directed by the Almighty, "through a long series of authoritative announcements, which centred very remarkably upon a coming Person, and fed continuously by the Messianic belief, which was in truth interwoven with the deepest life of the people." The Messianic doctrine was unfolded through four progressive stages—three within, and a fourth beyond the limits of the Old Testament Scriptures. In the first stage, which ended with Moses, the personal rank of the Messiah is not defined, though personal characteristics gradually emerge, and the Divinity not expressly asserted is, to minds properly attuned to discover it, implied. Now, in affirming the presence of a Messianic element in the Old Testament, Mr Liddon is on the side of truth : there is such an element, Divine in its origin and purpose, and progressively expanded beneath the influences of a Providential Will; but the prophetic intimations in which it is embodied, and more especially the earlier ones, are much less direct and definite than Mr Liddon imagines. To what an extent his zeal blinds him to the greatest difficulties, and causes him to intrude the ideas of dogmatic Christianity into regions where they are utterly out of place, may be gathered from his summary of Pentateuchal Messianic announcements, among which he confidently reckons a much disputed and quite unprovable interpretation of Gen. xlix. 10.

"In that predicted victory over the Evil One ; in that blessing which is to be shed on all the families of the earth ; in that rightful sway over the gathered peoples ; in the absolute and perfect teaching of that Prophet Who is to be like the great Lawgiver while yet He transcends Him,—must we not trace a predicted destiny which reaches higher than the known limits of the highest human energy? Is not this early prophetic language only redeemed from the imputation of exaggeration or vagueness by the point and justification which are secured to it through the more explicit disclosures of a succeeding age?" (p. 79).

But I am concerned with those texts only which are supposed to notify, more or less clearly, Messiah's Deity. Mr Liddon descries many such, but in almost every passage he handles, he neglects the contexts, and withdraws from their historical and textual surroundings a few words susceptible of an extreme sense. "The promise of a Kingdom to David and to his house *for ever*— (2 Sam. vii. 16), a promise on which, we know, the great Psalmist rested at the hour of his death (2 Sam. xxiii. 5)—could not be fulfilled by any mere continuation of his dynasty on the throne of Jerusalem. It implied, as both David and Solomon saw, some Superhuman Royalty." Now here—(1.) The utmost meaning is put into the phrase *for ever*, a phrase which, though it may denote eternity, depends for its precise force on the association in which it is employed, and is often used rhetorically to denote prolonged but limited duration. That David understood it in the limited meaning may be conjectured from verse 19, where he says: "Thou hast spoken of Thy servant's house for *a distant time*," using a word which indicates mere remoteness (compare the *far off, far*, 2 Sam. xv. 17 ; Prov. xxv. 25 ; Isa. xiii. 5). (2) The context, verses 14 and 15, shows that the seed of David, in whom the promise was to be fulfilled, was not superhuman (comp. Ps. lxxxix. 30–33).

The language of neither the second nor the forty-fifth Psalm is, as a whole, and in strictness, applicable to Christ, although both Psalms contain expressions which may allegorically, and by fair accommodation, be applied to Him. Verse 9 of the second Psalm does not suitably portray the method and effects of Christ's government ; and the warlike attributes extolled in verses 3, 4, and 5 of the forty-fifth, are not befitting the person and character of the Prince of Peace. Both Psalms primarily refer to Solomon, or some other Jewish monarch, and celebrate, with the license of poetical exaggeration, that monarch's dominion and glory. The forty-fifth appears to be a nuptial ode on the occasion of a king's marriage with a king's daughter. There is, therefore, an original historical sense, and a real point of attachment among the personages and events of Jewish annals. No exposition can be correct which has not the primary historical meaning for its basis. The Messianic signification is secondary, ideal, and suggested.

The statement, Psalm ii. 7, "Thou art my Son, this day have I begotten Thee" (comp. Exod. iv. 22 ; 2 Sam. vii. 14 ; Ps. lxxxix. 27), cannot possibly intimate that Messiah was an Eternal Person within the Self-existent Substance, and does *not* prove that "His Sonship is not merely theocratic or ethical, but Divine." St Paul saw in our Lord's resurrection from the dead, the Messianic fulfilment of the Psalmist's words (Acts xiii. 33 ; with which compare Rom. i. 4). Verse 12 is not, in the New Testament, applied to Christ, and Mr Liddon entirely misstates its purport, when he says, "All who trust in Him (the Son) are blessed ; all who incur His wrath must perish with a sharp and swift destruction." *Kiss*, that is, *do homage to, the Son ;* and,

Offer pure homage, worship purely, are both admissible translations, though the latter seems entitled to the preference. The
Septuagint and the Vulgate have *lay hold of instruction*. But,
whether *Son* or *purely* be the better rendering, the anger depre-
cated is the anger of Jehovah, the trust enjoined is trust in Him.

The 6th and 7th verses of the forty-fifth Psalm are applied
by the writer of the Epistle to the Hebrews to Christ (i. 8, 9),
and in them, "Messiah is directly addressed as God."   Now
it might be enough to make the very obvious remark, that the
Jewish King, of whom the Psalmist was thinking, was not God,
and therefore, the word *Elohim* must either be understood in an
inferior sense, or verse 6 must be regarded as a parenthesis describing the Almighty's throne. But there, again, the translation is, in the opinion of competent judges, very debateable.
Many of the best Hebrew scholars render, *thy throne of God, i.e.,*
thy throne, given and protected by God ; or according to a not
infrequent usage, the name of God may be employed to convey
the notion of excellence and high distinction—*thy exalted throne.*
Against the Hebraists who dissent from the received translation,
the dictum of Dr Pusey would have small weight, even if it were
recommended by less contumeliousness and more charity than
appear in Mr Liddon's extract.

Mr J. J. S. Perowne, an excellent Hebraist, and one who
knows how to temper orthodox convictions with fairness, retains.
in his work on the Psalms, the vocative rendering, *O God*, but he
also remarks : "This rendering seems indeed, at first sight, to be
at variance with the first and historical application of the Psalm.
Can Solomon, or any Jewish King, be thus directly addressed as
God ?   We find the title given to rulers, kings, or judges,
(lxxxii. 6, 7): 'I said, Ye are *gods*' (see our Lord's comment, John
x. 35); xcvii. 7 ; Exod. xxi. 6. Calvin, indeed, objects that
Elohim is only thus used in the plural, or with some restriction,
as when Moses is said to be made a God (*Elohim*) unto Pharaoh
(Exod. vii. 1). But the word is evidently used of one person in
1 Sam. xxviii. 13, as is plain from Saul's question, ' What form
is *he* of ?' though our version renders, ' I saw gods ascending.'"

But whatever the true translation may be, the context demonstrates that the meaning which Mr Liddon seeks to establish,
cannot be the right one. How can a co-equal Person in the
Eternal Godhead be said to have a God, and to be by that God
" anointed with the oil of gladness above his fellows ?" Who are
His fellows or associates, if He is a necessary Form, &c., in the
inmost life of the Self-existent Being ? Mr Perowne, while ' most

unhesitatingly admitting that the words of the Psalm have a meaning which is only fully realized in Christ,' comments on verse 7 : " But this Divine King is nevertheless a distinct person from God himself—GOD, EVEN THY GOD, peculiar to this Book of the Psalms, instead of ' *Jehovah* thy God.' "

In the language of the seventy-second Psalm, which no New Testament writer has quoted or explained of Christ, there is a strongly ideal element, and the expression of inspired hopes and aspirations too pure and lofty to be realized in the reign of any one of the historical series of Jewish Sovereigns. But the ideal element was joined to, and grew out of, what was real. The poet's thoughts were engaged upon the accession of a contemporary monarch, to whose reign he looked forward with pious wishes and bright anticipations. We cannot suppose his language to have been simply and purely prophetic—detached from all significance and association in his own times. It is not of the kind to be literalized, and treated as accurate measured description, consciously designed to depict " the character and extent of the Messianic Sovereignty," still less to foretell that He would be " a King immortal, all-knowing, and all-mighty," and therefore, in the highest sense, Divine.

From the hundred and tenth Psalm, Mr Liddon makes this deduction : " The Son of David is David's Lord, because He is God ; the Lord of David is David's Son, because He is God Incarnate." The deduction is quite arbitrary. On the expression *my Lord* (*Adoni*) no stress can be laid. It is no more than a form of courteous designation and address commonly given to superiors. The Hebrew word employed expresses superiority in the most general sense, and when applied to the Almighty it is nearly always written *Adondi*, as in verse 5 of the Psalm now referred to. " Jehovah said to my lord," is therefore language which does not touch the question of Christ's Divinity ; and the protection and honour conferred by Jehovah, surely do not attest that he on whom they are conferred is by nature Jehovah's equal. It is a poor straining of language to say, " Messiah is sitting on the right hand of Jehovah, as the partner of His dignity." We may waive all inquiry about the authorship of the Psalm, and need not insist upon the probability that, by the expression *my Lord*, the poet meant his earthly sovereign. Granting, on the strength of Matt. xxii. 41–45, and parallels in Mark and Luke, that David, looking into the future of his progeny, was inspired to behold the Messiah, his acknowledgment of Messiah's superiority is no sort of proof he expected Messiah to be God. Messiah might be David's son, and also David's lord, without being Jehovah, David's God.

On the Messianic sense of the Psalms, the conclusion arrived at by Dr Davidson, is a good general reply to the method of interpretation adopted by Mr Liddon, and will commend itself to reverent and reflecting Protestant minds, not governed by orthodox or anti-orthodox theories. "Nothing should be allowed to stand in the way of the grammatical and historical interpretation, not even the letter of the New Testament, else truth and independence are sacrificed. In that case Scripture is injured or perverted. . . . The dead letter must give way to the living voice within, else God is dishonoured. In conformity with a right interpretation, we hold that no *direct, definite, conscious* prophecies of Messiah appear in the Psalms. There are unconscious ones—the indefinite longings and hopes for coming restoration—ideas of future completion and glory in the royal line of David. The New Testament writers quoted and applied such passages according to the current sense of their time, without thought of the original meaning. . . . We are not disposed to deny the operation of the Divine Spirit in leading the authors of the Psalms to select poetical images that might be accommodated to the Saviour. A principal point to be kept in view is the *ideal nature* of poetical pictures sometimes given by these lyric writers. Moments of higher inspiration came over them, when they were transported in spirit to future times, and spake in glowing terms of scenes resplendent with earthly glory. Starting from the praises of a present monarch, they were rapt in poetic vision, to paint the reign of some majestic one, to whom all the ends of the earth should do homage. These were to them but ideal scenes, the manifestation of far-reaching hopes and yearning desires engendered in minds of transcendent grasp" (*Introduction to Old Testament*, Vol. ii., pp. 286, 287).

In the third period, extending from the reign of Uzziah to the close of the Hebrew Canon, "Messianic prophecy reaches its climax; it expands into the fullest particularity of detail respecting Messiah's Human Life; it mounts to the highest assertions of His Divinity" (p. 83). The passages supposed to contain the fullest particularity of detail are subjected to Mr Liddon's usual method, and therefore made to mean anything and everything which suits his hypothesis. Sentences and descriptions detached from the contexts whereby their meaning is restricted and determined, become so many loose phrases, amid which the prior theory of the interpreter may be incased. Fragmentary texts, taken from various places, are ingeniously dovetailed together, and made, by arbitrary combination, to announce or insinuate the doctrine for which a Scriptural dress is sought.   By such workmanship it is comparatively easy to clothe in the language of Scripture, conclusions which the expositor brings to the study of Scripture.

How pervadingly the previous conviction underlies and shapes Mr Liddon's interpretations, may be illustrated by two examples, one in which the warping influence is dimly disclosed, the other in which it is glaringly conspicuous.   He thus paraphrases Isa. xi. 3 : "He will not be dependent like a human magistrate upon the evidence of His senses ; He will not judge after the sight of His eyes, nor reprove after the hearing of His ears ; He will rely upon the infallibility of a perfect moral insight."   The possession of a Superhuman Nature and Divine attributes is here suggested ; but when we turn to the words of the prophet in the second, and the earlier part of the third verse, we perceive immediately there is no foundation for the suggestion.   The Spirit of Jehovah resting on a human nature, gifting it with wisdom, and animating it with the fear of Jehovah, is the avowed source of the righteous judgment ascribed to " the Branch who grows from Jesse's roots." Being guided by the Spirit of God, he will " not judge according to the appearance, but will judge righteous judgment."

By a reference to Jer. xxxi. 31–35, Messiah is, without any conceivable excuse, confounded with Jehovah.   " Such is His Spiritual Power as Prophet and Legislator, that He will write the law of the Lord, not upon tables of stone, but on the heart and conscience of the true Israel."   Now, granting the passage does in a general manner relate to the Messianic period and its attendant spiritual blessings, how can that fact intimate that the anointed Prophet and Legislator, whose followers are to receive God's blessings, is God himself ?   The text says, " I (Jehovah) will write my law in their hearts," &c.

But I pass on to the texts in which prophecy " mounts to the highest assertions of Christ's Divinity."   Among these Isa. ix. 6 holds the foremost place, and Mr Liddon contends, the plain literal sense expressly names Christ "the Mighty God."   Now, the words, " *The* mighty God," would to both Jewish and Christian apprehensions be a description appropriate to the Supreme Being alone.   But in the Hebrew the definite article is not prefixed, and to say the sense requires it to be understood, is to assume the very point in dispute.   The article, therefore, since it does not appear in the original, and does not necessarily belong to the exact sense, must not be introduced. "Mighty God" is, no doubt, a literal translation, but certainly not the only admissible translation. Many of the best authorities are of opinion the word rendered *God* ought to be taken in a lower and more comprehensive meaning ; and any one who is able to consult a Hebrew Lexicon, may readily convince himself their opinion is not destitute of foundation. The presence of a proverbially minute Hebrew letter would establish the translation, *a mighty hero*, which Gesenius and others approve, and which the ancient versions of Aquila, Symmachus, and Theodotion sustain. The Alexandrine MS. of the Septuagint* has the rendering, *strong potentate*, or, dividing the words, *strong, a potentate*, where the adjective is more probably designed to be the equivalent of the term rendered in the Vulgate and English Versions, *God*. The Vatican MS. differs from the Alexandrine in not having any of the titles given in the Hebrew, and agrees with it in the ascription of one title which the Hebrew does not give. The Vatican reading is simply, " His name is called Messenger of great counsel" (perhaps, " of the great council.") The Septuagint translators do not seem to have considered the passage a prophecy respecting a future birth. Had they regarded the verbs as " perfects of prophecy, having a future meaning," they would probably have rendered them by future tenses, instead of *has been born, has been given*. The circumstance that no New Testament writer cites a passage so appropriately Messianic, favours the supposition that the Vatican reading stood in the Septuagint of apostolic days.

To return to the particular phrase on which Mr Liddon builds, *Mighty God*. If that translation were quite unquestion-

---

* This Version, and not the original Hebrew, is the source whence the great majority of the New Testament quotations from the Old are drawn. The Version itself is unquestionably older than any existing Hebrew MS. ; and no known Hebrew MS. dates so far back as the fourth and fifth centuries, to which, in all probability, the Vatican and Alexandrine MSS. of the Septuagint may be respectively assigned. The following extract is from the Article *Septuagint* in Smith's "Dictionary of the Bible :"— " We do not attribute any paramount *authority* to the Septuagint on account of its superior antiquity to the extant Hebrew MSS., but we take it as an evidence of a more ancient Hebrew text, as an eye-witness of the texts, 280 or 180 years B.C. . . . Thus, the Hebrew will sometimes correct the Greek, and sometimes the Greek the Hebrew ; both liable to err through the infirmity of human eyes and hands, but each checking the other's errors." Some of the differences between the Septuagint and the Hebrew are very broad and material. Quotations in the New Testament often differ both from the Septuagint and the Hebrew. With respect to the Hebrew Text, it should always be remembered that the vowel points, which were not employed till after the fifth Christian century, have the effect, in a multitude of instances, of imposing a particular sense.

able, it would not necessarily denote possession of the Divine Nature, but of Godlike strength and qualities. Titles are not. as a rule, definitions of nature, but pertain to offices, qualifications, and achievements. *Mighty*, or *heroic God*, may, as Dr Davidson explains, be "equivalent to a hero who fights and conquers like an invincible God." Isaac Leeser, in his corrected English Version,* so translates that the definite article becomes fairly introducible : "Counsellor of the mighty God, of the everlasting Father;" and in his Notes observes: "The only difficulty in the verse is the word *El*, which may as well be rendered, with Aben Ezra, *powerful*, as *God*." Dr Pusey, as cited by Mr Liddon, does not deny that in Ezek. xxxi. 11, *El* is used of Nebuchadnezzar, "*hero, ruler*, or *mighty one*, among the nations ;" and again, in the plural (Ezek. xxxii. 21), *strong among the mighty;* or, *most powerful of the strong* (Vulgate) ; see also Exod. xv. 11. It is quite possible that in these instances, and in Isaiah ix. 6, the word fully written would have the *Yod*, that exceedingly small Hebrew letter, whose presence would put an end to contentions. However, be the correct translation what it may, the context forbids the sense for which Mr Liddon contends. The prophet, when he wrote of a child's being born, and a son given, who should sit upon David's throne, could not possibly have meant that the child and son was the Lord of Hosts. He had no knowledge of the ecclesiastical Triad of later times, and though his language may be suited to facts and personages beyond the conscious range of his thoughts, it cannot define ideas utterly foreign to his mind.

The epithets; *Jehovah is our Righteousness* (Jer. xxiii. 5); and, Immanuel, *God with us* (Isa. vii. 14 ; Matt. i. 23); are, Mr Liddon asserts, "descriptive of our Lord's nature, and not merely appellative." As to the words in Jeremiah, there is room for very great doubt whether the title used is given to Messiah at all. The grammatical construction equally permits the title to be referred to Israel, or, to the Righteous Branch which Jehovah promises to raise unto David. The reference to Israel is supported by xxxiii. 15, 16, where Jerusalem is called by the same name, a fact which sufficiently shows the name is not descriptive of nature, and can furnish no argument whatever for the Divinity of Jesus. The two words, *Jehovah Tsidkenu*, ought, indisputably, to be connected by the verb substantive; *Jehovah is our Righteousness* is the true rendering, and the expression and its application

* Trübner & Co.

may be compared with the names given to altars (Exod. xvii. 15 ; Judges vi. 24). The Septuagint version is—" This is the name which the Lord shall call him, Josedek (*Lord of righteousness*), among the prophets ;" the Vulgate—both here and in chap. xxxiii. —" This is the name which they shall call him, Our righteous Lord."

With regard to Isaiah vii. 14, it is so very obvious the name Immanuel cannot predicate a personal, in contradistinction to a providential, presence of God, that Mr Liddon's reference to the text hardly deserves remark. But an ordinarily attentive reader of Isaiah vii. sees at once that the promise made for the encouragement of Ahaz, was a promise to be speedily, not remotely fulfilled. A child to be called Immanuel (*God with us*), in token of Divine guardianship and assistance, was soon to be born (comp. viii. 8). The terms of the promise are, also, thoroughly and manifestly inapplicable to Christ. The only blessing promised is the deliverance of Judah, implied in the desolation and abandonment of Syria and Israel, the land of whose kings Ahaz was afraid. Nothing spiritual, nothing worthy of our Saviour, nothing suitable to Him, is announced. The writer of the first chapter of the First Gospel, or the inserter of the quotation from Isaiah, took the passage in a loose and typical sense, and his application of it is in no respect decisive. The Hebrew word employed is not that which is often used for virgin in the strict sense, but a less exact word, which means no more than a young, marriageable woman (Gesenius, Fuerst, Davidson), and is so translated by the Septuagint four times out of six, though not in Isaiah vii. 14, where they may have thought the young woman designated, to have been unmarried when the prophecy was spoken. It is used in Prov. xxx. 19, which seems to be connected in sense with verse 20. It has a masculine form—" a young man" (1 Sam. xvii. 56 ; xx. 22), a plural derivative from which denotes "youthful age, or period" (Job xx. 11 ; xxxiii. 25 ; Ps. lxxxix. 46 (45) ; Isa. liv. 4).

Zechariah xiii. 7 does not refer to Christ, and therefore does not " term Him the Fellow or Equal of the Lord of Hosts." Our Saviour did not apply the passage in its original sense, or say it was prophetic of Himself (Matt. xxvi. 31 ; Mark xiv. 27). He merely quoted a portion of it, as an appropriate description of what was then about to take place, the point He had chiefly in view, being the dispersion of His disciples in consequence of His trial and death. *The man of my fellowship,* to whom Zechariah's words referred, was a Jewish King, " so called by God, He

being also King of Israel" (Fuerst); the association is in the
Kingly office, and in that alone. The historical sense appears to be
a declaration of the Divine anger against a bad shepherd or ruler.
Perhaps, as Dr Davidson suggests, "the prophet may refer to
Pekah, whose reign was most disastrous to the people of Israel.
When the shepherd had been smitten and the sheep scattered,
Jehovah would turn His hand toward the poor, weak, afflicted
ones, and have compassion on them." The Vatican Septuagint
Version is, "Awake, O sword, against my shepherds, and against
a man who is my citizen, saith the Lord Almighty, smite ye the
shepherds, and draw out the sheep." The Alexandrine copy
agrees more closely with the Hebrew, but has the rendering,
"against a man who is my citizen."

It is a pity Mr Liddon has done Dr Pusey the unkindness of
bringing forward one of the weak, untenable arguments, wherein,
in his book on Daniel, he has allowed his prepossessions, or, as he
would say, his faith, to dictate to his scholarship.* There is no
proof the word rendered *my fellow* had been "disused and was
revived out of Leviticus." The statement involves the inadmissible assumption that, between the date of Zechariah and the
time when the Book of Leviticus received its final editing and
emendations, there was a long interval. Whatever may have been
the date of the Pentateuch in its earliest shape, all Hebrew
scholars are agreed that as it now stands there is no important
difference between its language and that of later books written
shortly before the return of the Israelites from the Babylonish
captivity. This fact points to the substitution of more modern
for ancient forms of expression. And if the absence of the word
in question, between Leviticus and Zechariah, proves it had fallen
into disuse, what does its absence from the other Pentateuchal
books, supposed to be contemporary with Leviticus, and written
by the same hand, prove? It is a puerile forcing of a word
which signifies companionship, association, friendship, and not
primarily, or directly, identity of nature, to say, "In Leviticus
the word is used strictly of a fellow-man, one who is as himself.
The name designates one united indissolubly by common bonds

---

* The very unfavourable estimate formed by Ewald, and other learned
Hebraists, concerning Dr Pusey's critical knowledge in the language of which
he is a Professor, is, no doubt, caused not so much by deficient scholarship,
as by the special pleading, and reliance on wretched reasonings, into which
his downright uncompromising support of traditional orthodoxy sometimes
betrays him. His intellect and attainments are absolutely subservient to the
traditionalisms with which his piety is bound up. He is an earnest, saintly
man, worthy of all love and respect, except in his capacity as a theologian.

of nature, which a man may violate but cannot annihilate. When, then, this title is applied to the relation of an individual to God, it is clear that That Individual can be no mere man, but must be one united with God by an Unity of Being." We might as reasonably infer, the Lord of Hosts is human, because He calls a *man* His fellow, as infer, the man is of the same Uncreated Nature with the Lord of Hosts. Is it not a preposterous thing gravely to argue that, "man of my fellowship," stands for, " Divine Being Who is by nature One with Me ? "

In Zech. ii. 10–13 ; xii. 10, Mr Liddon discerns a reference, in the clearest language, to " Christ's Incarnation and Passion, as being that of Jehovah Himself." As to the verses in chap. ii., I must leave the clearness of the reference to those who are able to perceive it, and with regard to xii. 10, the Evangelist (John xix. 37) has, perhaps, followed the true reading : " They shall look on Him (not me) whom they pierced." Jehovah is the Speaker, and if the piercing is physical and literal, the person mourned over would seem to be the person pierced. But, surely, no prophet of Old Testament days could have spoken about piercing Jehovah, and bitterly lamenting over Him as though He were dead. " Many Hebrew MSS., and some old editions, read, ' look to *Him*,' which agrees with the Evangelist's quotation " (Davidson); but, for the reading of the received text, the external authority is strong. Leeser makes out a consistent sense, by supposing an ellipsis : " They will look up toward Me (for every one) whom they have thrust through ;" and explains in a note : " The objective case is omitted in the original : *whom they have pierced*, cannot be in apposition to *me*, because the next clause is, *they will lament for him*, not *me ;* hence it is clear that the objective, *every one*, must be supplied." Fuerst (*Lexicon*) assigns to the verb a secondary, metaphorical meaning, *to revile, to calumniate*, and in so doing comes very near the Septuagint translation : " because they have insulted (me)." The spirit of grace and supplication to be poured out upon the house of David and the inhabitants of Jerusalem, would cause them to look up to Jehovah with contrition, because in the rejection and slaughter of His prophets, they had insulted Him. In the New Testament application of the passage, a martyred prophet " is viewed as a type of the higher martyr, Christ."

By his reference to Hag. ii. 7, 9, Mr Liddon appears to indorse the translation, *Desire of all nations*, and to understand it of the Messiah. But that translation does not quite accurately express the meaning ; and the application to Christ is indisput-

ably wrong. Only two meanings are admitted by good Hebraists :
(1,) *the desirable or precious things—treasure of all nations;* (2,)
the choice of all nations—the noblest and best of all peoples. The
Septuagint translation is somewhat ambiguous, but it expresses
one or other of the two meanings just given. There is, therefore.
nothing to sustain the statement, "Haggai implies Messiah's
Divinity by foretelling that His presence will make the glory of
the second temple greater than the glory of the first." Haggai's
prediction is nowhere, in the New Testament, referred to Christ.

Mal. iii. 1, should not be disjoined from the question with
which the preceding chapter ends : *Where is the God of judgment or justice ?* A judicial advent of the *Almighty* is foretold.
the use of the Hebrew definite article with the otherwise general
title, *Lord (Adon)*, and the proprietorship of the Temple, fixing
the sense. The text, therefore, does not "point to Messiah as
the Angel of the Covenant, Jehovah, Whom Israel was seeking,
and Who would suddenly come to His temple" (p. 89). The
Angel or Messenger of the Covenant, and Jehovah, are evidently
distinct persons, the former being denominated (iv. 5) *Elijah the
prophet,* to whom John the Baptist answered (Matt. xi. 14 ; xvii.
12). "The verse before us asserts that Jehovah would send His
messenger to prepare His way—the messenger of the covenant
they wished ; and immediately after, the Lord Himself should
suddenly enter His temple—*He* shall come. But who may abide
the day of His coming, &c.? The *coming* refers to Jehovah Himself, not to His Messenger who is *sent.* Jehovah comes to punish,
purify, and refine (comp. iii. 17, 18). By connecting the clauses
of the verse with one another alternately, the whole becomes apparent : ' Behold, I will send My messenger, and he shall prepare
the way before Me ; even the messenger of the covenant whom
ye delight in ; and the Lord whom ye seek shall suddenly come
to His temple, behold He shall come, saith the Lord of hosts.'"
(Davidson, *Introduction, &c.,* Vol. iii., p. 344). If we leave the
arrangement of the clauses unchanged, and render the conjunctive
particle by its more usual meaning, *and,* instead of, *even,* we can then
refer *He shall come,* to *the Lord,* and obtain, with some obscurity,
the sense which the above transposition more clearly brings out.

After interweaving texts from the Old Testament in a manner
to make them appear to contain and enunciate the dogma he
advocates, Mr Liddon exclaims, "Read this language as a whole :
read it by the light of the great doctrine which it attests, and
which in turn illuminates it, the doctrine of a Messiah, Divine as
well as Human :—all is natural, consistent, full of point and mean-

ing." By "as a whole," he means, "as I have selected and packed it." Not a passage he quotes in relation to Christ's Divinity will, when legitimately interpreted by its context, bear the meaning he thrusts into it. His appeal to the Old Testament is simply a string of audacious assertions, arrayed in phrases picked from this place and that, just such fragments being torn out of a Psalm, or Prophetic book, as will serve his purpose. Of this he seems to have a dim consciousness, though he is not at all ashamed of it, and fails to perceive how injuriously it affects his cause. He complains that, "It is possible to avoid any frank acknowledgment of the imposing spectacle presented by converging and consentient lines of prophecy, and to refuse to consider the prophetic utterances, except in detail and one by one; as if, forsooth, Messianic prophecy were an intellectual enemy whose forces must be divided by the criticism that would conquer it." The complaint is highly characteristic, and reveals the mind of one who has sunk the judge and inquirer in the advocate. How can we ascertain the meaning of prophetic utterances otherwise than singly and in detail? The true sense of each one must be discovered before we can classify them, or assign to each its place in a scheme embracing the whole. They cannot be fairly blended, or mutually strengthen each other, until each has been ascertained to have a definite and concordant meaning. They cannot acquire by combination a sense different *in kind* from that which belongs to each individually. The objection to Mr Liddon's argument is, that the passages which he imagines his selected fragments to represent, have not the definite and concordant meaning required. They are not, for the purpose he has in view, properly cumulative, and reciprocally corroborative evidences, but vague, unconnected, and often discordant materials. No doubt, if, forgetting the specialties of the Hebrew intellect, of Jewish culture, and Eastern diction, we look for philosophical ideas, and precise guarded expression, we may be tempted to think the wording of prophecy "overstrained and exaggerated," and reasonable interpretation of it "insipid and disappointing." But the presence in the Old Testament Books of a Messianic element, and of statements designed by God to receive in Christ their highest fulfilment, may be freely and even urgently recognised, while the obviously truthful confession is not withheld: "It is impossible to suppose that the mystery of the Incarnation was distinctly revealed and clearly understood under the Old Testament dispensation. God does not thus make haste with men" (Perowne on *Psalm* xlv.)

To minds filled with the impressions of traditional orthodoxy, rational expositions of Scripture must, for the most part, seem flat and unsavoury. Agreement with their prepossessions is, to such minds, the measure of truth and spirituality—disagreement well nigh the sole source of difficulties. Calm investigation and rational judgment are not the instruments employed in reaching conclusions, and no faultiness is seen in a method of interpretation which proceeds on the supposition that the Sacred writers, while at one moment in the current of ideas belonging to their age, were at the next moment carried quite above and beyond it, and prompted to use language which was to themselves either meaningless, or had a meaning which contradicted their most cherished convictions. It is sophistry and subterfuge to refer to Rabbinical literature, and say, " In that literature nothing is plainer than that the ancient Jews believed the expected Messiah to be Divine, with a belief notoriously based upon the language of the Prophets and Psalmists." *Divine* is an ambiguous word, and may signify much less than the proper Deity of the One Uncreated Being. In what sense does Mr Liddon use the word? The question is not whether some of the Jews have recognised in Messiah Godlike qualities, or imagined Him to exhibit and exercise some of Jehovah's attributes; but, have they apprehended Him to be truly and properly God, equal to, and in Essence the same with, Jehovah? Assuredly they have not. The Jews have always believed in One God, and One only. To them, the Lord of Heaven and earth has ever been not merely One Nature, but One Individual Being. They have never, either in Old Testament or subsequent times, acknowledged a Godhead embracing distinctions of Persons, and if they had ever believed Messiah to be truly God, they must have expected the One Almighty Infinite Spirit would personally clothe Himself in flesh, and dwell among men. Can Mr Liddon affirm they ever did expect this? Can he produce the testimonies which enshrine such an expectation, and name the document where Jews have taught, or even conjectured, that Messiah and Jehovah are One and the same Being? If he cannot, the language in which he refers to Rabbinical literature is unwarranted and deceptive. He has trusted too implicitly to the representations of Schöttgen, on whose "*Horæ Hebraicæ et Talmudicæ*," well informed and prudent scholars now place a much abated reliance. The enormous improbability that Jews would imagine the Divine Nature to comprise more than One Personal God, interdicts an easy credence to the statements of zealous partisans, who descry distinctively ecclesiastical theories in the flighty mysticism of Rabbis by whom Christianity was despised.

Mr Westcott, in his chapter on "The Jewish Doctrine of Messiah" (*Introduction to the Study of the Gospels*), does not permit orthodox convictions and desires to beguile him into assertions incapable of proof, and of Schüttgen he says : " He has accumulated a most valuable collection of Jewish traditions; but, apart from minor inconsistencies, he exhibits no critical perception whatever of the relative value of the authorities which he quotes, and often seems to me to misinterpret the real tenor of their testimony. The writers who have followed him have for the most part confirmed his errors."

The *Book of Zohar*, written or compiled in the thirteenth century (Schüttgen suspects by a Christian), is one great fountain of arguments for coincidences and resemblances between Rabbinical opinions and the Church's revelations. Westcott judges Schüttgen's deductions from this Kabbalistic compilation to be unwarranted ; and in a paragraph on " False Interpretations of Zohar," writes : "Pantheism lies at the basis of Zohar. At the same time, speculations on the Divine Nature are necessarily so vague, that recent theologians have found in Zohar the whole of Christianity. The two natures of Messiah, and His threefold office, are said to be symbolized ; and those more abstruse questions as to the Person of Christ which agitated and divided the Church, are said to be anticipated and decided in the mystical dogmas of *Simeon ben Jochai*" (the reputed author of *Zohar*).

In the Jewish Messianic hopes and conceptions up to the time of Christ's coming, Mr Westcott affirms, " The essentially Divine Nature of Messiah was not acknowledged ; " and, from his treatment of Rabbinical literature generally, it is clear he regards as not proven, all the positions which Dr Davidson, in the Article before quoted, pointedly denies. The best ascertained results of the evidence appear to be summarized in Dr Davidson's words :—

"Following out the hints given in the Book of Daniel, some later Jews conceived that Messiah was concealed with the Father, existing before His appearance to men, the Lord and Judge of all. Highest of the creatures of God, he was the Divine Representative, enthroned in surpassing dignity. Sometimes, again, he was considered a great prophet, the Instructor of the peoples ; or the true Adam, re-appearing to bring back the paradisiacal state. It is impossible to discover a distinct vestige of the belief among the Jews that he was God or truly Divine. None supposed that he was to be of the same or similar substance with the Father. Why? Because it was contrary to their Monotheism. And we are safe in asserting, that no modern Jew interprets the Old Testament in a sense involving the Divinity of Messiah's person. . . . It has been supposed that *the Word (Memra) of Jehovah,* in the Targums, or Jewish paraphrases of the Old Testament, is identical with the Messiah; and therefore, the expression has been used for doctrinal purposes. But the alleged identity is baseless. . . . *The Word of Jehovah* is nothing more than Jehovah Himself, His will going forth into action, His self-revealing agency."

"The will of God in action, His Word taking effect, was the initiative stage of that speculation to which the Jews, ignorant of second causes or the laws of nature, were unavoidably led. By degrees, the Word, or Self-revelation of God, became so prominent, that Jehovah himself receded from view, and the operative power virtually took His place, as a Person by whom He was manifested, a Mediator between the Creator and creature. Such is the process by which the mediative element tended to personality, and terminated in an outward agent."

"In Jewish literature, so far as we know, no identification of the *Memra* of Jehovah with the Messiah occurs. It might be shown that it is sometimes identified with the Shekinah; but the latter was only the visible presence of Jehovah, not a person. As to the correspondence of the *Memra* with the Greek *logos* in John i. 1, and its denoting the same thing, we believe, with Prideaux, that it is precarious to urge it."

"When the Jews are told, that had their forefathers not been swayed by prejudice, they would have perceived 'their promised Messiah was to be the Son of God, co-equal with God, and that he was revealed as such in their own Scriptures,' they know the worth of an assertion *contrary* to their Scriptures."

The exposition which distils the dogma of Christ's Deity from the Old Testament, is remarkably abnormal, and requires the warrant of another revelation to indorse its peculiarities. Indubitably, every maxim of reason is inverted, and all acquaintance with human feeling and intelligence is set at nought, when a faith so fundamental and constantly reiterated as the Hebrew faith in God's Unity, is assumed to be modified by the darkling insinuations of a few phrases which, if they are not decidedly metaphorical, are decidedly ambiguous, and are made to carry in orthodox commentaries the least probable amongst all their possible senses. And if the authors of the New Testament Scriptures had wished to find, and been satisfied they could find, in the Old, evidence for the Godhead of Jesus, such as later exposition concocted, surely they would have adduced something more pertinent than Isaiah vii. 14, and Psalm xlv. 6, 7. In the last chapter of the Gospel according to Luke, the risen Jesus is related to have explained to two of His disciples, " in all the Scriptures the things concerning Himself ; " and again " to have opened the understanding of the apostles, that they might understand the Scriptures." Is there the faintest token of His having drawn upon a store of Messianic prophecy which "mounts to the highest assertions of His Divinity ? "

CHAPTER IV.

Brief criticism of the argument entitled, " Our Lord's work in the world
a witness to His Divinity."—Christ's authority and kingship.—Characteristic " originality and audacity" of His teaching and plan.—Evidence
for the contemplated universality of His kingdom.—Difficulties attaching to the supposition that genuine words of Christ are recorded in
St Matt. xxviii. 19, 20.—Are the " Synoptical accounts of our Lord's
Nativity in *essential* unison with the Christology of St John's Gospel ?"
—The argument concerning the " Doctrine of the Eternal Word in the
Prologue of St John's Gospel " examined.—Strong contrasts between
the accounts in the Synoptists, and the last Gospel, of the time and
manner in which our Lord's Messiahship was freely made known.—
The reasonable conclusion from a general view of his Gospel is, that
the latest Evangelist did not intend in his Prologue to affirm the absolute Deity of the *Logos* or *Word*.

MR LIDDON has made a Lecture entitled, " Our Lord's Work in
the World a Witness to His Divinity," preliminary to the discussion of the New Testament witness concerning Christ's nature
and person. This arrangement is hardly the natural one in a
simple search after truth, but, for the aims of mere advocacy, it
has manifest advantages. In dealing with Christianity as a
grand fact in the history of mankind, there is room for much
striking general statement, wherein the inconveniences of accuracy
and attention to details may be avoided, and an impression
favourable to the reception of a particular dogma may be produced. Outlined descriptions of the Kingdom of God, of the
broader features of Christianity, and its success in the world,
may easily be thrown into a shape adapted to the theory that
Christ's proper Deity is the appropriate explanation of every
fact, the solution of every difficulty. They may also be easily
thrown into other shapes, and made to point to different and less
definite conclusions. Creeds which have far less than Christianity has to make them acceptable to the intellect and religious
sentiments of mankind, have spread rapidly, and acquired enduring, extensive, and not easily explicable prevalence. Nothing
more than a very disputable opinion is set forth in the sentence :
" The truth which really and only accounts for the establishment

in this our human world, of such a religion as Christianity, and of such an institution as the Church, is the truth that Jesus Christ was believed to be more than Man, the truth that Jesus Christ is what men believed Him to be, the truth that Jesus Christ is God" (p. 146). If the simpler moral and spiritual truths which compose the main substance of Christ's teaching are fundamental laws of human life, borne witness to by the Spirit of God in the human reason and conscience, then, the general language wherein Christ speaks of the Kingdom of God, and the actual triumph of the Gospel, may both be accounted for by recognising the hand of Our Father in Heaven, and seeing in Christ—not His Equal and a sufficient substitute for Him—but His Son, and Servant, and Messenger, furnished by His Spirit to do His work, and to become our Lord, and Guide, and Pattern, in the path which leads to Him.

There are two or three points in the third Lecture which call for remark; the rest of its reasonings will become valueless if the argument in the succeeding Lectures can be shown to be fallacious.

Christ's authority and Kingship in the Kingdom of God, are spoken of in terms which would be justifiable only when Christ had been proved by the clearest evidence to have claimed absolutely Divine dignity, and to have set Himself before men as the highest and sufficing Object of their adoration. But, as a matter of fact, He did nothing of the kind. It is assumption and exaggeration of the grossest sort to say, " He deliberately proposes to rule all human thought, to make Himself the Centre of all human affections, to be the Lawgiver of humanity, and the Object of man's adoration " (p. 116). Where is there the semblance of proof He did so? He knew that He bore God's commission, that God was with Him, and that His Father's work, in which He was the Instrument, would be prosperous and indestructible; but He never claimed to be, by inherent independent right, the supreme Ruler of mankind. His perfect filial dependence—His unwavering faith in One greater than Himself—His realizing consciousness of His Divine mission, and the presence with Him of " His Father and our Father, His God and our God "—explain the breadth and boldness of His words, when He speaks without directly naming the One Supreme Fountain of all His lordship and power. Mr Liddon must be aware, however much his mind may be saturated with expositions which he conceives to be authoritative, that to quote detached magisterial and regal expressions of Christ's, for the purpose of insinuating He knew himself to be God, and wished, with some reserve, to impart the knowledge to His followers, is to twist and misrepresent the whole tenor of His recorded language. The Kingdom is avowedly His, in a subordinate, not in the highest sense; His Kingship is delegated, not independent and supreme; "His Father appointed unto Him the Kingdom" (Luke xxii. 29), and gave to Him authority and power (Matt. xi. 27; John iii. 35; xiii. 3; xvii. 2, and following verses, which explain xvi. 15). Our Lord speaks continually of *the Kingdom of Heaven* and *the Kingdom of God*, but rarely calls the Kingdom His own, though, in all but the highest sense, it is so. The expression, *my Kingdom*, occurs, I believe, in the language ascribed to Christ, only four times in the Gospels; once in Luke xxii. 30, and three times in a single verse, John xviii. 36; and the expression, *His* (the Son of Man's) *Kingdom*, occurs only twice. The attempt, therefore, to infer Christ's Deity from His claims to Sovereignty is quite futile. If the nine-tenths of His language which are explicit, may be allowed to elucidate the other tenth, He is Lord and King under God, and in an acceptation which in no degree suggests His Deity, but implies that, in relation to God, His sovereignty is secondary, official, and conferred.

Mr Liddon considers, "the formation of an organized society was of the very essence of the work of Christ;" and, from the teaching of Christ himself, would fain elicit the lines of a definite and extended organization. A Kingdom of souls, a spiritual Society—"whose original laws are for the most part set forth by its Founder in His Sermon on the Mount," and "whose visibility lies in the fact of its being a society of men, and not a society solely made up of incorporeal beings such as the angels"—is, of course, very flexible with respect to its "governmental organization," and is the very subject for a daring manipulator of texts. Our Lord's declaration that they who confessed or denied Him before men, would be by Him confessed or denied "before His Father in Heaven," and "before the angels of God" (Matt. x. 32, 33; Luke xii. 8, 9), is translated into, the "insistance with great emphasis upon the payment of homage to His Invisible Majesty, outwardly, and before the eyes of men;" and we are apprized, "He provides His realm with a visible government, deriving its authority from Himself, and entitled on this account to deferential and entire obedience on the part of His subjects. To the first members of this government His commission runs thus:—"He that receiveth you receiveth Me" (Matt. x. 40; comp. Luke x. 16). It is the

King Who will Himself reign throughout all history on the thrones of His representatives; it is He Who, in their persons, will be acknowledged or rejected. Now, all this extortionate deduction, so far as it bears on Mr Liddon's main purpose, the ascribing of absolute, highest supremacy to Christ, is excluded by the words of immediate context; "and he that receiveth me, receiveth Him that sent me" (see also Mark ix. 37 ; John xiii. 20). The climax is the reception of "the One God and Father," "The Blessed and Only Potentate," Whose great Apostle Christ is. Here, as elsewhere, Christ studiously leads to One higher and greater than Himself, and carefully shuts out the idea which His modern interpreter, by mutilated quotation, inserts.

In speaking of the originality of our Lord's design and teaching; of "His isolation in early life;" and, " His social obscurity," —Mr Liddon unduly expands very insufficient information, and builds with very slight materials. But, granting that our Lord's mind was never cultivated by training in the schools of Gentile or Jewish speculation, yet, He was profoundly versed in the Canonical and Apocryphal books of the Old Testament, and brought to their study a heart and intellect capable of extracting and assimilating their richest moral and spiritual treasures. To congenial minds inhabited by the Holy Spirit, no kind of truth is so suggestive, and admits of such manifold application, as moral and spiritual truth. To unfold that truth and throw it into new practical forms, did not betoken an originality too vast for Divinely-aided humanity; and the vision of an universal faith, and the establishment of such institutions as Baptism and the Lord's Supper, did not express conceptions so unique and transcendent as to necessitate an Uncreated Person. Christ's foresight that His death and resurrection would be springs of life in the society of His followers, may be explained by prophetic inspiration, without fabricating a Personal Incarnation of Deity. The originality of our Lord's plan has, however, too indirect a bearing on the doctrine of His Divinity, and the plan itself, so far as His own acts and words exhibit it, is too vague a matter to need more than a passing remark. The definiteness and details of organization seem to me to exist solely in subsequent additions; a starting point is mistaken for a prolific germ, and external accretions, more or less congruous, are not discriminated from the unfoldings of intrinsic, vital growth. But on this part of his subject, Mr Liddon, though he strives to contribute to the scope of his argument, commits himself to few precise statements. His aim is rather to suggest and insinuate, and so, predispose the mind of the trustful reader for the reception of what is to follow. Yet an early paragraph of his third Lecture contains an admission in which some readers will see a pregnancy beyond his intention :—" Doubtless there were great saints in ancient Israel; doubtless Israel had prayers and hymns such as may be found in the Psalter, than which nothing more searching and more spiritual has been since produced in Christendom."

The " audacity of Christ's plan," is, we are told, " observable, first of all, in the fact that the plan is originally proposed to the world, with what might appear to us to be such hazardous completeness. The idea of the Kingdom of God issues almost as if in a single jet, and with a fully developed body, from the thought of Jesus Christ. Put together the Sermon on the Mount, the Charge to the Twelve Apostles (St Matt. x. 5–42), the Parables of the Kingdom, the Discourse in the Supper-room (St John xiv., xv., xvi.), and the institution of the two great Sacraments, and the plan of our Saviour is before you. And it is enunciated with an accent of calm unfaltering conviction that it will be realized in human history " (p. 113). Mr Liddon's notion of " a single jet," must be singular ; but perhaps a single jet, when theologically expounded, signifies an intermittent, varied, and eddying stream. Let any one carefully read and compare the utterances referred to, and he will discover neither hazardous completeness, nor perfect consonance, but progressive, perhaps fluctuating thought. The " fully developed body " is imported into the thought of Jesus Christ, from ecclesiastical dogmas and developments. Does the injunction (Matt. x. 5), " Go not into the way of the Gentiles, and into any city of the Samaritans enter ye not; but go rather to the lost sheep of the house of Israel " (see also 23d verse), inaugurate the preaching of a world-wide religion?

An eagerness to find in Christ's words well-defined predictions of the universal spread of His religion, causes the real meaning to be unconsciously overstepped. When the poor woman anointed Him, our Lord did not " simply announce that the act would be told as a memorial of her throughout the world " (Matt. xxvi. 13 ; Mark xiv. 9), but said conditionally, wherever in the whole world the Gospel should be preached, there her conduct would also be narrated. Knowing that the faith and service He enjoined, were the faith and service in which all mankind might find regeneration and communion with God, Christ, confiding in His heavenly Father's love to man, no doubt expected the propagation of His religion among the nations of the earth, but the expression of this expectation is a different thing from designed and formal prediction that in every part of the world His Gospel should be preached. The saying (John x. 16), " Other sheep I have, which are not of this fold," &c., does not amount to an announcement that from all the districts of the globe our Lord will gather sheep, and become the One Shepherd of all men. Later opinions, and after events, cause us to stretch to the utmost the significance of the words ascribed to Him. The true, conscious, original meaning may have been narrower and less defined than the sense we affix. And if after the fashion of expositors, we were to be urgent about verbal minutiæ, we could not forget that in John xvii. 9, 20, our Lord is made to declare, " He prays not for the world, but for His then existing Apostles, and those who, through their word, were believing on Him;" the true reading having the present participle. We are bound to notice that, in Matt. xv. 24, He is made to say, " I was not sent but to the lost sheep of the house of Israel ; " and again, in xix. 28, is made to promise His Apostles that " when He should sit in the throne of His glory, they also should sit upon twelve thrones, judging the twelve tribes of Israel."[*] In Matt. xxiv. ; Mark xiii. ; Luke xxi., the language attributed to Christ himself, though highly figurative and perplexing, imports plainly enough that His second coming, and the end of the world (literally, *winding up of the age*), were to follow very closely after the destruction of Jerusalem, and to take place before the generation which heard His words had passed away : see also Matt. x. 23 ; xvi. 27, 28 ; John xxi. 23 ; and the numerous passages in the Epistles and Apocalypse, which show how, in the expectations of the Apostolic age, Christ's second coming was not remote, but very nigh. The apparently conflicting statements in Matt. xxiv. 14 ; Mark xiii. 10, where our Lord is represented to have said, " That the Gospel must be first preached unto all nations " (see also Luke xxiv., 47), are explained—(1.) by the fact that in Matthew's record a term is used which does not signify *world* in the

----

[*] With Protestants who believe that Christ " not having the Holy Spirit given unto Him by measure," was morally and spiritually perfect, free criticism of the Gospel history is a necessity. If we are to hold to the faith that His character was spotless and lovely, the Christian perception, which His teaching and example have enlightened, must be at liberty to weed the records concerning Him. For instance, which is, to a venerating and rational mind, the more probable conclusion, that two Gospels preserve a legendary story (Matt. xxi. 18, 19 ; Mark xi. 12–14) ; or, that Jesus, under the stimulus of disappointed hunger, cursed a fig-tree for being fruitless at a season when the presence of fruit would have been unwonted?

modern acceptation, but the regions anciently known to be inhabited and civilized; the Roman Empire seems to be its widest New Testament meaning; (2.) by St Paul's description of the extent to which, towards the end of his career, he considered the Gospel to have been already diffused (Col. i. 6, 23).

Matt. xxviii. 19, 20, is a passage too uncertain to be quoted in a controversial work, without some attempt to vindicate its genuineness from the very grave doubts which other portions of the New Testament compel us to entertain. Mark xvi. 15, which only in part agrees with it, is in that concluding section which every scholar knows to be an extremely questionable fraction of the Second Gospel; and the other Gospels do not in any degree sustain it. The words, *uttermost part of the earth* (Acts i. 8), are not determinate. *Earth* may there have the restricted sense before referred to. Bloomfield, having an eye, I presume, to the after narrative, writes in the spirit of a reconciler: "The expression was probably understood by the Disciples of that part of the East only, namely, Syria. But our Lord, doubtless, meant it of the *whole world*." And, if any such plain command had been issued by Christ, how could there have been, as Acts x. and xi. demonstrate there was, hesitation, doubt, and surprise, regarding the admission of the Gentiles to Christian gifts and privileges? Let any ordinarily intelligent and fair-minded man, whose attention has been called to the subject, read the notices of the first preaching of the Gospel to the Gentiles, and then ask himself whether it is credible (if the Acts of the Apostles is trustworthy history) that our Lord had, at a most impressive time, and under most impressive circumstances, uttered the words which Matt. xxviii. 19, 20, puts into his mouth? It is simply inconceivable the Apostles should have forgotten such a charge, or have failed to adduce it in a difficulty, which, if it had not totally prevented, it would in a moment have set at rest. Yet there is no trace of recollection of, or reference to, the grand and solemn commission, in whose exact wording Mr Liddon finds the occasion for an outburst of declamatory rhetoric (p. 117). It is noticeable, moreover, that St Paul, when he writes concerning the duty of preaching the Gospel to the Gentiles, and the Christian equality of Gentile and Jew, never appeals to the great Master's decisive parting injunction, an injunction on which, if genuine, the duty of teaching all nations must have been felt in large measure to rest. Supposing that injunction to have been really given, the distinction between the Apostleships of the circumcision and the uncircumcision (Gal. ii. 7–9), must have been purely nominal, arbitrary, and unauthorized.

But this, though sufficient, is not the whole evidence against the genuineness of the passage. The Acts and Epistles contain several references to Christian Baptism, but no vestiges of the formula, " In the Name of the Father, and of the Son, and of the Holy Ghost." It is, indeed, next to impossible to believe, in the face of Acts viii. 16 ; xix. 5 ; Rom. vi. 3 ; Gal. iii. 27 ; 1 Cor. i. 13–15, that the Christians of Apostolic days used the formula.* Baptism *into the Name of Jesus Christ*, and *into Jesus Christ*, is not Baptism after the form prescribed at the close of the First Gospel. There must have been in the words with which Christian Baptism was at first administered, a distinctly prominent, not to say exclusive, connection with the Name of Christ, and the idea of Christ's leadership ; for upon any other supposition, St Paul's remonstrance with the sectarian Corinthians,—" Is Christ divided, was Paul crucified for you, or were ye baptized into the name of Paul ?"—would be, in its final clause, pointless and inexplicable. If St Paul had known that his converts had been baptized " into the Name of the Father, &c.," how could fear have crossed his mind, lest " any should say he had baptized into his own name ?" The worst instructed convert from heathenism could scarcely confuse the Names of Father, Son, and Holy Ghost, with the name of a missionary by whom Baptism had been administered. And how, we may well ask, could St Paul have written, " Christ sent me not to baptize, but to preach the Gospel " (1 Cor. i. 17), if our Lord had, by His own parting directions, sent His Apostles to baptize, no less positively than He sent them to teach ? That St Paul was not one of the original eleven is no satisfactory reply : he could hardly have been ignorant what commission they had received, and his own separate commission, coming from the same Master, and relating to the same work, is not likely to have differed from theirs in an important point.

The introductory statements of the fourth Evangelist, seem to Mr Liddon perfectly reconcilable with the narratives given by the first and by the third. " The accounts, then, of our Lord's birth in two of the synoptic Evangelists, as illustrated by the sacred songs of praise and thanksgiving which St Luke has

* To the texts above referred to, may be added Acts ii. 38, x. 43 : though the use of a different preposition makes the contrast with Matt. xxviii. 19, less clear and certain.

preserved, point clearly to the entrance of a superhuman Being into this our human world. Who indeed He was, is stated more explicitly by St John; but St John does not deem it necessary to repeat the history of His Advent. The accounts of the Annunciation and the Miraculous Conception would not by themselves imply the Divinity of Christ. But they do imply that Christ is superhuman; they harmonize with the kind of anticipations respecting Christ's appearance in the world, which might be created by St John's doctrine of His pre-existent glory. These accounts cannot be forced within the limits, and made to illustrate the laws, of nature. But, at least, St John's narrative justifies mysteries in the synoptic Gospels which would be un-intelligible without it; and it is a vivid commentary upon hymns, the lofty strains of which might of themselves be thought to savour of exaggeration" (p. 249).

Now, persons who give the subject a calm and impartial attention, can scarcely fail to observe that there is, to say the least, a great appearance of discrepancy between the accounts of the Nativity, and the announcement of the Fourth Gospel,—*the Logos became Flesh.* That announcement agrees with the doctrine which recognizes in Christ no real complete personal humanity; but the plain meaning of the two Synoptists is, that a human person was brought into existence by a miraculous conception and birth. There is nothing whatever in the synoptical narrative to show the person of Christ to have been superhuman in the sense of being pre-existent, and independent of mortal birth.* The inferences from the Evangelical Canticles,

* Some prominent points in the diversities entailed by the seemingly diverse conceptions of Christ's person entertained by the Synoptists and the last Evangelist, are brought together in the following extract from Dr Davidson's very instructive and much-needed *Introduction to the Study of the New Testament:*—"In conformity with the doctrine of the Incarnate Logos, everything is avoided in the Fourth Gospel that would favour the idea of Christ's development in knowledge and virtue. He is perfect at first, and all that implies growth is carefully kept out of sight. The traditions that represent Him as a descendent of David, the genealogies in Matthew, His birth at Bethlehem, the adoration of the Infant by the Eastern Magi as King of the Jews, and the miraculous conception, are absent. The fact that Jesus was baptized by John His inferior, is also omitted. The Incarnate Word cannot be exposed to the temptation recorded in the Synoptists; nor need a heavenly voice to attest His Sonship. . . . The entire account of His passion is also adapted to show that the Word made flesh was the Lamb of God who takes away the sin of the world. He does not pray, 'Father, if it be possible, let this cup pass from me;' but, 'The cup which my Father hath given me, shall I not drink it?' nor would He say, 'Father, save me from this hour,' since He had come for that hour. He knows the traitor from the beginning, and proceeds to the place whither Judas is about to come, to show His obedience to the Father. His enemies fall to the ground

in the first chapter of the third Gospel, are as ill-grounded as is the inference from the prophetic name *Emmanuel*, in which Mr Liddon discovers an intimation of "the full truth, that Christ is the Son of God, as being of the Divine Essence" (p. 247). It is simply untrue that in the song of thanksgiving attributed to Zacharias, "the new-born Saviour is the Lord, whose forerunner has been announced by prophecy" (Luke i. 76) ; *the Lord*, there, is, quite obviously, *the Highest, the Lord God of Israel*, to Whom the whole Canticle is addressed.

The prologue of the fourth Evangelist has naturally a conspicuous place in Mr Liddon's argument. "By the word Logos," he says, "St John carries back his history of our Lord to a point at which it has not yet entered into the sphere of sense and time. . . . At a point to which man cannot apply his finite conception of time, there was—the Logos or Word. When as yet nothing had been made, He *was*. What was the *Logos?* . . . . The term Logos denotes, at the very least, something intimately and everlastingly present with God, something as internal to the Being of God as thought is to the soul of man. In truth, the Divine Logos is God reflected in His own eternal Thought ; in the Logos, God is His own Object. This Infinite Thought, the reflection and counterpart of God, subsisting in God as a Being or Hypostasis, and having a tendency to self-communication,—such is the Logos. The Logos is the Thought of God, not intermittent and precarious like human thought, but subsisting with the intensity of a personal form. . . . What was the relation of the Word to the Self-Existent Being ? He was not merely $\pi\alpha\rho\grave{\alpha}$ $\tau\tilde{\omega}$ $\Theta\epsilon\tilde{\omega}$, along with God (xvii. 5), but $\pi\rho\grave{o}\varsigma$ $\tau\grave{o}\nu$ $\Theta\epsilon\grave{o}\nu$ (i. 1, 2). This last preposition expresses, beyond the fact of

when He says, 'I am He ;' and He dies uttering the triumphant cry, 'It is finished.' He does not partake of the paschal supper, because He was himself the true passover. . . . Before Pilate, the synoptical King of the Jews is transformed into a Sovereign, whose kingdom is truth. Simon of Cyrene does not appear, because the idea of exhaustion and faintness would be derogatory. 'Eli, Eli, lama Sabacthani,' is also eliminated from the gospel. No external prodigy enhances the grandeur of His death. No earthquake, no rending of rocks, or of the temple-vail, appears. His body is laid in the tomb by two men of distinction, and embalmed at great cost, contrary to the synoptical account. After His resurrection He presents himself without previous notice to Mary Magdalene, and then to the ten. Angels do not announce Him to the disciples. . . . These observations show that the Gospel was not meant for history. It was composed in another interest than the historical. . . . Speculative considerations are paramount. There is no human development, no growth of incidents or course of life. The transactions are in the realm of thought. The Word enshrined in His earthly tabernacle flashes out splendour on the people, indicating the eternal and all-embracing light which is to purify the world" (Vol. ii., pp. 343-345).

co-existence or immanence, the more significant fact of perpetuated inter-communion.* The Face of the Everlasting Word, if we may dare so to express ourselves, was ever *directed towards* the Face of the Everlasting Father. But was the Logos then an independent being, existing externally to the One God? To conceive of an independent being, anterior to creation, would be an error at issue with the first truth of monotheism; and therefore Θεὸς ἦν ὁ Λόγος. The Word is not merely a Divine Being, but He is in the absolute sense God. Thus from His eternal existence we ascend first to His distinct Personality, and then to the full truth of His substantial Godhead" (pp. 227-229).

I have quoted Mr Liddon at length, because I am quite unable to understand, and would not willingly misrepresent him. He seems to me to be entangled among words, and to have lost his hold upon intelligible ideas. His language makes more enigmatical than ever, the grand enigma, that the Self-existent Nature is One Indivisible Substance enfolding a Plurality of Persons, each of Whom possesses "the totality of the Divine attributes."

In the beginning, and, *from all eternity*, may be theologically, but are not rationally, convertible phrases. *Logos* is evidently a term of most mutable and difficult, not to say incomprehensible significance; *Word: Infinite Thought; God reflected in His Own eternal Thought;* and yet, a Person whose distinct personality leaves unimpaired the personality of the Everlasting Father God, Whose Word and Thought he is:—who can understand this revelation of the Logos, or follow its Oxford expounder? Must we not conclude; either, the writer of the fourth Gospel did not know his own meaning, or, used his terms in senses lower than, and different from, the senses assigned by Mr Liddon? It is impossible for any man not illumined by light beyond that which reason and Scripture furnish, to speak confidently about the expression commonly translated, *The Word was God*. *Logos* is most obscure, and the name *God* is without the article, while the article is prefixed in the phrase *with God*, which stands immediately before, and immediately after. This omission of the article creates an ambiguity quite unaccountable if the writer had wished to avouch that the Word is absolutely, in the fullest and highest acceptation, God. Winer remarks (Sec.

---

* πρὸς does not express "immanence" or internal annexation, and the radical signification, *towards*, is not invariably retained in the sense. There can be no doubt about the justice of Winer's observation, "Sometimes πρὸς with a noun in the Accusative, appears to lose the import of the Accusative, and to signify simply *with*, particularly before names of persons, as in Matt. xiii. 56; John i. 1; 1 Cor. xvi. 6."

xix. 1): "The Article could not have been omitted, if John had intended to say that the Logos was ὁ θεός (the God), as in this passage θεός alone was ambiguous. That John designedly omitted the article is apparent, partly from the distinct antithesis, *with the God*, and partly from the whole description of the Logos." Dr James Donaldson,* in his *Critical History of Christian Literature, &c.*, after noticing that no translation into English can exactly represent difficulties which the words of the first verse of the fourth Gospel suggest, writes :—

"That John does not assert that the Logos was one, or of the same nature which *the* God, is plain from his use of θεός without the article. The unity of the Divine Nature in God and Christ may be a satisfactory explanation of John's statement, but it is not what John states. The word θεός, as we shall see in treating of Justin Martyr's use of the term, and in many other cases, was very widely applied. It was sometimes applied to man when perfected. It was applicable to any being possessed of supernatural powers ; especially was it applicable to a being who was worshipped.† And perhaps what John meant to do, and certainly what he seems to do here, is to make a very wide general statement that the Logos was Divine. He does not obviate any of the difficulties which might arise from the assertion. As far as John's statement goes, we are bound to believe that the Logos is a Divine Being ; but we go beyond John's statement when we either assert that there are two Gods of equal glory and of the same substance, or that there is but one Divine Being, but two persons. John's assertion is of the vaguest and most general nature. . . . It seems scarcely possible not to identify the statement in John's introduction with Philo's doctrine. But we are not bound on that account to suppose that John accepted the whole of Philo's doctrine. His words, *and the Word was a God*, do not state that the Logos was a second God" (Vol. ii., Introduction, pp. 41-43).

Dr Davidson, in his recent *Introduction to the New Testament*, judging "the balance of evidence to be clearly against the fourth Gospel's authenticity," naturally sees, in some of its dubious ex-

* Joint editor with Dr Roberts of Messrs Clarks' very serviceable series of translations, "The Ante-Nicene Christian Library." "The History of Christian Literature," &c., is published by Macmillan.

† In giving reasons for the necessity of "a fresh definition at Nicæa," Mr Liddon tells us, "In the Arian age, it was not enough to say that Jesus Christ is God, because the Arians had contrived to impoverish and degrade the idea conveyed by the Name of God so completely as to apply that sacred word to a creature " (p. 434).

pressions, such an approach to the full Deification of Christ as might be expected from a Christian writing towards the middle of the second century, with the purpose of affirming and exalting Christ's pre-existent Being. In his analysis of the Gospel's contents, he says : "The Logos was a concrete person before the world existed, not becoming so at the Incarnation. As reason becomes speech, so when the eternal reason manifests itself, it is as the Logos; not necessarily hypostatic, but such in the Gospel. *When* the Word issued from the Divine Essence, *i.e.*, *was begotten*, whether from eternity or not, the Evangelist forbears to say. . . . It is observable that the appellation *the Word* does not occur in the speeches of Jesus himself; but that is no argument against its being synonymous with Christ. . . . The Father and the Son are both *God:* but the Father alone is *absolute God*, filling up the whole idea. The Son is *a God*, not God absolutely; and does not exhaust the conception" (Vol. ii. pp. 325, 327).

The use of θεός without the article, in looser and inferior senses, is illustrated by John x. 33, 35 ; Acts xii. 22 ; xxviii. 6; 2 Thess. ii. 4. The difference between *a god*, and the Almighty Creator, is obvious in these texts, and readers of the Greek Testament will notice how, in immediate contexts, θεός with the article is used to denote the Most High. The speculative, nebulous title, *the Word*, is not given to Christ in the fourth Gospel after the 14th verse of the first chapter, though the ascription to him of pre-existence and exalted dignity is plain throughout. But if the Evangelist had a firm and coherent conception of the Word's true personal Deity, it is strange that he makes John the Baptist, into whose mouth he puts very explicit testimony to the Person and work of Jesus, declare (iii. 34) Jesus to have been the recipient of the Spirit, in unmeasured gift. How could a Being " Who is in the absolute sense God," require or receive the Holy Spirit ? We can understand how the visible descent of the Spirit to which the Baptist refers (i. 32, 33), might be, in the Evangelist's view, no more than a miraculous attestation to John that Jesus was the Messiah and Son of God, but to seek in the gift of the Spirit any qualification for Christ's work as the Messenger of God, or any explanation of the fact of His speaking the words of God, is inconsistent with the idea of His complete and Essential Divinity. If our Lord's manhood had been " of Itself an individual Being," instead of " a vesture which He folded around His Person," we should still have been at a loss to imagine what office the Spirit could have in endowing or regulating a Nature already indissolubly linked to the Nature of Very and Eternal God. Was the Logos dormant, and did the Third Person in the Blessed Trinity undertake the work, not only of causing the conception of Christ's Humanity, but of guiding and sanctifying that Humanity after its junction with the Second Person of "the mysterious Three Who yet are One?" If Christ's ministerial endowments, or any portion of His perfect holiness, resulted from the presence with His human nature of God's Spirit, what activity and influence had the Eternal Word, " Who is One in Essence with the First and the Third of the Persons or Subsistences." Who together compose the Indivisible Self-existent Substance? The action of the Holy Ghost, in the enrichment or sanctification of our Lord's Humanity, is out of harmony with the doctrine of the Incarnate Logos enunciated at the outset of the fourth Gospel. It would be out of harmony, even on the supposition that Christ had a human person to be enriched and sanctified ; it is far more out of harmony according to the orthodox dogma which Mr Liddon repeats ; "the Person of the Son of Mary is Divine and Eternal." To assume John the Baptist used the words which the Evangelist records, and was mistaken in doing so, would remove the difficulty, but would not altogether accord with the extensive knowledge and full attestation of Christ's heavenly descent and mission, which the speeches ascribed to the Baptist indicate. But however that may be, the Holy Spirit is, in the Synoptical Gospels, represented as exercising an influence on, and standing in a relation to, Christ, quite inconsistent with His impersonal Humanity and proper Deity. " He was led by the Spirit into the wilderness to be tempted of the devil " (Matt. iv. 1 ; Mark i. 12 ; Luke iv. 1) ; and afterwards " returned in the power of the Spirit into Galilee " (Luke iv. 14). Our Lord himself appropriates the words of Isaiah : " The Spirit of the Lord is upon me, because He hath anointed me," &c. (Luke iv. 18) ; and the writer of the first Gospel declares, that in Him was fulfilled the promise of God through the same prophet, " I will put My Spirit upon Him, &c." (Matt. xii. 18) ; Christ also claims to " cast out devils by God's Spirit" (Matt. xii. 28). St Peter, when proclaiming the Gospel message, puts prominently forward, God's having " anointed Jesus of Nazareth with the Holy Ghost, and with power" (Acts x. 38). And the teaching of St Peter on this point is the more important, since to him had been revealed the fact, that Jesus was " the Christ, the Son of the Living God" (Matt. xvi. 16). He was not likely to go astray, or to fall short, in apprehending the true character and dignity of our Lord's Being, and yet he does not hesitate to affirm, " God anointed" Him with "the Holy Spirit and power." *

There is, therefore, a want of unison between the doctrine which Mr Liddon believes to be set forth in the beginning of the fourth Gospel, and the doctrine which is exhibited by St Peter, and the three earlier Evangelists. The device of a distinction between Christ as God, and Christ as man, is not much to the purpose; for Mr Liddon tells us, our Lord's Manhood was not personal, but was taken into closest union with his Deity; and he clings to " the fact, upon which St John insists with such prominence, that our Lord's Godhead is the seat of His Personality" (p. 259); and so, we are brought face to face with the conclusion, God led God, and anointed God with God! Surely, unless we are content to resign our reason and judgment in deference to some higher authority, a choice between the guidance of the fourth Gospel, and the prior narrations, is here forced upon us. From which are we to collect our dogmatic knowledge of Christ's personal rank? The writer of the last Gospel does more than supplement his predecessors : if the orthodox interpretation of his language is right, he corrects them, and takes ground which convicts them not merely of reservation, but of ignorance and blundering, on a vital point. For Protestants, who hold Scripture to be the Divine and sufficient Rule of Faith, there is no way of escape : they must either esteem the Logos doctrine a misty speculation, or depress other portions of the New Testament while they exalt what they conceive to be a contribution from St John.†

And, when we are examining the Scripture testimony respecting Christ's nature, it is scarcely possible for us to pass by unnoticed, the strong contrast between the Synoptic and the supposed Johannine accounts of the time and manner in which our Lord's Messiahship was freely made known. In Matt. xvi. 16, Peter's confession, " Thou art the Christ, the Son of the living God," is declared to have been prompted by a revelation from

---

* In Acts i. 2, Jesus is said either to have " commanded," or " chosen " the Apostles, *through* or *by means of the Holy Spirit*, where the difficulty attaching to orthodox faith is not removed, but brought into view, by the widely-accepted commentary ; " Jesus as *man*, is represented as acting by the authority, and with the co-operation, of the Holy Ghost." Where was the Infinitely Divine Person, the Logos?

† The Church of England is not in this dilemma, because, by the imposition of Articles and Creeds, she practically denies the sufficiency of Holy Scripture as a Rule of Faith, notwithstanding certain well-known expressions in her theory. Her weakness is, that she combines two inconsistent and mutually exclusive principles.

Heaven. The narratives in Mark viii. 29, and Luke ix. 20, do not add the words, *the Son, &c.*,* but in them, as well as in the first Gospel, the confession is followed by an injunction from Christ to conceal the fact of His Messiahship. The fourth Gospel is decidedly at variance with these representations. In the first and third chapters, our Lord's Messianic character and authority are recognised and acknowledged by John the Baptist with an amplitude, repetition, and precision, which aggravate to the utmost the difficulty involved in the message which the fame of Christ's miracles induced John to send from the prison ; " Art Thou He that should come, or do we look for another?" (Matt. xi. 3 ; Luke vii. 19.) In the first chapter, Andrew tells his brother Simon Peter, " We have found the Messias " (ver. 41) ; Philip conveys in effect the same information to Nathanael (ver. 45 ;) and from Nathanael the acknowledgment is extorted, " Rabbi, Thou art the Son of God ; Thou art the King of Israel " (ver. 49). And, on the part of Christ himself, there was no delay, carefulness, or reserve, in advancing His pretensions. At the opening of His public life, before John was cast into prison (iii. 24), He acted and spoke unreservedly ; expelled the money changers from the Temple ; foretold His own death and rising again (chaps. ii. and iii., comp. Matt. xxi. 12, xvi. 21, and parallels in Mark and Luke) ; avowed to Nicodemus His work, office, and Divine Sonship (iii.), and before the earliest period to which Peter's confession of the Messiahship, and the accompanying charge, *to tell no man that he was Jesus the Christ,* can be referred, declared explicitly to the woman of Sychar, that He was the Messiah (iv. 26), and left her fellow-citizens with the knowledge that He was indeed the Saviour of the world (ver. 42).

Now, no man whose prejudices are sufficiently moderate to permit him to give a verdict according to evidence, can deny the serious irreconcileable discrepancy into which diversity of narrative here passes. On the common-sense principle of preferring three witnesses to one, we are unavoidably conducted to an unfavourable appreciation of the fourth Gospel's historical fidelity, and are confirmed in the suspicion, that the writer made many state-

* Mr Liddon in his first Lecture (p. 10), builds an argument on the supposition that Peter's confession was made in the precise words given by Matthew. To the words which Mark and Luke omit, he attaches very great importance. But, how came two Evangelists, one of whom was, according to early tradition, the companion and reporter of Peter, to leave out of their records a statement of great significance, on a subject of the highest interest? Whose report is the strictly accurate one? John vi. 69, differs from all the other accounts, the true reading there, being, *Thou art the Holy (One) of God.*

ments from a speculative and ideal, rather than from a properly historical, point of view. But though his idealism may be hazy, and not unfolded with firmness of grasp and entire consistency of detail, he must, nevertheless, be allowed to have had a good general notion of his own sentiments and object; and, if he designed in his prologue to teach, that the Word who arrayed Himself in a human vesture was an Everlasting and Co-equal Person in the Divine Substance, he would not be likely to bring to the front expressions in which Christ himself avows inferiority, subordination, and dependence. It is quite certain, however, he does bring forward such expressions (expressions which I shall hereafter have occasion to quote), and his openly alleged aim is, not to prove Jesus is God, but to produce the belief that *Jesus is the Christ, the Son of God* (xx. 31). The ambiguity caused by the omission of the article before $\theta\epsilon\delta\varsigma$ (i. 1), is not, therefore, the sole reason for concluding the last Evangelist did not intend to affirm the Word's absolute Deity. The reasonable supposition that he knew, with some degree of exactitude, his own meaning, and did not unwittingly furnish materials for his own refutation, leads to the same conclusion. And, further, if he aimed at investing *the Word* as a Personal Being, with the entire attributes of Godhead, he cannot rationally be cleared of "an error at issue with the first truth of Monotheism;" because reason assuredly, and perhaps dogmatic theology likewise, pronounces to be inadmissible the only interpretation of his language which would then satisfy Monotheism, namely; *the Word was the God with Whom the Word was.*

CHAPTER V.

Discussion of texts supposed "expressly to assert the doctrine of Our Lord's Divinity;" viz., 1 John v. 20; Titus ii. 13 : Romans ix. 5; Philippians ii. 6-11.—Examination of Mr Liddon's exposition of passages in the Epistles to the Colossians and Hebrews, and in the Apocalypse.

AMONG "the comparatively few texts expressly asserting the doctrine of Our Lord's Divinity," Mr Liddon reckons 1 John v. 20 ; Titus ii. 13 ; Rom. ix. 5 ; in which he believes Christ to be designated—*the True God ; the Great God ;* and, *God over all, Blessed for ever.* If these epithets were descriptions of Christ, they would, undoubtedly, proclaim His Deity, but there is not adequate reason for supposing them to refer to Him. No person acquainted with Greek, will deny that the verbal constructions in the texts in question are ambiguous, and do not determine whether the titles are to be understood as descriptions of Christ, or descriptions of the Eternal Father. Not to mention other scholars whose judgment is entitled to weight, Winer, the standard authority on the Grammar of the Greek Testament, pronounces decidedly against the notion that our Lord Jesus Christ is necessarily, or more probably designated, in either of the three texts. All that can be said in behalf of Mr Liddon's interpretation is, that the wording, simply as such, admits it, and that ecclesiastical writers, after A.D. 190, for the most part approve of it. But the only testimony worth attention, Ante-Nicene testimony, is, in the form in which it has come down to us, nothing more than the opinions of a few individuals who had a dogmatic purpose to serve. It is far too scanty and one-sided to be considered duly representative of the age, and, in relation to texts employed in controversy, is, in Protestant eyes, perhaps less valuable than the private opinion of Mr Liddon. An interpretation which the natural force of language does not demand, and the Scriptures themselves do not show to be probable, is not confirmed by references to two or three Fathers of the third century.

The Anglican Version of 1 John v. 20, obscures the sense by

inserting the word *even*. The sacred writer teaches : " The Son of God has come, and has given us an understanding that we may know *Him Who is True* (literally, *the True*), and we are in *Him Who is True*, (being) in His Son Jesus Christ. This is *the True* God and Eternal Life." The concluding sentence more fully defines *the True One*, in Whom we are, through being in His Son Jesus Christ.* To be in God, is to have a reverent and filial love towards Him, and to be the objects of His approving love ; and in this condition faithful Christians are, through being in Christ, that is, through believing in Christ, and being members of that Church or Society in which Christ is, by Divine gift and decree, Lord and Head. The sense is plain enough to unbiassed minds ; indeed, the only consistent method of escaping it, is by supposing *God* to be the unexpressed nominative to *has given;* and, *the True*, to be a title of Christ—a conjecture advocated by Bishop Burgess, and quoted with approval by Bloomfield. Throughout the Epistle, *God*, and the *Son of God*, are clearly distinguished, and spoken of as two individuals—persons in the intelligible, and not in the ecclesiastical acceptation. In v. 11 God is declared to be the Giver, and His Son the channel of eternal life ; " God has given unto us eternal life, and this life is in His Son" (comp. Rom. vi. 23, where the original is, *in Christ Jesus our Lord*). God, the Father, is *Eternal Life* (that is, the Author and Source of eternal life), in the higher and primary sense, and *the True God* is an epithet which nothing short of imperative grammatical construction can justify us in understanding of another than Him (comp. John xvii. 3 ; 1 Thess. i. 9, 10).

The venturesome allegation : " St John's picture of Christ's work, in this first Epistle, leads up to the culminating statement that Jesus himself is the True God and the Eternal Life" (p. 239), will be appreciated as it deserves by careful readers of the Epistle. Mr Liddon denies that the interpretation he contends for effaces the distinction between the Father and the Son. " After having distinguished *the True* from *His Son*, St John, by a characteristic turn, simply identifies the Son with *the True God*. To refer this sentence to the Father, Who has been twice called *the True*, would be unmeaning repetition. . . . St John does not say, This is the Father, but, This is the True God. *The*

---

* The fully expressed meaning undoubtedly is : " That we may know the True (God) ; and we are in the True (God), &c." There is no identification of Nature and Substance between *the True God* and *His Son*. For the phrase, *in God*, see 1 John iv. 13-16.

True God is the Divine Essence, in opposition to all creatures. The question of hypostatic distinctions within that Essence is not here before the Apostle. Our being in the True God depends on our being in Christ, and St John clenches this assertion by saying that Christ is the True God himself." When the Apostle made his "characteristic turn" from the individual Father to the Divine Essence, Which includes both Father and Son, it is difficult to understand what was before his mind, if the existence of hypostatic distinctions was not. But possibly Mr Liddon means, that the Apostle reckoned on his readers' knowledge of a dogma prominent in the Church's oral teaching, and therefore did not feel called upon to elucidate a distinction which was sufficiently familiar and simple to be gathered from the passing allusion of an ambiguous phrase.

The pronoun (*οὗτος*) *this,* is sometimes to be joined, not with the nearer, but with the more remote antecedent, a fact illustrated by John vi. 48–50; Acts iv. 11; 2 John, ver. 7. After laying down the general rule, that nearness of position does not decide the pronoun's reference, Winer remarks (*Grammar of the New Testament, &c.,* Sec. 23); "In 1 John v. 20, *this is the True God,* refers to *God,* not *Christ* (which immediately precedes), as the older theologians, on doctrinal considerations, maintained; for, in the first place, *True God,* is a constant exclusive epithet of the Father; and, secondly, a warning against idolatry follows, and *True God* is invariably contrasted with *idols.*" In the earlier part of Section 34, Winer again alludes to the text, and says; "*The True* stands for God; the notion is grammatically complete, and the individual specially meant in Biblical diction, is to be ascertained from other passages."

In Titus ii. 13, our Authorized Version inaccurately puts *the glorious appearing,* for *appearing of the glory;* in other respects it answers more truly to the original than the version, "Looking for the blessed hope and appearing of the glory of our Great God and Saviour Jesus Christ, Who gave Himself for us." Mr Liddon says, "The grammar apparently, and the context certainly, oblige us to recognise the identity of *our Saviour Jesus Christ* and *our Great God.* As a matter of fact, Christians are not waiting for any manifestation of the Father. And He Who gave Himself for us can be none other than our Lord Jesus Christ " (p. 315). Here, the only context to which reference is made, is, in its chief feature, strangely misconceived. The text does not speak of any personal manifestation or appearing of God, but of a manifestation of God's glory. Did Mr Liddon forget that Christ himself had declared (Matt. xvi. 27 ; Mark viii. 38 ; Luke ix. 26), that His coming would be *in the glory of His Father ?*   Did he forget that St Paul (1 Tim. vi. 14-16), speaks of *the appearing of our Lord Jesus Christ,* as an event " which in His own times He will show, Who is the Blessed and Only Potentate, the King of kings and Lord of lords, Who only hath Immortality, Whom no man hath seen, nor can see ? "   The New Testament Scriptures explicitly announce, the appearing of Christ will be determined by the Father's will, and attended with an exhibition of the Father's glory. There is, then, no sort of warrant for the assertion, " The context certainly obliges us " to identify *the Great God* with *Jesus Christ.* The preceding and subsequent parts of the Epistle, plainly recognise the distinction between God and Christ.   Only a few sentences further on (iii. 4-6) ; *God our Saviour,* and *Jesus Christ our Saviour,* are associated in a manner which forcibly brings out the truth that God is in the principal and absolute, Christ in the secondary and instrumental sense, our Saviour. We may give up all attempts to ascertain the meaning of a canonical writer if it is possible for that writer to call Christ *our Great God,* and then with an interval of half-a-dozen sentences, to tell us of *God* imparting gifts of grace through Him who is *our Great God.*   Yet, Mr Liddon is able to cite from Bishop Ellicott, the opinion, that " the subsequent allusion to our Lord's profound Self-humiliation, accounts for St Paul's ascribing to Him, by way of reparation, a title otherwise unusual, that specially and antithetically marks His glory."   And, while the Bishop is too sound a scholar to hold there is grammatically anything more than a presumption in favour of this interpretation, he nevertheless, for other reasons, sees in this text a " direct, definite, and even *studied* declaration of the Divinity of the Eternal Son." Without any disrespect to the Bishop, we may, I think, conclude that in this instance, his wishes greatly stimulated his perceptive powers, and prompted him to risk the feeblest of surmises, and the most unfounded of assertions.   The " grammatical presumption " arises from the omission of the article before *Saviour ;* but the pronoun *our,* (literally *of us*), gives that name sufficient distinctness, assuming (what it is impossible to deny), the appellation *our Saviour Jesus Christ* to have usually denoted a person distinguished from God.*   " *The* Saviour of us,"

---

* When the difference of office or person is well known, the definite article is often omitted in English.   If, after visiting some public Institution, I were to say, " I saw the governor and chaplain," no one would imagine I meant only one person, though grammatically my words would bear that meaning.

would have been more perspicuous, but the article was not indispensable to mark the different individualities of *the Great God* and *our Saviour Jesus Christ.* Winer, when stating in the later editions of his Grammar, his deliberate adherence to his previously expressed judgment, writes : " Doctrinal conviction, deduced from Paul's teaching, that the Apostle could not have called Christ *the Great God,* induced me to show that, at the same time, there is no invincible obstacle of a grammatical nature to our taking the words, *and of our Saviour, &c.,* as a second subject. Examples, such as I have quoted (Sec. xix. 2), will at once satisfy the impartial inquirer that the article was *not* necessary before *Saviour.*" The opinion which Winer here repeats, he had already stated by saying : " The article is omitted before *Saviour,* because the word is made definite by the genitive, *of us,* and the apposition *precedes* the proper name (Jesus Christ) : of *the Great God and our Saviour Jesus Christ.*" Winer adds, "Similar is 2 Pet. i. 1, where there is no pronoun with *Saviour;* " a text which Mr Liddon explains to mean (p. 301), " He is our God and Saviour Jesus Christ ;" although in verse 2, a part of the same sentence, *God,* and *Jesus our Lord,* are indisputably distinguished from each other.

Rom. ix. 5, receives a good deal of Mr Liddon's attention, and in three lengthy notes he defends the mistaken punctuation, and consequent mistranslation, which stand in our Authorised Version. The older Greek MSS., being almost entirely unpunctuated, are no guides in a case where differences of punctuation entail differences of meaning. Any stop of greater length than a comma, after the word *flesh,* makes the final clause of the verse an independent statement concerning God, the Father. Lachmann, Tischendorf, Jowett, and many other critical editors and expositors, prefer the stopping which awards the ascription of Supreme Deity and Eternal Blessedness to the Almighty ; and suppose the Apostle to have added to the list of Jewish privileges, a thankful recognition of His goodness and power by Whom those privileges had been bestowed—*He who is God over all, (is) blessed for ever.* Such a recognition of the Divine bounty and Omnipotence, is a natural and appropriate appendix to the mention of advantages among which Christ's birth in our nature was included. There is nothing in the verbal construction of the verse to settle the application of the final clause. Grammatically it may be a continued description of Christ, or, an independent proposition relating to God. The omission of the verb substantive accords with usage, and presents no difficulty. In translating Greek

into English, the word *is* has very frequently to be supplied.
Assertions about "the natural meaning of the passage," and
carpings at "anti-theological interest," are utterly misplaced,
and, in Mr Liddon, peculiarly unbecoming.   He may be most
profoundly convinced of the truth of his own views, and the
soundness of his own reasonings, but his book is pervaded by
prejudgments, and he is the last man who should accuse others of
bias. As Bampton Lecturer, under voluntary obligation to vindicate a particular dogma, grammatical possibility may be to him
proof enough for any interpretation which can be turned to account,
and he may quite conscientiously believe, when verbal ambiguity
renders two or more senses admissible, the true sense must be
that which best suits his object.   But the fact is patent; men
who are, at the very least, his equals in every qualification
entitled to respect, unhesitatingly affirm the interpretation which
he refuses to allow.

If there were no other considerations to influence our decision,
the arguments on which Mr Liddon relies might have some little
weight, but as the case actually stands, they are singularly insufficient.   He thinks the concluding words of the verse must be
referred to Christ, in order to complete the antithesis implied in
the expression *as to the flesh*. The answer is, antithesis, as such,
may not have been the leading thought in the Apostle's mind,
but simply limitation.   By human descent and family kinship,
Christ belonged to the Jews.   To that extent He was *from them*,
but to that extent only.   There was a higher spiritual origin,
and a more universal relationship, which had no proper connection with privileges distinctively Jewish.   The higher and wider
aspects of Christ's Being are glanced at through restrictive terms,
but not defined.   A few lines before the text under discussion,
when St Paul calls the Israelites his kinsmen *as to the flesh*, he does
not complete the antithesis ; and again, in 1 Corinthians x. 18,
when he speaks of *Israel as to the flesh*, he does not unfold the
idea which the limiting phrase suggests.   And in Romans i. 4,
where the contrast between the bodily and spiritual parts of
Christ's Being is expressed, there is no assertion that He *is God
over all, blessed for ever*, but a description of a very different
kind, which clearly distinguishes Him from God.   "*As to the
flesh*, He is the seed of David ; *as to the spirit of holiness* (that is,
His holy spiritual nature), He is mightily shown to be the Son
of God, by the resurrection from the dead."   The resurrection of
our Lord from the dead is, by St Paul, frequently and uniformly
attributed to the power of God, the Father, and in the commenc-

ing paragraph of the Epistle to the Romans, as well as throughout the Epistle, distinction between God and Christ is unmistakably indicated.

Another of Mr Liddon's arguments is, that in the text in question the word *blessed* is put after the name *God*, whereas in the doxologies of both the Septuagint and the New Testament, it precedes the name. On this fact great stress is laid, but if the position of the adjective were peculiarly irregular, the New Testament has too many instances of irregular arrangement, for irregularity to be a safe ground of inference. Olshausen, an orthodox and able expositor, considers the position of *blessed* to be of no importance ; and Winer, who on such a point is no mean judge, says (Sec. lxi. 3) ; "Only an empirical expositor could regard this antecedent position as an unalterable rule ; for, when the Subject constitutes the principal notion, especially when it is antithetical to another Subject, the Predicate may and must be placed after it, (comp. Ps. lxvii. 19. Sept.) * In Romans ix. 5, if God is referred to, the position of the words is quite appropriate, and even indispensable, as some critics have pointed out."

A remark with which Mr Liddon concludes one of his notes, is, I should imagine, quite original, and is certainly unanswerable. He supposes that if the reading were so altered as almost to compel the reference of the final clause to Christ, the reference would not be disputed. "We may be very certain that, if ἐπὶ πάντων Θεός (*God over all*), could be proved to be an unwarranted reading, no scholar, however Socinianizing his bias, would hesitate to say that ὁ ὢν εὐλογητός, &c. (*He who is blessed, &c.*), should be referred to the proper name which precedes it " (p. 314).

The reasons against the interpretation for which the Bampton Lecturer contends, are, taken together, amply sufficient to decide the doubt which mere verbal construction admits. Already, in the Epistle to the Romans (i. 25), St Paul had applied to the Almighty the phrase *blessed for ever*, and in 2 Corinthians xi. 31, he gives the same words the same application. The whole phrase is never by any New Testament writer used of Christ, and Christ is never called εὐλογητός. There are other words descriptive of blessedness, but that particular word is retained for the One God and Father alone. Mr Liddon tries to explain this fact by observing ; "as regards εὐλογητός, the remarkable fewness of

---

* Mr Liddon, if I understand him rightly, objects against Winer's reference to the Septuagint 67th Psalm (Eng. Ver. 68th), that the reading not being literally after the Hebrew, is probably corrupt. But both the Vatican and Alexandrine MSS. have the adjective presumed to be interpolated, and variations from the Hebrew Text are very common in the Septuagint.

doxologies addressed to Christ might account for the omission." But if the sacred writers knew our Lord to be truly God, identical in Essence with the Father, why should doxologies addressed to Him be remarkably few, and destitute of a term which common usage had appropriated to God? The omission would not, in itself, be decisive against real reasons on the other side, but it outweighs all the pretexts which Mr Liddon has been able to put forward.

After the allusion to "the remarkable fewness of doxologies addressed to Christ," the passage in a subsequent part of the same Lecture (p. 328), speaking of "thanksgivings and doxologies poured forth to the praise of Jesus Christ," should not have been permitted to remain. The only texts referred to in justification of that passage, are Romans ix. 5, perhaps xvi. 27 ; 1 Timothy i. 12 ; the latter of which is an expression of gratitude to Christ, immediately preceded by the mention of God, and followed at a very brief interval by a formal doxology to *the King of the Ages, Incorruptible, Invisible, alone God.*

The description, *God over all,* cannot be understood of our Lord Jesus Christ without violence to the analogy of St Paul's doctrine, and inconsistence with his habitual use of language.* In Romans iii. 29, 30, he reminds us, the One God is God of both Jews and Gentiles, and so implies His highest dominion over all men ; and, in xi. 36, he asserts the exclusive supremacy of God the Father, by declaring, *of (from) Him, and through Him, and to Him, are all things.* Elsewhere, he calls God *the only God,* and *the Blessed and Only Potentate.* (Romans xvi. 27; 1 Timothy i. 17 ; vi. 15.) He tells us "That there is to us (Christians) but *One God,* the Father, of (from) Whom are all things, and we for Him ; and *one Lord Jesus Christ,* through whom are all things, and we through Him" (1 Cor. viii. 4-6) ; and again, that there is *One God and Father of all, Who is over all, &c. :* and yet again, that *God is the Head of Christ* (Eph. iv. 6 ; 1 Cor. xi. 3).

A number of other passages might be cited, showing the subordination of Christ, and the consequent improbability that St Paul would term Him *God over all;* and almost every page of the Apostle's writings might be appealed to for proof that, in his view, God and Christ were distinct individuals, possessing different natures, and not Forms in One and the same Supreme, Self-existent Essence ; and, although the term Θεός (God), may, without

---

* "Had St Paul ever spoken of Christ as God, he would many times have spoken of Him as such, not once only, and that by accident."—*Professor Jowett's Commentary.*

the article, mean less than absolute Deity, yet it is not, in the diction of St Paul, once given simply, and without qualification, to Christ. The received reading in Acts xx. 28, and also in 1 Tim. iii. 16, is generally admitted to be incorrect; in Titus ii. 13, *the Great God* is the Eternal Father, and the only other text in which St Paul has been imagined to assert Christ's Deity in direct terms is Rom. ix. 5. And in handling this text, Mr Liddon himself is driven, when he looks at the evidence of the Son's subordination and separate personality, to invoke the subtle distinction between the Father personally, and the Divine Substance Which is assumed to embrace both Father and Son. St Paul, he observes, " does not call our Lord ὁ ἐπὶ πάντων Θεός (*the God over all*)—the article would lay the expression open to a direct Sabellian construction.* St Paul says that Christ is ἐπὶ πάντων Θεός (*God over all*), where the Father, of course, is not included among the *all things* (1 Cor. xv. 27); and the sense corresponds substantially with Acts x. 36, Rom. x. 12. It asserts that Christ is internal to the Divine Essence, without denying His personal distinctness from, or His filial relation to, the Father."

Now, here, the texts assumed to have a corresponding sense are not parallel. The title *Lord* is not equivalent to *God*, except when used of Jehovah, the Almighty One. It is a title which, taken alone, describes dignity, but does not fix the rank and degree of the dignity, and nothing can be clearer than that it does not, in connection with the name of Jesus Christ, denote Deity. The repeated expression, *the God and Father of our Lord Jesus Christ*, and the manner in which St Paul (1 Cor. viii.; Eph. iv.) individualises the *One God* and the *one Lord*, prove the term *Lord*, when applied to Christ, not to mean *God*. Christ may be, as in Acts x. 36, called *Lord of all*,—that is, of both Jews and Gentiles, without being *God of all*. In Rom. x. 12, it is very far from evident Christ is designated *the same Lord of all*, being, in that connection, most probably Jehovah, the God of both Jews and Gentiles, 'Who is rich in mercy,' and 'no

---

* In a previous note, Mr Liddon, after stating that the text was understood in the early Church by Irenæus, Tertullian, and others, to apply to Jesus Christ, adds: "It seems probable that any non-employment of so striking a passage by the Catholics, during their earlier controversial struggles with the Arians, is to be attributed to their fear of being charged with construing it in a Sabellian sense." After the middle of the second century, controversial wants, and controversial fears, undoubtedly had great influence, and regulated interpretation.

A far less probable, but not wholly improbable, mode of punctuation and rendering, is; *Of whom came Christ according to the flesh, who is over all. God is blessed for ever.*

respecter of persons.' The texts, therefore, to which Mr Liddon refers, do not in any degree sustain his interpretation of Rom. ix. 5 ; and as to a difference of meaning between ὁ θεός and θεός, the difference is not a puzzling and imaginary one between the Personal Father and the Divine Essence, but (when the absence of the Article is designed to mark a difference) between *the God* and *a god—God* in the absolute and exclusive, and *god* in an inferior and figurative sense. This distinction rarely appears in modern writings, but the Old Testament Scriptures exhibit many instances of it in the employment of the name *Elohim ;* and perhaps it may be the key to the meaning of a few New Testament passages, where the want of the article before θεός creates an ambiguity, and can be explained neither by grammatical rule nor common usage. But a nice discrimination between Deity as an Essence or Nature, and Deity in the Person of the Almighty Father, is purely arbitrary and fanciful. There is no particle of evidence to support it ; and if, in Mr Liddon's judgment, our Master Jesus Christ could not be, without perilous inaccuracy, styled "*the* God over all," why does he take advantage of verbal uncertainty to insist that Christ is styled "*the* great God " and "*the* true God." The presence of the article unquestionably renders these latter expressions " open to a direct Sabellian construction."

In his Notes on the Epistle to the Romans, the Bishop of Lincoln (Dr Wordsworth), considers that, in ix. 5, ὁ ὤν is a title of Jehovah (comp. Sept., Exod. iii. 14), and should receive a special emphasis. " The words contain a distinct truth, and assert the eternal *pre-existence* of Christ, and are very appropriately added after the mention of His *Incarnation.* He Who *came* of the Jews, according to the *flesh*, is no other than ὁ ὤν, the BEING ONE, JEHOVAH."

Dean Stanley, on 2 Cor. xi. 31, remarks : " For the doxology, introduced by the solemn feeling of the moment, compare Rom. ix. 5, and i. 25 "—intimating, apparently, his concurrence with the opinion that the clause in debate should be regarded as an ascription of praise to the One God, the Father Almighty. He adds : " ὁ ὤν is used so frequently in the Septuagint, and by Philo, as a translation for JEHOVAH, that the phrase in this passage and Rom. ix. 5, if not used precisely in that sense, at any rate has reference to it."

If the words are equivalent to *Jehovah*, the independence of the clause, and the improbability of the conjecture which attaches it to Christ, are increased ; but the New Testament does not fur-

nish one example wherein the words are, with any approach to
clearness, a title equalling *Jehovah.*   The more usual construction
appears to me to be the true one, and upon the supposition that
the passage has peculiarities, the article, though separated, may
belong to θεός, and the literal sense may be, *The God Who is
over all, &c.*

If we are to gather the sense of the New Testament from a
thorough, candid, and rational investigation of its contents, I do
not see how we can persuade ourselves that 1 John v. 20, Titus
ii. 13, Rom. ix. 5, are descriptions of Christ, and assertions of
His Godhead.   If the decisions of an ecclesiastical, extra-scriptural authority are held to impose doctrines, and to supersede
rational judgment in the understanding of Scripture, then, of
course, the case is different ; but Mr Liddon has ventured upon
Protestant ground, and appeals to the Bible as the Rule of Faith
and document of proof. On this ground he can make out no claim
to the texts above referred to.   His attempt to claim them
merely exposes his weakness, and urgent need of direct evidence
on behalf of his dogma.   The texts must be carried over to the
other side, and added to the list—already an insuperable barrier
to the conclusiveness of merely Scriptural arguments for our
Lord's Deity,—the list which denominates the Almighty Father
by exclusive terms, *the One God and Father ; the only true God :
the only God ; the Blessed and Only Potentate.*

In commenting on Phil. ii. 6-11, a passage of undoubted
obscurity and difficulty, Mr Liddon contends :—

" The force of St Paul's moral lesson in the whole passage
must depend upon the real Divinity of the Incarnate and Self-
immolating Christ.   The point of our Lord's example lies in His
emptying Himself of the glory or ' form ' of his Eternal Godhead.
Worthless, indeed, would have been the force of His example, had
He been in reality a created Being, who only abstained from grasping tenaciously at Divine prerogatives which a creature could
not have arrogated to himself without impious folly " (p. 316).
There is considerable confusion of thought here.   Passing over,
for the moment, the assumption that *form of God* means " glory
of Eternal Godhead," and granting that *the being equal to God,*
or, as the phrase would be better translated, *the being like,* or,
*as God,** carries a corresponding meaning, what room is there

* Macknight properly translates, *to be like God,* and says : " Whitby has
proved in the clearest manner that ἴσα is used adverbially by the Septuagint
to express *likeness,* but not *equality,* the proper term for which is ἴσον."
This latter term does not necessarily, and always, denote *equality.*

for the idea that Christ "abstained from grasping tenaciously at
Divine prerogatives?" They were His irrelinquishably. He held
them by the indefeasible right of Essential Nature. Did St Paul
think so loosely, and write so inaccurately, as to employ, in suggesting mere suspension of manifested Majesty, the expressions,
emptied himself ; deemed it not a thing to be greedily seized, or *appropriated ?** The reality of Deity cannot be emptied out; for
even the Almighty cannot divest Himself of His own inherent
perfections. The Apostle did not intend to intimate an abdica-
tion of Deity, and his words are ill suited to intimate the veiling
of a glory which potentially, and in all its real basis, could not
be abandoned. And, premising that in relation to Divine
mysteries all Scripture is true, and all the Canonical writers
agreed, are we in a position to affirm, Christ "emptied Himself" of his pre-incarnate glory? In the fourth Gospel, that
glory is declared to have been manifested, and to have shone
forth in the sight of His disciples (i. 14 ; ii. 11). How far the
exercise of Divine prerogatives in heaven was affected by the
circumstance of Christ's having emptied Himself, and abstained
from grasping tenaciously at them, I do not dare to conjecture. Mr
Liddon, perhaps, could say something upon the topic, starting from
the position, "the Son of Man, while yet speaking upon earth,
was in heaven" (John iii. 13) ; but, however that may be, if we
are to believe the latest Evangelist, we must understand the
phrase *emptied Himself*, with abatements. The glory of the superhuman nature was exhibited in and through the veil of flesh.
The exhibition was no doubt on a different stage, in a modified
fashion, and before a new circle of spectators, but we are assured
that it took place. Mr Liddon himself enlarges (p. 232) on the
manner in which "St John's writings" proclaim a showing forth
of the Divine glory in the sphere of Christ's earthly life. "The
Word reveals the Divine Essence ; His Incarnation makes that
Life, that Love, that Light, which is eternally resident in God,
obvious to souls that steadily contemplate Himself. . . . The
Life, the Love, the Light are the ' glory ' of the Word Incarnate
which His disciples ' beheld,' pouring its rays through the veil
of His human tabernacle. The Light, the Love, the Life, constitute the ' fulness ' whereof His disciples received ; " and were
therefore, we may presume, the glory of which our Lord is re-

---

* This is the more probable meaning of the word rendered in the Authorised Version *robbery*. If the sense robbery is retained, St Paul's statement
would, from Mr Liddon's point of view, amount to the truism, that Christ
did not think it robbery to show Himself to be what He really was.

ported to have said (John xvii. 22), *The glory which Thou gavest me, I have given them* (comp. verses 5 and 24).

Mr Liddon perceives that *form of God* is not a description strictly synonymous with *God*, any more than *form of a slave* is a description strictly synonymous with *slave*. He therefore considers "*form of God* is apparently the manifested glory of Deity, implying of course the reality of the Deity so manifested." But when the fact has once been avowed, that *form* does not stand for *nature*, the sense is seen to be too uncertain for any " of course" inductions. Granting exalted personal pre-existence to be predicated, and not representative capacity and authority, there is no assignment of definite, co-equal rank. To say, one person is in *the form* of another, is quite obviously a different thing from saying, the two persons are identical in nature, or stand in the same place and condition. Both the phrases employed, *form of God*, and *the being like God*, seem to have a purposed and very significant vagueness. The subject of Christ's pre-incarnate Being and dignity was before the Apostle's mind. If he had been able to aver, and had wished to aver, that Christ was God, he could have done so in simple, straightforward language. The scope of his argument called for a distinct indication of the height from which Christ stooped, in becoming incarnate. There was every motive to assert in terms Christ's Deity, yet St Paul deliberately avoided the assertion, and was content with the glorification of indefinite, ambiguous circumlocutions.

The use of the Greek article is too little a matter of rule for any satisfactory argument to be built upon its absence in the passage I am now examining. Its presence is certainly not indispensable to show that the Supreme Being is referred to in Phil. ii. 6, but as certainly it would not be superfluous. If the article had not been omitted before the words *form* and *God*, the meaning which Mr Liddon seeks in the text would have been less occult and more probable. When, in verse 9, the God by Whom Christ is highly exalted is named, the article is prefixed. *The form of the God*, and *the being like the God*, would have been, in their Greek shape, expressions much better suited to imply the dogma of Christ's Essential Deity. As the text stands, room is left for doubt whether St Paul may not have intended to contrast, in very general terms, a superhuman, spiritual, glorious existence, with a humble human existence—*a Divine form* with *a servile form*. The latter expression does not directly imply Christ's manhood, which is indicated by the subsequent words, " being made in the likeness of men ; " and, " being found in fashion as a man." The same general conception, presented with yet greater indefiniteness, appears in 2 Cor. viii. 9, where the Apostle declares, that " Christ, though rich, for our sakes became poor." The object in both passages is to inculcate, through Christ's example, a moral lesson of humility, benevolence, and self-denial. The Person and conduct of our Lord are set forth in their ethical aspect, and no well-defined, accurate notion of His pre-incarnate condition and rank can be fairly extracted. We cannot know more of the Apostle's mind than his language distinctly imparts. That he did not design to teach, either directly or by implication, the doctrine of Christ's proper Deity, he makes abundantly evident. Jesus Christ and God are, throughout his reasoning, separate individual Beings. There is no hint that One Divine Nature comprised them both. God is said to have " highly exalted Christ, and given Him a Name which is above every Name ; " and in the confession : " Jesus Christ is Lord," a tribute is paid " to the glory of God the Father." The Apostle's words at once recall his positive and perspicuous statement in an earlier Epistle : " To us there is but One God, the Father, and one Lord, Jesus Christ" (1 Cor. viii. 4-6).

If St Paul's opinions, when he wrote to the Philippians, had risen to the level of ecclesiastical orthodoxy, he believed Jesus Christ to be personally Very God, lacking no attribute of Godhead, and he must, in such case, be understood to teach that, because God assumed a vesture of body, soul, and spirit,—became as much man as He could without becoming a human person, and submitted His impersonal Humanity to death upon the Cross—" therefore, God highly exalted God, and gave God a Name," &c. If to any rational mind this wears a look of absurdity, I am not accountable for the absurdity. I only state what must have been St Paul's meaning, supposing him to have been able to think consistently, and to have known Christ to be truly God, " equal to the Father as touching His Godhead." Should it be said, Our Lord's Humanity was exalted, the answer is, there was no human person to exalt ; and, if there had been a human person, how could that person, when taken into inseparable union with Essential Deity, be capable of exaltation at the hands of personally distinct Essential Deity ?

If with some MSS. we read, " *the* Name which is above every name," the argument will not be affected. Whatever the exaltation and the name are, the fact remains, that the

Apostle depicts them, not as inalienable attributes of Godhead, but as gifts bestowed by God.

The general diction of the Philippian Epistle lends no support whatever to the notion that the author saw in Christ a second personal God, or ascribed to Him equality with God. God is the Object of thanksgiving and prayer (i. 3 ; iv. 6). It is He Who, " having begun a good work in us, will carry on that work until the day of Jesus Christ" (i. 6). " Fruit of righteousness is, through Christ, to His glory" (i. 11). He is the Source of salvation, and of the energy in virtue of which our part in the work of salvation is accomplished (i. 28 : ii. 13). He is the inward Revealer (iii. 15); and the primal Giver of peace (iv. 7, 9). Of Him St Paul writes : " My God will supply all your need, according to His riches in glory, in (or by) Christ Jesus.—To our God and Father be the glory for ever and ever" (iv. 19, 20).

The Pauline benedictory salutation (i. 2) does not equalise or identify God and Christ as sources of grace and peace, but by descriptive appellation marks the difference between *God our Father*, and *our Lord Jesus Christ.* The name Christ (iv. 13) is interpolated, the true reading being, *in Him Who strengtheneth me.*

There is in Col. i. 15-17 (comp. 2 Cor. iv. 4), "a magnificent dogmatic passage," containing "perhaps the most exhaustive assertion of our Lord's Godhead which is to be found in the writings of St Paul. The Colossian Church was exposed to the intellectual attacks of a theosophic doctrine, which degraded Jesus Christ to the rank of one of a long series of inferior beings, supposed to range between mankind and the Supreme God. Against this position St Paul asserts that Christ is the *Image of the Invisible God.* The expression, *Image of God*, supplements the title of ' the Son.' As ' the Son,' Christ is derived eternally from the Father, and He is of One Substance with the Father. As ' the Image,' Christ is, in that One Substance, the exact likeness of the Father, in all things except being the Father. The Son is the Image of the Father, not as the Father, but as God : The Son is ' the Image of God.' The *Image* is indeed originally God's unbegun, unending reflection of Himself in Himself ; but the *Image* is also the Organ Whereby God, in His Essence invisible, reveals Himself to His creatures. Thus the *Image* is, so to speak, naturally the Creator, since creation is the first revelation which God has made of Himself. Man is the highest point in the visible universe ; in man, God's attributes are most luminously exhibited ; man is the image and glory of God (1 Cor. xi. 7).

But Christ is the Adequate Image of God ; God's Self-reflection in His Own thought, eternally present with Himself. As the *Image*, Christ is the πρωτότοκος πάσης κτίσεως ; that is to say, *not* the First in rank among created beings, *but* begotten before any created beings. That this is a true sense of the expression is etymologically certain " (p. 317).

We are here carried into the cloudy region of theological metaphysics, where language and understanding part company. To all appearance. Mr Liddon has convinced himself, and would fain persuade others, St Paul aimed not only to exalt Christ above angels, and to point out His priority to every other creature, but also to assert His Godhead. Yet very little examination is needed to ascertain that the Apostle's language can by no reasonable construction be made to allege or imply Christ's Deity. The phrases employed are very far from being tantamount to delineations of the Most High ; they clearly bespeak difference and inferiority. The term *Image* denotes resemblance, without marking the kind and extent of that resemblance. In its most extreme sense it does not signify *sameness*, and, as St Paul uses it, the features constituting the likeness are left undefined. Mr Liddon indulges in the too common practice of interpreting Scripture by inflating indefinite epithets. According to his exposition, the title *Son* displays an identity of Substance with the Father, and the title, *Image of God*, an exact likeness to God. *The Son* has the Father's Uncreated Nature ; *the Image* is after the closest lines of complete similitude. Now, this is purely arbitrary,—a rash and presumptuous stretching of diction, which properly describes, not Divine, but human relations. *Son of God* is, manifestly, an analogical and figurative expression ; and the adjective, *only-begotten*, which the latest of the Canonical writers joins with it, enlarges the figurativeness, even while giving a degree of uniqueness and intensity to the relation indicated. What is *begetting* on the part of God, if being *alone begotten* is the specific difference which sunders the beloved Son from the many sons, who, in the realm of created life, are *begotten* and *born* of God ? It is not from Scripture, rationally interpreted, men have inferred the proposition that the *only-begotten* Son is, in virtue of His Sonship, a Person within the Incommunicable and Imperishable Essence. They have brought elaborated conceptions to Scripture, and have grafted them on to a few mystic and metaphorical words. The very phrases by which the Sacred writers seem to shun explicitness and precision, become, beneath the hands of interpreters, most explicit and precise. For converting *Image* into a synonym for exact and adequate likeness, there is really no reasonable pretext. No special emphasis is given to the noun, as in Heb. x. 1 ; no defining adjective is used ; and St Paul does not even prefix the Article, and call Christ *the Image* of God, but *an Image*, just as he had, in 1 Cor. xi. 7, called man (comp. James iii. 9). The addition to the name of God, of the epithet *invisible*, does not strengthen the expression, or render it more expressive than that which is, in the first Corinthian Epistle, applied to man. Since the Essence of God is invisible, the visible image of God cannot be identical with His Essence. I cannot even imagine what sort of distinct, objective personality, is to be understood by " God's unbegun, unending reflection of Himself in Himself ; His Self-reflection in His Own thought, eternally present with Himself." The fault may be in my own powers of comprehension, but I strongly suspect, Mr Liddon mistook phrases for ideas.

The point is not one of much moment, but Mr Liddon is somewhat too confident in his affirmation that the original of the Authorised Version, *first-born of every creature*, means *begotten before any created beings*. To be first-born among, is, doubtless, to be born before ; but we depart from what is " etymologically certain" when we substitute *begotten* for *born*. Begetting, and bringing forth by birth, are, in their human significance, diverse. Neither can be in strictness attributed to the Almighty, but the attribution of the former is less conspicuously figurative than the attribution of the latter. Unconsciously, if not consciously, the Protestant theological dogmatist desires to reduce, as much as may be, the metaphorical aspect of the expressions into which the language of Scripture compels him to thrust his traditional theories concerning Christ's nature, and so he prefers *first-begotten* to *first-born*. There can be no dispute, however, that the more literal and customary meaning of the term employed by St Paul, is *first-born*. New Testament usage sanctions no other meaning. Our Lord is announced to have been originated or produced before all creation. But this is all that is announced respecting His origin. The text does not say, the birth of the Son, who is *Image of the Invisible God*, was not some creative process, though that process preceded, and may in unexplained ways have differed from, what is commonly called creation : it does not say, the Son was an inherent Form or Person in the Divine Substance, eternally present with the Father. Rather. it implies by the words *Son*, *First-born*, *Image*, the prior and distinct existence of an originating God and Antitype, Who, by an act of His own Will and Power, became in some way a Father, and produced a Representative of Himself. Expositors who can discern in the words *Son, first-born, only-begotten,* a disclosure of identity of nature between God and Christ, are curiously unable to discern the vastly more obvious disclosure, that God is in some very real sense the Originator of Christ, the Cause of Christ's existence. If the Son is verily a necessary and everlasting Personal Being, comprised in the Divine Essence, Equal to, and of One Substance with, the Father, then *first-born* and *only-begotten* are thoroughly empty phrases, about the most senseless and unmeaning which could have been devised to express the relations of eternally co-existing and Substantially identical Persons in the Godhead. The loose figurativeness of the language is transparently manifest in everything except in indicating that God was prior, and God the Producer ; but Mr Liddon draws his theology from the metaphor, and excludes from consideration the one simple, intelligible fact, on which the metaphor is based.

To avoid superfluous discussion, I do not mention some fairly probable explanations of the passage ; but certainly, the expression *first-born of all creation,* most naturally denotes the position and pre-eminence of primogeniture among created beings and things, and cannot be understood as a denial that the Son was created by God. To suppose the Apostle intended to set forth Christ's Deity by calling Him *born before,* or *first-born of, the whole creation,* is to invite contempt for the Apostle and his language. It is not thus the Church has proclaimed her dogma, and no man in his senses would dream of teaching Christ's Godhead in such a fashion. The use of πρωτότοκος is illustrated by Exod. iv. 22 ; Jer. xxxi. 9 ; Rom. viii. 29 ; Col. i. 18 ; Heb. xii. 23 ; Rev. i. 5.

A man committed to the task of extracting a revelation of our Lord's Deity from the pages of the New Testament, is naturally tempted to invest with peculiar and augmented significance the statement (Col. i. 16), that all things have been created *in Christ, by Christ,* and *for Christ.* If, with Mr Liddon, we translate ἐν, *in,* we give to the first of these expressions a metaphysical and mystic import ; but whatever creating *in Christ* may signify, the act of creating must be referred to the Father, Who, in emitting, originating, or producing His Son, contemplated and prepared for the production of the Universe. The most accomplished of systematic theologians would probably shrink from the proposition that Christ himself created all things in Himself. If we translate ἐν, *by*, it will then undoubtedly point to secondary, instrumental agency.

With regard to the next expression, *by*, or *through Christ*, the preposition therein employed (διά, with the Genitive case), may indeed be used of the principal cause (Rom. xi. 36 ; Heb. ii. 10 ; 1 Cor. i. 9 ; and perhaps Gal. iv. 7), but is much more frequently and regularly used of the subordinate cause, when it corresponds to our *by means of, through*. Nothing can be plainer in St Paul's writings, and throughout the New Testament, than the ascription of creation to God as the Primary, Principal, ultimately Efficient Cause (Acts xiv. 15, xvii. 24, 28 ; Rom. xi. 36 ; 1 Cor. viii. 6 ; Eph. iii. 9). The two or three passages (John i. 3 ; Col. i. 16, 17 ; Heb. i. 2), which attribute creation to Christ, attribute it in an inferior, secondary sense. The statement : " Christ is the One Producer and Sustainer of all created existence," is a very hyperbolical mode of saying, He is the agent through whom, in some manner not explicable by us, God produced and sustains all things. Taking the statement rigorously and literally, it is palpably false, and also unscriptural. Mr Liddon himself admits ; " The Eternal Father is the ultimate Source of all life."

The third of the expressions, *for Christ* (εἰς), betokens created things to have a reference to Christ, he being, under God, and by God's gift and appointment, their Lord and Head. In Rom. xi. 36, after the statement, all things are *from God*, all things are said to be *for Him ;* but it is puerile to contend that the general indication of aim and reference contained in the preposition must have strictly the same force in the two instances. The different Persons, God and Christ, suggest the different ranges of meaning to be assigned. A dogma must be in extremities when its defenders cling to a possible sense of a single preposition, in a single text. The whole tenor of Scripture proves created Intelligences to be *for God*, and *on account of God* (Heb. ii. 10), in an acceptation in which they are not *for Christ. Glory, thanks, spiritual sacrifices, fruits of righteousness*, are " to God and His honour, through (διά) Jesus Christ " (Rom. xvi. 27 ; 1 Cor. xv. 57 ; Col. iii. 17 ; 1 Peter ii. 5 ; Phil. i. 11). We are taught, "The Lord God Almighty is worthy to receive glory, and honour, and power, because He has created all things, and on account of His Will they were and were created " (Rev. iv. 11). The guiding purpose of the Christian's life is " that in all things God may be glorified, through Jesus Christ " (1 Peter iv. 11). Other texts of the same or similar purport might be cited, but these are sufficient, and by their light Mr Liddon's adventurous exposition of the words, *for him,* may be read: "Christ is not, as Arianism afterwards pretended, merely an inferior workman, creating for the glory of a higher Master, for a God superior to Himself. He creates for Himself; He is the End of created things, as well as their immediate Source; and in living for Him, every creature finds at once the explanation and the law of its being. For ' He is before all things, and by Him all things consist ' " (p. 319).

The words adduced in the final sentence are no extenuation of what precedes. The Apostle does not introduce them as a reason or an explanation: *And, he is before, &c.* They affirm priority of existence, and imply pre-eminence in relation to created things; and by stating that all things stand together or consist (ἐν) *in* Christ, they to some extent expand, without illuminating, what had before been said, namely, that all things were created *in Christ.* It is impossible to determine conclusively the particular shade of significance which the writer intended to attach to the verb *consist.* The subject transcends the domain of definite conceptions, and the language is vague. But Mr Liddon has no right to depart from the meaning which he had just previously given to the preposition ἐν. In verses 16 and 17, one of the two translations, *by him,* and, *in him,* should be kept to. The former will denote instrumental agency; the latter will lift our thoughts into a dim ideal region, but will point back to the One Infinite Mind Whose wisdom and power created all things *in Christ,* and caused all things to stand together *in him.*

The 18th and following verses of the first chapter to the Colossians, Mr Liddon passes with scantiest comment. He is, no doubt, able to reconcile them with his dogma in a manner quite satisfactory to himself, but they have, to say the least, an appearance of incongruity with the position, that the greatness ascribed to Christ is due to his being Very and Eternal God. When He is magnified by the title *First-born from the dead,* His Divine Person is not the Object in view, and yet, since there is no other person than the Divine, *the first-born of all creation,* and *the first-born from the dead,* must be personally one and the same. In verse 19, the nominative to the verb *was well pleased,* is not expressed, but our Translators rightly supplied the ellipsis from the remoter antecedent (ver. 12), and the import of the language ill accords with the doctrine of our Lord's Con-substantial, Co-eternal, Co-equal Deity.

The word ($\pi\lambda\dot{\eta}\rho\omega\mu\alpha$), *fulness*, which is used in Col. i. 19, is used again ii. 9, where the *fulness of the Godhead* is said *to dwell in Christ bodily.* Mr Liddon expounds the latter text thus:—

"The entire cycle of the Divine attributes, considered as a series of powers or forces, dwells in Jesus Christ; and this, not in any merely ideal or transcendental manner, but with that actual reality which men attach to the presence of material bodies which they can feel and measure through the organs of sense;" and in a Note, he adds; "In this passage the *pleroma* must be understood in the metaphysical sense of the Divine Essence, even if in Col. i. 19, it is referred to the fulness of Divine grace. Contrast, too, the permanent fact involved in the present *dwells* of the one passage, with the historical aorist, *was well pleased,* of the other." The adverb *bodily* has its best explanation in our Lord's Humanity, and signifies *in bodily form.* The meaning, *really, substantially,* is not inadmissible, but finds stronger support in the authority of orthodox interpreters than in reason and philology. The expression, *fulness of the Godhead,* is not distinguishable from *fulness of God.* The word translated Godhead is not that which in Rom. i. 20, stands for the Divine Nature, but a term to which *Godship* would perhaps be the more exact English equivalent. It is, however, idle to imagine the author of the Epistle to have had a distinction of this sort in view. If we bring in the nice discriminations and verbal minutiæ of scholastic theology, it is erroneous to affirm that the Divine Essence *abides in Christ.* He is interior to the Divine Essence, and the precise statement of His Deity demands the announcement; *He is the fulness of the Godhead, in a bodily form.* Apart from the Divine Essence, there is, according to the theory Mr Liddon maintains, no personal Christ in whom the Divine Essence can dwell. But the attempt to wring a dogma out of a trivial difference in phraseology, is manifestly foolish. The *fulness* said to dwell in Christ, reasonably viewed by the light of Scripture, consists in the plentitude of exalted endowments of power and dominion, grace and sanctity, communicated from the Divine Nature of God to the human nature of Christ. Whether they were bestowed through the channel of a pre-existent spiritual Being, or imparted to the human nature directly by the Spirit of God, as the title, *the Christ* (or Anointed), and some texts of Scripture already appealed to (Matt. xii. 18; Luke iv. 18; John iii. 34; Acts x. 38), would lead us to conclude, is not here of practical moment; in either case, God was their Source and Giver. There is nothing to sustain the assertion that, *all the fulness of the Godhead* was incommunicable to any creature, and specifically different in kind from *all the fulness* which the Father was well pleased should dwell in Christ (i. 19), or from *all the fulness of God* unto (εἰς) which the Apostle prayed Christians might be filled (Eph. iii. 19). By phrases so nearly identical, the same writer cannot, without extra Scriptural light, be seen to convey conceptions so totally dissimilar, as are the influential presence of God in created persons, and the Incarnation of entire Personal Deity within the elements of an impersonal Humanity. In John i. 16, we are said to *have received of Christ's fulness,* and the contemplated end of Christian progress is the "coming unto a perfect man, unto the measure of the stature of *the fulness of Christ*" (Eph. iv. 13). In neither of these passages can *the fulness of Christ* mean "the Divine Essence," or, "the Divine Attributes, considered as a series of powers or forces." And the immediately subjoined context (Col. ii. 10), "And ye are filled full (or have your fulness) in Him," does not strengthen the opinion that *fulness of the Godhead* denotes essential, inherent qualities of the Divine Nature. The very close connection of the noun and verb is concealed from the English reader, owing to our Translators having rendered the latter, *are complete;* but in the Greek the noun is a derivative from the verb, and the two are as nearly allied as are *fulness* and *to fill* in our own language. Christians are made full from the fulness that is in Christ, but certainly do not share the absolute perfections of the Godhead. The *fulness* is denominated *fulness of the Godhead,* not because it is the cycle of the Almighty's Essential, Incommunicable Properties, but because it flows from God, and is God's gift. Professor Moses Stuart, the great American champion of Mr Liddon's dogma, freely acknowledged this in his Fifth Letter to Channing. "In Eph. iii. 19, the Apostle exhibits his fervent wishes that the Christians of Ephesus might be 'filled with all the fulness of God.' By comparing this expression as applied to Christ in Col. i. 19, ii. 9, with John. i. 14, 16, and Eph. i. 23, it appears evident that, by the *fulness of God* is meant the abundant gifts and graces which were bestowed on Christ, and through Him upon His disciples." The results of holiness which God has abidingly and completely effected in Christ, He (according to the theology of the Colossian and Ephesian Epistles) designs, through Christ, gradually to effect in His other spiritual, rational offspring. "The measure of the stature of the fulness of Christ," even, "all the fulness of God," is the height to which our Heavenly Father's loving wisdom will lift His obedient children, by the stages of long-continued progress.

The distinction between God and Christ, though not presented in the Epistle to the Colossians with all the definite clearness which appears elsewhere in the New Testament, is nevertheless marked in a fashion not easily reconcilable with the assumption that the writer, in exalting our Lord Jesus Christ, intended to equalise Him with God. In the opening sentences, the Deity is designated "God our Father," and, "God the Father of our Lord Jesus Christ:" in iii. 17, the precept is given, "Do all things in the name of the Lord Jesus, giving thanks to God, the Father, through him;" and in iv. 3, there is an exhortation to pray that God would open a door for speaking the mystery of Christ; the mystery "wherein are hid all the treasures of wisdom and knowledge" (ii. 3). If St Paul was inspired to believe, with an uniform and steady faith, that Christ is a Person or Form within the Essence of the Divine Nature, this language, and the general style of his references to God and Christ throughout the Epistle, are very perplexing, and by no means calculated to exhibit and propagate his faith.

By what rational method Mr Liddon can have reached the following conclusion, I am utterly unable to conceive :—" Although throughout this Epistle the title *Logos* is never introduced, it is plain that the *Image* of St Paul is equivalent in His rank and functions to the *Logos* of St John. Each exists prior to creation ; each is the One Agent in creation ; each is a Divine Person ; each is equal with God, and shares His essential Life ; each is really none other than God." The *Logos* and *Image* may approximate nearly, though the former is a step in advance, and, to each, an existence prior to creation generally, may be ascribed : the rest of the description is due to Mr Liddon's traditional faith and lively imagination.

The Prologue of "St John's Gospel," and the opening chapter of the Epistle to the Hebrews, are, in Mr Liddon's opinion, the only passages in the entire compass of the New Testament which are adequately parallel to the "exhaustive and magnificent dogmatic passage in the Epistle to the Colossians." The speculative Christology with which the fourth Gospel commences has been already alluded to, and also that application of words from the 45th Psalm, by which "Christ is expressly addressed as God" (Heb. i. 8). But the doctrine deduced from a misapplied, and perhaps mistranslated phrase,* is set aside by the plain sense of the subsequent context ; *thy God hath anointed thee, &c.*

* Dr Davidson repeats in his *Introduction to the New Testament* his opinion that the sense of the Hebrew is, "Thy *God's*, or *Divine throne*, is for ever and ever." Isaac Leeser also renders, in Psalm xlv. : "Thy throne, given of God."

The language of the writer to the Hebrews dilates remarkably under Mr Liddon's manipulation. "Christ in His crucified, but now enthroned Humanity, is seated at the right of the Majesty on high (i. 3); He is seated there, as being Heir of all things (ver. 2); the angels themselves are but a portion of His vast inheritance. The dignity of His titles is indicative of His essential rank (ver. 4)." How can Christ's being seated at the right hand of God, intimate he is God? Do not the very terms in which His exalted position is described, show him not to be interior to the Divine Majesty, but exalted by It? How does Christ become Heir of all things?—in virtue of inherent Deity, or, by the decree of "His Father and our Father, His God and our God?" The author of the Epistle tells us, God constituted or appointed Him Heir of all things. How can the supreme rank of Essential Godhead be indicated by the statement, "He became so much better than the angels, as He hath inherited (or obtained) a more excellent name than they?" Mr Liddon himself admits the reference is to the exaltation of our Lord's Humanity. The superior excellence of Christ's Name, is enforced and illustrated in verse 5, by an application of language which Christians, possessing the knowledge that Christ is Eternal God, cannot readily apply to His Divine Essence ; *Thou art my Son, this day have I begotten thee* (see also v. 5). And again *I will be to him, as,* or *for* (εἰς), *a Father, and he shall be to Me as,* or *for* (εἰς), *a Son* (comp. 2 Cor. vi. 18). If it is said, begetting in time (*this day*), refers to Christ's assumption of human nature, or, to His resurrection in that nature ; then, the Sonship is no token of Deity, and does not unveil an Uncreated Entity. The present Bishop of Lincoln (Dr Wordsworth), in his Article, *Son of God* (Smith's *Bible Dictionary*), expounds the passage with his accustomed decision and lucidity : "But, in a still higher sense, that title (Son) is applied by God to His only Son, begotten by eternal generation (see Ps. ii. 7, as interpreted in the Epistle to the Hebrews, i. 5 ; v. 5) ; the word *to-day*, in that passage, being expressive of the act of God, with Whom is no yesterday, nor to-morrow." *To-day*, therefore, in Divine phraseology addressed to men, excludes any definite particular time. The wonder is that a word so superfluous and misleading should have been introduced, but its presence may remind us of the difference between Divine and human diction.

Verse 13 raises the question ; To what personal Being is the language addressed, *Sit thou on My right hand, till I make thine enemies thy footstool?* Is it addressed by God to Co-equal, Consubstantial God, or, is it addressed to the impersonal Humanity in which one of the *Forms, Distinctions,* or *Persons* of the Godhead, arrayed Himself? This is a point which must be settled before inferences are drawn. If the writer of the Epistle imagined Deity was accosting Deity, his credit for spiritual discernment and common sense is impaired; if he believed the man Christ Jesus was accosted, his inspiration did not develop orthodox apprehensions of Personality, and his language does not contribute to establish the dogma that Christ is, in the most absolute sense, Divine.

On the expression, "This day have I begotten thee," Mr Liddon bestows no attention. He understands the term, *the Son of God,* or *the Son,* to refer to our Lord's only personal nature, the pre-incarnate, and seeks the full sense of the term in the imagery of the third verse. "That the Son is One with God, as having streamed forth eternally from the Father's Essence, like a ray of light from the parent fire with which it is unbrokenly joined, is implied in the expression, *effulgence of His glory.* That He is both personally distinct from, and yet literally equal to, Him of Whose Essence He is the adequate imprint, is taught us in the phrase, *imprinted image of His Substance.** By Him, therefore, the universe was made (ver. 2); and at this moment all things are preserved and upheld in being by the fiat of His almighty word (ver. 3)" (p. 322).

Now, in this commentary, ideas are interpolated, and facts are misrepresented. There is nothing implied or taught about *eternal* streaming forth, and *unbroken junction.* The figurative delineation might have been invested with a more definite, special, and exclusive character by the use of the Article; but " the Son *in* or *by* (ἐν) whom God has spoken," is called only *an emanation, &c., an impression, &c.* The writer of the Epistle was sufficiently master of Greek to know how to express in that language clear

---

* Mr Liddon quotes the Greek of the expressions, *effulgence, &c., imprinted image, &c.,* without translating. *Person* in the Authorized Version is certainly incorrect ; *substance* is a better translation, but the word employed carries no assurance that the writer had the particular conception *Essential Nature,* rather than the more general conception *Being,* in his thoughts. The same word occurs (iii. 14) in the phrase " beginning of our *confidence :*" and again (xi. 1), in the badly-rendered phrase, "faith is the *substance.*" &c. On the two expressions from which Mr Liddon argues, Conybeare and Howson give the following notes :—

(1.) " Not *brightness* (A.V.), but *emanation,* as of light from the sun. The word and idea occur in Philo."

(2.) " Literally *impression,* as of a seal on wax. The expression is used by Philo concerning the Eternal Word.'

and precise thoughts, with clearness and precision. He tried to set forth what in his conception was our Lord's most intimate relation to God, and he employed, in its vaguest form, very vague and figurative diction. The implication and the teaching of unity and equality, as well as personal distinctness, may be quite manifest to Mr Liddon, but from ordinary understandings they are impenetrably hidden.

In the statement, "by Him (Christ), therefore, the universe was made," advantage is taken of verbal ambiguity. The literal translation of the text is, *through whom also, He (God) made the ages*, where it is not at all probable the word *ages* signifies *the universe*, though it is perhaps possible, but still very unlikely, the word signifies *worlds*, that is, the present and future abodes of mankind. A reference to Heb. xi. 3, by no means settles the question, the sense being there also undetermined. The more radical and closely connected senses of the word, *period of duration, age, dispensation*, appear in the Epistle, and more especially in vi. 5, and ix. 26, in the latter of which the usual and proper term for *world*, occurs in the expression, *foundation of the world.* Professor Stuart, in the first of his *Essays on Words relating to Future Punishment*, writes : "I had myself, before I gave the topic an extended and minute investigation, been accustomed to suppose that in Heb. i. 2, xi. 3, the *universe* must be meant, particularly because the plural number is there employed ; but a minute inquiry into the grounds of such a rendering, has convinced me of my mistake." The plural number is employed in ix. 26, *at the end of the ages.*

Mr Liddon again avails himself of verbal ambiguity when he says, "All things are preserved and upheld in being by the fiat of His (Christ's) almighty word." The phrase, *word of His power*, may possibly refer to the power of the Son, but more naturally and probably refers to the power of the Infinite Father. The dubious construction of the Greek is exactly represented in the Anglican Version.

On the ground of a misapplied and mistranslated quotation from Psalm xcvii. 7, Mr Liddon speaks of "the honours which the heavenly intelligences themselves may not refuse to pay Christ, even when He is entering upon His profound Self-humiliation (ver. 6)." We need not inquire how the heavenly intelligences could need the injunction, *let all the angels of God worship Him.* Whether their intelligence was, or was not, equal to the task of discerning the Almighty and Self-existent Substance through the veil of human flesh, is a question beyond the range of our knowledge. The error in the application of the Psalmist's words, " worship Him all ye gods (*elohim*)," is obvious to every reader of the 97th Psalm. Some suppose a Septuagint reading of Deuteronomy xxxii. 43, preserved in the Vatican MS., but probably spurious, is the source of the quotation ; but this supposition does not help the matter, since in Deuteronomy xxxii. the Messiah is not, directly or indirectly, alluded to. There is but one conclusion which a rational judgment can sanction,—the Canonical writer applied an Old Testament passage erroneously.

A similar decision must be given respecting the citation in verses 10–12, which Mr Liddon uses as a testimony to " Christ's relationship of Creator both to earth and heaven." Reference to the 24–27 verses of the 102d Psalm demonstrates that the author of the Epistle to the Hebrews was mistaken. The afflicted Psalmist's plaintive entreaty is poured forth to God, the One God whom the Jews worshipped, and not to Messiah.

But it may be urged, these citations from the Jewish Scriptures are at any rate evidence of what the writer of the Epistle himself thought concerning Christ's nature and dignity. Opinions enforced by palpably bad reasons are not generally of much value, but the citations, when compared with the language which pervades the Epistle, are rather proofs the writer did not think deeply, and knew too little of his theme to treat it consistently. If he believed that Christ in His pre-incarnate and alone personal Being, was addressed in the language he had just quoted from the 102d Psalm, how could he with consistency immediately add (ver. 13), referring to the beginning of the 110th Psalm, " To which of the angels said He (God), at any time, Sit thou on my right hand, until I make thine enemies thy footstool ?" How could he, conformably with the doctrine of Christ's Personal Co-equal Godhead, describe Him in the terms made use of in ii. 10–. 13 verses ? How also, if he had grasped the conception that Christ is Very and Eternal God, could he have written (ii. 18 ; iv. 15 ; v. 7 ;) of our Lord's having suffered, being tempted,— tempted in all points like as we are ; and having offered up prayers and supplications, &c. ? God cannot be tempted by evil (James i. 13), and the elements of a created Humanity, which Christ drew around his Divine Person, could not, in any real sense, expose the Self-existent Infinite Spirit to the temptations of finite creatures. ' Temptations endured by Almighty God,' is language akin to blasphemy, but, if Christ's temptations were not endured by Almighty God, by what person were they endured ?

If His "prayers and supplications, with strong crying and tears," were not offered up by Almighty God, by what person were they offered up?

In Heb. iii. 2, "Jesus, the Apostle and High Priest of our profession," is said to have been faithful to Him who appointed Him, and His superiority to God's servant Moses is illustrated (ver. 6) by the fact that He is over God's house as a son. The English Version misleads by translating, *his own house;* the original is, *His* (God's) *house*, Whose house Christians are (comp. 1 Cor. iii. 16 ; vi. 19 ; 2 Cor. vi. 16).

It is impossible to reconcile the language respecting our Lord's priesthood according to the Order of Melchisedec, in the fifth chapter, and five chapters next ensuing, with any sort of clear, intelligent faith in His Deity. Mr Liddon sees "a superhuman Personality more than hinted at in the terms of the comparison which is instituted between Melchisedec and his Divine Antitype. History records nothing of the parents, of the descent, of the birth, or of the death of Melchisedec ; he appears in the sacred narrative as if he had no beginning of days or end of life. In this he is 'made like unto the Son of God,' with His Eternal Pre-existence and His endless days. This Eternal Christ can save to the uttermost, because He has a Priesthood that is unchangeable, since it is based on His Own Everlasting Being" (p. 338). Arguments of this kind only provoke a smile. The description given of Melchisedec (vii. 3) is singularly fanciful and exaggerated. He is said explicitly to be "without father, without mother," to have "neither beginning of days nor end of life ;" and then, the perpetuity of His priesthood is described by exactly the same phrase by which (x. 12), the perpetuity of Christ's session at the right hand of God is described. And why, in quoting Heb. vii. 24, 25, are the important words, "Them that come unto God, through Him," omitted? Is it because they distinguish between Christ and God, in a manner unsuited to Mr Liddon's deductions?

But the errors into which the writer of the Epistle to the Hebrews has fallen, do not call for the supposition that, on the subject of Christ's pre-incarnate rank, his thoughts were so utterly ignorant and confused, as to render the general prevailing tone of his language not indicative of the opinions to which his mind inclined. A few perverted and inconsistent interpretations of the Old Testament Scriptures certainly do not justify us in pronouncing him altogether speculative, visionary, and unreasonable. In addition to the evidence already adduced, I think the subjoined passages sufficiently reveal that their author did not hold, or intend to impart, the theory ;—Christ is Essential and Consubstantial God, in Nature One with, and Equal to, the Father.

" How much more shall the blood of Christ, who through the Eternal Spirit (perhaps, Holy Spirit) offered Himself without spot to God, cleanse your conscience from dead works to the service of the living God " (ix. 14). " Ye are come to the general assembly and church of the first-born (πρωτοτόκων), who are enrolled in heaven, and to God the Judge of all, and to the spirits of just men made perfect, and to Jesus, mediator of a new covenant " (xii. 23, 24).

" May the God of peace, Who brought again from the dead our Lord Jesus, the great Shepherd of the sheep by the blood of an everlasting covenant, make you perfect in every good work, to do His will ; working in you that which is well pleasing in His sight, through Jesus Christ " (xiii. 20, 21). The Greek admits the rendering, " The Shepherd of the sheep, great by the blood," &c., but the other rendering is, I think, to be preferred.

Mr Liddon conceives that, in the statements of the first chapter of this Epistle, " We recognise a Being, for Whose Person, although It be clothed in a finite Human Nature (iii. 2), there is no real place between humanity and God " (p. 323). Assertions of this kind prompt the inquiry—What do we know of the intermediate terms of the series intervening between earthly humanity and God ? But experience shows that ignorance of the grounds on which his proposition ought to rest need never hinder a man from affirming an orthodox conclusion to be contained in Scripture. If, having first derived our dogma from other sources, we come to the reading of the Epistle fully convinced such a Being as Mr Liddon discovers is, and must be, depicted, then, doubtless, we shall recognise him ; but unbiased, reasonable investigation will not lead to the recognition. The general tone and scope of the sacred writer are, according to all ordinary rules of apprehension, plainly at variance with the assumption of his belief in the proper Deity of Jesus Christ. Mr Liddon is thoroughly persuaded that in various portions of the New Testament, the Divine prerogatives (that is, true Deity) of Christ, are explicitly asserted, and therefore does not speak ironically when he says, " While the Epistle to the Hebrews lays even a stronger emphasis than any other book of the New Testament upon Christ's true Humanity, it is nevertheless certain that no other book more explicitly asserts the reality of His Divine prerogatives."

Now, a careful examination of the passages in the Epistles to the Philippians, Colossians, and Hebrews, to which Mr Liddon appeals, does something more than show the failure of his appeal to evoke the response he seeks. It throws suspicions of the gravest kind upon his doctrine, and raises difficulties which admit of no solution, short of denial that the Scriptures, rationally understood, are a true and sufficing Rule of Orthodox Faith. A really candid, logically-minded investigator, feels himself driven, however reluctantly, to one of two conclusions—either Orthodoxy has taught for doctrines unwarranted and extra-Scriptural speculations, or the Canonical writers were directed by a controlling inspiration of concealment, preparative to the Church's mission as the living and authoritative Revealer and Teacher, through Which, to the end of time, the light of dogma was to be dispensed. According to one of these conclusions, Mr Liddon's doctrine may be true and tenable, and on the ground on which it is tenable, I leave it quite unchallenged. I only contend that in Scripture alone it has no adequate logical basis, and cannot possibly be deduced by methods of rational interpretation. Assume there is in the Church an authority co-ordinate with, and in some respects superior to, Scripture, and, so far as I am concerned, the controversy is at an end. I do not wish to enter upon the question whether the claims of Church authority can be satisfactorily vindicated. Mr Liddon exposes himself to criticism by not avowing that he interprets from the ground of ecclesiastical light and prerogative, not from the ground of reason. He wants to be thought rational when he is ecclesiastical, but the two conditions are different; the latter is held by many to be the nobler and more enlightened condition, but it is specifically distinct from the former.

There can be no doubt the writers of the Epistles named above designed to exalt Christ, and to avouch His superiority to angels, and to all the productions of any creative or administrative energy which they supposed the Father to have exercised through Him. If they had dared to proclaim, and had desired to proclaim, His Godhead, surely (looking at the subject from the reasonable, and not the ecclesiastical point of view) they would have done so. They would not, when the topic was specially before their minds, have wrapt their faith in figurative phrases, and have shunned giving simple and distinct utterance to the thought which lay nearest their hearts. Men who are convinced Christ is God, are not apt to be reticent or ambiguous when discoursing of His dignity. Approximations on this subject may be fairly construed as evidences the writers could not do more than approximate. They might be moving in the direction of the doctrine ultimately laid down by the Church, but their thoughts were still in the nature of guesses and speculations ; and conscious lack of knowledge restrained them from definite allegations. If the New Testament contains no statements which, in their rational meaning, amount to negation of Christ's Deity (a point to be hereafter examined), microscopic germs of the doctrine of His Deity may perhaps be discernible in the vague, obscure, metaphorical expressions which Mr Liddon seizes upon, and expands ; but on the most favourable supposition, the doctrine itself, in a developed, intelligible, precise shape, is absent. We must seek for it as a revelation, beyond the limits of Scripture, and then bring it to Scripture, as a key of knowledge, and a clue to meanings which unaided reason could never detect.

The Christology of the Apocalypse is treated with Mr Liddon's accustomed heedless rhetoric, and readiness of assumption. " The representation of the Person of our Saviour in the Apocalypse, is independent of any indistinctness that may attach to the interpretation of the historical imagery of that wonderful book. In the Apocalypse, Christ is the First and the Last ; He is the Alpha and the Omega ; He is the Beginning and the End of all existence (Rev. i. 8 ; ii. 8 ; xxi. 6 ; xxii. 13). He possesses the seven spirits or perfections of God (iii. 1). He has a mysterious Name which no man knows save He himself (xix. 12). His name is written on the foreheads of the faithful (iii. 12 ; comp. ii. 17); His grace is the blessing of Christians (xxii. 21) " (p. 243).

Out of the four texts included in the first of the above references, there is only one (ii. 8), in which it is certain Christ is the speaker. Hengstenberg, who fancies the diction of the Apocalypse to have been framed with the intention of exhibiting Christ's " equality to God in power and glory " (*Commentary on Apocalypse*, Eng. Trans., Vol. i., p. 107), is of opinion that, in i. 8, xxi. 6, xxii. 13, Christ in His personal distinctness is not the speaker, but " God in the undivided Unity of His Being, without respect to the difference of Persons ; " an opinion which the contexts in the two former instances sustain, though, in the latter, the speaker is doubtful. There is, therefore, only inadequate warrant for the announcement " Christ is the Alpha and Omega ; He is the Beginning and End of all existence." In i. 8, the Speaker is shown by the true reading to be the Lord *God*, the Almighty, and the words *beginning and end* are very doubtful ; the descriptive clauses with which verse 11 commences must also be omitted.   Christ is called *the first and the last*, and to these epithets in i. 17, and ii. 8, is appended the statement, He *was dead and is alive*, a statement which could not rationally be made of a Person Who is the Almighty's Equal in nature, power, and glory.   And the titles *the first and the last* are not, even if synonymous with *the Alpha and the Omega, the beginning and the end*, necessarily predications of Supreme Deity.   Jesus Christ is "the First and the Last, the Beginning and the End," in relation to the Church, in which He is the *Foundation* and the *Head* (1 Cor. iii. 11 ; Eph. i. 22, ii. 20, iv. 15) ; and the Faith, of which He is *Author and Finisher* (Heb. xii. 2).   The titles may be suitably applied both to the Lord God, and to Christ, but the significance in each application will be determined by the nature, attributes, and offices of the Being described.   That our Lord Jesus Christ is, under His Father, and by His Father's ordination, the commencement and consummation of the Church, is unquestionably the teaching of the New Testament.   When Scripture proof shall have been presented that Christ is not the highest originated spirit, the noblest and most lavishly enriched production of His Father's Wisdom, Will, and Might, it will be time enough to argue that comprehensive designations assigned to Him have the same exclusive and singular force which they have when assigned to the Almighty.

Christ is called (iii. 14), *the beginning of the creation of God*, a most inexcusable and dangerous appellation, if St John knew Him to be severed by the immeasurable chasm of Self-existence from all the creatures of God ; for the phrase cannot fairly be denuded of its simple, *primâ facie* sense, *the first created Being*.

Where is the warrant for transforming the *seven spirits* into the *seven perfections of God?*   The writer of the Apocalypse begins his address to the seven Churches (i. 4) with the pious aspiration—"Grace and peace be unto you, from the Almighty, and from the seven spirits which are before His throne, and from Jesus Christ, the faithful witness, the first-born of the dead." In iii. 1, the possession of the seven spirits of God, and of the seven stars or angels of the seven Churches (i. 20), is ascribed to Christ.   The 5th verse of chap. iv., symbolizes the seven spirits by seven lamps of fire burning before the throne ; and the 6th verse of chap. v. says, the seven horns and seven eyes of the Lamb (the Lord Jesus), are the seven spirits of God sent forth into all the earth.   There is here no justification for surmising the spirits to be attributes or perfections of the Almighty.   The only motive for such a surmise is the desire to transfer to Christ essential properties of the Divine Nature. If the writer did not mean to indicate seven separate, created, ministering spirits, he meant to typify the varied operations of the One Holy Spirit. The latter was more probably his purpose. Dr Davidson remarks : " Seven spirits are said to be before the throne of the Almighty, meaning the seven highest spirits ; an idea taken from the Zoroastrian religion into the Jewish, as we see from Zechariah (iv. 2–10), but modified in the Hebrew conception, so that in the Apocalypse the seven spirits represent the One Spirit of God" (*Introduction to New Testament*, Vol. i., p. 337). The prerogative of Christ in the distribution of the Holy Spirit's gifts is indisputable, but such prerogative is assuredly no proof of His Deity. It appertains to the regency and delegated control which the One God and Father has bestowed.

A comparison of passages shows the reference to Christ's "mysterious Name" (xix. 12) to be quite irrelevant to Mr Liddon's object. From ii. 17, we learn, that to him who overcometh, Christ will " give a white stone, and on the stone a name written which no one knoweth saving he that receiveth it." In iii. 12, Christ is made to say, " Upon him that overcometh I will write the Name of my God, and the name of the city of my God, and my new Name." Again, in xiv. 1, the hundred and forty-four thousand are introduced, who (according to the true reading) have " the Lamb's Name, and His Father's Name, written on their foreheads." These texts evince that we are not at liberty to argue from the reception and bearing of a name, to the possession of a nature. Christ is denominated *the Word of God*, and is said to have " on His vesture, and on His thigh, a name written, King of kings, and Lord of lords" (xix. 13 and 16 ; comp. xvii. 14) ; expressions which leave no doubt the writer proposed to attribute to Christ a very high exaltation, and to assign Him a special nearness to God, but they do not rise to the height which the doctrine of Christ's Essential Godhead requires. That doctrine, though mysterious, and beyond the reach of reason, is, nevertheless, capable of very simple unequivocal statement, and no man who held it, would (unless designedly reserved) resort to cloudy periphrasis, vague imagery, and inferential metaphors. Mr Liddon finds no difficulty whatever in putting a plain assertion of Christ's Godhead into at least half-a-dozen different shapes, and there is no ground for conjecturing poverty of language prevented the Apocalyptic Seer from doing the like.

When quoting the passage ascriptive of the titles, " King of kings, and Lord of lords," Mr Liddon connects with it a reference to 1 Tim. vi. 15, and rightly, if the titles are not Names of God "written upon" Christ, inasmuch as a comparison of the texts brings into view the wide difference between the Almighty Father and the glorified Jesus, *the Prince of the kings of the earth* (i. 5). Christ may be, subject to the Most High, *King of kings, &c.,* but He is not *The Blessed and only Potentate Who alone hath Immortality.* The difference of the descriptions is more instructive than their partial agreement. With regard to the "mysterious name," Dr Davidson says :—

"The new name is the unutterable name, yet the name does not imply that the *nature* of Jehovah belongs to Messiah. It is an old Rabbinic tradition, that the appellation Jehovah belongs to three things—the Messiah, the righteous, and Jerusalem; which is proved by Jer. xxiii. 6 ; Isa. xliii. 7 ; Ezek. xlviii. 35. It is highly probable that the Apocalyptist alludes to this tradition, because the faithful are represented as having the name of God, and that of the New Jerusalem, and the new name of Messiah, written on their foreheads, which name is Jehovah. Besides, the angel *Metatron*, in Jewish doctrine, is also called 'Jehovah,' showing that the title is given to creatures" (*Introduction to New Testament*, Vol. i., p. 333).*

When Mr Liddon writes : "His (Christ's) grace is the blessing of Christians (xxii. 21)," I presume he wishes his readers to draw the inference, Christ is God, but the inference is groundless. No truthful expositor of Scripture will deny Christ's function as the channel and minister of favour and spiritual blessings from God ; and since God has invested Him with authority, and made Him Head of the Church, the wish that favour and blessing from Him may be with Christians, was a most natural and pious wish for

* "The *Metatron* in Jewish conception was one of the three highest angels, who was permitted to sit in the divine chamber and write down the virtues of the Israelites. His name is like that of his Master, *i.e.*, *Shaddai* (*Mighty One ; Almighty*). The distinction made between him and other angels is, that he sits with God in the innermost apartment, while the rest hear the divine command before the veil. Hence he is called *Prince of the Face, i.e.*, who stands before God. . . . The relation of the Metatron to the Shekinah is fluctuating. . . . He may have been a kind of Mediator, the revealer of Jehovah, the investiture of the Shekinah ; but he was never thought of as *properly Divine.* Instead of participating in God's Essence, he was His instrument. While explaining the Angel of Jehovah by Metatron, later Jews, far from making him Jehovah's fellow, God eternally proceeding from the unseen Creator, have believed that he was a created angel of exalted rank" (Dr Davidson, *Theological Review*, January 1870).

Mr Westcott, in treating the same subject (*Introduction to the Gospels*), coincides with Dr Davidson in judging "Schöttgen's arguments resting on the convertibility of the terms *Shekinah, Metatron,* &c., with *Messiah,* to be unwarranted."

Apostles to express ; but where in these facts is the excuse for the deduction, Christ is God, and therefore the Supreme Independent Source of spiritual gifts? Scripture nowhere exhibits Him in such a character, and if Mr Liddon were in the habit of looking to contexts, he would have observed that in the concluding paragraph of the Apocalypse, God and the Lord Jesus are mentioned in a manner which strongly marks their distinct individualities.

Mr Liddon sees the climax of Apocalyptic significance in " the representation of Christ in His wounded Humanity upon the throne of the Most High.   The Lamb, as It had been slain, is in the very centre of the court of heaven (v. 6) ; He receives the prostrate adoration of the highest intelligences around the throne (v. 8), and, as the Object of that solemn, uninterrupted, awful worship (v. 12), He is associated with the Father, as being in truth one with the Almighty, Uncreated, Supreme God (v. 13 comp. xvii. 14)."   Now, in vii. 17, the Lamb is represented as being in the midst of the throne ; and in xxii. 1 and 3 verses, " the throne of God and of the Lamb" is mentioned ; but the association with God upon His throne is illustrated and explained by the language of ii. 26, 27 ; iii. 21 : " He that overcometh, and keepeth my works unto the end, to him will I give power over the nations (or Gentiles), and he shall rule them with a rod of iron, as earthen vessels are shattered ; as I also have received of my Father." " To him that overcometh will I grant to sit down with me on my throne, as I also overcame, and have sat down with my Father on His throne."   Mr Liddon seems to have neglected these texts, feeling, perhaps, they were not suited to elucidate his argument, though he would be the last to question the accuracy, wisdom, and profound meaning of the language which St John has ascribed to our Lord.

With respect to " the prostrate adoration of the highest intelligences round the throne," it should be borne in mind, the chorus of praise to the Lamb,—" The Lion of the tribe of Judah and the root of David " (v. 5),—is in connection with the opening of a book which he receives from the hand of God.   The association with God in the reception of prostrate homage appears only in chap. v. ; elsewhere such homage is limited to the Lord God Almighty, and injunctions are given to worship Him.   The terms of the new song in which the worthiness of the Lamb is celebrated, virtually exclude the idea of His Godhead : " Thou art worthy to take the book, and to open the seals thereof ; for thou wast slain, and hast redeemed unto God by thy blood from out of every kindred, and tongue, and people, and nation, and hast made them a kingdom and priests unto our God (comp. i. 6), and they shall reign upon the earth." Again, in v. 12, " Worthy is the Lamb that was slain to take (or receive) the power, and riches, and wisdom," &c. ; and in v. 13, and elsewhere, *He that sitteth upon the throne* is clearly distinguished from *the Lamb.* There is no trace of identity, or unity of nature, and a very manifest separation of persons.

Few men who had read the Revelation of St John carefully through, would have ventured to affirm, even in University Sermons on our Lord's Divinity, that Christ is therein represented " as being in truth one with the Almighty, Uncreated, Supreme God." If a theologian can bring himself to the conviction Christ is, in the Apocalypse, on a level with the Lord God Almighty, argument will, of course, be unavailing ; he is clothed in armour of prepossession which neither facts nor reasoning can penetrate.

Besides the texts to which allusion has already been made, the following will help to throw light on the Apocalyptist's estimate of our Lord's Person, and on his ascription of an unrivalled supremacy to God, as the One Uncreated Source and Possessor of Majesty and power.

"A revelation of Jesus Christ, which God gave unto Him," &c. (i. 1). "Jesus Christ hath made us a kingdom and priests unto His God and Father " (i. 6).

In iii. 12, the glorified Saviour repeatedly uses the expression *my God,* an expression which, according to the true reading, he also uses iii. 2.

In xv. 3 and 4, we find "The song of Moses, the servant of God, and the song of the Lamb," addressed to the Lord God Almighty, Who is called *alone Holy.*

The distinction between *our God,* and *His Christ* (or *Anointed*), is marked in xi. 15 ; xii. 10. The separate individualities are also seen in xii. 17 ; xiv. 4 and 12 ; xx. 6 ; xxi. 22.

Among Christians versed in the traditional dogmatic analysis of the Divine Nature, recognition of distinct Personalities in God and Christ may, without risk, be couched in language which, when taken alone, is almost necessarily open to misconstruction. But the New Testament Scriptures addressed recent converts with a view to their edification, and, by Protestant supposition, address also all Christians as long as the world shall last, for the very purpose of affording doctrinal proof and verification ; yet neither guarding explanation nor unambiguous avowal is provided to shelter the separate personal designations of God and Jesus Christ from the invasions of imperfect knowledge and hostile thought.

CHAPTER VI.

Illuminative action of the Holy Ghost, and presumed resulting unity of
  Apostolic doctrine—The 'incidental expressions implying a high
  Christology in St James's Epistle,' considered—Supposed evidence
  favourable to the dogma of Christ's Godhead, in St Peter's Missionary
  Sermons—Difficulty involved in the constant ascription of our Lord's
  Resurrection to the power of the Almighty Father—How far are John
  ii. 19, x. 18, able to bear out the summary assertion, "Christ raises
  Himself from the dead?"—Argument from the Missionary Sermons
  continued—Argument from St Peter's General Epistles—'St Jude's
  implications that Christ is God'—Rational statement of the evidential
  purport of the documents referred to in this Chapter.

THE *full* recognition of Christ's Godhead by the Apostles, Mr
Liddon refers to the enlightening influences of the Holy Spirit
imparted subsequently to Christ's ascension.

"The Holy Spirit (St John xiv. 26 ; xv. 26 ; xvi. 13, 14, 15),
was to bring the Words and Works and Character of Jesus before
the illuminated intelligence of the Apostles. The school of the
Spirit was to be the school of reflection. But it was not to be the
school of legendary invention. Acts, which, at the time of their
being witnessed might have appeared trivial or commonplace,
would be seen, under the guidance of the Spirit, to have had a
deeper interest. Words, to which a transient or local value had
been assigned at first, would now be felt to invite a world-wide
and eternal meaning. 'These things understood not His disciples
at the first' (St John xii. 14–16), is true of much else besides
the entry into Jerusalem. Moral, spiritual, physical powers which,
though unexplained, could never have passed for the product of
purely human activity, would in time be referred by the Invisible
Teacher to their true source ; they would be regarded with awe
as the very rays of Deity.*

---

* Mr Liddon seems here to forget that our Lord, in connection apparently
with a contemplated increase of His own power (the power of Essential Godhead ?) through His going to the Father, is said by the Fourth Evangelist to
have declared : "He that believeth on me, the works that I do shall he do
also ; and greater than these shall he do, because I am going to the Father,"
&c. (John xiv. 12 ; comp. St Matt. xxi. 21). The writer of the Acts regards
both Christ and the Apostles as the Almighty's instruments in miraculous
works, God wrought *through Him*, and *through them* (ii. 22 : xv. 12 ; δια, with
the genitive case in both instances). That any of Christ's first followers saw,

"Thus the work of the Spirit would but complete, systematize, digest, the results of previous natural observation. Certainly it was always impossible that any man could 'say that Jesus was the Lord but by the Holy Ghost.' The inward teaching of the Holy Ghost alone could make the Godhead of Jesus a certainty of faith as well as a conclusion of the intellect. But the intellectual conditions of belief were at first inseparable from natural contact with the living Human Form of Jesus during the years of His earthly Life. Our Lord implies this in saying, 'Ye also shall bear witness, because ye have been with Me from the beginning.' The Apostles lived with One Who combined an exercise of the highest miraculous powers with a faultless human character, and Who asserted Himself, by implication and expressly, to be personally God. The Spirit strengthened and formalized that earlier and more vague belief which was created by His language; but it was His language which had fallen on the natural ears of the Apostles, and which was the germinal principle of their riper faith in His Divinity" (pp. 271–72).

When a portion of St John xvi. 13 is quoted as the very words of Jesus himself, we are naturally led to ponder the reason given for the Spirit's being a guide in all the truth : *he will not speak from himself ; but whatsoever he shall hear, he will speak.* Is this language properly applicable to the Third of the Co-equal Persons in the Divine Substance, or likely to have been used by the Second ?

When, again, the expression of St Paul (1 Cor. xii. 3), *No man can say that Jesus is Lord, but by the Holy Ghost,* is appropriated, what excuse is there for insinuating that the expression intimates the Godhead of Jesus ? The acknowledgment of Christ's Lordship is, by the Apostle, opposed to the assertion, Jesus is accursed,—an assertion which no man Divinely inspired can make ; and, in verses 5 and 6, *the same Lord,* and *the same God,* are as clearly distinguished as are the ministrations or services in the Church over which the former presides, and the spiritual operations of which the latter is the source. The immediate context demonstrates *Lord* and *God* not to have been in the writer's intention synonymous, and further, the first Epistle to the Corinthians contains apparently invincible testimony St Paul did not believe Christ to be God.

or were at all disposed to see, in His miracles, tokens of His personal Deity, is an idea not rationally deducible from the language of Scripture. That the Church, after the Apostles' days, may have been led by the Spirit to discern and teach more than the Scriptures reveal, I do not deny.

But detailed criticism of the flaws and assumptions which disfigure the extract I have made, is superfluous. I am concerned only with the more prominent features of Mr Liddon's method and argument. His statement invites us to look for the signs of completeness, system, and mental digestion in the pages of the New Testament, regarding the great topic upon which he discourses. The premiss that Scripture sets forth with practical explicitness all necessary Christian doctrine, binds the orthodox Protestant to the estimate which is here advanced respecting the work of the Spirit.

In conformity with this estimate, therefore, Mr Liddon detects implications and assertions of Christ's Deity in the Epistles of SS. James, Peter, and Jude.

" The *engrafted word* (James i. 21) is the very substance and core of the doctrine ; it is He in Whom the doctrine centres ; it is the Person of Jesus Christ Himself, Whose Humanity is the Sprout, Shoot, or Branch of Judah, engrafted by His Incarnation upon the old stock of humanity, and sacramentally engrafted upon all living Christian souls. . . . St James's doctrine of the Engrafted Word is a compendium of the first, third, and sixth chapters of St John's Gospel ; the word written or preached does but unveil to the soul the Word Incarnate, the Word Who can give a new life to human nature, because He is Himself the Source of Life " (p. 289). A glance at the context ought to have suppressed this reckless empty verbiage. From verses 17 and 18, we learn that the Father of Lights, the Giver of every good and perfect gift, begat us of His own will, by the word (*logos*) of truth. The word is just afterwards described as the *engrafted* or *implanted word*, which is able to save our souls, and we are exhorted to be doers of it, and not self-deceiving hearers only. Incontestibly, the *implanted word* is the message and teaching of God, in the Gospel. That St James's few words are a compendium of the first, third, and sixth chapters of the latest Evangelist, is a discovery of great originality and magnitude, but unfortunately altogether incapable of verification.

To the compendious allegation, St James "appears to apply the word *Lord*, throughout his Epistle, to the God of the Old Testament and to Jesus Christ, quite indifferently," exception may be taken. The Epistle has throughout a markedly Hebraistic complexion. The author's mind is possessed by the language and tone of the Old Testament, to which he continually refers. We cannot be sure, therefore, that by the denomination *Lord* simply, he ever means other than the Almighty God. The strong probability no doubt is, that when he mentioned the coming of the Lord (v. 7, 8), he had in view the expected coming of Christ, but even there his thoughts may have been directed to a visitation of God, and his phraseology may have been employed in the Jewish rather than the distinctively Christian meaning. When he adduces the prophets who spoke *in the name of the Lord* (v. 10) as examples of suffering and patience, he evidently alludes to the Divinely-commissioned teachers of the earlier Covenant, and when he enjoins prayer, and the anointing of the sick *in the Name of the Lord*, since it is certain the prayer was to be addressed to the Most High, and not to Christ, the presumption is, that, in verses 14 and 15, the word *Lord* is put for God. In verse 12 of the first chapter of the Epistle, *the Lord* is interpolated, and the connection in which verse 7 stands, shows *Lord* to be there a title of God. An attentive reading of the Epistle leads us to conclude, Jesus Christ is not called simply *Lord*, until the last chapter, and perhaps is not so called there. But if he had been, the fact would have carried no sort of indication of his Godhead. Believing St James's teaching to harmonize completely with St Paul's, Mr Liddon should have remembered St Paul's fundamental and unconditionally avowed position ; to Christians *there is one God, the Father, and one Lord, Jesus Christ* (1 Cor. viii. 4-6 ; Eph. iv. 6 ; 1 Tim. ii. 5). The title *God* of course includes the title *Lord*, but there is a pitiable violation of reason and evidence involved in the inference, God and Christ are in nature and dignity identical, because each is denominated *Lord*. If the Scriptures teach anything unambiguously to a docile and intelligent mind, they teach that Christ's lordship and the Almighty's Lordship rest on different bases. The former, whatever may be its extent, is derived, imparted, and subordinate ; the latter is absolutely underived, independent, and supreme. *God has made Jesus both Lord and Christ* (Acts ii. 36), *has highly exalted him, and given him a name which is above every name, &c.* (Phil. ii. 9). St Paul, who uniformly attributes the resurrection of Christ to the power of God the Father, declares that, *to this end Christ both died and lived, that He might have lordship over both dead and living* (Rom. xiv. 9). That our Lord's dominion, however vast and transcendent, is distinguished from the dominion of the Almighty, by derivation and bestowal, is a scriptural truth which may indeed be explained away, but cannot be denied. And even to minds tied and bound by predeterminations, the constant want of reference to the ground of inherent eternal Godhead, must appear most puzzling. How does it come to pass that Evangelists and Apostles, under the completing and systematizing tuition of the Spirit, ascribe to donation and investiture, the empire and the might which, by the hypothesis of Christ's proper Deity, attach to His Essential Personal Being, no less than to the Being of the Everlasting Father? If the doctrine of Christ's Personal Divinity was an item in the primitive Gospel message, and if the Scriptures contain the faith originally delivered to the saints, it is an utterly inexplicable thing that our Lord's power and lordship should not often be annexed to His Ineffable Unoriginated Nature, from which they would inevitably and inalienably flow.

The true reading of iv. 12, most probably is: *One is the Lawgiver and Judge, Who is able to save and to destroy;* and Mr Liddon supplies the following commentary: "Especially noteworthy is St James's assertion that the Lord Jesus Christ, the Judge of men, is not the delegated representative of an absent Majesty, but is Himself the Legislator enforcing His own laws. The Lawgiver, he says, is One Being with the Judge Who can save and can destroy; the Son of Man, coming in the clouds of heaven, has enacted the law which He thus administers." There is here a purely gratuitous, and totally improbable assumption. The One Lawgiver and Judge is Almighty God, in Whom alone the prerogatives of judgment and legislation ultimately and independently reside. The most exalted estimate of Christ's prerogative is that, through Him the precepts of God are communicated (John vii. 16, 17; viii. 26, 28; xii. 49, 50; xiv. 10, 24), and through Him as a delegate and representative the function of judgment is exercised. His own teaching, as understood by His Apostles, was, *He is ordained by God the Judge of quick and dead* (Acts x. 42): *through Him God will judge the secrets of men* (Rom. ii. 16); and so His judgment-seat is the judgment-seat of God (comp. Rom. xiv. 10, where the correct text is *judgment-seat of God,* with 2 Cor. v. 10). To Him *the Father has given all judgment,* and, *has given Him authority to execute judgment also;* not because He is the Original Lawgiver, and in nature one with, and equal to, the Father; but *because He is the Son of Man* (John v. 22, 27). From the Old Testament, the Apostle James would certainly learn that the One Lawgiver and Judge is the Lord of Hosts; and nothing in the Gospel (presuming always that the New Testament sufficiently exhibits the Gospel), would so modify his knowledge as to warrant the supposition his language was intended to denote any other than God Most High. The fundamental agreement of SS. Paul and James would, we may fairly conclude, cover the doctrine which the former proclaims (Acts xvii. 31), " God has appointed a day, in which He will judge the world in righteousness by the Man whom He hath ordained; having given assurance to all men, in raising Him from the dead."

Those who yield themselves to obey the messages of God sent to mankind in and through Christ, are at once the servants or slaves of God, and the servants or slaves of Christ. In serving their Master, Christ, they become acceptable servants of God, bringing forth the fruit of righteousness, which is through Jesus Christ to His glory (Rom. xiv. 18 ; Phil. i. 11). The pervading Scriptural conception is, that, in keeping the sayings and following the example of our Lord, we render service to God. Until the revelation dispensed through the post-Apostolic Church, concerning Christ's Person, has engrossed our minds sufficiently to supersede the rational meaning of the revelation given in the New Testament, we must look upon the service of God as the higher end to be reached in, and by means of, the service of *the Captain of our salvation*—the Son by whom God has in these last times addressed and instructed us. Indisputably, the Apostles write as if they designed to lead us through Christ, up to our God and Father. Only the supernaturally aided insight of the Church, disclosing truths practically new, can detect a design to equalize God and Christ as Objects of Christian service. The habitual sequence of Apostolic thought, from whatever point of view the Christian's standing was surveyed, was ; *Ye are Christ's, and Christ is God's : the Head of Christ is God* (1 Cor. iii. 23 ; xi. 3) ; *through Christ we have access to the Father : He brings us unto God* (Eph. ii. 18 ; 1 Tim. ii. 5 ; Heb. vii. 25 ; 1 Pet. iii. 18). Mr Liddon, however, does not weigh evidence ; he loses sight of everything but the exigencies of the tenet he has undertaken to uphold, and without misgiving, gravely observes ; " St James, although our Lord's own first cousin, opens his Epistle by representing himself as standing in the same relation to Jesus Christ as to God. He is the slave of God and of our Lord Jesus Christ."

In a similar style of extortionate deduction and exaggerating perversion we are told : " St James hints that all social barriers between man and man are as nothing when we place mere human eminence in the light of Christ's majestic Person ; and when He names the faith of Jesus Christ, he terms it with solemn emphasis, ' the faith of the Lord of Glory,' thus adopting one of the most magnificent of St Paul's expressions, and attributing to our Lord a Majesty altogether above this human world." Now, it is hard to understand what valid pretext there is for affirming, the Apostle places mere human eminence " in the light of Christ's majestic Person," when he rebukes an unchristian deference to worldly distinctions of rank and wealth. The influence of our Lord's ethical teachings, which have descended to us through the First Gospel, is clearly traceable in St James's Epistle, and the motive of his language may be more probably found in Christ's precept—*all ye are brethren* (Matt. xxiii. 8), and in the primary Christian duties of brotherly love and humility.

In James ii. 1, the appellation *Lord* is not repeated before the words, *of glory.* The Greek is literally, *the faith of our Lord Jesus Christ of Glory,* and to this literal rendering the Vulgate Version adheres. It is far from certain our Authorized Version has, by inserting *the Lord,* conveyed the true sense, though the construction which joins *glory* with *Lord,* is, I think, to be preferred. There is no justification, however, for Mr Liddon's peremptory assertion, the words *must* be so joined. He ought to have been well aware that, *of glory* frequently has been, and may quite fairly be, construed with *the faith.* Macknight renders, *the faith of the glory of our Lord Jesus Christ,* remarking that in so doing, he follows the Syriac translation. Mr Liddon's aim is, I presume, to suggest supremacy in the realm, and authority in the apportionment of glory; but the phrase on which he builds is, by the pretty general verdict of interpreters, both ancient and modern, best understood as a Hebraism for *glorious Lord.* He himself admits, "*of glory* may be an epithetal genitive, such as constantly follows the mention of the Divine Name;" but if it is equivalent to *glorious,* its explication as applied to Christ would seem most naturally to be, *Who has been glorified,* and it would refer to His exaltation, and investiture *with glory* (1 Tim. iii. 16; 1 Pet. i. 21).

But whatever rendering is given to the phraseology in question, when we turn to "one of the most magnificent of St Paul's expressions" (1 Cor. ii. 8), we discover a context utterly at variance with the inference of St Paul's intention to put *God,* and the *Lord of Glory,* on one level of Uncreated Nature and Dignity. The connection of thought may possibly be, that Christ is the Lord of *our glory,* spoken of in the earlier portion of the same sentence; but at any rate, there is no excuse for the innuendo, Lord means God, and, *the Lord of glory* is synonymous with *the God of Glory* (Acts vii. 2)—or with *the God of our Lord Jesus Christ, the Father of Glory* (Eph. i. 17). That " our Lord's Majesty is altogether above this human world," is a circumstance which has no decisive bearing on the point at issue, namely, the origin of His majesty, and its quality in relation to the Majesty of the Eternal One.

“A few passing expressions of the lowliest reverence disclose the great doctrine of the Church respecting the Person of her Lord, throned in the background of the Apostle’s thought.   And if the immediate interests of his ministry oblige St James to confine himself to considerations which do not lead him more fully to exhibit the doctrine, we are not allowed, as we read him, to forget the love and awe which veil and treasure it, so tenderly and so reverently, in the inmost sanctuary of his illuminated soul.” The doctrine is too far in the background, and too closely veiled, for the eyes of the most inquisitive rational discernment, though its position of inaccessible obscurity admirably harmonizes with the existence of an authoritative Church, inspired to bring to light hidden things, and prohibit reason from the exposition of the Sacred Writings.   An immovable conviction that St James must have held the doctrine, notwithstanding all he says, or does not say, is the only explanation of the statement : “ St James’s recognition of the doctrine of our Lord’s Divinity is just what we might expect it to be, if we take into account the immediately practical scope of his Epistle.   Our Lord’s Divinity is never once formally proposed as a doctrine of the faith ; but it is largely, although indirectly, implied.   It is implied in language which would be exaggerated and overstrained on any other supposition.   It is implied in a reserve which may be felt to mean at least as much as the most demonstrative protestations ;” in other words, it is most impressively inculcated by not being specified.

What the sentiments of St James really were, and whether he held the Godhead to be an Entity comprising co-equal Forms or Persons, one of Whom Jesus Christ is, may be gathered, not merely from the entire absence of formal propositions of a dogma which specially needed positive enunciation, but also from expressions and statements which present the Almighty Father as the One Supreme Object of prayer, and faith, and devout regard. The customary separate mention of God, and the Lord Jesus Christ, with which the Epistle opens, is in itself an indication of separate individuality, and seemingly not in accordance with the idea that both the Persons named are truly God, being included in one and the same Divine Nature.   Prayer for wisdom is to be directed to God ; and religion, pure and undefiled, is *before the God and Father* (i. 5, 27).   God has chosen the poor in the world to be rich in faith, and heirs of the kingdom which He has promised to them that love Him (ii. 5 ; comp. i. 12). Faith that there is One God, or *that One is the God*, is commended (ii. 19), without a word of precautionary instruction showing *One* not to mean One Person, but One Substance comprehending Equal Persons. We are reminded : With the tongue bless we *the Lord and Father*, and therewith curse we men who are made after the similitude of God (iii. 9). Attachment to a sinful world is contrasted with devotion to God, and God is recognized as the source of grace and mercy (iv. 4-8). Throughout the Epistle there is not the faintest trace of an indication of the writer's knowing more than One personal God, Whom he denominates *the God and Father ; the One God ; the Lord and Father ; the Lord of Sabaoth (Hosts)*, (v. 4).

On the two stages of St Peter's recorded teaching, represented respectively by his missionary sermons in the Acts of the Apostles, and by his general Epistles, Mr Liddon expatiates largely, infusing into the Apostle's language senses quite foreign to a reasonable interpretation. St Peter is admitted to have spoken " of our Lord's Humanity with fearless plainness."

" But this general representation of the Human Nature by Which Christ had entered into Jewish history, is interspersed with glimpses of His Divine Personality Itself, Which is veiled by His Manhood. Thus we find St Peter in the Porch of Solomon applying to our Lord a magnificent title, which at once carries our thoughts into the very heart of the distinctive Christology of St John. Christ, although crucified and slain, is yet the *Leader* or *Prince of Life* (Acts iii. 15). That He should be held in bondage by the might of death was not possible (ii. 24). The heavens *must* receive Him (iii. 21); and He is now the Lord of all things (x. 36). It is He Who from His heavenly throne has poured out upon the earth the gifts of Pentecost (ii. 33). His Name spoken on earth has a wonder-working power ; as unveiling His Nature and office, it is a symbol which faith reverently treasures, and by the might of which the servants of God can relieve even physical suffering (iii. 16 ; iv. 10). As a refuge for sinners, the Name of Jesus stands alone ; no other Name has been given under heaven, whereby the one true salvation can be guaranteed to the sons of men (iv. 12). Here St Peter clearly implies that the religion of Jesus is the true, the universal, the absolute religion. This implication, of itself, suggests much beyond, as to the true dignity of Christ's Person. Is it conceivable that He Who is Himself the sum and substance of His religion, Whose Name has such power on earth, and Who wields the resources and is invested with the glories of heaven, is notwithstanding in the thought of His first apostles only a glorified man, or only a super-angelic intelligence? Do we not interpret these early discourses most naturally, when we bear in mind the measure of reticence which active missionary work always renders necessary, if the truth is to win its way amidst prejudice and opposition? And will not this consideration alone enable us to do justice to those vivid glimpses of Christ's Higher Nature, the fuller exhibition of Which is before us in the Apostle's general Epistles?" (p. 293.)

Now this quotation is a sample of the sophistical pleading, the overstrained deduction, and the intrusion of extraneous ideas, which too generally characterize Mr Liddon's exegesis. When we calmly examine the several texts to which he appeals, we find contexts which, for the most part, bar out the interpretation he strives with such pertinacity to introduce. The title *Leader* or *Prince*, does not betoken the position of Deity, in the possession and bestowal of life, but the function of Guide and Chieftain in the way which leads unto life. It is employed in Heb. ii. 10; xii. 2; and we should especially compare Acts v. 31, where St Peter uses the same title, and preaches that God has exalted Christ to be a *Leader* and a Saviour. A commentary which exhausts the range of admissible significance may be found in the words; *the gift of God is eternal life in Christ Jesus Our Lord* (Rom. vi. 23). *God has given unto us eternal life, and this life is in His Son* (1 John v. 11). St Peter prefaced his application of the title by proclaiming that the God of the Patriarchs had glorified His servant Jesus, the holy and righteous Man whom the Jews had denied, and to whom they had preferred a man who was a murderer. The human character of our Lord was evidently in the mind of the Apostle, when he rapidly contrasted Christ's moral purity and excellence with the guiltiness of Barabbas, thereby giving a sharper edge to the accusation; *ye killed the Leader of Life, whom God has raised from the dead.* The nature in which our Lord underwent death, was certainly not His Divine Nature; but the description *Leader of Life* is immediately conjoined with the fact of His death, and followed by the oft-repeated declaration (see Acts ii. 24; iv. 10; v. 30; x. 40): 'God raised Him from the dead,'—a declaration which defies comprehension on the hypothesis of Christ's being accounted Very and Eternal God. If we do not take the standing ground of a Church-authority not amenable to reason, we must perceive in the fact of Christ's resurrection by the Almighty Father's power, as in the fact of His being anointed by God with the Holy Ghost (x. 38), an implication He is not absolutely God. The human soul and spirit of Jesus, when withdrawn through death from the flesh, were, according to the Church's teaching, indissolubly joined to a Personal Deity possessing the undiminished attributes of Godhead; what necessity and what room were there, then, for the intervention of another Personal Deity in bringing about the resumption of the flesh? If the Petrine Christology agreed with the traditionally Johannine, and if the Logos is, in the full and perfect sense, God, how came the Logos to be quiescent, and, so to speak, handled by another, in the great event of His resurrection? When attempts are made to put the Church's dogma concerning Christ's Person on the basis of reasonable deductions from Scripture, this question may be quite reverently, and is sure to be persistently, pressed. Definitions which the language of the Sacred Writings is said to prompt and certify, force the inquiry upon us, and, after human words have been applied with confident exactness to the most mysterious of subjects, we have no right to shield ourselves, under the plea of inscrutable mystery, from the direct consequences of our own verbal propositions. The ascription of Christ's Resurrection to the might of His own inherent co-equal Godhead, is what reason, starting from the doctrine of His Deity, compels us to expect, but Scripture disappoints reason, by making the Resurrection an act of the Almighty Father. This is a point about which steady faith and intellectual honesty cannot afford to shuffle. If, on the one hand, interpretation belongs to a province as much beyond reason as is the most recondite subject-matter of Divine revelation, then, we are bound to confess the fact, and to recognize in the Church's dogmatic instruction, not the rational expansion and definition of clearer intellectual apprehension, but supplementary revelation, completing and rendering operative, an otherwise defective Rule of Faith. Orthodox exposition is, in that case, not to be judged by the intellect, but to be accepted submissively, as given from Above through the instrumentality of the Church. But if, on the other hand, interpretation is within the sphere of rational judgment and research, then, the constant Apostolic assertion that the Almighty Father raised Christ from the dead, is pregnant with suggestions adverse to the doctrine of Christ's proper, personal, Deity.

Mr Liddon indeed, relying on John ii. 19; x. 18, summarily asserts, in his Fourth and Seventh Lectures, 'Christ raises Himself from the dead;' and thus sets two statements in the Fourth

Gospel, against about twenty unequivocal passages in the Acts and the Epistles. The Synoptic Gospels, moreover, contain no hint that our Lord ever spoke the words, *Destroy this temple, and in three days I will raise it up.* If He had spoken those words, there would have been as much of truth as falsehood in the charge, which is in Matt. xxvi. 60 ; and Mark xiv. 57 ; imputed to false witnesses. But what is of far more consequence is the fact that the explanatory clause, *He spoke of the temple of His body,* &c., added by the fourth Evangelist (ii. 21), is in itself improbable and unsuitable, and, judging from the applications of Old Testament language in Acts ii. 27–32 ; xiii. 33–37, *the Scripture which the disciples believed,* did not harmonize with the opinion ; 'Christ raised Himself from the dead.' Neander and Ewald, in their *Lives of Christ,* though they both hold St John to have been the author of the Gospel which bears his name, set aside the Evangelist's exposition as being only an accommodation of words whose original and designed import was different. An instance of similar departure from the sense of the speaker quoted is. Neander thinks, observable in John xviii. 9 ; and his own view of " the most natural and apparent interpretation of the words, *Destroy this temple, &c.,*" is substantially conveyed in Ewald's statement of Christ's " precise meaning in that riddle,"—" Your whole religion, as it rests on this temple, is corrupt and perverted ; but *He* also is present, who, when it passes away. as it must pass away, will easily restore it again in far higher Majesty, and thus is able to accomplish, not merely a common miracle as you ask, but the very highest miracle."

With respect to John x. 18, the brief expression, *I have power to take my life again,* is entitled to no weight against the multitude of concurring texts which explicitly affirm Christ to have been raised from the dead by the Father. And further, whatever power may be ascribed to Christ in any portion of the New Testament, that power is not said to be essentially inherent, independent, and self-originated, but imparted by, and derived from, the Father, and is, therefore, not the power of One Who is by nature God, but of one who is exalted and aggrandized by God.

It is difficult to believe Mr Liddon could have imagined he was helping his argument, when, citing Acts ii. 24, he said, " That Christ should be held in bondage by the might of death was not possible;" and added in a Note, " This 'impossibility' depended not merely on the fact that prophecy had predicted Christ's resurrection, but on the dignity of Christ's Person, implied in the existence of any such prophecy respecting Him." The supposed glimpses of Divine Personality vanish, the moment we examine the passage in which the words cited stand: " Jesus the Nazarite, a man proved unto you (to be) from God, by miracles, and wonders, and signs, which God did through Him in the midst of you, ye have taken and by wicked hands have crucified and slain ; whom God hath raised up, having loosed the pains of death, because it was not possible that He should be holden of it ;"—then follows a quotation from the 16th Psalm, together with an intimation that, with prophetic foresight of Christ's resurrection, David prayed to God, " Thou will not leave my soul in Hades, neither wilt Thou suffer Thy holy one to see corruption " (comp. Acts xiii. 35–37).   The human nature of Jesus, and the power of God acting upon it, are exclusively and conspicuously present in the passage.   How is " the dignity of Christ's Person " (by which Mr Liddon means His Godhead), implied in the existence of a prophecy that God would not leave him in Hades, nor suffer His flesh to see corruption ; and, in the fulfilment of the prophecy, announced by St Peter, *This Jesus hath God raised up ?*[*]

The context, again, dispels the insinuation Mr Liddon seeks to convey through the words, *whom the heavens must receive until the times of restitution of all things* (iii. 21).   I do not see what is gained by putting a special emphasis on *must*, since that word is no more specially emphatic than two or three other words in the sentence.   The Apostle exhorts his hearers to repentance and conversion, ' that their sins may be blotted out ; that so times of refreshing may come from the face of the Lord, and He may send Jesus Christ, *whom the heavens must receive, &c.*'   The language of Moses is then applied to Christ : " A prophet shall the Lord your God raise up unto you from among your brethren, as He raised up me," &c. ; and, after a general reference to the Old Testament prophecies, the discourse concludes with the statement,

* The reading of the Hebrew in Psalm xvi. 10 is debated.   On the whole, the evidence seems to me to favour the Received Text ; *Thy holy one.*   But in the matured and final judgment of Dr Davidson, "The proper reading is *holy ones or saints ;* not the singular, *Thy holy one ;* showing that it refers to the pious generally.   *Suffering His pious ones not to see the grave,* is, *to deliver them from the peril of death* " (*Introduction to Old Testament,* Vol. ii., p. 279). This decision is re-stated in an Article on English Versions of the Bible (*Theological Review,* April 1866).   " *Thine holy one* is not the textual but the marginal reading.   The former is, *Thy holy* or *pious ones,* which we know to be the reading of the Masorah, and the true one."   The Septuagint has the singular.   Whether the Hebrew term, translated by the Septuagint *corruption,* is rightly translated, is very doubtful, and reference to the Lexicons shows that Dr Davidson has strong reasons for affirming—"The word does not mean *corruption,* but *the grave ;* and therefore the rendering in Acts ii. 27 is incorrect."   Mr J. J. S. Perowne, translates, *to see the pit,* conceding that *the grave* is indicated.

"unto you first. God having raised up His servant ($\pi\alpha\iota\varsigma$), sent Him to bless you in the turning away every one of you from your iniquities." There is here no glimmer of Deity veiled by Manhood.

In the verse just quoted, and also in Acts iii. 13 ; iv. 27, 30, *servant* is the correct rendering, and should be substituted for *son*, and *child*, in the English Version. When applied to David, Acts iv. 25, the word is rightly rendered, and in Matt. xii. 18, our translators have given the true sense. The point is not a disputed one. Archbishop Trench and other most orthodox scholars, candidly admit, the Authorized Version is wrong in not translating $\pi\alpha\iota\varsigma$ $\Theta\epsilon o\tilde{v}$, *servant of God*, 'whenever in the New Testament it is used of Christ.'

Acts x. 36, does not assert Jesus Christ to be "Lord of all things," but far more probably, Lord or Master of *all persons*, both Jews and Gentiles ; and the title stands in a passage referring to 'the word which God sent unto the children of Israel, preaching good tidings through Jesus Christ.' God is also said 'to have anointed with the Holy Ghost and with power Jesus of Nazareth, who went about doing good, and healing all who were oppressed by the devil, because God was with Him. When the Jews had slain Him, God raised Him up on the third day, and He commanded His Apostles to preach that He has been appointed by God, Judge of quick and dead.' If words and apparent connection of thought can indicate the absence of a particular idea, we may be sure the idea of Christ's Godhead was not in the Apostle's mind when he called Christ *Lord of all*.

In adducing Acts ii. 33, Mr Liddon really mutilates a text by omitting the part which does not fit his purpose. To say, "it is Christ Who from His heavenly throne has poured out upon the earth the gifts of Pentecost," may suggest Christ is God, but St Peter's recorded language suggests nothing of the kind. "This Jesus hath God raised up, whereof we all are witnesses ; therefore, being exalted by the right hand of God, and having received of the Father the promise of the Holy Ghost, He hath shed forth this which ye see and hear." What pretence do these words afford for discerning an implication that Christ is God ? He is exalted by God's right hand, and receives from God the gift (see also i. 4) which He is said to have poured forth on His first disciples. Whatever may be the office of Christ in the distribution of spiritual gifts to His Church, St Peter saw in God the primary and ultimate Giver of the Holy Ghost (Acts viii. 20 ; xi. 17).

The manner in which Mr Liddon expatiates on the Name of

Christ, is another instance of stilted exposition and neglected context. "The nature and office unveiled" by the name, *Jesus Christ the Nazarite*, are assuredly not the nature and office of absolute Deity; and the whole account (iii. 6–16), abundantly evinces that the wonder-working potency associated with the Name of Christ, was not the intrinsic might of Christ's actual Godhead, but a potency imparted by the God Who had raised and glorified His servant Jesus. The miracles wrought by the hands of the Apostles, whether coupled with the employment of Christ's Name or not, were wrought by God (xix. 11), and the inference to which Mr Liddon invites unwary and prepossessed readers is dissipated by the recorded Apostolic prayer entreating God to "stretch forth His hand for healing, and for the doing of signs and wonders, *through the Name of His holy servant Jesus*" (iv. 30).

When Mr Liddon says: "as a refuge for sinners the Name of Jesus stands alone," &c., he manifestly endeavours to put upon St Peter's language an extreme significance, regardless alike of the textual connection of the words to which he appeals, and of that 'proportion of the faith' which Scripture exhibits. The noun *salvation* and the verb *to save*, are frequently used in the New Testament of safety and deliverance from temporal and bodily evils, as danger, infirmity, sickness, death; and this primary and natural meaning the context would lead us to affix in Acts iv. 12. The English Version darkens the sense by translating the same verb differently in the 9th and 12th verses. To represent the original accurately, one expression, either *made whole*, or, *saved*, should have been employed in both cases. If in the 9th verse we render, *by what means he is saved*, we are guided to the sense of *saved* in the 12th verse, and perceive it to refer primarily, if not exclusively, to physical soundness. Any other or higher sense is secondary, and is not the more probable and natural meaning. Mr Liddon's argument proceeds upon an assumption which many eminent and orthodox commentators have seen to be untenable.

But, granting that St Peter in almost consecutive sentences used the same verb in different senses, and passed from the lower to the higher and more comprehensive import, what ground is there for the momentous inferential interpretation which Mr Liddon imposes? Where, in the New Testament, is Jesus set before us as the ultimate Source of our safety, and the highest Object of our faith and worship? Invariably God is above and beyond Him, and He is depicted as being only ministerially, instrumentally, and in virtue of the Almighty Father's gifts and appointment, the Captain of our salvation. The fact is an eminently plain one, and some of the ample evidence which illustrates it has been already quoted in the course of this examination. Jesus Christ is not " Himself the sum and substance of His religion " in any acceptation which interferes with the supreme devotion of heart and life to the service of our Heavenly Father. If reason and common sense are not banished from the office of expounding the Sacred Writings, God is ' the sum and substance of Christ's religion,' in a loftier, deeper, and broader sense than Christ himself is. Repentance, faith, hope, love, obedience, prayer, and thanksgiving are, in their highest forms and aspects, directed towards God. St Peter gave his view of the subject in few words, when he described Christians as those who, through Christ, believe on God Who raised Him from the dead, and gave Him glory ; that their faith and hope might be toward God (1 Pet. i. 21) ; and again, when he taught that Christians, as a holy priesthood, offer up spiritual sacrifices, acceptable to God, through Jesus Christ (ii. 5).

It seems a disingenuous and unworthy proceeding, to infuse into one text of dubious wording, a meaning which can draw no support either from the immediate context, or from other portions of Scripture. The words from which Mr Liddon deduces so largely—" neither is there salvation in any other ; for there is no other Name under Heaven given among men, whereby we must be saved "—do not, when spiritually understood, exclude the Name and working of our Father in Heaven ; they do not elevate Christ to an equality with God, but relate to God's grand gift to men, in Christ, and are, if reasonably interpreted, in perfect agreement with St Paul's doctrine—" There is One God, and one Mediator between God and men, a man, Christ Jesus, who gave Himself a ransom for all " (1 Tim. ii. 5).

The Epistles of St Peter are pronounced by Mr Liddon, to " exhibit Christian doctrine in its fulness, but incidentally to spiritual objects, and without the methodical completeness of an oral instruction. Christian doctrine is not propounded as a new announcement ; the writer takes it for granted as furnishing a series of motives, the force of which would be admitted by those who had already recognized the true majesty and proportions of the faith."

Now, here, the real *status* of ecclesiastical tradition and authority with reference to the dogmas of Orthodoxy is hinted at, though not adequately acknowledged. Mr Liddon does not boldly relieve himself from the fatal obligation of proving that the doctrine he advocates is consistent with a reasonable interpretation of the Apostle's language, and he is constrained, after the usual fashion, to fabricate a semblance of reasoning, by inflating texts and extorting inferences.

From the expression *the Spirit of Christ in them* (1 Pet. i. 11), we have the large induction; "The prophets of the Old Testament were Christ's own servants, His heralds, His organs. He Who is the Subject of the Gospel story, and the living Ruler of the Church, had also, by His Spirit, been Master and Teacher of the prophets. Under His guidance it was that they foretold His sufferings. It was the Spirit of Christ Who was in the prophets, testifying beforehand the sufferings of Christ and the glories that would follow" (p. 295). This exposition may doubtless claim the approval of a host of Orthodox commentators, whose theology is so much a theology of inference from isolated and ambiguous phrases; but far more probably, *the Spirit of Christ* here means the prophetic spirit anticipating Christ, the Spirit of God, pointing to Christ, and Christ's religion. Before any other explanation can be rationally accepted, proof is needed that Christ was, by the instrumentality of the Holy Ghost, the Inspirer of the Old Testament. The very name, *Christ*, or *Anointed*, by which our Lord is designated, seems to connote the action of the Holy Spirit upon Him, and is, so far, discordant with the idea St Peter was thinking of His pre-incarnate condition, or designed to inculcate that He spoke by the Holy Ghost through the prophets. The Scriptural point of view respecting prophetic inspiration is indubitably that of the author of the Epistle to the Hebrews; "God, Who spoke in time past to the fathers in (or by) the prophets, hath, at the last of these days, spoken unto us in (or by) a Son."

Mr Liddon says; "Here, Χριστοῦ (of Christ) is clearly a genitive of the subject." The clearness is limited to his own assertion. On the primary import of the Greek genitive, a large diversity of significations is engrafted, and in the New Testament the objective genitive is, at the least, as frequent as the subjective. The *Spirit of Christ*, in the few instances where it, or some convertible phrase, is used, neither necessarily nor probably denotes the Spirit imparted by, and issuing from, Christ. *The Spirit of His Son* (Gal. iv. 6), which God sends forth into Christian hearts, is equivalent to the effect of that influence which ' forms Christ in us' (iv. 19), ' conforms us to His image' (Rom. viii. 29), and, through which ' Christ dwells in our hearts by faith' (Eph. iii. 17). In a word, the *Spirit of Christ*, without which no man can truly belong to Christ, is Christ's temper and disposition of mind, and results from 'the indwelling presence of the Spirit of Him who raised Jesus from the dead' (Rom. viii. 9–11). It is the product of 'the law of the Spirit of Life' in those who are in Christ Jesus (verses 1 and 2).

If, in Phil. i. 19, the genitive were undoubtedly subjective in the words, *the Spirit of Jesus Christ*, the text would do no more than point to Christ as the Head of the Church, exercising functions and dispensing gifts bestowed upon Him by the Father.

In 2 Cor. iii. 17, 18, the reference is manifestly to the underlying spiritual meaning of the Old Testament, as opposed to the letter; and the expressions, *the Spirit of the Lord*, and *the Lord is the Spirit*, have no bearing on the question whether the Holy Ghost is ever said to be subjectively Christ's, in a manner which would imply Christ's Godhead.

According to Mr Liddon, 1 Pet. i. 7, 8, testifies, "it is the Person of Jesus in Whom the spiritual life of His Church centres;" yet the previous verses (3–5) leave no room for doubt that the Church's spiritual life centres more truly and profoundly in Him who stands related to Christ as *God and Father*, and by Whose power Christians are kept through faith unto salvation : "Blessed be the God and Father of our Lord Jesus Christ. Who, according to His great mercy, hath begotten us again unto a lively hope, by the resurrection of Jesus Christ from the dead," &c.

The minds of the first Christian converts must have been very thoroughly imbued with the dogma of our Lord's Deity, before they could have seen in the words, *which things angels desire to look into* (1 Pet. i. 12), the pregnant significance Mr Liddon detects.

"If the Christ of St Peter had been the Christ, we will not say of a Strauss, or of a Renan, but the Christ of a Socinus, nay, the Christ of an Arius, it is not easy to understand what should have moved the Angels with that strong desire to bend from their thrones above, that they might gaze with unsuccessful intentness at the humiliations of a created being, their peer or their inferior in the scale of creation. Surely the Angels must be longing to unveil a transcendent mystery, or a series of mysteries, such as are in fact the mystery of the Divine Incarnation and the consequences which depend on it in the kingdom of grace. St Peter's words are sober and truthful, if read by the light of faith in an Incarnate God; divorced from such a faith, they are fanciful, inflated, exaggerated" (p. 296).

Since the 'things' referred to are said to have been announced by the first heralds of the Gospel, we may gather from the " unsuccessful intentness " of the angelic gaze, that angels in heaven have a feebler insight into Divine mysteries than saints upon earth. That St Peter believed the work of man's redemption and spiritual advancement to merit the attentive observation, and engage the deep interest and active ministry of angels, will hardly be denied, and his faith quite explains his language. The fancifulness, inflation, and exaggeration, are the illusions of his modern expositor.

From the Bampton Lecturer's point of view, no aspect of Christ's work can be mentioned without some implication of His perfect Divinity. The exhibition of His suffering Manhood implies His Godhead. After noticing some passages in which " St Peter lays especial stress both on the moral significance and on the atoning power of the Death of Jesus Christ," Mr Liddon argues, " Certainly this earnest recognition of Christ's true Humanity as the seat of His sufferings is a most essential feature of the Apostle's doctrine ; but what is it that gives to Christ's Human acts and sufferings such preterhuman value ? Is it not that the truth of Christ's Divine Personality underlies this entire description of His redemptive work, rescuing it from the exaggeration and turgidity with which it would be fairly chargeable if Christ were merely human or less than God ?" (p. 298.)

The reprehensible neglect of context which mars Mr Liddon's exegesis, and discredits the theology he defends, so far as that theology is made to lean upon Scripture, has led him into the error of imagining the *logos* or *word* of the Living and Enduring God (1 Pet. i. 23) to be the Person of Christ. But *logos* is often used for the spoken or written Word,—the message of God,— and there is every reason to conclude that in the phraseology of St Peter, it is synonymous with the ῥῆμα or ' *word* of the Lord' mentioned in the quotation from Isaiah in the immediately consecutive verses,—the Word which has been preached in the Gospel. In the expression translated *milk of the word* (ii. 2), an adjective derived from *logos* is used, and the term *logos* occurs in ii. 8, where the better rendering is, *who stumble, obeying not the word ;* and again, in iii. 1 ; *if any obey not the word, they may without a word, &c.*

In conjecturing the Petrine personal Christ to be the Logos, Mr Liddon finds an explanation of the subjection of angels and authorities unto Him, and remarks ; " He is not said to have been taken up into heaven, but to have gone up thither, as though by His Own deed and will." The Apostolic statement is; "Baptism doth now save us (not the putting away filth from the flesh, but the answer of a good conscience towards God) through the resurrection of Jesus Christ, who is on the right hand of God, having gone into heaven; angels and authorities, and powers being subjected unto Him" (iii. 21, 22). A fact is here stated simply, without allusion to the mode of its accomplishment. Does Mr Liddon wish, by taking advantage of open verbal construction, to bring this statement into conflict with St Peter's constant and explicit teaching, 'God raised Jesus from the dead and exalted Him?'

And, as to the subjection of angels, &c., on the supposition that Christ is truly God, it is unmeaning to say they have been, or are, *made subject unto Him*, such language being suitable only to the position of one whom God has exalted, not to the everlasting indefeasible supremacy of God Himself.

The doxology (1 Pet. iv. 11) is *not* directed to Jesus Christ, but to 'the God Who is in all things to be glorified through Jesus Christ.' The unscrupulous eagerness with which Mr Liddon, in the face of probability, appropriates ambiguous language, is the reverse of convincing.

Whether the Second Epistle, traditionally inscribed with St Peter's name, is really an Apostolic composition is very problematical; but Mr Liddon assumes its genuineness, and works up fragments of it into his pleadings. "St Peter's second Epistle, like his first, begins and ends with Jesus. Its main positive theme is the importance of the higher practical knowledge of our Lord and Saviour Jesus Christ (i. 2, 3, 8; ii. 20; iii. 18). . . . . The prominence given to the Person of Christ, in this doctrine of a *knowledge* of which His Person is the Object, leads up to the truth of His real Divinity. If Jesus, thus known and loved, were not accounted God, then we must say that God is in this Epistle thrown utterly into the background, and that His human messenger has taken His place." There is, for the minds of candid and thoughtful readers, no sort of hint anywhere in the Epistle, that the writer accounted the Person of Christ to be God, or held the subsequently-promulgated paradox of Plurality in Unity, and Unity in Plurality.

The uncertain meaning of the words (2 Pet. i. 1) which Mr Liddon renders, *Our God and Saviour Jesus Christ*, has been already noticed. The Greek is susceptible of his version, but the clearly separate individualities of *God*, and *Jesus our Lord*, in the next verse, seem quite decisively to prescribe the sense, *of our God, and of our Saviour Jesus Christ.* The Codex Sinaiticus* reads, *of our Lord and Saviour Jesus Christ,* which is perhaps the original Text, and is certainly a description so often repeated, that its employment is a characteristic of the Epistle (i. 11 ; ii. 20 ; iii. 2, 18).

In his anxiety to show that " Christ's power is spoken of as Divine," Mr Liddon altogether misapprehends the purport of expressions in i. 3. The pronoun *His,* there refers to God, Whose " Divine power is said to have given unto us all things that belong to life and godliness, through the knowledge of Him (*i.e.*, Jesus Christ) who hath called us by His own glory and excellence." An exhortation is added, to the end Christians may not be " idle nor unfruitful as regards the knowledge of our Lord Jesus Christ " (ver. 8). Escape from the pollutions of the world is joined with *the knowledge of the Lord and Saviour Jesus Christ* (ii. 20) ; and the Epistle closes with an exhortation to grow in grace and *knowledge of our Lord and Saviour Jesus Christ.* The balance of probability, therefore, strongly inclines to the opinion, that in the expression, *the knowledge of Him who hath called us, &c.* (i. 3), our Lord Jesus Christ is referred to, and not, as Mr Liddon conceives, " The Eternal Father.'

The following extract consists mainly of assumptions and gratuitous affirmation :—

" Christ's power is spoken of as Divine ; and through the precious things promised by Him to His Church (must we not here specially understand the Sacraments?) Christians are made partakers of the Nature of God (i. 3, 4). To Christ, in His exalted majesty, a tribute of glory is due, both now and to the day of eternity (iii. 18). Throughout this Epistle, Jesus Christ is constantly named where we should expect to find the Name of God. The Apostle does not merely proclaim the Divinity of Jesus in formal terms ; he everywhere feels and implies it." In i. 4, *very great and precious promises* are mentioned, and the reasonable evidence these promises are the Sacraments is on a *par* with the evidence, " Jesus Christ is, throughout the Epistle, constantly named where we should expect to find the Name of God." The mental condition to which one of these conclusions is probable, is, no doubt, profoundly receptive of the other.

The point is unimportant, but there is room for great doubt

---

* I depend on Mr F. H. Scrivener's most useful little volume, *A Full Collation of the Codex Sinaiticus with the Received Text of the New Testament* (Bell and Daldy).

K

whether the tribute of glory at the end of the Epistle is to the day of *eternity.* The exact phrase used in the original, is without articles, does not occur elsewhere in the New Testament, and is a difficult one to translate literally, but αἰών signifies a period of time of undefined duration, *an age,* and not eternity, and the more probable sense is "to the day *of the age;*" *i.e.,* until the beginning or the ending of whatever era *the age* may be. The doxologies (1 Pet. iv. 11 ; v. 11) both have αἰών in the plural, and in the former instance, certainly, reduplicated (*ages of ages,* or, *ages beyond ages*). To take for granted that the term simply, and in the singular, means eternity, is to presume on the reader's ignorance or carelessness.

The proclamation of Christ's Deity in "formal terms" is utterly wanting in St Peter's Epistles, and a diffused feeling and implication of the dogma can be detected by those alone who have learned through evidence perfectly apart from the Apostle's language, what convictions must have filled his mind. Whether he had departed from the standing ground of Hebrew Monotheism, or was inspired to allot to Christ a personal existence within the Eternal Uncreated Essence, may be inferred from the fact, that he never once calls Christ *God,* but distinguishes between Him and God in a manner which not merely reserves, but suppresses the truth, if Christ be really God.

The Eternal One is *the God and Father of our Lord Jesus Christ* (1 Pet. i. 3) ; to Him prayer is to be directed (i. 17) ; and a principal feature of the faith attained through Christ, is to believe that God raised Christ from the dead, and gave Him glory (i. 21). Any ability we possess is to be esteemed and employed as God's gift, so that in all things He may be glorified through Jesus Christ (iv. 11). They who are called to suffer according to God's will, are to commit their souls to Him as to a faithful Creator (iv. 19) ;—all are to humble themselves under His mighty hand, that He may in due time exalt them ; casting all their care upon Him, because He careth for them (v. 6, 7) ; and the Apostle's petition for his afflicted brethren was, that " after they had suffered awhile, the God of all grace, who had called them unto His eternal glory in Christ, would Himself perfect, stablish, and strengthen them " (v. 10). Apart from express revelation, the natural conclusion of the first Christians would have been that the Being who was known on earth as Jesus of Nazareth was less than God, and with such a conclusion, St Peter's teaching, whether in the Missionary Sermons or the Epistles, contains not a word at variance. The latent significance, the subtle implications, the diffused underlying conviction of Christ's Veritable Deity, may be descried by minds ecclesiastically illuminated, but are totally shrouded from merely rational intelligence.

In commenting on the Epistle which bears the name of St Jude, Mr Liddon takes for granted, Christ is called "our only Sovereign and Lord Jesus Christ " (ver. 4). But the translation is very questionable. Winer pronounces against the opinion that grammatical construction confines the description to one Person, and considers two different Subjects may be referred to, since the word *Lord*, being made definite by the pronoun *our*, does not require the article. Conceding, as we must, the Name *God* in the Received Text to be an interpolation, the probability still is, two Persons, God, and Jesus Christ, are indicated : *the only Sovereign, and our Lord Jesus Christ.* We may justly ask for better warrant than ambiguous wording, before we conclude that Christ is called *our only Sovereign and Lord.* From the term rendered *Sovereign* (which, though sometimes applied to God, may mean no more than *Ruler, Master*), no inference can be drawn, but the adjective *only* appears to restrict the title to the One God and Father. In verses 20 and 21, Mr Liddon discerns these intimations : " The life of Christians is fashioned in devotion to the Blessed Trinity. It is a life of prayer ; their souls live in the Holy Spirit as in an atmosphere. It is a life of persevering love, whereof the Almighty Father is the Object. It is a life of expectation ; they look forward to the indulgent mercy which our Lord Jesus Christ will show them at His coming. Christ is the Being to Whom they look for mercy ; and the issue of His compassion is everlasting life. Could any merely human Christ have had this place in the heart and faith of Christians, or on the judgment-seat of God ? "

The excessive strain here put upon words is too palpable to need remark, and the question at issue is not whether the writer of the Epistle believed in a merely human Christ. Mere Humanity and absolute Godhead are not a pair of alternatives, one of which must be chosen. There is between Humanity and God, an unknown range of superhuman Existence ; and all the peculiar endowments of office, power, and majesty with which the Almighty has invested Christ, are, for genuine Protestants, to be measured neither by our guesses, nor by the necessities of traditional dogmatics, but by the statements of Scripture, so far as those statements are sufficiently plain and concordant to justify definite conclusions.

The final sentence of the Epistle is, in its true reading, inconsistent with the notion that in the heart and faith of the writer, Jesus Christ occupied the place of God. "Unto Him Who is able to keep you from falling, and to present you faultless and joyful in the presence of His glory; unto *the only God our Saviour, through Jesus Christ our Lord*, be glory, majesty, dominion, and power, both now and throughout all the ages."

There is a perfectly amazing one-sidedness, and consequent inconclusiveness, in the method of Mr Liddon's argument. He neglects implications directly and obviously against the doctrine he advocates, and argues as though that doctrine were too amply demonstrated to be seriously questioned, and might be assumed as a standard whereby to regulate interpretation. Beneath all his semblances of evidence, there lurks the assumption that evidence is superfluous, and that, write what they may, the Sacred Writers *must* be in harmony with the framers of the Nicene and Athanasian Creeds. Scripture is indeed illuminating, but only to the initiated; it is conclusive, but then it must be studied with the bias of a previous invincible conviction, and by the light of a revelation external to itself.

That SS. James, Peter, and Jude entertained a very high' conception of the Person and offices of Jesus Christ, whom God had ' raised from the dead, and clothed with glory' (1 Pet. i. 21), and who had when on earth, ' received from God the Father honour and glory' (2 Pet. i. 17), there can be no doubt; but they nowhere hint, even indirectly; ' Jesus is God Incarnate.' If they believed Christ to be God they have strangely repressed their faith, and have most ingeniously withheld both avowal and intimation of a doctrine which Christians in subsequent times have never really believed without frequently and earnestly proclaiming. Granting the competency of ecclesiastical tradition, and the inspired voice of a revealing Church, to make it a probable, or even a certain conclusion, that these earthly companions of our Lord conceived Him to be an Essential Form of Omnipotent Self-existent Deity, still the fact remains,—their faith does not appear in their Epistles. Nothing is gained by attempts to erect the Church's teaching on false grounds, on the contrary, faith is shaken, honest perception is blunted, and interpretation is degraded into a series of crafty contrivances to hide natural meaning and exhibit an ecclesiastical sense.

CHAPTER VII.

Dissection of the reasoning by which Mr Liddon endeavours to show that Christ's Deity 'is bound up with St Paul's whole mind,' and is implicitly taught throughout his Epistles—In reality the Bampton Lecturer refuses to take the point of view which St Paul's writings, and other New Testament Scriptures, incessantly present—Doctrine of the Real Presence in the Holy Eucharist—Mistaken deductions from the Epistles to the Ephesians and Colossians—Some additional imaginary implications of a Christ Divine in the sense maintained by the Lectures—Adverse testimony of St Paul exhibited, and an appeal made from the ground of that testimony, to the honesty, intellectual conscientiousness, and common sense of Orthodox Protestants—Catholic Churchmen not liable to this appeal.

THE most irreclaimably biassed interpretation could collect from St Paul's discourses and Epistles but few expressions which can be made to wear the semblance of either announcing in terms, or plausibly suggesting, that our Lord Jesus Christ is Unproduced Eternal God, in Essential Being the same as, and equal to, the Almighty Father. The Pauline texts which Mr Liddon supposes directly to assert, or clearly to imply, Christ's Deity, have been already examined, and shown not to be fairly open to the construction he assigns. But, in handling St Paul's language, he builds, with much pretension, on a mass of indirect testimony, which, viewed in the shadow of his own prepossessions, seems to him to prove the doctrine of Christ's Deity was "bound up with St Paul's whole mind ;" and "irresistibly to imply a Christ Who is Divine." In attempting to draw out and illustrate the meaning which so deeply underlies the Apostle's writings, and is so wonderfully absent from the surface of his words, Mr Liddon expends pages of passionate rhetoric, the major part of which (regarded as argument, and not as mere declamation) is redeemed from being absolutely silly, only by being eloquent and sincere. In language frequently reiterated in substance, though varied in form, the conclusion is pressed upon us, that "the doctrine is inextricably interwoven with the central and most vital teaching of the Apostle ;" and that, "taking St Paul's teaching as a whole, it must be admitted to

centre in One Who is at once and truly God as well as Man"
(p. 324).

I shall not follow minutely every sentence of rapacious deduction from materials which are admitted to be unpronounced,
while they are held to be potently cumulative. My readers
will by this time have learned to know the method, and
appreciate the worth, of the reasonings I am reviewing. Wherever any prominence is given to the offices of Jesus Christ, and
our relation to Him as the God-exalted Ruler and Saviour of
mankind, there Mr Liddon detects the slightly-veiled presence
of the dogma he is bent on finding, and triumphantly proclaims
the inference, 'Christ must be God.' The antidote to his very
real, though undesigned sophistry, may, in most instances, be
discovered in the immediate contexts of the passages he produces.

What inference, bearing helpfully on his theme, Mr Liddon
imagines can be extracted from that " Sermon of St Paul's from
the steps of the Areopagus, which, at first sight, might seem to
be Theistic rather than Christian," is not easily discernible.
The sermon, he reminds us, " though insisting chiefly on those
Divine attributes which are observable in nature and Providence,
ends with Jesus. . . . The certainty of the coming judgment
has been attested by the historical fact of the resurrection of
Jesus ; the risen Jesus is the future Judge " (Acts xvii. 18–31).

The Apostle preached with great emphasis and clearness One
living and true *Lord of heaven and earth*, the Creator, Ruler,
Sustainer, and Father of all mankind, and finished his discourse
by declaring, "God now commands all men everywhere to repent,
because He has appointed a day in which He will judge the world
in righteousness by a Man whom He hath ordained ; having
given unto all men assurance in raising Him from the dead." If
this language be in perfect harmony with the persuasion, 'Jesus
Christ is God,' what conceivable words can be out of harmony
with that persuasion ?

The Apostle's address to the Presbyters on the strand of
Miletus (Acts xx. 18–36), "moves incessantly round the Person
of Jesus. He protests that to lead men to repentance towards
God, and faith towards the Lord Jesus Christ (ver. 21), had
been the single object of his public and private ministrations at
Ephesus." How does this intimate that in St Paul's conception
Jesus Christ was God? The phraseology rather excludes the
intimation. The supreme devotion of heart and mind are
claimed for God, and belief is demanded with reference to the

office and work of the beloved Son and Servant whom God had raised from the dead, and made both Lord and Christ. The repentance and faith referred to, are a comprehensive description of Christian belief and conduct; and, measured only by the hints which his farewell address at Miletus supplies, the Apostle's teaching would appear to have been of a very undogmatic and practical kind.

The discreditable, though possibly unconscious tendency to strain and inoculate every turn of expression, is displayed in the paraphrase of verse 24 in the same discourse :—" The Apostle counts not his life dear to himself, if only he can complete the mission which is so precious to him, because he has received it from the Lord Jesus." The recorded words are: "That I may finish my course, and the ministry which I have received from the Lord Jesus, to bear witness of the gospel of the grace of God,"—where the special preciousness of the mission is, certainly, as fairly ascribable to its subject-matter, as to its reception from the Lord Jesus. No doubt it was prized by the Apostle on both grounds.

In referring to verse 28, Mr Liddon injudiciously clings to the wrong reading, which seems to affirm, " God purchased the Church with His Own Blood." To sustain the phrase, *blood of God*, the concurrence of all ancient MSS. would scarcely suffice, whereas, in fact, a majority of the MSS. whose antiquity carries weight, have the reading, *The Church of the Lord, which He hath purchased with His own blood.* Though Mr Liddon himself adopts the erroneous wording, he briefly indicates in a Note the condition of the external evidence. If *Church of God* were undoubtedly genuine, we might still, I think, with a very high degree of probability, regard *Christ* as an unexpressed nominative to *has purchased*; unexpressed, because so very obvious. To use the passage at all as a proof text, in arguing for the dogma of our Lord's Divinity, is among the absurdities which grow out of abundant conviction and scanty evidence.

The circumstances which accompanied, and immediately succeeded St Paul's conversion, are touched in Mr Liddon's accustomed fashion ; and fragments of the narratives in Acts xxii. and xxvi. are duly marshalled and manipulated to introduce the query, " Who can fail to see that the Lord, Who, in His glorified manhood, thus speaks to His servant from the skies, and Who is withal revealed to him in the very centre of of his soul (Gal. i. 15, 16), is no created being, is neither saint nor seraph, but, in very truth, the Master of consciences, the

Monarch Who penetrates, inhabits, and rules the secret life of spirits, the King Who claims the fealty, and Who orders the ways of men ?"

The utter groundlessness of the induction, that *Jesus the Nazarite*, the glorified Master of Christians, who appeared to Saul of Tarsus on the road to Damascus, and sent him forth to preach the Gospel, is, in Attributes and Essence, Veritable Deity, will be manifest to every reader who calmly peruses the narratives quoted. The words of Ananias, to whom also a vision of Christ had been vouchsafed, and of whose coming Paul had received an entranced foresight (Acts ix. 10–12), place the subject in 'the true light, and show how baseless is Mr Liddon's strained and stilted exposition. "The God of our fathers hath chosen thee to know His will, and to see the Just One, and to hear a voice from His mouth, because thou shalt be a witness for Him unto all men, of what thou hast seen and heard " (xxii. 14, 15). The perpetually recurring Scriptural conceptions of God's distinct supremacy, and our Lord's inferiority and instrumentality, are, surely, more present here than the ideas Mr Liddon cannot " fail to see."

In the appearance of Jesus to Paul, there was nothing to betoken our Lord to be either uncreated or super-angelic. He appears as a spiritual and glorious Being, clothed with authority and a mission from the Most High. If a suggestion as to the mode of our Lord's appearance is designed, it is scarcely accurate to say, "He speaks to His servant from the skies," the truer account would seem to be, He came from the skies to speak to His servant.

I cannot perceive the relevancy of the reference to Gal. i. 15, 16 : *It pleased God . . . . to reveal His Son in me.* Combine that statement as you will with the records of St Paul's conversion, visions, and conduct, how can the conclusion be reached ; Christ is the Supreme and Divine " Master of consciences, the Monarch Who penetrates, inhabits, and rules the secret life of spirits," &c. ?

To what purpose is the remark ; " St Paul's popular teaching is emphatically a ' preaching of Jesus Christ ' (Acts ix. 20, xvii. 3, 18, xxviii. 31 ; comp. Acts v. 42 ; 2 Cor. iv. 5) ?" Doubtless it is so, but the fact of Christ's filling a place of peculiar emphasis and prominence is very far indeed from proving Christ to be God. In what sense does the Apostle preach Christ ? and on what doctrine concerning Christ does he insist ? Does he anywhere, in a single phrase of clear, unequivocal meaning, proclaim,

' Christ is God ?'   Does he anywhere put Him on an equality with God ?   Does he anywhere, even in the later Epistles and the strongest passages, represent Him as being greater than God-appointed, God-endowed, God-exalted ?   His whole Apostolic labour was a devoted spiritual service of God, in the Gospel of His Son (Rom. i. 9); the faith he seeks to establish, and to which he gives the promise of justification, is faith in Him Who raised up Jesus our Lord from the dead (iv. 24 ; x. 9, 10) ; the peace he announces, is peace with God, through our Lord Jesus Christ, through whom we have access into the grace wherein we stand (v. 1, 2) ; the very core of the Gospel was, in his view, the overflowing grace of God, and God's gracious gift in the man Christ Jesus, abounding unto mankind (v. 15–17); his thanksgivings habitually went up to God for the grace given in Christ Jesus ; and his ground of Christian assurance was, that faithful is the God Who calls us into the fellowship of His Son, Jesus Christ our Lord (1 Cor. i. 4, 9).   The company of be-lievers is God's husbandry, and God's building ; the true minis-ters of the Church, who lay the one foundation, Christ Jesus, are labourers of God ; and the climax of Christian privilege and security is expressed in the formula, *Ye are Christ's and Christ is God's* (1 Cor. iii. 9, 11, 23; comp. Eph. ii. 18–20).   The Church is the Body of Christ, but it is a Body in which God supremely governs, and sets the various members according to His own wise Will (1 Cor. xii. 18, 27, 28).   The dominion of Christ is declared to be an imparted and delegated dominion ; to be at length delivered up to the God and Father, to Whom the Son shall be Himself subject, that God may be all in all (xv. 24–28).   He who establishes us with respect to Christ, and anoints us, is God (2 Cor. i. 21).   Of the crucified Christ, whom the Apostle gloried in preaching, he could announce, that though He was crucified through weakness, yet He is alive through the power of God (xiii. 4) ; an announcement in which language is strangely used, if Christ be, Himself, personally God.   When the Apostle claims a superhuman origin for his Apostleship, he sees a height yet beyond the Master, Jesus Christ, even God, the Father, Who raised Christ from the dead (Gal. i. 1 ; comp. Eph. i. 1) ; and when he states most pregnantly the purpose for which Christ became our Redeemer, he tells us that purpose was in fulfilment of the Will of our God and Father (Gal. i. 4).   The spiritual blessings which Christians receive in Christ, are ascribed to *the God and Father of our Lord Jesus Christ ;* to Him St Paul's prayers for gifts of wisdom, enlightenment, and spiritual strength are directed ; and to Him the endless tribute of glory in the Church, and in Christ Jesus, is acknowledged to be due (Eph. i. 3, 17, 18 ; iii. 14–21).

The list of texts denoting the Apostle's " emphatic preaching of Jesus Christ " not to have been a preaching which either expressly affirmed or tacitly implied Christ's Deity, might be easily extended. Turns of thought and diction out of keeping with faith in any Godhead but the Father's, meet us at every step, in closest connection with statements which proclaim the dignity and offices of Christ.

The dogma of our Lord's Deity being assumed to be recognised and fixed in St Paul's mind, his remarkable mode of inculcating it, is felt to be a problem which calls for some attempt at solution. Putting, for the moment, all evidence on the other side out of the account,—if the Apostle's thought and teaching moved so continually round the Person of an absolutely Divine Christ, his rare use of ambiguous expressions, which even the resolute faith and cultivated ingenuity of centuries, have been able plausibly to isolate and enlist, and his entire abstinence from clear and definite avowals of Christ's Deity, become to the eye of reason, convincingly indicative that, either purposely or under constraint of inspiration, he withheld the tenet which the Church afterwards made the centre of her dogmatic system.

Mr Liddon, indeed, argues :—" Our Lord is always the Apostle's theme ; but the degree in which His Divine glory is unveiled, varies with the capacities of the Jewish or heathen listeners for bearing the great discovery. The doctrine is distributed, if we may so speak, in a like varying manner over the whole text of St Paul's Epistles. It lies in those greetings (commencements of all the Epistles, see also 2 Cor. xiii. 13 ; 2 Thess. ii. 16) by which the Apostle associates Jesus Christ with God the Father, as being the source, no less than the channel, of the highest spiritual blessings. It is pointedly asserted, when the Galatians are warned that St Paul is ' an Apostle not from men, nor by man, *but* by Jesus Christ and God the Father.' It is implied in the benedictions which the Apostle pronounces in the Name of Christ without naming the name of God (Rom. xvi. 20, 24 ; 1 Cor. xvi. 23 ; Gal. vi. 18 ; Phil. iv. 23 ; 1 Thess. v. 28). It underlies those early apostolical hymns, sung, as it would seem, in the Redeemer's honour. . . . It alone can explain the application of passages, which are used in the Old Testament of the Lord Jehovah, to the Person of Jesus Christ ; such an application would have been impossible unless St Paul had renounced his belief in the authority and sacred character of the Hebrew Scriptures, or had explicitly recognized the truth that Jesus Christ was Jehovah Himself visiting and redeeming His people" (p. 327).

A little examination detects the unsoundness of this reasoning. The benedictory greetings do not involve the supposition; Jesus Christ, " being the source no less than the channel of the highest spiritual blessings," is God. According to the teaching of Scripture, He is not, as the Almighty Father is, the original primary source of any spiritual blessing whatever, but, in virtue of the Father's gifts, the secondary and instrumental source. His whole function between God and us is ministerial, and He can bestow nothing which He has not Himself first received from the *One God and Father Who is over all* (Matt. xxviii. 18 ; Acts ii. 36, v. 31 ; Phil. ii. 8–11 ; Eph. i. 20–22). There is but one way in which the language of Scripture can be rationally harmonized, namely, by starting from the position to which a multitude of texts lead, that Christ is made of God the Channel, and is furnished by God to be the Dispenser, of gifts of grace. Hopeless confusion is introduced, and every dictate of sound reasonable interpretation suffers violence, when unexplained association is dilated into antagonism with explicitly avowed recipiency and subordination. The exaltation and the endowments, of which the Canonical penmen held Christ to have been the recipient, fully account for every expression which points to Him, either as a source or a channel of grace and peace, and, at the same time, leave uncrossed the numerous statements which exhibit the unrivalled, unapproachable, supremacy of the Father, as the One Independent, Self-sufficing Fountain of every good and perfect gift. Taking into view the whole of the New Testament phraseology bearing on the point, the natural, probable, and amply sufficient meaning of the expression, *grace* or *favour of our Lord Jesus Christ*, is the loving approval attaching to faithful discipleship, together with all the blessings of which the great High Priest and Apostle of our profession is the minister to those who are *heirs of God, and joint-heirs with Christ* (Rom. viii. 17).

I am not inclined to dispute whether, in the passages referred to, Christ is contemplated as a Dispenser and Channel of grace ; but an expositor, less ready than Mr Liddon is to clutch at a possible meaning of an ambiguous phrase, might object that, in the great majority of the texts adduced, the Greek will bear the translation, *from God, the Father of us, and of the Lord Jesus Christ ;* and that some proximate contexts (2 Cor. i. 3 ; Eph. i. 3 ; Col. i. 3) tend to sustain the translation. But, without taking exception to the generally received and more probable rendering, the immediate contexts above mentioned, *Blessed be the God and Father of our Lord Jesus Christ,* do seem conclusively to shut out the idea that, in associating Christ with the Father in benedictory salutations, the Apostle was impelled by the underlying thought, or proceeded on the tacit assumption, of Christ's Deity. With regard to Gal. i. 1, one thing which the Apostle there "pointedly asserts," is, God the Father raised Jesus Christ from the dead ; but the words, *Who raised Him from the dead,* being opposed to the desired inference, do not appear in Mr Liddon's quotation. St Paul having pronounced his Apostleship not to be *from* men, as the commissioning source, nor *through* any man, as an intermediate authority, it seems not improbable, his fully expressed meaning would be, "but through Jesus Christ, and (*from*) God the Father."

The phrase, *the grace of our Lord Jesus Christ,* is, to Mr Liddon's mind, vastly pregnant with acceptable significance. In his delineation of "the implied Christology of the Epistles to the Corinthians," he concludes with the exclamation, "Would St Paul impart an Apostolical benediction ? In one Epistle he blesses his readers in the Name of Christ alone ; in the other he names the Three Blessed Persons ; but *the grace of our Lord Jesus Christ* is mentioned, not only before *the fellowship of the Holy Ghost,* but even before *the love of God*" (1 Cor. xvi. 23 ; 2 Cor. xiii. 14). If such exceedingly weak pleading was pardonable in a University pulpit, it should not have been allowed to appear in print. Did the thought never strike Mr Liddon, that, presuming the arrangement of the latter benediction to have a designed and special purpose, the purpose might have been to ascend from more diffused and general forms, to a more concentrated and particular form, of spiritual blessing. The fellowship of the Holy Ghost is the highest result, and the most precious inward individual realization, of all that the favour of Christ, and the love of God, can bestow.

When Mr Liddon caught at the concluding benediction of the first Corinthian Epistle, he should have observed how, to the pious wish for the presence of Christ's favour, St Paul adds the words, *My love be with you all in Christ Jesus.* Are we absurdly to infer the Apostle's possession of superhuman capacity and dignity? He might appropriately have written, "The love of God be with you all in Christ Jesus."

But association of names, and the mention, under identical

terms, of attributes and relations whose force and extent vary
with the persons indicated, are the poorest arguments for equality
of rank and nature.   Are the holy angels put on a level with
Christ, and with the Father, when, in Luke ix. 26, the glory of
the Son of Man, and of the Father, and of the holy angels, is
spoken of in one and the same sentence ?   Do the angels of God
acquire a Divine dignity by the association in Rev. iii. 5 ?
(Comp. Matt. x. 32 ; Luke xii. 8 ; Mark viii. 38.)   Did the
Apostles, presbyters, and brethren, equalize themselves with the
Holy Ghost in authority, when they wrote, *it seemed good to the
Holy Ghost, and to us ?* (Acts xv. 28.)   Did St Paul intend to
suggest the parity of those he named, when he used the adjura-
tion, *I charge thee before God, and Christ Jesus, and the elect
angels ?* (1 Tim. v. 21.)   The writer of the Epistle to the Hebrews,
in describing the gloriousness of the heavenly Jerusalem, names
together, " God the Judge of all ; spirits of just men made perfect ;
and Jesus, Mediator of a new covenant " (xii. 23, 24) ; but what
sane person would imagine these inhabitants of heaven to be
compeers, because they are grouped in a recital of celestial at-
tractiveness and splendour ?   The remarkable fact that spirits of
just men are " mentioned even before " Jesus the Mediator,
merits Mr Liddon's thoughtful observation.   Again, in Rev. xiv.
10, the revelation imparted by angelic lips to St John, not only
joins the angels with the Lamb, as spectators of the fiery torments
of the wicked, but also significantly mentions the presence of the
angels " even before " the presence of the Lamb.*

The early Apostolical hymns to which Mr Liddon refers, are
supposed to be contained in 1 Tim. i. 15 ; iii. 16 ; 2 Tim. ii.
11–13 ; Titus iii. 4–7 ; Eph. v. 14 ; and students who have not
yet acquired the faculty of seeing anywhere and everywhere
whatever they may wish to see, can decide for themselves what
doctrine " underlies " these fragmentary anthems.   In 1 Tim.
iii. 16, the corrupted reading, *God,* too little defensible even for
Mr Liddon's appropriation, must of course be cancelled.

The specimens cited, of " the application to the Person of
Christ, of passages which are used in the Old Testament of the
Lord Jehovah," are, Joel ii. 32, in Rom. x. 13; and Jer. ix. 23,
24, in 1 Cor. i. 31.

In taking for granted St Paul applies the words of Joel to Christ,

---

* According to the reading adopted in Dean Alford's Revised Version
(1 Thess. iii. 2), Timothy is denominated a *fellow-worker with God.* But,
doubtless, the Dean never guessed his amended text and translation might
involve the Deification of Timothy.

Mr Liddon treads in the steps of numerous orthodox commentators, who, having such slender materials in Scripture for the concoction of the Church's dogma, are actuated by an unconscious bias, and build upon doubtful surmises as though they were indubitable facts. Candid examination of St Paul's argument, shows there is by no means adequate ground for asserting he intended the words of Joel to designate Christ. The prophet's language is most likely quoted in its true original sense, and designates Jehovah. Looking carefully to the preceding and subsequent contexts of Rom. x. 13, we soon perceive Mr Liddon should have put conjectural opinion in the place of confident assertion. Verse 11 repeats in part a quotation just previously made (ix. 33) from Isaiah xxviii. 16, and relates to Christ, the foundation-stone in the spiritual Zion. *The same Lord of all* in verse 12 (comp. Rom. iii. 29, 30 ; and, amending translation, ix. 5) is the Supreme God Who raised Christ from the dead (ver. 9) ; Who lays the foundation-stone in Zion ; is *rich in mercy* (Eph. ii. 4), and *no respecter of persons* (Acts x. 34). The promise (ver. 13) is to all of every nation who call upon His Name, that is, acknowledge and serve Him. Verse 16 notices parenthetically the unbelief of the Jews, and in the ensuing verses there is a reference to the Gentiles, and their case is contrasted with that of the Jews. The issue of the exposition Mr Liddon indorses is, that the foundation-stone laid by Jehovah, is Jehovah Himself ! The passage is not altogether free from obscurity, and may, therefore, be snarled over by predetermined theologians, but to extort the inference, 'Christ is Jehovah,' is certainly to make controversial convenience, and not probability, the standard of interpretation.

To connect Jer. ix. 23, 24, with 1 Cor. i. 31, for an argumentative purpose, is quite beyond the license of even theological special pleading. The words of Jeremiah, according to the Septuagint Version, which here agrees with the extant Hebrew Text, are, " Let not the wise man glory in his wisdom, &c., but let him that glorieth glory in this, to understand and to know that I am the Lord, Who doeth mercy, and justice, and righteousness upon the earth, because in these things is my pleasure, saith the Lord." If St Paul really had this portion of Jeremiah in view, and remembered its original sense, the natural connection of his thought would have been, that God's goodness and mercy were exercised in sending Jesus Christ to become unto us the channel of wisdom, and righteousness, &c. (see 1 Cor. i. 30), and that, therefore, the only ground of boasting is in God, Who enriches us, through Christ, with every spiritual blessing.

It is strange that the phraseology, " Jehovah visiting and redeeming His people," did not recall to Mr Liddon's mind the words,
*and hath raised up a horn of salvation for us, in the house of His
servant David.* If Christ is the *horn of salvation,* then Jehovah
visited and redeemed His people by providing another, not by
coming Himself (Luke i. 68, 69 ; comp. vii. 16) ;—and further,
the verb translated *visited,* is properly, *looked upon,* and does not,
when applied to God, in any degree convey the idea of Personal
presence, as distinguished from Providential observation and
care. From Luke ii. 29–31, we learn that Simeon, inspired by
the Holy Ghost, saw in Christ the God-prepared Salvation or
Saviour. The ecclesiastical meaning may be, ' Jehovah raised up
and prepared Himself,' but it is not the natural meaning, nor
can we accept it, without confessing the incompetence of reason
rightly to understand what is apparently the plainest language of
Scripture.

In a rush of irrelevant declamatory questions, Mr Liddon
sophistically argues that, because in the provinces of judgment,
justification, and redemption, Christ is certainly more than mere
man, therefore He is God. The conclusion does not follow from
the premisses, and if we calmly consult in their entirety the passages embodying the expressions on which Mr Liddon depends,
we see that the Apostle believed Christ to be removed from, and
subordinate to, absolute Deity, no less assuredly than he believed
Him to be removed from, and superior to, ordinary Humanity.
There is a feeble, unreflecting rationalism running in the wake
of an assumption, involved in the question, " If Jesus Christ be
more than man, is it possible to suggest any intermediate position between Humanity and the throne of God, which St Paul,
with his earnest belief in the God of Israel, could have believed
Him to occupy?" (p. 329.) We are not called upon to suggest
anything, but to accept in its plain natural sense, language of the
Sacred Scriptures which freely and often ascribes Christ's dignity,
offices, and powers, to the Almighty's gift and appointment.
Such language denotes how, in the hearts and thoughts of the
Canonical writers, Christ *did* occupy an intermediate position
between Humanity and the throne of God. It solves Mr Liddon's difficulty, and exposes the futility of the argument by which
he persistently strives to enforce the alternative, ' if Christ be
not mere man, He must be Very God.' The presupposition involved in texts which exalt Christ and His functions, without
alluding to the ground of His exaltation, is, not His Deity ; but,
His recipiency from Deity (explicitly avowed in other texts), of

peculiar dominion, authority, and endowments. Mr Liddon's knowledge is not only more extended and precise than that of the Apostles, but runs upon a different line. Their language, reasonably apprehended, intimates that they held Christ to fill, in virtue of conferred qualifications, an unique and exceptional position of spiritual Headship and Mediation between God and man. But Mr Liddon perceives the idea of such a position to be inadmissible. He is able to gauge the capabilities of possible Being, between man and the Self-Existent One, and, in the absence of revealing statements, and in the face of opposing implications, he can deny that any place exterior to the Unoriginated Substance, may be consistently found for Christ's Person. It is in vain Apostles discriminate our Lord from God, in a manner which implies the actual division of separate individual existence : it is in vain they indicate Christ's derivation, origination, and dependence : it is in vain they refer Christ's lordship and capacity to the Father's decree, the Father's action, and the Father's gifts : it is in vain St Paul affirms, with repetition, emphasis, and in the most exclusive terms, the Divine Unity. Mr Liddon pronounces,—" If Christ be not God, St Paul cannot be acquitted of assigning to Him generally a prominence which is inconsistent with serious loyalty to monotheistic Truth." The Apostle earnestly believes in One Divine Nature, and imparts his belief in unequivocal terms ; he earnestly believes also (according to Mr Liddon's hypothesis), that Christ is mysteriously internal to, and comprised in, the One Divine Nature ; but he imparts his belief by utterly abstaining from explanation and avowal, and by repeatedly employing language which means rationally nothing, if it does not mean, Christ is individually, and in the real ordinary acceptation of the words, distinct from God, inferior to God, and a recipient of sovereignty and endowments at God's hands. I have already stated this more than once in substance, but Mr Liddon's repetition, in various guises, of the same vicious argument, compels repetition on my part. He resolutely ignores the obvious Scriptural solution of what appears to him a difficulty ; and, having taken for granted the point to be proved, proceeds on the assumption that the allusions which magnify our Lord, and give prominence to His Person, offices, and claims, in the work of redemption, and the government of the Church, must of necessity involve His Supreme Divinity. Whatever Apostles may have written, or left unwritten, Mr Liddon's reason decides,—God could not have produced Christ, and have qualified Him by pre-incarnate and incarnate endowments for the place Scripture assigns Him. The Omnipotent One cannot, in the profoundly cognizant philosophy of Mr Liddon, be conceived to have appointed any Being next to Himself, who is not also Himself. The limits and methods of Creative might, the extent to which the Great Parent can inspire and inhabit His highest rational and spiritual offspring, are so exhaustively exhibited in man, and in the scanty knowledge which the Scriptures communicate respecting angels, that Mr Liddon can definitively mark the boundary, and say where the manifestation of Divinity in dependent Being terminates, and where the Self-existent Independent Substance comes Personally forth in the entirety of Its attributes, to fold around Itself the vesture of created Form.

" There is no room in St Paul's thought for an imaginary being like the Arian Christ, hovering indistinctly between created and Uncreated life ; since, where God is believed to be so utterly remote from the highest creatures beneath His throne, Christ must either be conceived of as purely and simply a creature with no other than a creature's nature and rights, or He must be adored as One Who is for ever and necessarily internal to the Uncreated Life of the Most High " (p. 310).

The doctrine of the Real Presence in the Holy Eucharist, which Catholics, as opposed to Protestants, so deeply cherish, implies and encourages faith in the tenet, which is Mr Liddon's theme. He is, therefore, quite consistent in assuming the literalness of the phraseology employed by St Paul (1 Cor. x. 16 ; xi. 27, 29). " The broken bread and the cup of blessing are not picturesque symbols of an absent Teacher, but veils of a gracious yet awful Presence ; the irreverent receiver is guilty of the Body and Blood of the Lord, Which he does not discern " (p. 330).

Among the difficulties which, from the Protestant point of view, encumber this exposition, is the fact of its taking for granted the existence, on the subject of the Eucharist, of precise and explicit oral teaching to which the Acts and Epistles do not in any way allude. Before the terms, *Body* and *Blood*, could be understood to signify an actual though invisible presence of Christ's Incarnate Person, a vast amount of preliminary instruction, of a unique and not easily comprehensible kind, would be requisite. The marvel is that the Corinthians, being sufficiently familiar with the dogma of the Real Presence, to accept in this sense St Paul's words, should have fallen into so shockingly irreverent a fashion of celebrating the central, highest, and overwhelmingly awful act of Christian worship. The more simple and natural meaning of the Apostle's words is, undoubtedly, the figurative, symbolical meaning, which Mr Liddon repudiates.

What conceivable point is there in the following remark and references ?—"In the allusions to the Three Most Holy Persons, which so remarkably underlie the structure and surface-thought of the Epistle to the Ephesians, Jesus Christ is associated most significantly with the Father and the Spirit (i. 3, 6, 13 ; ii. 18 ; iii. 6 ; comp. iii. 14-17)." In citing from the first of the texts referred to, Mr Liddon warily omits the title *God.* The words, *the God and Father of our Lord Jesus Christ* (i. 3), and also the words, *the God of our Lord Jesus Christ, the Father of glory* (i. 17), do, doubtless, contain a most significant association, displaying the subject, as well as the filial, relation in which Christ stands to the Almighty King. That our Lord is *the beloved* of God ; that Christians are sealed with the Holy Spirit ; and that, through Christ, both Jews and Gentiles have introduction or access by One Spirit unto the Father, are announcements from which no ordinary process of deduction can elicit the inference, Christ is internal to the Uncreated Life of the Most High. But Mr Liddon's estimate of "the allusions to the Three Most Holy Persons" in the Ephesian Epistle, is more guarded than that of a deservedly eminent contemporary elucidator of Holy Writ. Dean Alford, in teaching *How to study the New Testament,* says, " The whole Epistle to the Ephesians is a magnificent apostolic comment on the doctrine of the Holy Trinity, as the Divine Persons are concerned in the work of our redemption. Those who deny that doctrine must either set aside this Epistle altogether, or must tear out of it all meaning and coherence." Yet, the Epistle not only calls the Almighty Father, *the God of our Lord Jesus Christ,* but proclaims also, that " there is *one Lord,* one faith, one baptism, *One God and Father* of all, Who is over all, and through all, and in all" (iv. 5, 6). But the measure in which the holding of the Church's doctrine, when unaccompanied by a frank recognition of the Church's dogmatic authority, can warp and bias earnest, able minds, is painfully visible in Orthodox Protestant comments on the *Sacred Book.* Their authors set aside perspicuous and exact information ; they strip language of all probable meaning ; they wrest thought out of all coherence, and then, with amusing effrontery, charge upon others the very kind of outrages of which they themselves are guilty. No exposition of the Epistle to the Ephesians can be faithful and consistent, which does not recognize, along with our Lord's highly exalted dignity, His separation from, and inferiority to, the Self-existent One. The sole ultimate Supremacy, and originating Energy of God, as the Giver of grace, and the primary Sovereign Ruler in all the arrangements and dispensations of creation and redemption, are so uniformly conspicuous throughout the Epistle, that it is astonishing how even the prejudices of theological training, hardened by the corroborating assent of numbers, can be blind to them. In this as in every other New Testament document, *the God and Father*, to Whom we are admonished to give thanks, in the Name of our Lord Jesus Christ (v. 20), appears to be the only *God* with Whom the writer was acquainted.

Some detached texts from the Colossian and Philippian Epistles are made to swell the inferential argument, by deductive processes which I need not again particularize. The treatment of two texts, however, deserves special notice. On the ground of Col. ii. 3 (i. 19; ii. 9 being referred to as confirmatory), we are informed; " In the Epistle to the Colossians, Jesus Christ is said to possess the intellectual as well as the other attributes of Deity." Now, even as the text is commonly read, we are quite at liberty to translate; *in which (mystery) are hid all the treasures of wisdom and knowledge.* But the words, *of the Father, and of the Christ*, are of very doubtful genuineness. *Of God, Father of Christ*, and *of the God of Christ*, are the better readings, from the more ancient MSS. Dean Alford strikes out the doubtful words, and reads simply, *of God*, leaving no choice but to join the relative pronoun with *mystery*, and render *in which*, or *wherein;* for the mere grammatical possibility of referring the relative to God, need not be considered. On the whole, therefore, probability is heavily against Mr Liddon's interpretation of the passage, to say nothing of the strain involved in the identification of *all the treasures of wisdom and knowledge*, with the intellectual attributes of Deity.

The other text is Phil. ii. 10, wherein Mr Liddon conceives it to be " expressly said, that all created beings in Heaven, on earth, and in hell, when Christ's triumph is complete, shall acknowledge the Majesty even of His Human Nature." Now, as everybody is aware, this text, read in the original, has, *in the Name, &c.*, and it is far from certain, *in the Name of Jesus* means *at the Name.* The Apostle's meaning may have been, that, in the Name of Jesus, as Lord and Leader, the whole race of Man, both in Heaven, on earth, and in Hades, should worship God (comp. Rom. xiv. 11). In Col. i. 20, God is said *to reconcile unto Himself all things, on earth, and in heaven, through Christ*, —an apostolic statement, the exact sense of which is difficult to penetrate. But whether in virtue of the exaltation and the Name bestowed by the Father, Christ was Himself to receive the homage of the hosts who people the seen and unseen realms ; or was to be their Leader and Master in the adoration of *the Blessed and Only Potentate ; His God and their God*,—is a point about which, while attention is directed to one text alone, discussion is sure to be inconclusive and unprofitable.   Mr Liddon's argument is palpably weak, because, influenced by a pardonable anxiety to restrict the phrase, *God highly exalted Him*, &c., to Christ's human nature, he has made that nature Personal, whereas his own repeated definitions affirm our Lord's human nature to have no individual personal Being, but to be folded as a garment round a Divine Person.

Returning again to the indispensable assumption, that a Christ not truly God can fill no exceptional special place and office between man and God, Mr Liddon exclaims in a triumphantly defiant strain ; " Substitute, if you can, throughout any one of St Paul's Epistles, the name of the first of the saints, or of the highest among the angels, for the Name of the Divine Redeemer, and see how it reads.   Accept the Apostle's implied challenge. Imagine for a moment that Paul was crucified for you ; that you were baptized in the name of Paul ; that wisdom, holiness, redemption, come from an Apostle who, saint though he be, is only a brother man.* . . . Why is it that when coupled with any other name, however revered and saintly, the words of Paul repecting Jesus Christ must seem not merely strained, but exaggerated and blasphemous ? " (p. 339).

The paltry fallaciousness of this, and much more of the like kind, needs no detailed exposure. The argument does not touch the point at issue, but simply amounts to the inquiry, Why can you not substitute for a Being whom God has sent, and qualified, and highly exalted for the accomplishment of a particular purpose, some man, or some angel, whom God has not so sent, and qualified, and exalted ?   And the proximate context of one passage from which Mr Liddon draws (1 Cor. i. 13), involves intimations utterly at variance with his deduction.   How could the divided Corinthians have used the names of *Paul*, and *Apollos*, and *Cephas*, and *Christ*, in distinctive party cries, if they had been taught to believe in Christ's Godhead ?   Would the

---

* The turn here given to 1 Cor. i. 30, if not the result of inadvertence, is something worse.   The Apostle wrote : "Of God are ye in Christ Jesus, who has become wisdom to us *from God, &c.*," the preposition implying *sent from*.

A just perception of the origin and meaning of much of St Paul's language, is shown in a remark of Professor Jowett, on Gal. i. 1 ; "The whole work of Christ, in all its parts, becomes an attribute of God."

most ordinary intelligence, and the least particle of reverent feeling, have allowed professions of attachment and discipleship to Apostles and Evangelists, to be associated and balanced, with professions of attachment and discipleship to Christ? Would not the declaration, *I am of Christ*, have been at once, and justly, felt to condemn and silence every factious watchword? St Paul’s ‘implied challenge’ does not hint that Christ is God. The evidence desiderated from the Canonical Writings is definite acknowledgment, or, at the very least, plainly probable implication, of Christ’s Deity. Mr Liddon meets the requirement by practically ignoring the passages which definitely ascribe Christ’s sufficiency to the Father’s plan and gifts, and by dragging inferences, more desperate than ingenious, out of vague and elastic materials. The process is only a variety of the familiar isolation, packing, straining, neglect of contexts, and intrusion of senses. Obscure, ambiguous, plastic, and figurative phrases are laid under contribution, and thus, arguments are fabricated to show—“A Divine Christ is implied in St Paul’s account of Faith;” and again, “in his account of Regeneration;” and that, “the doctrine of our Lord’s Divinity is the key to the greatest polemical struggle of the Apostle’s whole life—the controversy with the Judaizers.” Neither man nor angel having received a commission and endowments resembling those which God is expressly said to have bestowed on Christ, the Apostolical diction will, confessedly, fit neither man nor angel, and therefore; “my brethren, what becomes of this language, if Jesus Christ be not truly God?” (p. 348.) In the minds of those already convinced beyond all doubt and misgiving, that Christ is truly God, Mr Liddon’s pleadings will perhaps create satisfaction, but in the minds of those who study the Apostle’s words, and seek with open-mindedness to ascertain his meaning, they will create amazement.

Is one unprepossessed searcher of the Apostle’s writings, likely to be persuaded by wily manipulation of clauses, rent from the thought involved in closely adjacent expressions, that St Paul entertained the dogma of Christ’s Godhead, because he sets forth Christ as an Object of faith? It is the chicanery of polemics, and not sound reasoning, to start from the tacitly-assumed or loosely-stated premiss, ‘God alone is the Object of Christian faith.’ In the highest sense He is so; but is there no lower sense, and may not the Messiah, and the *One Mediator* between the *One God* and mankind, have an altogether exceptional standing, and unwonted claims? The truly pertinent question is—Does the

Apostle avow or enjoin belief in Christ as God ? Reasonable exposition can find no such avowal or injunction. Only by marvellously distorting inferences, and remorseless scorn for context, can the conclusion be made decently plausible : " In the spiritual teaching of St Paul, Christ eclipses God, if He is not God ; since it is emphatically Christ's Person, as warranting the preciousness of His work, which is the Object of justifying faith. Nor can it be shown that the intellect and heart and will of man, could conspire to give to God a larger tribute of spiritual homage than they are required by the Apostle to give to Christ " (p. 344).

Texts, which must regulate rational interpretation, clearly conduct to a conclusion totally different from the preceding. The condensed summary of St Paul's testimony, both to Jews and Greeks—" Repentance toward God, and faith toward our Lord Jesus Christ" (Acts xx. 21), plainly implies the supremely higher faith and duty, of which the One God and Father is the Object. And the Roman Christians are taught to regard themselves, as " being justified freely by God's grace, through the redemption that is in Christ Jesus, whom God set forth as a propitiation, through faith in (by ?) his blood, &c., that God may be just, and the Justifier of him who is of faith in Jesus " (Rom. iii. 24–26).

The commencing words of Romans v., duly read in their connection with verse 24 of the previous chapter, show that, in St Paul's mind, justifying faith was faith " on Him who raised Jesus our Lord from the dead," in strict keeping with another lucid statement in the same Epistle (x. 9)—" If thou shalt confess with thy mouth the Lord Jesus, and shalt believe in thine heart that God raised Him from the dead, thou shalt be saved." The saints, and faithful brethren also, at Colossae, are instructed to reckon themselves "raised with Christ in their baptism, through the faith in the operation of God, Who raised Him from the dead " (Col. ii. 12).

Faith in Jesus as God's Son and Messenger, and by God's edict, and in virtue of God's endowments, our Redeemer, Teacher, and Example here, and in his exaltation at God's right hand, the earnest of our glory hereafter, is confessedly among the items of a full Pauline faith in the Almighty Father, and the Almighty Father's methods. And this faith agrees with the doctrine dictated in those Canonical documents which Mr Liddon more particularly prizes. Characteristic features of Christian faith and knowledge are ; that " Christ came forth from, and was sent by, the Father" (John xvi. 27 ; xvii. 25) ; and, that " Jesus is the Christ, or Messiah, the Son of God " (John xx. 31 ; 1 John v. 1). If belief in Christ has the promise of everlasting life, it is in consequence of the loving purpose and will of Him Who gave and sent Christ (John iii. 16 ; vi. 40 ; 1 John iii. 23) ; and Jesus Himself is recorded to have said; " This is the work of God, that ye should believe in Him whom He sent." " Believe (or, ye believe) in God, believe also in me " (John vi. 29 ; xiv. 1). The very statements which magnify Jesus most, are, unless interpretation be dominated by distinct extra-Scriptural disclosure of His Deity, singularly inconsonant with the conception of His Deity. But, in the Lectures I am examining, argument is supposed to have prepared for the assertion,—

"It would, then, be a considerable error to recognize the doctrine of our Lord's Divinity only in those passages of St Paul's writings which distinctly assert it. The indirect evidence of the Apostle's hold upon the doctrine is much wider and deeper than to admit of being exhibited in a given number of isolated texts ; since the doctrine colours, underlies, interpenetrates the most characteristic features of his thought and teaching. The proof of this might be extended almost indefinitely " (p. 348).

Why not *quite* indefinitely? The presumed "evidence " is put together without regard to contexts, logic, or common sense.

Before quitting the subject of St Paul's testimony, candour and honesty require us to examine searchingly some prominent features which, from Mr Liddon's stand-point, are more prudently evaded than discussed. My use of the seemingly positive witness which the New Testament furnishes against the dogma of our Lord's proper Deity, has hitherto been allusive and incidental, rather than detailed and direct. I have had occasion to expose the weakness of the defences, rather than actively to assail the position defended. But there are texts in the writings of St Paul which have no rational significance at all, if they do not exclude the doctrine for which Mr Liddon contends. I argue, of course, from the Protestant ground, that Holy Scripture contains a Revelation addressed to the human intelligence, and is a sufficient Rule for the instruction of the human mind in matters of Faith, as well as of practice. From the Catholic ground, that Scripture is only a subordinate factor in a complex Rule, and is constructed by Divine Wisdom to be valueless in relation to the mysteries of the Faith, apart from the Church's authoritative interpreting voice, merely logical deductions have manifestly no place, and merely rational conclusions no weight. The weakness of Mr Liddon's book results from the fact of his not avowedly standing upon the Catholic ground, but writing as though reason could follow the steps, and reach the decisions of ecclesiastical inspiration, in ascertaining the sense of documents which are themselves adapted by inspiration to veil their meaning from every gaze but that of Divinely-illuminated ecclesiastical insight. I disclaim the notion that, in criticising his pleas, I am dealing with the broad and comprehensive question, whether his doctrine is true or false ; I deal only with the narrow and partial question, whether it can or cannot be proved from Scripture, by proofs which the human understanding can comprehend and accept. My clerical brethren will readily perceive the wide difference between the two questions ; and signs are not wanting that educated laymen are awakening to perceive capability of Scripture proof, to be no necessary credential of the profound mysteries on which the Orthodox presentation of Christian faith and worship turns.

But, descending from the higher Catholic level, to Protestant principle, and the intelligence common to man ; if the dogma of Christ's Godhead had been broached in St Paul's days, and he had wished to deny it, his formal negative might, indeed, have been more pointed in shape, but scarcely more positive in substance, than some expressions which he has actually employed. Of course, a theory has been elaborated to explain away the opposition,—so palpable to the unsuppressed intellect,—between Church dogma and Apostolic teaching. The distinctive form of St Paul's Christology leads him, we are apprized, to insist upon the truth of our Lord's Humanity, and to dwell upon Christ's Manhood as the Instrument of Mediation between God and Man.

" It is as Man that Christ is contrasted with our first parent ; and it is in virtue of His Manhood that He is our Mediator, our Redeemer (1 Tim. ii. 5, 6), our Saviour from Satan's power, our Intercessor with the Father (Heb. ii. 14 ; v. 1). Great stress, indeed, does St Paul lay upon the Manhood of Christ, as the instrument of His mediation between earth and heaven, as the channel through which intellectual truth and moral strength descend from God into the souls of men, as the Exemplar wherein alone human nature has recovered its ideal beauty, as entering a sphere wherein the Sinless One could offer the perfect world-representing sacrifice of a truly obedient Will. So earnestly and constantly does St Paul's thought dwell on our Lord's Mediating Humanity, that to unreflecting persons his language might at times appear to imply that Jesus Christ is personally an inferior being, external to the Unity of the Divine Essence. Thus he tells the Corinthians, "that Christians have one Lord Jesus Christ as well as One God (1 Cor. viii. 6). Thus he reminds St Timothy that there is One God, and One Mediator between God and man—the Man Christ Jesus, Who gave Himself a ransom for all (1 Tim. ii. 5, 6). Thus he looks forward to a day when the Son Himself also, meaning thereby Christ's sacred Manhood, shall be subject to Him That put all things under Him, that God may be all in all (1 Cor. xv. 28). It is at least certain that no modern Humanitarian could recognize the literal reality of our Lord's Humanity with more explicitness than did the Apostle, who had never seen Him on earth, and to whom He had been made known by visions which a Docetic enthusiast might have taken as sufficient warrant for denying His real participation in our flesh and blood " (pp. 305-307).

But this limitation of obnoxious texts to our Lord's mediating Manhood admits of no justification. To the unbiassed expositor it must seem purely arbitrary, and nothing better than an expedient for reconciling with a foregone dogmatic conclusion, language of which the simple natural meaning is adverse. And the expedient is not reinforced by bold affirmations about the "Apostle's general teaching," and specious concessions that, "particular texts, when duly isolated from that teaching, may be pressed with plausible effect into the service of Arian or Humanitarian theories." The particular texts in question lose none of their *primâ facie* rational significance, when studied in the closest connection with their contexts; and their sense is, besides, too specific and complete for any isolation to affect it. When we examine them, the perverse sophistry of the pleading which seeks to shun their force, becomes very evident.

" None other is God except One. For though there be that are called gods, whether in heaven or upon earth (as there be gods many, and lords many), yet to us there is One God, the Father, of (from) Whom are all things and we for (unto) Him, and One Lord, Jesus Christ, through Whom are all things, and we through Him " (1 Cor. viii. 4-6).

Now here, in the reference to the heathen gods and lords, there is an allusion to the division into greater and lesser deities, the imaginary superhuman powers, celestial and terrestrial, of the idolatrous pantheon. In that classification the *lords* were, doubtless, inferior to the *gods*, and were supposed to hold intermediate places and offices between the gods and mankind; they were often, only deified creatures. The Apostle, therefore, introduces the distinction between the One God, and the One

Lord, of Christians, in a manner which must inevitably have
taught the Corinthians to deem Christ external, and inferior,
to the Godhead, unless they were in possession of some secret
and explicit oral teaching which adequately neutralized the
subtle and designed inaccuracy of the Written Word. And,
besides, the Apostle's language is in itself a direct, unconditional
declaration, "*there is no God but One*, namely, *the Father.*"

Mr Liddon feels the opposing weight of the text, and in a
Note to p. 306, has condescended to quibble as follows : " Here,
however, (1.) *Lord*, as contrasted with *God*, implies no necessary
inferiority, else we must say that the Father is not *Lord*;*
while (2.) the clause, *through Whom are all things, and we
through Him*, which cannot be restricted to our Lord's redemptive work without extreme exegetical arbitrariness, and which
certainly refers to His creation of the Universe, places Jesus
Christ on a level with the Father. Compare the position of διὰ
(*through*) between ἰξ (*of* or *from*) and εἰς (*for*), Rom xi. 36
(compare Col. i. 16). Our Lord is here distinguished from the
One God as being Human as well as Divine." This is indeed
the weakest of shuffling evasions. *Lord*, though in itself a lower,
and by no means exclusive designation, (see Matt. xv. 27 ; xxi.
30 ; xxvii. 63 ; Luke xvi. 3, 5, 8 ; xix. 33 ; John xii. 21 ; xx. 15;
Acts x. 4 ; xvi, 16, 19, 30 ; xxv. 26 ; Rev. vii. 14), is, when
used of the Almighty, equivalent to *God*, simply because it is
so used ; but *God* is the supreme title of dominion, and covers
all imaginable rights and claims of Lordship.

The fact of all things being instrumentally *through* Christ,
does not put Him on a level with the Father, *from Whom are
all things*, but allots Him, so far as a brief expression can, a
distinctly secondary inferior position, by implying He was the
ministerial channel, and not the original Source and Possessor
of creative power. In what sense and manner the Apostle
believed Christ to have been the Father's Instrument in creation

---

* The argument that the title *Lord*, being often applied to the Father, is
not necessarily inferior to *God*, though contemptible enough, is, in form, a
shade better than that which Bloomfield borrowed from Dr Pye Smith :
"The Deity of Christ can no more be denied because the Father is here
called the One God, than the dominion of the Father can be denied because
the Son is called the One Lord." Bloomfield continued : " By this mode of
expression it is intimated that Father and Son are one God, and one Lord, in
the Unity of the Godhead." Exactly so, to those whom carelessness or
prepossession qualifies to receive the intimation ; but, then, by what other
mode of expression, short of formal negation, could it be intimated that
the Father and Son are *not* "one God, and one Lord, in the Unity of the
Godhead ?"

(if, indeed, the text refers to creation generally), we cannot say. Perhaps his ideas on the subject were no clearer than our own ; but, when we are interpreting his language, we have no warrant to deny, in the teeth of his words, that Christ was an Instrument, because to our understandings, creation, through instrumental agency, appears incomprehensible or unlikely. The case stands thus : with unmistakeable clearness and abundant frequency, creation is, in Scripture, ascribed to God. In a very few phrases of somewhat obscure meaning, instrumental constructive action seems to be also ascribed to Christ. That the Omnipotent Father is the primary Fountain of Creative Energy, Will, and Might, is, therefore, indisputably a revelation contained in Scripture. If Mr Liddon admits the Father's having made Christ His Instrument in the work of creation, and then contends that, because the power of the Highest was exerted through Christ, therefore Christ is on a level with the Highest, his reasoning needs no refutation.

The assertion, " The One Lord is distinguished from the One God, as being Human, as well as Divine," is purely gratuitous. If Christ is really God, His Humanity is not the seat of His distinct personality, and does not annul or lower His Deity. Evidence of the greatest weight and strength is necessary to render feasible the conjecture ; St Paul's language to the Corinthians was the utterance of a sincere man, whose fully expressed faith would have been, " to us there is One God, and One Lord *Who is both God and Man.*" The additional proposition imports a new and confusing element, which, in the absence of cogent proof, only blind prejudice will be content to accept.

A text parallel to that just examined is Eph. iv. 6, the sense of which undoubtedly is ; " God is the God and Father of all in every conceivable respect, exerting power *over* all, acting *through* all, and dwelling *in* all" (Winer). The way in which the Apostle's language divides Him from the *one Lord*, would seem to have been devised for the very purpose of misleading and bewildering the intellect, if they are both enclosed in the same Nature, and bound together by inseparable unity of Being. But the text has been, by theological dogmatists, explained to imply the existence and activity of the whole Trinity, in the following fashion : " *Over all* as Father ; *through all* by the Word ; and *in all* by the Holy Ghost," a commentary which strikingly exhibits the effect of the later and extra-Scriptural stages of Revelation, in irradiating the earlier, and bringing hidden things to light.

The restricting of the description—*a man Christ Jesus who gave Himself a ransom for all* (1 Tim. ii. 5, 6) to our Lord's Mediating Humanity, is mere caprice, exercised in subservience to dogmatic exigency. Elsewhere, Mr Liddon insists, the doctrine of Christ's Godhead is requisite to 'redeem from exaggeration, the New Testament representations of the effects of His Death.' It is needless to inquire whether this way of putting the case is empty verbal structure, or the expression of real ideas. To me it appears to be mainly the former, but it is among the accredited methods of showing how the Canonical writers mean what they do not say. With genuine theological readiness to construct from his own ignorance, and draw upon his own imagination, Mr Liddon asks, in his final Lecture, " How was a real reconciliation between God and His creatures to be effected, unless the Reconciler had some natural capacity for mediating, unless he could represent God to man no less truly than man to God ?" (p. 478). St Paul, then, we must presume, contemplated only one side of this natural capacity, when he declared to Timothy; *there is One God, and one Mediator between God and men, a Man, Christ Jesus, who gave Himself a ransom for all.* But is it not in the highest degree improbable that St Paul should, in such a passage, omit all reference to our Lord's Divine Personal Being, and with misguiding inexactness, style Christ's Humanity *Himself ?* He writes of the One individual God of all mankind, and the one individual Mediator between God and mankind, and he calls the Mediator *a Man.* It may be argued ; if Christ's pre-existence be admitted, the fact of His Humanity does not exclude His possession of another nature, and Mr Liddon does remark (p. 312), that the phrase " *was manifested in the flesh* (1 Tim. iii. 16), at least implies that Christ existed before this manifestation." Whether the phrase really carries the asserted implication is very debateable, even if we leave out of our reckoning the important circumstance, that the reading, *which was manifested,* instead of, *who was manifested,* is found in the Latin Vulgate, and is otherwise not devoid of authority. But granting the implication of pre-existence, the fact remains,—in their simple, primary, unadulterated import, the words, *there is One God and one Mediator, &c.,* do exclude the Mediator from the Unity and Nature of Deity. If St Paul intended Timothy to infer the One Mediator was God, or God-man, there is nothing he may not have intended, and no connection is traceable between his language and his thoughts ; *One* may be the negation of unity ; *God* may mean *Man,* and *Man* may mean *God.*

In this same First Epistle to Timothy are two other passages which remarkably illustrate the extreme latency and reserve of Scriptural inspiration on the topic of Christ's Deity. One of these passages precedes, by only a few sentences, that already discussed, and is a doxology, wherein the Almighty is styled *Incorruptible, Invisible, Alone God* (i. 17). And in conjunction with this doxology, we cannot fail to notice, how the previous verse contains the statement; *that in me Jesus Christ might show forth all long-suffering, &c.*, a statement from which it might be argued, that Christ Jesus was believed to wield the prerogatives of Divinity, and so was, in the deeper thought of the Apostle, identified with God. But the immediately subsequent recognition of the *Invisible Only God*, forbids the argument, and indicates that, in the mind of the Apostle, Christ was not elevated to the height of Godhead.

The second passage to which I refer, is, what Mr Liddon justly considers to be, "the richest and most glorious of the doxologies occurring in St Paul's Epistles" : "Till the appearing of our Lord Jesus Christ, which in His Own times He will show, Who is the Blessed and Only Potentate, the King of kings, and Lord of lords, Who only hath immortality, dwelling in light unapproachable, Whom no man hath seen, nor can see ; to Him be honour and power eternal " (vi. 15, 16).

If the announcement, whose direct force is met with capricious conjectures about exclusive reference to our Lord's mediating Manhood, is read in connection with these doxologies which mark the opening and closing thoughts of the writer when composing the Epistle, there is no legitimate escape from concluding the Apostle to have meant in all plainness and sincerity, just what he said, when he reminded Timothy ; *there is one God, and one Mediator between God and men, a man, Christ Jesus.*

Mr Liddon's treatment of 1 Cor. xv. 28, is of a kind which would be denounced with unmeasured severity if it were employed in heterodox instead of orthodox advocacy. Presuming the Apostle's faith to have been that which the Church afterwards set forth, the natural sense of the expression, *the Son Himself*, would be, the Divine Son Who is " The Father's Equal, in that He is partaker of His Nature ; the Father's Subordinate, in that the Equality is eternally derived." To make the expression point exclusively to Christ's Sacred Manhood, is to indulge in very easy but perfectly unwarranted assumption. It points to Christ's entire Incarnate Being, and the connection in which it stands evinces, as far as words can evince, that the Apostle held that Being to occupy in relation to God, not only a place of economical orderly subordination, but a place of essential, natural inferiority. That our Lord's Humanity is the sole subject of the objectionable verb which bespeaks inferiority, may be " the opinion of St Augustine, St Jerome, Theodoret," and after them, of a long array of commentators who have sacrificed common sense and consistency to a controversial purpose. But repetition does not change assertion into proof, and if the Apostle wrote as a reasonable man to reasonable men, he designated Christ's Person in Its completeness, and not merely the enveloping created elements, which never had an individual existence apart from the Divine Personality. The mental confusion springing out of theological definitions when they are not aids to a submissively receptive faith, is to be seen in the fact that a clear, honest, and unreserving thinker, as St Paul is supposed by Protestants to have been, can be imagined to have known Christ's Person to be wholly Divine, and yet to have written, in a number of passages, as though the Manhood were, in distinction from the Divinity, a Personal Agent and Subject. Mr Liddon is not altogether blind to the dilemma, and seeks immunity through jugglings which tell their own tale. He starts boldly from a misinterpreted text ; " A writer who believed our Lord to be literally God (Rom. ix. 5), could not have supposed that, at the end of His mediatorial reign as Man, a new relation would be introduced between the Persons of the Godhead. The subordination ($\varkappa\alpha\tau\grave{\alpha}$ $\tau\acute{\alpha}\xi\iota\nu$) of the Son, is an eternal fact in the inner Being of God. But the *visible* subjection of His Humanity (with which His Church is so organically united as to be called *Christ* (1 Cor. xii. 12), to the supremacy of God, will be realised at the close of the present dispensation" (p. 306). How can Christ reign as Man when he possesses no Personal Manhood ? And, what visible subjection can there be of a Humanity linked indissolubly to Essential Godhead ?—unless, indeed, Mr Liddon will go so far as to affirm *the Son Himself* to be a sublime personification of ' the Church organically united with Christ's Humanity.' No cleverly raised dust of verbiage can hide the fact that in the Apostle's meaning, *God*, in verse 28, is the individual *God and Father* to Whom, according to verse 24, the Son will deliver up the Kingdom. Whatever obscurity may surround St Paul's summarily announced anticipation, this much at least is clear,—he held Christ's dominion to be conferred, and returnable after its purposes should have been accomplished, to Him Who conferred it : " God hath put all things under him : then cometh the end when He shall have delivered up the Kingdom to the God and Father."

The uniformly pervading conception which penetrates and shapes all the New Testament representations of Christ's Royalty distinctly reappears. Christ is highly exalted, delegated, Divinely equipped, and sustained, by the Father, and therefore, in His loftiest elevation and most exceptional capacities, is not God, or God's Equal, but God's Instrument, ruling under and for God. During the Mediatorial reign the Father retains His singular and unapproachable Sovereignty. "In saying all things are put under Christ, it is manifest that He (God) is excepted Who did put all things under Him" (ver. 27). The notion of some inscrutable Equality of Nature, combined with eternal derivation (whatever that may be) and formal subordination, is manifestly not what lay behind and prompted the Apostle's words, presuming always, his words were designed to impart and reveal, and not, for the Church's sake, to reserve and conceal, his mind.

The absolute superiority of God, together with the real and intelligible, and not merely formal and verbal inferiority of Christ, are clearly implied in two other passages of the first Corinthian Epistle, *Ye are Christ's, and Christ is God's* (iii. 23). *The head of every man is Christ, and the head of Christ is God* (xi. 3).

The Unity of God is incidentally affirmed by St Paul (Rom. iii. 30 ; Gal. iii. 20); and in Rom. xvi. 25-27, there is a form of doxology, sharply distinguishing between Jesus Christ, and Him Who is able to establish us according to the Gospel, *the Only Wise God.*

St Paul's Epistles contain the designation, five times repeated (Rom. xv. 6 ; 2 Cor. i. 3 ; xi. 31 ; Eph. i. 3 ; Col. i. 3), *the God and Father of our Lord Jesus Christ,* a designation not easily explicable if St Paul knew that Christ was Himself God. The same designation is found in the writings of another Apostle (1 Pet. i. 3). St Paul also speaks of *The God of our Lord Jesus Christ, the Father of glory* (Eph. i. 17).

Do not the often recurring phrases, *God the Father ; God our Father ; our God and Father,* when taken together with the texts which have in the last few pages been under consideration, and with the fact of St Paul's never in one single passage calling Christ *God,*[*] overwhelmingly denote the Apostle to have known

---

[*] I think I am now fairly entitled to affirm this, notwithstanding the ambiguity of Rom. ix. 5 ; Tit. ii. 13. If these texts could be perfectly isolated, grammatical construction would leave the question whether they refer to the Father, or to Jesus Christ, open ; and the considerations arising from habitual Pauline thought and language are conclusively against the latter reference. After a survey of St Paul's writings, the attempt to erect two ambiguous ex-

no God but the Father, however lofty his conceptions may have been of Christ's Person, dignity, and dominion?

And further, can we, after largest allowance for exaggeration, incidental to earnestness and rapid style, reconcile with the Apostle's presumed faith in Christ's Godhead, the form of the injunctions in which he exhorts wives to obey their husbands? Could a believer in the superlative claims of Christ's Godhead have written: "Wives, submit yourselves to your own husbands, as to the Lord. For the husband is the head of the wife, even as Christ is the Head of the Church. But as the Church is subject to Christ, so let the wives also be to their husbands, in everything?" (Eph. v. 22-24). Would not reverence and sound discretion forbid Mr Liddon, or any other orthodox divine, to use such language?

Again, the Apostle reminds the Galatian Christians how they did not despise him, *but received him as an angel of God, as Christ Jesus* (Gal. iv. 14). After every allowance, this language must appear distasteful and unseemly to a mind inhabited by the orthodox faith. Is it likely St Paul would have used such phraseology, if he had himself believed, and had instructed the Galatians to believe, 'Christ Jesus is truly God?' Assuming the Galatians to have been taught, the Lord Jesus is *the Great God*, and, *God blessed for ever;* with what respect, veneration, adoration, may we imagine they would have received Him! Did they accord to the Apostle a reception which, even in the greatest heat of composition, and the freest exaggeration of Eastern rhetoric, might be, without palpable falsehood and irreverence, compared to the reception they would have accorded to One Whom they held to be God Almighty?

Taking St Paul's teaching as a whole, and bringing to the study of it unprejudiced rational investigation, a conclusion contrary to the doctrine Mr Liddon advocates seems inevitable. The Bampton Lectures do not, after the manner of some older treatises on the same side of the controversy, indulge freely in abuse of those who differ, but the bitterness which assumes denial of Christ's Deity to issue from enmity to Him and His Gospel, and from a disposition to cavil at and reject Scripture testimony concerning Him, is not entirely absent. It is, however, as a rule, strangely misapplied, and comes with a very ill grace from expositors whose distinctive tenet compels them habitually to do

pressions into explicit declarations of Christ's Godhead, is seen to be ridiculous, unless we start from some postulate which removes the work of interpretation from the hands of reason.

violence to the plain force of Scripture language. From the ground of St Paul's writings, an appeal may be justly made to the honesty, intellectual conscientiousness, and common-sense, of all Protestants who, being persuaded the Apostle knew, and designed to promulgate, truth as it is in Jesus, claim him as a witness for the Divinity of Jesus. If Mr Liddon ever preaches from any of that class of Pauline texts which are *primâ facie* adverse to the Church's dogma, does he not find it needful first of all, to explain away the apparently obvious sense and implication, and to show "unreflecting" hearers how the Apostle could not have really meant what he seems to say? Does he not feel the necessity of furnishing from his own resources, the information which the Apostle withholds, and the judicious caution which the Apostle lacks? Would he, without resorting to defensive and modifying explanation, employ, as the Apostle does, phraseology which distinguishes sharply between the *One God*, and the *one Lord?* Would he assert the Unity of the Godhead, using seemingly exclusive and contrasting terms, in the very same sentences which refer to and name Jesus Christ? If St Paul's language had not the sanctity of Canonical authority, and were now for the first time introduced, would it not be denounced as dangerous, heretical, and even pointedly counter to the ecclesiastical definitions of faith? Is it at all such language as might be expected to issue from the mind and pen of a truthful, and ordinarily prudent, orthodox man? Would any orthodox preacher be contented simply to draw it together, and recite it, without fencing, neutralizing, comments? The circumstance that in Apostolic days the doctrine of Christ's Deity was a novel doctrine, ‘a great discovery to be borne by the capacities of Jews and heathens,’ did not make its lucid avowal the less, but the more needful, and rendered every apparently conflicting statement doubly perilous. If Mr Liddon were restricted to St Paul's diction, could he make the dogmatic trumpet give a certain sound? Could he frame explicit unambiguous inculcation that our Lord is truly God? The exact defining phrases of ecclesiastical theology are all extra-Scriptural, and have, in truth, been devised to supply the deficiencies of the Canonical phraseology. Not to mention more scholastic and abstract terms, the appellation *God the Son* occurs nowhere in the Scriptures. Yet, given the position, ‘Christ is indeed God,’ and that appellation arises by natural, inevitable suggestion, and is sure to be often substituted for the Scriptural *Son of God*, which, if not emptied of intrinsic meaning, cuts away the attributes of eternity and independent, Self-contained Subsistence.

M

Protestants, who accept the Church's definitions respecting Christ's Person, have therefore, clearly, no right to upbraid their brethren who reject them. Men who dare not repeat without supplementary and guarding additions, numerous, simple, and distinct Scriptural utterances; men who have learned from experience the inadequacy of Scripture terms for the due expression of an Orthodox faith, lay themselves open to well-merited and not stinted retort, when they venture to charge their opponents with hostility to Gospel truth, and unwillingness to be guided by the Sacred Writings.

The increasing body of Protestants, whose consciences, a rational understanding of the Scriptures they diligently search, teaches to deny the proper Deity of Christ, do not fancy they possess materials enabling them to differentiate with exactitude Christ's pre-incarnate nature from the nature of all other spiritual intelligences; but they believe, on the strength of testimony which many of them, in common with their Orthodox brethren, hold to be inspired and revealing, that our Lord's Being is in its every aspect, originated, derived, produced, subordinate, and dependent; and, therefore, indubitably *not* the Eternal, Self-existent Essence, whatever else it may be. The Bible, they conceive, instructs them to affirm with unhesitating confidence, 'Christ is *not* Very God;' and, adhering consistently to Protestant principle, they attach little importance to the ecclesiastical revelation which would rectify their error by superseding their intellect, and showing them how the letter and manner of Scripture are more mysterious and supernatural than any matter which Scripture contains. The fundamental faultiness of Protestantism in relation to the tenets of Nicene theology is, doubtless, the notion that the Word of God in the Bible is directly addressed to the reason and the heart of all who will with devout care study it. But the Catholic Churchman knows that the Bible is the Church's Book, and that, withdrawn from the Church's light, its revelations cannot be read aright. The reserved and concealed meaning of the inspired penmen, the inspired Church draws forth. In the Spirit they speak mysteries, in the Spirit also, the Church interprets.

And this rule of interpretation is singularly exemplified in the instance of those particular texts of St Paul which are, Mr Liddon concedes, liable to be pressed with plausible effect into the service of erroneous theories. Rationally, according to the customary laws of thought and language, there is no excuse whatever for eliminating the apparently plain sense of St Paul's words, by imagining he was anxious to insist on so recondite a truth as the reality of our Lord's Manhood, or anxious duly to recognize a doctrine so hard to understand and retain, as the derivation of Christ's Sonship from the Person of the Father.

The discourses of St Paul preserved in the Acts of the Apostles, can hardly be pronounced, even by the most penetrating of ecclesiastically-minded commentators, to exhibit our Lord's Deity more convincingly than do the Pauline Epistles, but then, the Acts being a Canonical document, its records were moulded by the characteristic inspiration of secretiveness and reserve, and may, therefore, contain no samples of the Apostle's ordinary manner of preaching. Starting from the Church's assurance that the dogma of our Lord's Godhead was always a most vital, prominent part of the faith delivered to the saints, we must surmise St Paul's oral teaching to have been in general marked by such a vivid and earnest inculcation of the dogma, that his hearers, through dwelling upon it disproportionately, were exposed to peril from specious heresies which controverted the reality of Christ's Human Nature, and were also liable to forget how a Divine and Necessary Being, comprised in the Self-existent Substance and lacking no attribute of Deity, was, nevertheless, derived, and relatively subordinate. To the Protestant mind this surmise wears an air of arbitrariness, but it aids the Catholic to discern the descent through the Church, of the grand truth of St Paul's oral teaching, while his Epistles are seen to guard against once-attractive errors, which portions of his oral addresses were wrested to sanction.

CHAPTER VIII.

The title *Son* as expressive of relationship to God.—Supposed indications in
the Old Testament, of a Divine Sonship internal to the Being of God.
—Synoptists' use of the title *Son of God.*—Mr Liddon's attempt to
show that *the Son* is identical with *the Logos* or *Word,* and that the
two descriptions complete and guard each other.—The expanded title,
Only-begotten Son.—Weakness of Mr Liddon's position metaphysically.
—His view of the bearing of the miracles upon the question of Christ's
Person.—His deductions from the Self-assertion exhibited in the first
or Ethical stage of our Lord's teaching.—Difficulties connected with our
Lord's exposure to temptation, &c.—Mr Liddon's arbitrary, evasive
treatment of a troublesome saying reported by two Evangelists.—In-
ferences drawn from the authoritativeness of Christ's teaching.—Did
He ratify the Pentateuch as a whole?

IN a note (p. 10), illustrating the use of the title *sons,* in the Old
Testament, to express relationship to God, Mr Liddon says :—

"The singular, *My Son, The Son,* is used only in prophecy of
the Messiah (Ps. ii. 7, 12 ; and Acts xiii. 33 ; Heb. i. 5 ; v. 5),
and in what is believed to have been a Divine manifestation,
very probably of God the Son (Dan. iii. 25).   The line of David
being the line of the Messiah, culminating in the Messiah, as in
David's One perfect Son, it was said in a lower sense of each
member of that line, but in its full sense only of Messiah, ' I
will be to Him a Father, and He shall be to Me a Son' (2 Sam.
vii. 14 ; Heb. i. 5 ; Ps. lxxxix. 27).   The application of the title
to collective Israel in Hos. xi. 1, is connected by St Matthew (ii.
15), with its deeper force as used of Israel's One true Heir and
Representative.   Compare, too, the mysterious intimations of
Prov. xxx. 4 ; Ecclus. li. 10, of a Divine Sonship internal to the
Being of God."

These statements are perhaps worthy of a few remarks.   The
Hebrew being confessedly ambiguous, and the Septuagint and
Vulgate Versions, together with some of the best modern Hebraists, being against the translation, *Kiss the Son,* it is not the
part of either sound scholarship or prudence to insist that Ps.
ii. 12, refers to the Messiah.

Until the phrases *God the Son,* and *a Son of God,* shall have
been shown to be interchangeable, there cannot be the faintest

reasonable pretence for thinking a manifestation of *God the Son* is described in Dan iii. 25.   Does Mr Liddon imagine Nebuchadnezzar, or the writer who relates his words, to have had any conception of such a manifestation ?

In quoting for a controversial purpose 2 Sam. vii. 14; Heb. i. 5, it should in fairness be remembered, the exact force of the Hebrew, the Septuagint, and the New Testament Text, is : " I will be to Him as (or for) a Father, and He shall be to Me as (or for) a Son."   Mr Liddon wishes his readers to see an averment of Paternity and of Sonship of the strictest, closest kind, but overlooks the circumstance that in the language, accurately rendered, such a sense does not exist.   Even in its English shape, the text does not amount to, " I am His Father, and He is My Son."

How the full significance of Ps. lxxxix. 26, 27, can ally itself advantageously with the requirements of Mr Liddon's theme, I am not at all able to perceive.   The words spoken through the Psalmist, are, " He shall cry unto Me, Thou art my Father, my God, and the rock of my salvation.   Also, I will make Him My First-born, higher than the kings of the earth."   (See likewise the preceding and subsequent contexts.)

If the first Evangelist has, in his application of Hos. xi. 1, brought out the real intention of that passage, the fact may be taken as an additional symptom of the total incapacity of reason to understand the utterances of inspiration.   The prophet's words must be quite wrenched away from their context, and from all the ostensible train of his thought, before they will bear the sense imposed in Matt. ii. 15.*   The difference by no means suffices to prove, the Evangelist quoted either inexactly, or from a faulty text, but the Septuagint Version, which in all probability was made from a Hebrew Text older than that in use when the first Gospel was written, reads ; *out of Egypt I called his children.*

---

* Such an application of Old Testament phraseology as that in Matthew ii. 15, is quite in the style of second and third century Christian writings, but hardly in keeping with the generally superior caution and insight of the Evangelists.   Is it not due to the Evangelists that we should ascribe any manifestly erroneous use of Old Testament expressions, not to them, but to editors and transcribers whose copyings were anterior to the oldest Manuscripts and Versions now extant?   That the best Text of the present day faithfully represents the Evangelical narratives in their first form, may be, to Orthodox apprehensions, a wholesome belief for the multitude, but will not commend itself to the minds of men who have attentively considered the subject,—a subject about which there is either strange ignorance, or most conscientious lying for God, on the part of not a few popular theological writers.

If intimations of a Divine Sonship internal to the Being of God are contained in Prov. xxx. 4 ; Ecclus. li. 10, their mysteriousness is most unquestionable ; but here, again, we should bear in mind how in Proverbs, the Vatican Septuagint reads, *what is the name of his children ?* instead of, *what is his son's name ?* The Alexandrine MS. has, *what is the name of his child* (τέχνον) ?

A man who is able to discover in the expression, *the Lord, the Father of my lord,* in the last chapter of Ecclesiasticus, an intimation of a duality of Co-equal Persons in the Almighty Nature, may be expected to cling to his discovery with much tenacity. The expression is obscure, which, assuming the inspiration of the book, is, so far, an argument that it was designed to contribute through the Church to the revelation of deep Christian mystery.

Mr Liddon contends :—

"In the Synoptic Gospels Christ is called the Son of God in a higher sense than the ethical or than the theocratic. In the Old Testament, an anointed king or a saintly prophet is a son of God. Christ is not merely one among many sons. He is the Only, the Well-beloved Son of the Father. His relationship to the Father is unshared by any other, and is absolutely unique. It is indeed probable that of our Lord's contemporaries many applied to Him the title *Son of God* only as an official designation of the Messiah ; while others used it to acknowledge that surpassing and perfect character which proclaimed Jesus of Nazareth to be the One Son, Who had appeared on earth, worthily showing forth the moral perfections of our Heavenly Father. But the official and ethical senses of the term are rooted in a deeper sense, which St Luke connects with it at the beginning of his Gospel. 'The Holy Ghost shall come upon thee,' so ran the angel-message to the Virgin-mother, 'and the power of the Highest shall overshadow thee : therefore also that Holy Thing Which shall be born of thee shall be called the Son of God' (St Luke i. 35). This may be contrasted with the prediction respecting St John the Baptist, that he should be filled with the Holy Ghost even from his mother's womb (i. 15). St John then is in existence before his sanctification by the Holy Spirit ; but Christ's Humanity Itself is formed by the agency of the Holy Ghost" (p. 247).

The precise reason assigned in the third Gospel, for calling Christ *the Son of God,* is, that an immediate direct action of Divine power took the place of God's customary working through the established laws of human paternity. According to St Luke, Christ is the Son of God, because the Almighty, in a miraculous and exceptional way, caused His conception in the Virgin's womb. In virtue of His miraculously-produced human nature, He is in a special manner God's Son. Yet, in his fifth Lecture, a few pages before the passage last quoted, Mr Liddon strenuously argues, *the Son* is identical with the *Logos* or *Word* :—

"The Word is also the Son. As applied to our Lord, the title *Son of God* is protected by epithets which sustain and define its unique significance. In the Synoptic Gospels, Christ is termed the *well-beloved* Son. In St Paul He is God's *Own* Son (Rom. viii. 3 and 32). In St John He is the Only-begotten Son, or simply the Only-begotten. This last epithet surely means, not merely that God has no other such Son, but that His Only-begotten Son is, in virtue of this Sonship, a partaker of that incommunicable and imperishable Essence, Which is sundered from all created life by an impassable chasm. If St Paul speaks of the Resurrection as manifesting this Sonship to the world (Acts xiii. 32, 33 ; Rom. i. 4 : compare on the other hand, Heb. v. 8), the sense of the word *Only-begotten* remains in St John, and it is plainly defined by its context to relate to something higher than any event occurring in time, however great or beneficial to the human race. . . . Each of these expressions, the Word and the Son, if taken alone, might have led to a fatal misconception. . . . The bare metaphors of *Word* and *Son*, taken separately, might lead divergent thinkers to conceive of Him to Whom they are applied, on the one side as an impersonal quality or faculty of God, on the other, as a concrete and personal, but inferior and dependent being. But combine them, and each corrects the possible misuse of the other. The *Logos*, Who is also the Son, cannot be an impersonal and abstract quality ; since such an expression as the Son would be utterly misleading, unless it implied at the very least the fact of a personal subsistence distinct from that of the Father. On the other hand, the Son, who is also the Logos, cannot be of more recent origin than the Father, since the Father cannot be conceived of as subsisting without that Eternal Thought or Reason Which is the Son. Nor may the Son be deemed to be in any respect, save in the order of Divine subsistence, inferior to the Father, since He is identical with the eternal intellectual Life of the Most High. Thus each metaphor re-enforces, supplements, and protects the other. Taken together, they exhibit Christ before

His Incarnation as at once personally distinct from, and yet equal with the Father; He is That personally subsisting and ' Eternal Life, Which was with the Father, and was manifested unto us' (1 St John i. 2)." (Pp. 233–235).

With whatever ingenuity, and clothing of graceful diction, this kind of speculation is presented, its factitious and baseless character cannot be concealed. Before we can truthfully allege the terms *Word* and *Son* to be mutually sustaining, supplementary, and guarding, the former must be shown to suggest lucid and definite ideas. Are not words put for things in a very shallow and foolishly pretentious way, when the Personal Son is defined to be, "that Eternal Thought or Reason without Which the Father cannot be conceived of as subsisting;" and again, is affirmed to be "identical with the Eternal Intellectual Life of the Most High." If the Father is personally God, and the Son also personally God, then clearly the Eternal Thought, or Reason, or Intellectual Life of the Most High, is double. As the case stands, the designation *Logos* is so vague that the pre-conceptions of any unflinching dogmatist, or random theorist, may be thrust into it. No hint is given by the Evangelist why Christ is called *the Word*, and Christ is not recorded to have ever called Himself by that name.* In handling such a term nothing can be grasped by the intellect, and the theological spinner draws either from independent knowledge, or an active imagination, the materials of his web. The fact that so much of the weight

---

* Mr Liddon sees in this fact an argument for the accurately historical character of the last Evangelical narrative. "If St John had been creating a fictitious Jesus designed to illustrate a particular theosophic speculation, he would have represented our Lord as announcing His Divinity in the terms in which it is announced in the Prologue to the Gospel." But does this conclusion follow? The Evangelist may have moulded and amplified selected facts and sayings, to suit an honestly-entertained theory, and yet may have felt himself debarred by existing beliefs and documents from putting his own speculations explicitly into the mouth of Jesus. If, moreover, we do not, in submission to the Church, exclude all really inquisitive criticism, we have no right to assume that the matter of the fourth Gospel generally, is in unison with its Prologue understood as the majority of Christians understand it. Whether the work of the latest Evangelist is a consistent whole, and whether its details are reconcilable with the Synoptic records, are questions which must, from the Protestant ground, be decided by free and patient inquiry. Our knowledge about the earliest forms of Christian literature is very scanty, and we cannot extricate our slender materials from the gloom of a dim twilight. We may, of course, easily construct after the pattern of our own fixed opinions, and weave scraps and fragments into an artificial and imposing chain; but our duty is to pronounce, with tolerant diffidence, a verdict true according to such evidence as we possess.

of Mr Liddon's edifice is made to rest on an epithet which is applied to Christ only in the first fourteen verses of the Gospel which the Church pronounces to be St John's, is very significant. *The Word of Life* (1 John i. 1), and *the Word of God* (Revelation xix. 13), are titles to which it is comparatively easy to affix a meaning,—the offices of Christ in proclaiming the doctrines of life, and the messages of God, being adequately explanatory. But no thoughtful man, who is careful to have ideas behind his words, will venture to speak confidently about the never-repeated and extremely opaque expression, commonly translated, *the Word was God.* To Mr Liddon this one expression is indispensable, and prolific of meaning, the maxims of his exegesis apparently inculcating, not only, that the Canonical documents have a peculiar organic unity, but also, that the key to vital doctrine is supplied by the rarest and darkest phrases of a single writer.

That the designation *Son of God* is sufficiently distinctive to be an indication of Divinity, or, to " suggest the reproduction in the Son of all qualities of the Father," sober judgment will shrink from affirming in the face of such texts as Matt. v. 9, 45 ; Luke xx. 36 ; Rom. viii. 14, 19 ; ix. 26. And the protecting, sustaining, defining epithets, *beloved, own, only-begotten,* to which Mr Lidden points, do not help his argument, to say nothing of the fact, that the application of the last named to Christ, is confined to the Fourth Gospel and the First Epistle of John (John i. 14, 18 ; iii. 16, 18 ; 1 John iv. 9), documents, in both of which Christ is designated *the Son,* and, *the Son of God,* with great frequency. What is, upon every reasonable interpretation of Scripture language, so fatally against Mr Liddon's dogma, is the constant employment of the word *Son,* to denote our Lord's relationship to God. The track of Old and New Testament usage, along its whole extent, demonstrates filial relationship to the Almighty, to have been ascribed to beloved and favoured, but created and dependent, beings. The very last way of teaching a Jew to esteem a particular personage in very truth *God,* would have been to call him *Son of God.* To say, Sonship implies identity of Nature, is, moreover, to press the loose analogy furnished by the conditions of human life, beyond the limits which reverence and common sense prescribe. Neither in its simpler forms, nor in its Johannine expansion, *only begotten Son,* does the filial title warrant raids of presumptuous fancy into recesses of the Divine Nature.

Mr Liddon leans on the term *only-begotten,* and after remarking with Tholuck, that in Luke vii. 12 ; viii. 42 ; ix. 38 ; Heb.

xi. 17 ;* it signifies "that which exists once only, that is, singly
in its kind,"—he leaps to the conclusion ; "God has one Only
Son Who by Nature and necessity is His Son." But this is obviously nothing better than blindly rash, not to say irreverent,
deduction. The very utmost the term can indicate, is that the
mode of Christ's origination or production was, in some sense
unique, not, certainly, that the Divine Nature includes arrangements for an ineffable reproduction, doubling, and propagation of
Itself in the entirety of Its attributes. And Mr Liddon must be
conscious that, interpreted rationally, and by the light the Bible
itself seems to afford, the term probably means, in any application which is not very definitely physical and literal, *well-beloved,
specially dear.* The Hebrew word corresponding to *only, only-
begotten,* is frequently rendered in the Septuagint Version, *beloved*
(Gen. xxii. 2, 12, 16 ; Jer. vi. 26 ; Amos viii. 10 ; Zech. xii.
10 ; Prov. iv. 3). In Pss. xxii. 20; xxxv. 17, Fuerst and Gesenius
take the word to denote *life* or *soul,* life being at once most
dear, and to its possessor *the only* thing of its kind. The Septuagint Translators render, in these two instances, *my only-begotten ;* the Anglican, *my darling,* with the marginal alternative
my only one. In Judges xi. 34, and Ps. xxv. 16, the Greek Version has *only-begotten.*

Looking at these facts, we see there is no firm ground for the
confident assurance Mr Liddon feels about the sense of that adjective which is, in its literal and primary meaning, *only-begotten.*
It may be equivalent to *beloved, dearest ;* certainly, Isaac was
not in strictness Abraham's *only* or *only-begotten son* (Heb. xi.
17), but had brothers older and younger (Gen. xvi. 15 ; xxv. 2).
Our Lord being styled in the synoptical Gospels *the beloved Son*
(comp. Col. i. 13) the question naturally arises, whether the epithet applied to Him in the Fourth Gospel, and the First Epistle
of John, is to be understood in harmony with the other Scriptures, or regarded as a supplementary and higher title, a step on-
wards, in the progressive revelation of our Lord's Person. On
the word *begotten,* no stress can be legitimately laid, because the
very writings which call Christ *only-begotten,* say, Christians are
begotten of God. (John i. 13 ; 1 John iii. 9 ; iv. 7 ; v. 1, 18).

Granting, however, that our Lord's Sonship is solitary and exceptional, still it is Sonship, and the reality of the filial relation
is, we must confess, rather intensified than lowered by the Johan-

* The only places, besides the five previously referred to, in which the
word occurs in the New Testament. Since St Luke uses the adjective, the
fact of his *not* applying it to our Lord, is the more noticeable.

nine epithet. And does not Sonship, just in proportion to its reality, suggest posteriority, derivation, and some sort of dependence. The difficulty with which Mr Liddon fails to cope, is the reconciliation of Sonship with necessary Co-existence, Co-eternity, and equality of Attributes. When he admits; " The Son is in the order of Divine Subsistence inferior to the Father," and again ; " From the Father, Christ eternally receives an equality of life and power, and therefore, as being a recipient, He is so far subordinate to the Father " (p. 323), we may justly challenge him to give to his words a meaning which shall be intelligible, and at the same time not discordant with his dogma. If Christ is absolutely God, we simply darken counsel by words without knowledge, when we call Him a *recipient, subordinate,* and *begotten.* He has received nothing which could have been imparted, and nothing which could have been withheld. His existence is in no way whatever dependent on the Personal Father's power and Will, but He is, equally with the Father, everlastingly and necessarily comprised in the Self-existent Substance. The Divine Nature cannot be contemplated as having ever existed without Him. But, when sameness of Substance, Co-equality, Co-eternity, and Necessary Existence, have been predicated,—recipiency, derivation, origination, sonship, begottenness, inferiority, are terms conspicuously inapplicable, and divorced from every comprehensible idea. The employment of them puts an end to reasoning, the common ground of rational understanding being deserted, and words no longer available symbols for the conveyance of thought. As a metaphysical tenet, the doctrine Mr Liddon maintains necessitates perfectly contemptible shuffling and inanity. If the question were pressed ; How can Self-existent Being either impart or derive " equality of life and power ?" the answer would be ; the impartation and derivation were eternal,—' the Son was generated eternally.' And if (assuming the generation was some actual process) we were closely to inquire, what is meant by ' generated eternally,' as distinguished from generated in time, the final response must be,—not generated at all, in any mode man's understanding can conceive or human words describe. We do not cover, but rather lay bare the emptiness of our defining language, when we put a procedure supposed to be real, backward, and backward, to infinity. The introduction of that "unknown quantity," Eternity, is indeed, manifestly, only a verbal refuge from the contradiction involved in a Sonship which leaves the Father and the Son, the Originator and the Originated, enclosed in the same Unbegun, Undivided Essence, and yet, awards to each, Personal Being, and possession of the totality of the Divine Attributes. The Orthodox enunciation of the Deity of God's *Only-begotten Son*, is, in its metaphysical phases, a hopeless puzzle, from which merely rational minds must always retreat in compassion and despair.

Convinced that a reasonable interpretation of our Lord's sayings supports the Church's traditional faith, Mr Liddon declares boldly; "The Apostles lived with One Who asserted Himself, by implication and expressly, to be personally God" (p. 272). But for this declaration, as for so many of Mr Liddon's propositions, there exists only the slenderest and most imperfect basis— just enough to excuse the adhesion of an honest and strongly biassed mind, trained from childhood in a particular school of prevalent Christian thought,—but nothing more. Arguments against Orthodoxy, resting on similarly insufficient grounds, would be righteously received with derisive indignation, and be too speedily and effectively refuted ever to reappear.

Before entering upon " the very heart of our great subject, and penetrating to the inmost shrine of Christian truth," the question, namely, " what position did Jesus Christ, either tacitly or explicitly, claim to occupy in His intercourse with men ?"—Mr Liddon devotes a few pages to the consideration of Christ's miracles, in which he discerns, not merely evidential value, but " physical and symbolic representations of Christ's redemptive action as the Divine Saviour of mankind." He not only descries the more general indications of redemptive power, but, with piercing and consistent ecclesiastical intuition, detects foreshadowings of the central vitalities of the Church's system, the Holy Sacraments.

" The drift and meaning of such a miracle as that in which our Lord's *Ephphatha* brought hearing and speech to the deaf and dumb, is at once apparent when we place it in the light of the Sacrament of baptism (St Mark vii. 34, 35). The feeding of the five thousand is remarkable as the one miracle which is narrated by all the Evangelists ; and even the least careful among readers of the Gospel cannot fail to be struck with the solemn actions which precede the wonder-work, as well as by the startling magnificence of the result. Yet the permanent significance of that extraordinary scene at Bethsaida Julias is never really understood until our Lord's great discourse in the synagogue of Capernaum, which immediately follows it, is read as the spiritual exposition of the physical miracle, which is thus seen to be a commentary, palpable to sense, upon the vital efficacy of the Holy

Communion : compare St John vi. 26-59 ; and observe the correspondence between the actions described in St Matt. xiv. 19, and xxvi. 26 " (p. 157). Discussion of these views is quite needless, they occur in the Bampton Lecturer's argument, and I reproduce them in his own words.

No reasoner, worthy of the name, would see in our Lord's miracles proofs of His Deity. Faith in His Deity no doubt entails a most willing admission of the reality of preternatural incidents in His earthly life, but unquestioning acceptance of those incidents, though it accords with, certainly does not entail, the belief that He is God. Scripture never puts forward the idea of His Godhead to account for the wonders wrought by Him ; and to His Apostles, and other earliest followers, miraculous powers of vast extent were given. Our Lord's own view of the source of His miraculous powers, may be gathered from the records on whose infallible inspiration, and minute accuracy, Mr Liddon's mind reposes. (See Matt. xii. 28 ; Luke xi. 20 ; John x. 25 ; xi. 41, 42 ; xiv. 10, 12.) How completely the Apostles' and first disciples' views were in unison with their Great Master's, may be learned from Acts ii. 22 ; x. 38 ; and, Matt. ix. 8 ; Luke vii. 16 ; xxiv. 19 ; John iii. 2 ; vi. 14, 15 ; ix. 16, 33 ; xi. 22. Our Lord's habit of prayer to God, attested by numerous passages in the Gospels, and particular expressions of prayer and thanksgiving which He is related to have employed, are, assuredly, not in accordance with the idea ; He wrought His miracles in virtue of independent, underived energy. If He had claimed to possess such energy, that habit, and those expressions, would have seemed incongruous, but as the case actually stands, they are weighty indications He did not possess other than conceded powers. (See Matt. xiv. 23 ; Luke vi. 12 ; xxii. 31, 32, and many similar texts: Matt. xi. 25, 26 ; Luke x. 21 ; Matt. xxvi. 39-43, 53 ; John xii. 27, 28 ; xiv. 16 ; and xvii. throughout.) Yet, without distinctly affirming the inference of Christ's Divinity, from the miraculous element in the Gospel narratives, Mr Liddon pertinaciously suggests, the inference may legitimately be drawn.

" The Gospel narratives describe the Author of Christianity as the Worker and the Subject of extraordinary miracles ; and these miracles are such as to afford a natural lodgment for, nay, to demand as their correlative, the doctrine of the Creed. That doctrine must be admitted to be, if not the divinely authorised explanation, at least the best intellectual conception and *résumé* of the evangelical history. A man need not be a believer in order to admit, that, in asserting Christ's Divinity, we make a fair translation of the Gospel story into the language of abstract thought ; and that we have the best key to that story when we see in it the doctrine that Christ is God, unfolding itself in a series of occurrences which on any other supposition seem to wear an air of nothing less than legendary extravagance " (p. 160).

Now, if the Sacred Writings had failed to intimate that Christ's miracles were wrought by conferred power, and if they had clearly propounded the doctrine of His Divinity, and the doctrine had involved no special difficulties of its own, we might speak of it as 'the best intellectual conception and *résumé* of the evangelical history.' In matter of fact, however, the position that Christ is verily God, is not only *not* clearly propounded, but is loaded with intrinsic difficulties, and makes the Evangelical history teem with perplexities.   Will Mr Liddon commit himself to an avowal, that the supernatural incidents of the Gospel story are, in the light of human experience and probability, more reasonably explained by the assumption, Christ is the Almighty, than by the assumption, the Almighty furnished Christ with exceptional powers, and wrought through Him ? Is the best intellectual conception that which, without stringent necessity, presumes an intervention utterly new in kind, rather than one augmented and extended in degree ? But criticism is wasted on arbitrary and audacious conjectures. I leave my readers to think over them, and estimate them at what they are worth.

In the larger portion of his Fourth, and in a few paragraphs about the middle of his Fifth Lecture, Mr Liddon, pursuing his peculiar method, picks over, and deduces from, our Lord's own teaching as represented in the Gospels, and more especially in that Gospel which bears the name of St John. He prudently avoids reference to any presumed order in the events and sayings of the several histories, and contents himself with the general assertion, that there are, in Christ's teaching, two distinct stages or levels, the former of which, exhibited in the Sermon on the Mount, is mainly ethical and concerned with primary, fundamental moral truth.   Intellects and hearts which have not irrevocably succumbed to the Church's dogmatic claims, will probably recognize in the following eloquent summary of our Lord's wonderful Sermon, something more exalted and matured than merely 'broad and deeply-laid foundations of His spiritual edifice' : " A pure and loving heart; an open and trustful conscience ; a freedom of communion with the Father of spirits ; a love of man as man, the measure of which is to be nothing less than a man's love of himself; above all a stern determination, at any cost, to be true, true with God, true with men, true with self;—such are the pre-requisites for genuine discipleship; such the spiritual and subjective bases of the new and Absolute Religion; such the moral material of the first stage of our Lord's teaching" (p. 163).

And, in this first stage of our Lord's teaching there are two characteristics, the one negative and the other positive, both of which Mr Liddon conceives to be at variance with the supposition of His being less than Divine. The negative characteristic is, that, while in the words, "be ye therefore perfect even as your Father which is in Heaven is perfect" (Matt. v. 48) our Lord proposes the highest standard, and enforces absolute morality, He makes no confession of individual shortcomings, or of personal unworthiness thus to teach.

" Conscious of many shortcomings, a human teacher must at some time relieve his natural sense of honesty, his fundamental instinct of justice, by noting the discrepancy between his weak, imperfect, perhaps miserable self, and his sublime and awful message. He must draw a line, if I may so speak, between his official and his personal self; and in his personal capacity he must honestly, anxiously, persistently associate himself with his hearers, as being before God, like each one of themselves, a learning, struggling, erring soul. But Jesus Christ makes no approach to such a distinction between Himself and His message. He bids men be like God, and He gives not the faintest hint that any trace of unlikeness to God in Himself obliges Him to accompany the delivery of that precept with a protestation of His own personal unworthiness " (p. 163).

Now, to this artificial and vapid pleading, it might be a sufficient answer to say that, admitting fully the substantial authenticity and practical sufficiency of Christ's recorded sayings, we do not possess more than digests and fragments of His discourses. The Sermon on the Mount can hardly be imagined to have been delivered as a continuous whole, and in just the form in which it has descended to us. The parables, and other speeches, may also have had verbal settings of which we know nothing, and therefore, we are in no condition to affirm Christ may not at some time have used language of a kind to show that His moral perfection did not result from inability to sin, but from faithful devotedness, resignation, and love to the Heavenly Father, *owing to Whom He lived* (John vi. 57); by Whom He was sent; Who was ever with Him; Whose Spirit was upon Him, and of Whom

He himself declared, *the Father abiding in me doeth the works* (John xiv. 10).

Mr Liddon tacitly assumes a perfect man to be impossible, and the Creator unable to produce a morally unblemished human creature whose sanctity shall not be stimulated by a sense of sin. He takes for granted, the Almighty would not, and indeed could not, elevate His human offspring by showing forth in one man the true idea of human nature, the pure relationship of the human spirit to the Divine,—the sacred possibilities which Divine inspiration, and fully realised fellowship with God, can develop and mature. An exceptional man, an extraordinarily endowed man, a created Being who should be formed and furnished to bear high commission and office from the Almighty, and to be the channel of a world-wide and regenerating impulse,—the Master, Example, Redeemer, and Leader, in the way *to His Father and our Father, His God and our God*, such a Being, with inveterate and reiterated assumption, Mr Liddon excludes from the range of likelihood, and forces the alternative ; if Christ is not ordinary, sinful man, he is absolute, impeccable God. But if we are to approach the New Testament in the capacity of learners, no assumption can be more illegitimate ; none can be less suggested or sustained by canonical witness ; none can be more out of keeping with recorded facts and aspects of our Lord's life, and the avowed conceptions of the Sacred Writers concerning Him.

What was the meaning of our Lord's temptation, if, being Very God robed in a human vesture, he was utterly incapable of sin ? We can understand how a celestial spirit, or the most God-possessed of mankind, can feel the force of temptation, and be, in the resistance of temptation, a pattern to other creatures liable to be tempted, but Christ's temptation by the Devil was a deceptive and paradoxical farce if His personal moral perfection was the perfection of the Self-existent and infinitely Holy Nature. The author of the Epistle to the Hebrews, who preaches that, Christ is ' able to succour us, having been tempted Himself, tempted in all points like as we are, yet without sin ; and that, He learned obedience by the things which He suffered ' (ii. 18 ; iv. 15 ; v. 8) ; can be acquitted of gross irreverence only by being convicted of ignorance. Is it not something beyond the extreme of platitude and simplicity, for a writer, if he knew our Lord to be absolutely God, to tell us that He was not only holy, but *harmless, undefiled, and separate from sinners* (Heb. vii. 26) ?

Is St Peter's description of Christ's sinlessness, compatible with a conscious and devout perception of Christ's Deity? "He did no sin, neither was guile found in His mouth, when He was reviled, He reviled not again, when He suffered He threatened not, but committed (Himself, or them) to Him Who judges righteously" (1 Peter ii. 22, 23). We repeat this description (as we do Scripture language in general when it is not directly practical and devotional), without reflection, because it was written by an inspired Apostle; but is it such as an Orthodox believer could spontaneously employ?

And if the force which initiated and upheld the holiness manifested through our Lord's human garb, was the force of Essential, Personal Godhead, what was the meaning of His earnest prayer, "Father, if Thou be willing, remove this cup from me; nevertheless not my will, but Thine, be done?" (Luke xxii. 42-44; Matt. xxvi. 39-44; Mark xiv. 35-39). What veritable, honest import, was there in the cry from the Cross; "My God, My God, why hast Thou forsaken me"? (Matt. xxvii. 46; Mark xv. 34), if, "in Jesus the place of any created individuality at the root of all thought and feeling and will, is supplied by the Person of the Eternal Word," Who is in very deed God, lacking no attribute of Deity? However craving may be our anxiety to show that the Gospels teach what the Catholic Church has taught, is it fair and truthful to empty this language of its natural suggestions and rational significance? Granting for argument's sake, our Lord can be reasonably understood to have had, as the Church has decreed, a human will without a human person, yet what was that will as a conflicting power in presence of the boundless energy of the Will of the Divine Personality? How could the struggles of human fears, human weakness, and human volition, produce in a Co-equal Person of the Eternal Uncreated Essence, "the prayers and supplications, the strong crying and tears" (Heb. v. 7), offered up in the garden of Gethsemane? Why, too, does an Evangelist relate the appearance of an angel from Heaven strengthening Christ, in his hour of agony (Luke xxii. 43), if in Christ, an impersonal Humanity clad Personal, Self-existing Omnipotence? Something more than a string of glib and fluent assertions concerning the explicitness, variety, and vividness of the testimony borne by Scripture and the Church to the reality and truth of our Lord's Manhood, is necessary before any impartially reflecting mind can feel that these questions are properly met. It is easy to say, the subject is mysterious and many-sided (in the Church's view it is most emphatically so), but the point as to which Protestants require to be assured is,

N

that some sides and mysteries are *not* of purely human manufacture.   Before we can justly infer Christ's freedom from sin, to
have resulted from intrinsic, infinite holiness of Being, we must
at the least correct the Synoptic narratives, and deny that our
Lord put on appearances which were false, and uttered words
which could have no rational meaning.   Suppose Him to have
been in His Own Person the Father's Equal, and possessed of the
Divine attributes in their entirety, what is signified by the Father's
forsaking Him ; and if such desertion had been possible, what
difference could it have made ?   But suppose Him to have been
the offspring of the Father's Will, and Power, and Wisdom, and
to have been dependent on the Father, then, though mystery may
shroud the details of His Being, His prayers, and cry upon the
Cross, are seen to be natural, and full of appropriate, pathetic
meaning.

If, therefore, we had the right (as we have not), to assume that
Christ never ascribed His sinlessness to imparted strength, still,
the indirect evidence afforded by His temptations, His prayers,
and His explicitly-proclaimed reception of the Holy Spirit, would
enjoin the inference that His holiness, like His miracles, followed
from the anointing and gifts of God.   The difficulties attending
this aspect of the Church's theory, are handled, without being
at all relieved, in asseverations on the 'consistency of our Lord's
real Human Will with the Impersonality of His Manhood.'

"The regenerate man's lower nature is not a distinct person,
yet it has what is almost a distinct will, and what is thus a
shadow of the Created Will which Christ assumed along with
His Human Nature.   Of course in the Incarnate Christ, the
Human Will, although a proper principle of action, was not,
could not be, in other than the most absolute harmony, with the
Will of God.   Christ's sinlessness is the historical expression of
this harmony.   The Human Will of Christ corresponded to the
Eternal Will with unvarying accuracy ; because in point of fact
God, Incarnate in Christ, willed each volition of Christ's Human
Will. Christ's Human Will then had a distinct existence, yet Its
free volitions were but the earthly echoes of the Will of the All-
holy.   At the Temptation, It was confronted with the personal
principle of evil ; but the Tempter without was seconded by no
pulse of sympathy within.   The Human Will of Christ was incapable of willing evil.   In Gethsemane It was thrown forward
into strong relief as Jesus bent to accept the chalice of suffering
from which His Human sensitiveness could not but shrink.   But
from the first It was controlled by the Divine Will to which It

is indissolubly united, just as, if we may use the comparison, in a holy man, passion and impulse are brought entirely under the empire of reason and conscience. As God and Man, our Lord has two Wills; but the Divine Will originates and rules His action; the Human Will is but the docile servant of that Will of God which has its seat in Christ's Divine and Eternal Person. Here, indeed, we touch upon the line at which revealed truth shades off into inaccessible mystery " (p. 262).

In his First Lecture, Mr Liddon appears to see the explanation of Christ's freedom from sin, in His miraculous conception;—" Christ's Manhood is not unreal, because It is sinless; because the entail of any taint of transmitted sin is in Him cut off by a supernatural birth of a Virgin Mother; " and, even in his sweeping and rapid deduction from totally insufficient materials, though the impression he is aiming to produce is unmistakably manifest, he has, notwithstanding, enough of discreet caution left, to be content with the expressed conclusion, " This consciousness of an absolute sinlessness in such a Soul as that of Jesus Christ, points to a moral elevation unknown to our actual human experience. It is, at the very least, suggestive of a relation to the Perfect Moral Being altogether unique in human history" (p. 166).

But is there not a saying of Christ's, reported by two Evangelists,* which is, when fairly interpreted, a disclaimer of absolute, independent perfection? (Mark x. 17, 18; Luke xviii. 18, 19). When called *Good Master*, Jesus answered, *Why callest thou me good? none is good except One, that is God.* Are not these words, in their simple, natural meaning, the meaning in which those who heard must have apprehended them, an assertion clearly discriminating between Christ and God, and announcing goodness in its highest and widest sense to be predicable of none except the One infinitely good God? Mr Liddon thrice refers to these words of our Lord, and each time obtrudes a most arbitrary and baseless exposition, constructed on purpose to parry the plain force of language. In a Note to his First Lecture, he remarks, Christ " is not denying that He is good; but He insists that none should call Him so who did not believe Him to be God." In his Fourth Lecture, he couples the saying in question with the exposure of unreality and self-deception. " A disciple addresses Him as *Good Master*. The address was in itself sufficiently

---

* I omit reference to Matt. xix. 17, on account of the variety of reading in good MSS. The true text there, very possibly is, *Why askest thou me concerning what is good? There is One Who is good. But if, &c.* For another noticeable affirmation of the Divine Unity, see Mark xii. 29-34.

justifiable, but our Lord observed that the speaker had used it in an unreal and conventional manner. In order to mark His displeasure, He sharply asked, 'Why callest *thou* me good? There is none good but One, that is God.'" The Seventh Lecture presents again the same choice evasion—"The rebuke to the rich young man implies, not that Jesus Himself had no real claim to be called *Good Master*, but that such a title, in the mouth of the person before Him, was an unmeaning compliment."

These repeated references betray a solicitude to provide readers with a soothing interpretation of a troublesome text, but what reasonable extenuation is there for the manner in which Mr Liddon strives to shut out the inference that offends him? Doubtless, our Lord does not repudiate His own claims to real moral goodness, but He does, by the plainest implication, disown the possession of that particular kind of goodness which He ascribes to the One God. His meaning, as determined by the demands of dogma, and the light of ecclesiastical inspiration, I do not scrutinise, but as seen by the light of common intelligence and reason, His language seems necessarily to suggest; He is not God, and is not good with the Self-originated, Self-sustained, Infinite Goodness which belongs to God.

What supposition can be, to the eye of reason, more thoroughly unfounded and capricious than the supposition of Christ's words being a covert requisition for faith in His Own Godhead? He points from Himself to God. And, for laying an expository emphasis on *thou*, there is no semblance of decent pretext, either in the structure of the sentence, or in the context. The pronoun *thou* is not expressed in the original, otherwise than through the inflection of the verb—a strong indication no special stress upon it was designed. The customary mode of marking emphasis is the separate expression of the pronoun, and examples of emphasis, and suppressed antithesis, thus marked, are familiar to every student of Greek Testament grammar. (See Winer, Sec. xxii. 6.) The really emphatic word is, by every rule of probability, the pronoun *me*, and the antithesis is between Christ's goodness and God's. That the young ruler's address was unreal, conventional, and the utterance of unmeaning compliment, is exactly the reverse of the conclusion deducible from St Mark's record that, *Jesus beholding him, loved him;* and from the fact that he could not, without being *very sorrowful*, neglect to comply with Christ's requirements.

The other, or positive characteristic, of the first stage of Christ's teaching, consists in its tone of authority, and in the strongly marked contrast between His attitude and that of the ordinary expounders of the Jewish Code: "He taught the people as one having authority to teach, and not as their Scribes" (Matt. vii. 29).

"He takes up instinctively a higher position than He assigns to any who had preceded Him in Israel. He passes in review, and accepts or abrogates, not merely the traditional doctrines of the Jewish Schools, but the Mosaic law itself. His style runs thus: 'It was said *to* them of old time . . . . but I say unto you' (Matt. v. 21, and other verses) . . . The prophets always appealed to a higher sanction: the prophetic argument addressed to the conscience of Israel was ever, 'Thus saith the Lord.' How significant, how full of import as to His consciousness respecting Himself is our Lord's substitute, 'Verily, verily, *I* say unto you.' What prophet ever set himself above the great Legis-lator, above the Law written by the finger of God on Sinai? What prophet ever undertook to ratify the Pentateuch as a whole, to contrast his own higher morality with some of its precepts in detail, to imply even remotely that he was competent to revise that which every Israelite knew to be the handiwork of God? What prophet ever thus implicitly placed himself on a line of equality, not with Moses, not with Abraham, but with the Lord God Himself? So momentous a claim requires explanation if the claimant be only human. This impersonation of the source of moral law must rest upon some basis: what is the basis on which it rests?" (p. 167).

As to the authoritative manner of Christ's teaching, the dignity of His character, and office, and endowments, as the Anointed and Messenger of God, quite sufficiently explains it, without resorting to the hypothesis that he is Himself God. The speeches ascribed to our Lord in the Fourth Gospel, disclose a point of view widely different from Mr Liddon's, while they account for the didactic tone which he misinterprets. "My doctrine *is not mine, but His That sent Me.* If any one wishes to do His Will, he shall know of the doctrine whether it be of God, or whether I speak from myself" (John vii. 16, 17). "I do nothing from myself; but as the Father taught me, I speak these things. Ye seek to kill me, a man that hath told you the truth, which I have heard from God" (viii. 28, 40). "I have not spoken of myself; but the Father Who sent me, He has given me a commandment what I shall say, and what I shall speak; whatsoever I speak, therefore, as the Father has said unto me, so I speak"

(xii. 49, 50). "All things which I have heard from my Father, I have made known unto you" (xv. 15).   Other statements of similar force might be quoted from the Gospel, in which Orthodox theologians imagine there is a consistent presentation of *the Word*, as the personal Christ, and as being in the full and absolute sense, God ; but these are enough to show the gratuitousness of Mr Liddon's inferences from the mode in which Jesus Christ delivered His precepts.

But with no guide except the contents of the Sermon on the Mount, the straining, perversion, and confusion involved in Mr Liddon's reasoning are easily seen. Giving him, as his argument requires, the benefit of the doubtful translation, " *to* them of old time," what does he conceive Christ to have accepted, what to have abrogated ?   In referring to some of the Ten Commandments, was our Lord's object to show, they were inherently wrong and defective, or, that Jewish legislators had been for centuries engrafting upon them unspiritual, narrowing, and corrupting interpretations ?   If His teaching was aimed against Rabbinical misconceptions and falsehoods ; if He designed only to correct and countermand the superimposed blunders of human traditions, then, certainly, He neither 'set Himself above the Law written by the finger of God on Sinai,' nor ' placed Himself on a line of equality with the Lord God Himself,' and the whole form of His sayings betokens Him to have been dealing with the prescriptive explanations of men, and not with the eternal principles of rectitude, which the Commandments, rightly understood, embodied. His meaning was not an antithetical and annulling,—'*God* taught them of old time, but *I* teach you,' and, if His meaning was not this, what ' impersonation' was there of ' the source of moral law,' and what validity is there in Mr Liddon's reasoning ? Christ, no doubt, opposed His own precepts to a long-current mass of legislation and commentary.   In Matt. v. 22, 28, 32, 34, 39, 44, the *I*, is, as the Greek and context indicate, antithetical and emphatic, but there is, probably, a yet more pointed antithesis between the men of earlier generations who went no deeper than the letter, and those whom Christ was teaching to read the spirit of all injunctions truly Divine.   It was said to *them of old time*, but *I* say to *you*.   One section of His discourse (Matt. v. 39-42) seems to have a special adaptation to the relations in which the Jews stood to their Roman conquerors.

Mr Liddon was too eager, to be duly observant, when he connected the formula " Verily, verily, *I* say unto you," with the Sermon on the Mount.   The doubling of the asseverative word in our Lord's Discourses, is peculiar to the Fourth Gospel, and when, in the Sermon on the Mount, the word is used singly, it, and not the unexpressed personal pronoun, is evidently intended to carry the stress (Matt. v. 18, 26; vi. 2, 5, 16). I may add that, in the whole range of instances (between seventy and eighty), in which the single or duplicate *verily* occurs joined with *I say unto you*, there is not one where the pronoun *I* is separately expressed, or designed to be emphatic.

Whence is evidence producible for the innuendo, that Christ undertook to ratify the Pentateuch as a whole, or, that He put the stamp of His approval on the notion of its being, in its entirety, the handiwork of God? We know how in His judgment all the Law and the Prophets hang upon the two great commands, to love God supremely, and to love our neighbours as ourselves (Matt. xxii. 37-40; Mark xii. 29-34; compare Luke x. 25-28). Can any system of exegesis pretending to be rational and legitimate, gather under these commands, either the letter or the spirit of the unsifted mass of Pentateuchal enactments? Does not Christ Himself contrast a permission given in the Mosaic statutes (Deut. xxiv. 1), with the law and purpose of God expressed in the constitution of human nature? (Matt. xix. 4-8; Mark x. 4-9). Was the maxim, *Thou shalt hate thine enemy* (Matt. v. 43), a precept of Jehovah, because it unavoidably sprang out of, if it was not formally laid down in, passages of the Pentateuch (see Exodus xxxiv. 12; Deut. vii. 2; xxiii. 3-6; xxv. 17-19)? Can we really receive into our souls, the inestimable light which the Bible sheds on the Divine Nature and character, and then believe Exodus xxi. 20, 21; xxxii. 9, 10, to be in any sense God's words; or, the entire body of civil and ceremonial rules and injunctions contained in the Pentateuch, to be, without exception, His handiwork? If we cannot, are we not acting unfaithfully, and dishonouring our Heavenly Father's Adorable Name, when either in peevish anger and alarm, or, in the selfish supineness of lazy acquiescence, we repeat, and endeavour to propagate among the simple, our hobbling crotchet; every sentence of the Bible is identical with the Word of God.

CHAPTER IX.

Mr Liddon's view of the second stage of our Lord's public teaching depends almost entirely on materials peculiar to the Fourth Gospel.— These materials discussed in detail, and shown neither to warrant Mr Liddon's deductions, nor to contain the presumed dogmatic revelations of Christ's Co-equality and Essential Oneness with the Father. —No consciousness of Eternal Being is unveiled in John viii. 58, and there is no justification for coupling that text with Exodus iii. 14.

For his view of the second stage of our Lord's public teaching, Mr Liddon depends almost exclusively on statements attributed to Christ in the 'Gospel according to John ;' taking for granted these statements are really Christ's, and reported by the Evangelist with verbal exactitude. The great characteristic of this stage, he considers to be self-assertion, and his argument is framed to sustain the hypothesis, that our Lord's pretensions were so enormous, His self-assertion so energetic, comprehensive, and persistent, as to reduce us to the dilemma of either confessing His Godhead, or, denying His possession of ordinary moral virtues.

The evidence from which this dilemma is extracted, begins with a mosaic composed of detached fragmentary sayings, arranged without regard to context, and in neglect of everything but the advocacy of a foregone conclusion. And these artificially-clustered fragments are dilated and amplified by paraphrastic touches, lest readers should fail to instil due meaning into the brief, metaphorical, undefined, and abstract terms of the original.

We are reminded ; Christ "speaks of Himself as the Light of a darkened world" (John viii. 12 ; see also ix. 5 ; xii. 46), but we are not reminded ; He applies precisely the same description to His disciples (Matt. v. 14).*

The text, "I am the Way, and the Truth, and the Life, no man cometh unto the Father but by me" (John xiv. 6), is not

---

* If our Lord had said, *I am the salt of the earth*, the properties and effects of salt would, doubtless, have been thought to betoken how inapplicable the metaphor was to a creature, how exclusively suited to the Omnipresent and All-preserving Creator.

only inflated as preconceptions dictate, but torn asunder in order that it may be the more effectively manipulated. The final clause being a broad practical explanation of the preceding epithets, ought not to be dissociated from them, and there is, to most minds, a great difficulty in perceiving how the suggestion that Christ is God, can be contained in the fact that He is our Conductor to God. In the same discourse, also, only five verses previously, our Lord is made to distinguish Himself from God, when demanding faith in Himself as God's Messenger; "Ye believe in God, believe also in me;" words which Mr Liddon paraphrases; "He encourages men to trust in Him as they trust in God," but which, clearly, ought to be read by the light of the statements; "The words that I speak unto you I speak not of myself; the word which ye hear is not mine, but the Father's Who sent Me" (verses 10 and 24); "this is life eternal, that they may know Thee, the Only True God, and Jesus Christ whom Thou hast sent" (xvii. 3).

" Life is resident in Him in virtue of an undefined and eternal communication of it from the Father" (John v. 26). Life, in the passage referred to, is, far more probably, the power of distributing spiritual and eternal life to mankind. The Father, the sole primary Source and Giver of this life, has granted to the Son also to be a source and giver. But, admitting the other interpretation, the communication of the life is not said to have been eternal, and is defined in this important particular; it is a concession and gift, *the Father hath given to the Son,*—and, as a gift, obliterates the ideas of Co-equality and Self-existence. In the very same chapter too (verse 44), Christ is represented as speaking of *the Only God,* an exclusive designation which the English Version mistranslates *God only.* In the following chapter (vi. 57), the sustenance of our Lord's life by the Father is acknowledged in a very unequivocal way: "As the living Father hath sent me, and I live by the Father, so he that eateth me, shall live by me;" where "*by*" is equivalent to *on account of, owing to,* and the dependence of a Christian's spiritual life on Christ, is paralleled with the dependence of Christ's life on the Father.

A few phrases illustrative of Christ's self-assertion, are culled from the highly figurative and intensely cloudy discourse comprised in John vi. 32-63. To say, " My Father giveth you the true bread from Heaven; the bread of God is He which cometh down from Heaven and giveth life unto the world; I am the Bread of Life,—the Living Bread which cometh down from

Heaven and giveth Life unto the world ; I am the Bread of Life,
—the Living Bread which cometh down from Heaven" (verses 32,
33, 48, 51), is to use language into which vast significance may
be put, but which contains no hint of Deity.   When the explanatory clauses are added, " the Bread that I will give is my
flesh ; except ye eat the flesh of the Son of Man, and drink His
blood, ye have no life in you, for my flesh is meat indeed, and
my blood is drink indeed" (verses 51, 53, 55),—phraseology
perfectly incomprehensible is employed, unless we sweep away
its whole literal, natural meaning, and take license to think
what we will, from the thoroughly emancipating announcement,
—" It is the Spirit that quickeneth; the flesh profiteth nothing:
the words that I speak unto you are spirit and life" (ver. 63).*

"John iv. 14, points to a living water of the Spirit, which
Christ can give, and which will quench the thirst of souls that
drink it."   That text, no doubt, relates to *the gift of God* (ver.
10), bestowed in and through Christ, and offers no excuse for
the insertion of ideas about Christ's Godhead.   Jesus Himself,
and His teaching, were the gift of God ; the living water was
the doctrine of God which Jesus taught, and all the spiritual
blessings annexed to a sincere reception of the doctrine.   To
hear Christ's words, and to believe on the Father Who sent Him,
is to have the living water (v. 24).

In verses 23 and 24 of John iv. it is noteworthy, the Personal
Father is identified with the God Who is a Spirit, in a manner
quite foreign to the notion that the Nature and Name of God
cover any Form or Person besides the Father.

Protestants who have learned to substitute an intelligent
loyalty to their Great Master, for an indiscriminating adhesion to
every scrap of Evangelical testimony respecting Him, will probably hesitate before they see His exact words in John iv. 22 ;
or, again, in x. 8, with which compare Matt. v. 17-19.   The
latter of the two texts is a self-assertion Mr Liddon cites, but he
adroitly dilutes it by the addition which I italicise : " All who
came before Him He characterizes as having been, *by comparison
with Himself,* the thieves and robbers of mankind."

---

* Dr Schenkel, in his *Sketch of the Character of Jesus,* remarks :—"The
omission in the Fourth Gospel of the institution of the Lord's Supper, is explained by the circumstance that from his dogmatic point of view, the Evangelist could attach thereto only a relatively slight importance, in consistency
with his declaration that faith in the Saviour is the true eating and drinking
of His body and blood (John vi. 35, 47, 51)."
Certainly, the exposition which couples the Discourse in John vi. with the
doctrine of a real presence of Christ's Human Nature in the Holy Eucharist,
is only ecclesiastically. not rationally, sound.

The opening verses of John xv. are treated unfairly, by leaving out the important sentences : " My Father is the husbandman. Every branch in me that beareth not fruit, He taketh away ; and every branch that beareth fruit, He cleanseth it, that it may bear more fruit. Now ye are clean through the word which I have spoken unto you." To fill in, *ad libitum*, the more allegorical, and pass over the plainer, simpler expressions, is not to expound, but to distort. The superiority and Divine activity of 'the God and Father' are prominent, if the passage is not mutilated and perverted for the sake of Orthodox conceptions. Nothing short of an ineradicable persuasion that Jesus is God, can dispose a rational mind to find in the passage the faintest indications of His Godhead.

"He promises that all prayer offered in His Name shall be answered, ' If ye ask anything in My Name, *I* will do it ' (xiv. 14)." This text ought, undoubtedly, to be read in close con nection with the two preceding verses, and refers to miraculous powers even greater than those Christ had exhibited, which were to be vouchsafed to His disciples in consequence of His going to the Father. Our Lord did not direct that prayer should be offered to Himself ; and the avowed object of His action was the Father's glory (ver. 13); and in verse 16, He is made to say, " *I will ask the Father, and He shall give you*," &c. The Apostolical view of spiritual gifts as dispensed by Christ may be gathered from Acts iii. 33.

" He contrasts Himself with a group of His countrymen as follows: 'Ye are from beneath, I am from above: ye are of this world, I am not of this world (viii. 23).' Granting, Jesus here points to heavenly origin as well as to heavenly-mindedness, what semblance of an intimation is there that He is Almighty God, in Essence the Equal of the Father Who sanctified and sent Him (x. 36) ? In xv. 19, He declares, His disciples *are not of the world ;* and again, in xvii. 14 and 16, He twice affirms : *they are not of the world, as I am not of the world.* The expression *not of* (ἐx) *the world*, therefore, carries no implication of Deity. But men would perhaps be less inclined to infuse their own conceptions into verse 23, if they looked a little carefully at the words of verse 38. " I speak that which I have seen with My Father ; and ye do that which ye have seen with your father" (the devil, see ver. 44). The extreme freedom of this language ought to teach us caution, and to show the folly of intruding precise meanings amongst vague and figurative words. In what sense was the Devil the Father of the Jews ? In what sense were they ' of (ἐx) him,' and how had they, by sight or hearing, learned from him ? Surely not in any literal natural sense.

"Christ claims to be the Lord of the realm of death ; He will Himself wake the sleeping dead ; all that are in the graves shall hear His voice (v. 28, 29 ; vi. 39). He proclaims : ' I am the Resurrection and the Life ' (xi. 25)." The obscurity of the sense in v. 21-30, is ill-suited to any such brief and positive exposition. It is very far indeed from being certain a bodily resurrection is there referred to. The *now is*, of verse 25, appears to point distinctly to spiritual resurrection from the moral and metaphorical ' death of sin.'

When vi. 39, is interpreted through the dogma that a resurrection of the material body will be the lot of the whole human race, the connection of verses 37 and 39, either entails narrow and Calvinistic notions of salvation, or, presuming the Father's gift to cover all mankind (see xvii. 2), entails belief in universal salvation, because " *all* whom " the Father gives, will come to Christ, and of the entire gift, nothing will be lost, but the whole will be raised up at the last day. If Mr Liddon is not prepared to offer a clearly defined, and consistently Orthodox exposition, he does not, from the Protestant point of view, understand the text sufficiently well to justify reference to it for purposes of proof and illustration.

There is enough of uncertainty whether spiritual or bodily life and resurrection are intended in xi. 25, to preclude inferences. As the Divinely-sent and qualified Leader in the way to God ; as the Teacher of awakening truths which, when they are practically believed, conduct to eternal life, Christ might in the freedom of Eastern diction, have justly denominated Himself *the Resurrection and the Life*. When men charge the sayings ascribed to Him in the ' Gospel according to John,' with either broad literalism, or with the subtle accuracies or inaccuracies drawn from scholastic theology, they only show they have not studied the Fourth Evangelist with attention enough to understand his style, and elicit coherent, generally applicable, rules of interpretation. Their guiding maxim is the reinforcement of Orthodoxy, and beneath that most pliable of canons, metaphors become, as convenience may demand, either most metaphorical, or, singular combinations of pregnancy and precision. Their rule may be very discreet, and productive of excellent results, but it can have no claim to be rational, except as it follows in the train, and echoes the voice, of a Church instinct with Divine inspiration, and commissioned authoritatively to expound and reveal.

Assigning to the particle καθὼς (*as*), the utmost possible exactness and stretch of literal significance, and absolutely ignoring the fact, attested throughout the Christian Scriptures, that the first Christians did *not* honour the Son with the same kind and degree of honour with which they honoured the Father,—Mr Liddon asserts : " our Lord encourages men to honour Him as they honour the Father " (John v. 23) ; and again, a few pages further on, assures his readers that, by our Lord's words, " the obligation of honouring the Son, is defined to be just as stringent as the obligation of honouring the Father ; " and yet again, in a Note, remarks ; " if the honour paid to the Son be merely relative, if He be merely honoured as an Ambassador or delegated Judge, then men do *not* honour Him *as* they honour the Father " (p. 182).

Now, when a scholar interprets in this fashion, if, in the judgment of charity, we admit his honesty, we cannot think he displays his intelligence. Mr Liddon must know that the word on which he builds, is frequently used in the latest Gospel to signify a general and proportionate resemblance, rather than exact likeness, and equality in degree. Chapter xvii. affords examples in which he would certainly deny identity in kind, manner, and extent, to be indicated. In verse 11, Christ prays that those whom the Father has given Him, " may be one, *as* He and the Father are ; " and in verse 22, He is made to say, " the glory which Thou gavest Me, I have given them, that they may be one, *as* we are one." Verse 16 recounts the declaration, " they are not of the world, *as* I am not of the world ; " verse 18, " *as* Thou hast sent Me into the world, I also have sent them into the world ; " and verse 23, " Thou hast loved them, *as* Thou hast loved Me." In xv. 9, 10, we read ; " *As* the Father hath loved Me, I also have loved you ; continue ye in my love. If ye keep my commandments ye shall abide in my love, *as* I have kept the Father's commandments and abide in His love ; " and in xx. 21, " *as* the Father hath sent Me, I also send you." Will Mr Liddon strain the καθὼς in these examples, after the same puerile unscholarly fashion in which he strains it in v. 23 ? I do not press him with the circumstance, that one or two of the examples differ from the text he tortures, in having καί after καθὼς, and being thereby greatly increased in strength and precision, as descriptions of corresponding manner. In translating, I have neglected the true force of καί as virtually a comparative particle in the second member of the sentence. Indubitably, καθὼς alone, has not necessarily the sense Mr Liddon affixes. It may mean, *in proportion as, since, inasmuch as,* and for the latter meaning, Bloomfield's *Lexicon of the New Testament* rightly refers to John xvii. 2 ; Rom. i. 28 ; 1 Cor. i. 6 ; Eph. i. 4 ; Phil. i. 7. (See also Winer's remarks, *Grammar of New Testament,* Sec. liii. 8.) An exposition which hinges on the Conjunction *as,* is simply contemptible, and justly subjects the expositor to the suspicion of deliberately counting on the prejudices, the inattention, and the ignorance of his readers. A reference to the context puts the folly of Mr Liddon's explanation in a clear and strong light. In the course of the speech, whence the text imparting its revelation through that very luminous and precise word καθώς, is picked out, the Evangelist reports the following statements :—

" The Son can do nothing of Himself, but what He seeth the Father doing ; for whatever things He doeth, these also doeth the Son in like manner. For the Father loveth the Son, and showeth Him all that Himself doeth ; and He will show Him greater works than these, that ye may marvel. The Father judgeth no man, but *hath given* all judgment unto the Son. As the Father hath life in Himself, so *hath He given* to the Son to have life in Himself; and *hath given* him authority to execute judgment also, because He is the Son of Man. I can of myself do nothing ; as I hear, I judge, and my judgment is just ; because I seek not mine own will, but the will of Him that sent Me. If I bear witness concerning Myself, my witness is not true. There is another that beareth witness concerning Me, and I know that the witness which He witnesseth concerning Me is true " (John v. 19-32).

Now, if these words have any rationally ascertainable meaning, and were not designed either to deceive and bewilder, or, with reserving foresight to furnish a riddle for the Church's Divine light to solve,—can we imagine they were spoken by One Who knew Himself to be, in Nature and Attributes, the Eternal, Self-existent Father's Equal ?

The more probable rendering of the verse which Mr Liddon isolates and misinterprets, is ; " That all men may honour the Son, *since,* or, *in proportion as,* they honour the Father. He that honoureth not the Son, honoureth not the Father Who sent Him," exalted Him, and made Him worthy of honour.

We are reminded that, in Christ's teaching, " to love Him is a necessary mark of the children of God ; ' If God were your Father ye would have loved Me ' " (John viii. 42). The rest of the verse, which Mr Liddon omits, ought to be added : " For I came forth, and am come from God ; for I came not of Myself, but He sent Me." According to the Bampton Lecturer's dogma, the personal *I*, here, and elsewhere in Christ's speeches, can only denote the Divine Personality Which is of the Adorable, Incorruptible, Essence, identical in Nature and Perfections with the Almighty Father. But upon this supposition, the language becomes hopelessly inscrutable to reason, and evidently meant for the ecclesiastical, as distinguished from the rational mind. Love for our Lord Jesus Christ is, doubtless, a characteristic of the true children of God. Hatred to Christ may with truth be said to involve hatred to God (John xv. 23), but what bearing have these facts on the notion, ' Christ is God ?' The first Epistle of John emphatically teaches that to love our brethren is a necessary mark of the children of God, and affirms ; " if any one say, I love God, and hateth his brother, he is a liar, for he that loveth not his brother whom he hath seen, how can he love God Whom he hath not seen ? " (iv. 20.)

The self-assertion contained in the statement, " If ye love Me, keep *My* commandments " (John xiv. 15), does not, even when with Mr Liddon we have made *my* emphatic, transcend the claims of a Teacher conscious of a Divinely-given commission and endowments, and conscious also, that grievously false teaching prevailed around Him. The discourse which supplies the statement just quoted, supplies also a reason for remembering and obeying Christ's words, "The word which ye hear is not mine, but the Father's Who sent Me " (verse 24).

" The most representative document of the second stage of our Lord's teaching, is the Discourse in the supper-room," given in the 13th and four following chapters of the latest Evangelist.* " His subject in that discourse is Himself. Certainly He preaches, Himself in His relationship to His redeemed ; but still preaches above all and in all, Himself. All radiates from Himself, all converges towards Himself. The sorrows and perplexities of His disciples, the mission and work of the Paraclete, the mingling predictions of suffering and of glory, are all bound up with the Person of Jesus, as manifested by Himself. In those matchless words, all centres so consistently in Jesus, that it might seem that Jesus alone is before us ; alone in the greatness of His supramundane glory ; alone in bearing His burden of an awful, fathomless sorrow " (p. 172).

This is rhetorical, but is it true ? Any one who will with

---

* I include chapter xvii., in the Discourse, since, if the record is really historical, the prayer of Christ must have been addressed aloud to God, in the Disciples' hearing, for their instruction.

attentive care study the language attributed to Christ in the Discourse referred to, cannot fail to perceive the uniform prominence of the Father's supremacy, the Father's glory, and the Father's imparted gifts.   The highest self-assertion bespeaks dependence on Him, and falls very short of claiming equality, and identity of Nature with Him.   The self-proclamation culminates in the claim to have come forth from God (xvi. 27, 30 ; xvii. 8) ; the admission of that claim is the comprehensive aspect of Christian faith.   In terms not altogether perspicuous, but still practically clear as against the conclusion, ' the Son is Himself God,' the relation of the Son to the Father is intimated to be similar to that of the disciples to the Son (xiii. 20 ; xiv. 20 ; xv. 9, 10, 15 ; xvii. 22).

In xiv. 28, Christ's inferiority to the Father, and consequent exclusion from the One Self-existent Substance, is explicitly avowed.   "If ye loved me, ye would rejoice that I go unto the Father, for my Father is greater than I."   The manifest truth of the Father's superior greatness, should have taught the disciples to rejoice in the advantage and honour which their Great Master would gain by going to God.   There is nowhere in the Gospels the smallest particle of evidence the Apostles apprehended Jesus to be in very truth God, and the Father's Equal.   His assurance that the Father was greater than Himself, was therefore, undoubtedly, not intended to correct an erroneous opinion, or to disclose an unsuspected fact.   It was intended to remind the Apostles, by calling their attention to a most incontrovertible truth, that, in the desire to retain Him for what they believed to be their own profit, His exaltation and aggrandisement were being somewhat selfishly and unlovingly forgotten.   The acknowledged pre-eminence of the One God and Father, as compared with the greatness of Christ, being so palpable, reference to it at once suggested and enforced the thought that in departing to Him, Christ would be a gainer.   Reasonably understood the text will carry no other meaning.   Its whole rational significance turns on the implication that the inferiority of Jesus to the Father, is the broad and actual inferiority of receptiveness and dependence, not the narrow and nominal inferiority of such relative ineffable subordination, as may consist with sameness of Essence, and equality of Godhead.

Mr Liddon, with the highest capacity for a style of exposition which descries what is latent and overlooks what is obvious, observes ; the best of men would be "guilty of something worse than a stupid truism" if he should announce that God was " greater " than himself.

" Would he not seem to imply that he was not really a creature of God's hand? Would not his words go to suggest that the notion of his absolute equality with God, was not to be dismissed as altogether out of the question?   Should we not peremptorily remind him that the life of man is related to the Life of God, not as the less to the greater, but as the created to the Uncreated, and that it is an impertinent irreverence to admit superiority of rank, where the real truth can only be expressed by an assertion of radical difference of natures?   And assuredly a sane and honest man, who had been accused of associating himself with the Supreme Being, could not content himself with admitting that God was greater than himself.   Knowing himself to be only human, would he not insist again and again, with passionate fervour, upon the incommunicable glory of the great Creator?" (p. 200).

Simple truths which might, on account of their simplicity, be stigmatized as " stupid truisms," are not unfrequent in the Fourth Gospel, but, granting the words in question do obliquely imply Christ to be more than man, that does not impair their explicit assertion, He is less than God, or establish a rational likelihood that, *greater than I*, is equivalent to, *in one or two points slightly my superior*.   If our Lord were the Uncreated Father's Equal, and lacked no attribute of Godhead, how could the Father's excelling greatness illustrate His gain in going to the Father?   It might have been profitable to Him to have manifested again in Heaven the inalienable splendours of Deity which had for a while been shrouded upon earth, but the resumption of those splendours could not have been depended upon, or have been enhanced by, the comparative greaterness ' in the order of the Divine Subsistence,' of the merely Co-equal, Consubstantial Father.

Since all proof is wanting that our Lord's Apostles ever suspected Him of associating Himself with God, or, were disposed to pervert His words, after the manner of His Jewish foes, there is no fair pretext for imagining, that in speaking to them, He would shape His language with a view to malevolent and absurdly false calumnies.   Sane and honest men are not sensitively alive to foolish falsehoods which they know their friends do not believe ; and, if ridiculous charges are noticed, the simplest expression of simple truth is more dignified than repeated asseverations, and ' passionate fervour.'

In days when the intellect was less sceptical, and faith in mysteries more facile than now, the Father's superiority to the Co-equal Son was felt to be perplexing, and Mr Liddon directs his readers to Suicer's summary of Patristic arguments " against the Arian abuse" of John xiv. 28. "The μειζονότης of the Father is referred by SS. Athanasius, Gregory Nazianzen, Chrysostom, Basil, and Hilary, to His being the Unbegotten One ; by SS. Cyril, Augustine, Ambrose, and Leo, to the Son's humiliation as incarnate."

The former of these Patristic opinions brings no relief. Persons afflicted with common sense, and a determination to attach meanings to the phrases employed about sacred subjects, will conjecture that the difference between Unbegotten and begotten, is tantamount to the difference between Independence and dependence, Producer and produced, Creator and creature.

The latter opinion, which makes the phrase under discussion describe only diversity of condition, is nothing better than an elusive supposition, involving the utterly unsupported assumption, that the Apostles knew Jesus to be God. If they did not know Him to be God, the saying : " My Father is greater than I, because He is in glory, and I am in humiliation," would, for them, have come under that category of exceedingly plain truth which Mr Liddon calls ' stupid truism.' But the explanatory expansion is purely arbitrary, unless the Church has received a revelation outside the Canon of Scripture, with which all Canonical statements *must* be reconciled.

The text (John xiv. 28) can hardly be denied to be full of the perilous semblance of direct antagonism to ecclesiastical dogma, which so remarkably characterizes the higher scriptural teaching concerning Christ's Person. The methods and experience of commentators in handling this, and other passages, illustrate the duty of remorselessly subordinating the obstructive, as well as the exceedingly obscure, and at best, merely germinal enunciations of Holy Scripture, to the fully ripened and openly pronounced definitions of the Church. What unaided intellectual insight, what weary gropings of reason, could ever have convinced truthful and pious minds, that latent claims to absolute Deity, and Essential Equality with the Almighty Father, do not jar with the announcement, *My Father is greater than I !*

The concluding section of that ' most representative Self-assertion' which Mr Liddon brings into court, consists of a prayer to God, the whole tone and wording of which appear to be directly at variance with the supposition of there having been in our Lord's mind any reserved, underlying consciousness of proper, actual Deity. In His intercourse with the Almighty, some expressions betraying clearly His real Personal Rank, might naturally be expected.   But He not only prays that those whom the Father had given Him, may be, by the Father, kept in safety, sanctified, and united, but He prays also that He Himself may be glorified, and, using terms the most exact and definite, excludes Himself from the One Godhead in the statement : “ This is Life Eternal, that they may know *Thee, the Only True God*, and Jesus Christ whom Thou hast sent” (xvii. 3).   Combine this statement with the many others of the Discourse in the supper-room, which imply receptivity, inferiority, dependence, and then let reason, reverence, and common sense, decide whether the combination does not impart to all simplicity, intensity, and definiteness, by intimating the Father to be the *Only True* God, and Jesus Christ not to be in the highest, and absolute sense, God at all.   And more especially, combine it with the enunciation of the Father’s pre-eminent greatness.   Why is the Father greater than the Son ?   Because the Father is the *Only True God*, and not one of two or more Forms, Persons, or Subsistencies, each of Whom is enfolded with Him in the Unity of the same Nature, and is Co-equal, Co-eternal, Consubstantial, with Himself.   Unless it can be shown (as indubitably it cannot), that other portions of the Fourth Gospel aver, in unambiguous terms, Christ to be truly and essentially God, the very document in which Mr Liddon most confides, ought to have warned him against the suicidal folly of trying to build the grandly distinctive dogma of the Catholic Church, on the treacherous Protestant basis of reasonably-expounded Scripture.

The legitimate, natural, and most plain meaning of John xvii. 3 is, however, battled against and disguised, by devices of unblushing and laborious ingenuity.   After quoting the verse in a Note (p. 237), Mr Liddon argues :—

“ But here a Socinian sense is excluded—(1.) By the consideration that the knowledge of God *and a creature* could not be Eternal Life ; (2.) By the plain sense of verse 1, which places the Son and the Father on a level: What creature could stand before his Creator and say, ‘ Glorify me, that I may glorify Thee ?’ (3.) By verse 5, which asserts our Lord’s pre-existent *glory*.   It follows that the restrictive epithets *only*, *true*, must be held to be exclusive, not of the Son, but of false gods, or creatures external to the Divine Essence.”

With what scornful intolerance would this wriggling sophistry be trampled underfoot, if it were employed against a doctrine of Orthodoxy !   (1.) Christ is spoken of as the Ambassador through whom the Father communicates His will, makes known His messages of mercy, and establishes His kingdom. The knowledge of our Lord in this function, added to the knowledge of *the Only True God* Who sends Him (compare ver. 8), is declared to be the subjective condition and pledge of Eternal Life. The exclusive restriction immanent in the epithets *only, true,* is wholly unaffected by the association of Christ in the official capacity with which the Almighty had invested Him. Each of the Beings named is to be recognized, according to the terms of their respective designations, in His own proper character,—the Father as being *the Only True God,* and Jesus Christ as being the Father's *Messenger.*

(2.) The sapient assertion, ' The plain sense of verse 1, places the Son and the Father on a level,' would appear to have originated in the not very pardonable error of understanding the glorification of the Father by the Son, to be the same in kind with the glorification of the Son by the Father ; but the processes referred to, cannot be identical, or, similar. The *Only True God* glorifies His Servant Jesus (Acts iii. 13 ; 1 Peter i. 21), by raising Him from the dead, exalting Him to Heaven, and giving Him to be Head over all things in the Church (Eph. i. 22). This glorification cannot be reciprocated in kind ; but the Father is glorified by the Son, in the accomplishment of human salvation, in the realization of that reconciliation of man to Himself, in which He has made the Son His Instrument, the Pattern Image, and First-born among many brethren (Rom. viii. 29), the Captain of the salvation of the many sons brought unto glory (Heb. ii. 10). The mode in which the Son was to glorify the Father, is intimated, not obscurely, in the immediate context of the verse now in question : " Since Thou hast given Him power over all flesh, in order that He should give eternal life to as many as Thou hast given Him." From verse 4, we learn that the Son had already glorified the Father on the earth, by finishing the work which the Father had given Him to do. And when the different natures of the glorifying processes on the parts of the Creator and the creature are remembered, there is seen to be nothing unbefitting, in supposing even an ordinary human creature to stand before his Creator and say, ' Glorify me, that I may glorify Thee.' The highest end and duty of the Christian's existence in this world, is to glorify God, and the same (more perfectly attained and accomplished) will be the end and duty of his existence in the world to come. When the loving and obedient child of God, looks trustfully forward to the delights and employments of the Heavenly Home, what more suitable petition can ascend from his heart and lips, than, 'Glorify me, that I may glorify Thee?'

(3.) The reference to 'our Lord's pre-existent *glory*,' in verse 5, certainly does not denote that glory to be the inherent, irrelinquishable grandeur of Consubstantial, Self-subsisting Godhead. On the contrary, the *glory* is acknowledged to be a gift and boon from the Father. Consider, in conjunction with verse 5, the language of verses 22 and 24, and the utter unreasonableness of attempting to identify the conferred *glory* with the Majesty of true Deity, will be manifest. Theologians are rarely aware of the strength of their own educational and professional leanings, but no unsophisticated mind would ever have conjectured that John xvii. 3 does *not* shut out the meaning; 'Thee, the Only True God, and Jesus Christ, *the True God* Whom Thou hast sent.'

In forging his defensive weapons, Mr Liddon naturally dwells on John xiv. 23, and contends that Jesus virtually proclaims His own Deity, when He associates Himself with God, in the saying :—

" ' If a man love me, he will keep my words; and my Father will love him, and *We* will come unto him, and make *Our* abode with him.' Reflect : Who is this Speaker That promises to dwell in the soul of man ? And with whom does He associate Himself ? It may be true of any eminent saint, that ' God speaks not to him as to one outside Himself ; that God is in him ; that he feels himself with God ; that he draws from his own heart what he tells us of the Father ; that he lives in the bosom of God by the intercommunion of every moment.' But such an one could not forget that, favoured as he is by the Divine Presence illuminating his whole inner life, he still lives at an immeasurable distance beneath the Being Whose condescension has so enriched him. In virtue of his sanctity, he would surely shrink with horror from associating himself with God ; from promising, along with God, to make a dwelling-place of the souls that love himself ; from representing his presence with men as a blessing co-ordinate with the presence of the Father ; from attributing to himself oneness of will with the Will of God ; from implying that, side by side with the Father of spirits, he was himself equally a ruler and helper of the life of the souls of men " (p. 178).

Now, if the doctrine, 'Christ is God,' had any well-marked and adequate Biblical sanction ; if there existed any indications of its having been so familiar as to be the natural explanation of obscure and exceptional expressions, then, unquestionably, the text Mr Liddon handles so vigorously, might be fairly quoted as harmonizing and corroborative. But unsupported and counter-balanced, it has no argumentative weight, and the language of the near context (ver. 20), to say nothing of other passages in the last Gospel, might teach us to be cautious how we inject meanings into such phrases as, *abiding with, being in, and dwelling in.* "At that day ye shall know that I am in my Father, and ye in me, and I in you" (comp. xv. 4-7 ; xvii. 21, 23, 26). Unless, too, the hard exigencies of his position had coerced Mr Liddon to clutch recklessly at possible deductions, he would have noticed how verse 24 indirectly negatives Christ's Deity. "The word which ye hear, is not mine, but the Father's Who sent me." If Jesus and the Father are bound together by unity of Nature and Attributes, the 'word' is, in all strictness, as much Christ's as the Father's, and nothing is added to its dignity or sacredness, when it is in any sense disowned by the one, and transferred to the other. And even a Bampton Lecturer may be asked to re-member the twenty-eighth verse, before he proceeds to drag in theories through the twenty-third. Whether the Discourse in the supper-room is reported *verbatim,* or is a compilation of the Evangelist's from loose and imperfect data, of which we can never now know the original form, still, we may venture to surmise that, even the highest inspiration, in preparing materials for the exegetical offices of the Church, did not quite renounce rational coherence, and that, therefore, the relation implied in the asso-ciating words : " *We* will come, and make *Our* abode," is com-patible with the inferiority avowed in the saying : " *My Father is greater than I.*"

Mr Liddon is convinced, the claim to be universal Judge is irreconcilable with the capacities of any created intelligence. And if the question were simply a problem proposed to human reason and experience, much might be said for his view, but I must again remind him bare rationalism is inadmissible. In survey-ing, from the ground he has taken, the doctrine of our Lord's Divinity, we are not concerned with what reason alone makes probable, but with what the Sacred Writings, reasonably inter-preted, teach. And they teach with a clearness and accuracy which nothing can invalidate (short of a revelation more authori-tative and explicit than themselves), that the province of judg-ment belongs primarily to the Almighty, and that He delegates, commissions, and qualifies His Son, Servant, and Messenger, Jesus Christ, to act the part of Judge. ' To Him the Father *has given all judgment ; and given Him authority to execute judgment,* because He is the Son of Man (John v. 22, 27). He *is ordained of God* to be the Judge of the quick and the dead.   God has appointed a day in which He will judge the world in righteousness by *a man whom He has ordained* (Acts x. 42 ; xvii. 31).   God will judge the secrets of men, through Jesus Christ (Rom. ii. 16).'   The authors of these announcements may be quite mistaken, and far behind Mr Liddon in the scope and exactness of their information, but they announce plainly enough, that Jesus is, in the work of judging, God's Agent ; the Holder of an appointment from God, the Wielder of Divinely-consigned prerogatives. If judgment appertains to Christ's glorified condition as the Messiah,—*God has highly exalted Him ;* and, *made Him both Lord and Christ.*   He is not Judge in right of infinite, inherent, independent qualities, but in right of Divine ordination, and imparted gifts.   Orthodox Protestant expositors may, if they choose, pronounce this to be irrational, but they will argue more to the purpose, when they state what other meaning the words of Scripture will rationally bear.

That Evangelists and Apostles did not imagine the task of judging to demand the independent possession of the boundless resources of Deity, is evident from the fact of Christ's being made to promise that the Twelve (including Judas Iscariot ?) " shall sit on twelve thrones, judging the twelve tribes of Israel " (Matt. xix. 28),—a promise which St Luke repeats without specifying the number of thrones, but with the prefatory statement : " I appoint unto you a kingdom, as ($\varkappa\alpha\theta\dot\omega\varsigma$) my Father hath appointed unto me " (xxii. 28-30).   St Paul, also, was inspired to teach ; " the saints shall judge the world, and judge angels " (1 Cor. vi. 2, 3 ; comp. Rev. ii. 27 ; iii. 21).   These passages indicate, on the part of the Sacred Writers, a point of view different from that which Mr Liddon's rationalism furnishes, and a disability to perceive in the functions of judgment, duties necessarily beyond the range of created and Divinely-equipped intelligence.

If the foregoing considerations are fairly weighed, the concluding section of Matt. xxv., which Mr Liddon labours to utilize, cannot contribute to his argument.   But with respect to that section there is, obviously, something more to be added.   Supposing Jesus really to have uttered the sayings therein narrated, they must be taken together with their general context (for they terminate a series of closely-connected discourses), and compared with some other sayings which lead up to the emphatic predictions ; " Verily I say unto you, this generation will not pass away, till all these things be fulfilled " (Matt. xxiv. 34 ; Mark xiii. 30 ; Luke xxi. 32 ; compare also the very distinct statement in Matt. xvi. 27, 28). "Verily I say unto you, ye shall not have finished the cities of Israel, till the Son of Man be come" (Matt. x. 23). These texts are more than sufficient to make a sincerely truth-seeking cautious thinker pause, before he interprets the highly figurative and dramatic expressions contained in Matt. xxv. 31-46, of a coming to judge finally the human universe of quick and dead. And the whole probable bearing of purpose and language in chapters xxiv. and xxv. favours the opinion that, *the winding up (or conclusion) of the age,* which is so erroneously translated *the end of the world,* relates to the close of the Jewish Dispensation. Quietly to take for granted, in face of all the difficulties and uncertainty which hang around the phrases, *conclusion of the age ; coming of the Son of Man;* a yet future and universal assize to be intended, is a proceeding which can add no strength to a doctrine, and no credit to expositors who profess to find their guiding light in the Bible, and the Bible only.

"In dealing with separate souls, our Lord's tone and language," are, according to Mr Liddon, "not less significant" than in claiming to be universal Judge. "We will not here dwell on the fact of His forgiving sins (St Matt. ix. 6 ; St Mark ii. 10 ; St Luke v. 24), and of transmitting to His Church the power of forgiving them (St Matt. xvi. 19 ; xviii. 18 ; St John xx. 23)." For the ends of truth, however, we ought to dwell upon the texts referred to, so far as to note that, our Lord in replying to the murmuring thought of the Scribes ; 'Who is able to forgive sins except God only ?' hinted no claim whatever to Deity, but, employing the title which unequivocally denotes His Humanity, said; "that ye may know that *the Son of Man* hath power *on earth* to forgive sins," &c. Some of his auditors fancied He was arrogating a prerogative of the Almighty. He answered by an explicit confession of his Manhood, and affirmed His power to forgive sins, with the restricting clause, *on earth.* Neander comments : "God forgives the sins in heaven, but Christ, as Man, announces the Divine forgiveness. *Son of Man* and *on earth* are correlative conceptions." The context shows that the forgiveness the Son of Man had power to grant, to have been in effect, the removal of present disease, which either really was, or was believed by the Jews to be, inflicted as the punishment of transgression (comp. John v. 14 ; ix. 2, 34; Luke xiii. 2-5).

If the power of forgiving sins was transmitted to the Apostles, and in succession from them to the Church, then clearly, the possession of it does not necessarily involve the possession of Divine attributes, and the fact to which Mr Liddon points, tells against his argument.

The call of Christ, *Follow Me*, which occurs several times in the Gospels ; and the words, " He that loveth father or mother more than Me, is not worthy of Me.   If any man come to Me, and hate not his father, and mother, and wife, and children, and brethren, and sisters, yea and his own life also, he cannot be my disciple " (St Matt. x. 37 ; St Luke xiv. 26), are construed :— " It is clear that He treats those who come to Him, as literally belonging to Himself, in virtue of an existing right.   He commands, He does not invite, discipleship . . . . . It is impossible to ignore this imperious claim on the part of Jesus to rule the whole soul of man.   Other masters may demand a man's active energies, or his time, or his purse, or his thought, or some large share in his affections ; but here is a claim on the whole man, on his very inmost self, on the sanctities of his deepest life " (pp. 175, 176).   The stream of eloquence then expands into a succession of vehement interrogatories, whose form may be readily guessed.

Such studied inflation of language which, when justly interpreted, carries a much lower meaning, scarcely deserves attention. The contexts amply testify the complete absence of any approach to an assertion of inherently Divine right.   As the Messenger of God, and the Teacher of Truth, our Lord's commission and office quite justify the tone and cast of the language ascribed to Him, without resorting to the conjecture that He spoke from a reserved, underlying consciousness of Godhead.   If He knew Himself to be the preacher of the highest moral and spiritual verities ; if He felt that the Father had sent Him ; that the Father was with Him ; and that He was doing the Father's work,—His self-consciousness fully suffices to explain and vindicate the sayings which Mr Liddon loads with alien inferences, instead of equitably expounding.   Antagonism to existing earthly ties and relationships, inevitably waited on faithful discipleship to a spiritual Leader and Reformer Who came to purify and elevate old truths, and to proclaim truths practically new.   Decision, promptitude, the renunciation of worldly interests, and, in some cases, of home affections, may certainly be due tributes of allegiance to spiritual light and truth, without suggesting more than the inspiration and Divine Mission of the Instructor through Whom the light and truth are sent.

I find it very difficult, almost impossible, to comprehend how any man can have studied the Gospels, and yet have brought himself to pen such sentences as : " How can Christ bid men live for Himself, as for the very End of their existence ? How can He rightly draw towards Himself the whole thought and love, I do not say of a world, but of one single human being, with this imperious urgency, if He be indeed only the Christ of the Humanitarian teachers, if He be anything else or less than the supreme Lord of life ? " Where is there a tittle of proof Christ did anything of the kind ? In what discourse, honestly read by the light of near context, and the plain general purport of the Gospel records, did He ever put Himself on a level with God, or claim rights necessarily Divine ? Assuredly not in any utterance which Mr Liddon has been able to cite. But the poor sophistry of a bastard rationalism, to which I have before adverted, is beneath Mr Liddon's declamation. His traditional faith and pious credulity, having accepted conclusions destitute of Scriptural ground, retain his understanding to plead there is no place or rank for Jesus between actual Godhead and ordinary Manhood. Jesus Christ is in nature merely a human fellow-creature, or, he is in Nature the Adorable, Uncreated One ; and to the measures of these alternatives all Scripture must be forcibly contracted or forcibly stretched. Would it not be more reverent, as well as more logical and convincing, to say boldly : the Church Universal has been guided from Above to decree that Christ is ' Very God,' and by so decreeing, has provided a pregnant, paramount, unerring rule of interpretation, and a clue to senses of Scripture otherwise inaccessible ?

Mr Liddon, however, believes he can adduce something stronger than doubtful deductions and rhetorical special pleadings. The statements and claims in which the truth is latent, are, to our " positive moral relief," explained by declarations explicitly asserting Christ's Godhead. The comparative paucity of " the solemn sentences in which our Lord makes that supreme revelation," is acknowledged, but, " entering as He did perfectly into the actual conditions of our human and social existence, He exposed Himself to a triple scrutiny, and met it by a correspondingly threefold revelation. He revealed His Divinity to His disciples, to the Jewish people, and to His embittered opponents, the chief priests and Pharisees " (p. 177).

One instance of this revelation is our Lord's response when " Philip preferred to Him the peremptory request, ' Lord, shew us the Father, and it sufficeth us.' Well might the answer have thrilled those who heard it. ' Have I been so long time with you, and yet thou hast not known Me, Philip ? He that hath seen Me hath seen the Father ; and how sayest thou then, Shew us the Father ? Believest thou not that I am in the Father, and the Father in Me' ? (St John xiv. 9, 10). Now what this indwelling really implied is seen in our Lord's answer to a question of St Jude (verse 23)." The argument from the answer to St Jude's question has been already examined. And the utter futility of the appeal to the reply given to Philip, is easily demonstrated. According to the Evangelist, Jesus had just previously (verse 6) distinguished Himself, personally and officially at any rate, from the Father. He then had added, "If ye had known Me, ye would have known my Father also, and from henceforth ye know Him, and have seen Him."* This declaration drew from Philip a request which seems to have originated in the mistake of understanding literally the words, *have seen*. The rejoinder Jesus is represented to have made, was either a definite affirmation that He is personally the Father, and that, therefore, in Him the Father was beheld by the bodily senses (but see 1 John iv. 12 ; 1 Tim. vi. 16), or else it was a figurative statement that He is, through the Father's benefactions and indwelling, the Moral Image of God, and the Manifester of His teaching, character, and purposes. Even Orthodox Protestant theologians, when out of their pulpits, will not deny that it was the latter, and if so, it carries no intimation of equality of Attributes, unity of Nature, identity of Substance. That our Lord must not be supposed to have intended to equalize, or Essentially to identify Himself, with the Father, is evident from the sentence which follows next after Mr Liddon's quotation, " the words that I speak unto you, I speak not from myself, but the Father Who dwelleth in Me, *He doeth the works*" (an equally good reading is, *doeth His works*). See also verse 24.

Men who have strenuously toiled to sustain, by such arguments as the case admits, the idea that Christ's Deity is so set forth in Scripture, as to be sufficiently within the cognizance of devout and diligent intellects interpreting in accordance with the common laws of thought and diction, have perceived the weakness of inferences drawn from our Lord's " language in the supper-room to St Philip." Professor Stuart (Fourth Letter to Channing) wrote :

" The expression of Jesus that *the Father is in Him, and He in the Father*, I do not understand as asserting His Divine Nature in a direct manner. It is a phrase which is used to ex-

* Winer (*Grammar of New Testament*, Sec. xl. 4) observes that this last clause must he rendered literally : *from this time ye know Him, and ye have seen Him;* not paraphrased ; *ye will soon know, and as it were see Him.*

press the idea that any one is *most nearly and affectionately
united with God* (See 1 John iv. 16, where it is applied to Christians; also verses 12, 13, and 15)."

The error of the explanation which deduces the Essential
Unity of Christ and God, from the phraseology under consideration, is displayed, not alone by the context (John xiv. 20), and
other texts to which I have already referred, but also by Matt. x.
40; xxv. 40; John vi. 56; 1 John iii. 6, 24; 3 John 11).

The knowledge and the sight of the Father, and the mutual
indwelling between the Father and Himself, to which the words
of Jesus relate, are to be looked for in disclosures of God's Will,
and manifestations of His character and power.   And if the other
reasons, whose cumulative force unanswerably dispels the interpretation Mr Liddon would impose, did not exist, we should still
be bound to remember how in the same discourse and chapter,
there stands the very intelligible avowal, *the Father is greater
than I*, an avowal which, whether it contrasts Christ's purely
pre-incarnate, or His whole composite Being, with the Father's
Deity, is a declaration that He is Personally less than God, and
therefore, not Divine in the senses of the Nicene and Athanasian
Creeds.

Another instance of our Lord's "explicit and supreme revelation of Himself," is presented as follows.   When the Jews saw
a breach of the Sabbath-day in the healing of an impotent man,
and in the injunction given him to take up his bed and walk,—

"Jesus justified Himself by saying, 'My Father worketh
hitherto, and I work.' 'Therefore,' continues the Evangelist, 'the
Jews sought the more to kill Him, because He not only had
broken the Sabbath, but said also that God was His Own
Father, making Himself equal with God' (StJohn v. 17, 18). Now
the Jews were not mistaken as to our Lord's meaning. They
knew that the Everlasting God 'neither rests nor is weary;'
they knew that if He could slumber but for a moment the universe would collapse into the nothingness out of which He has
summoned it.   They knew that He 'rested on the seventh day'
from the creation of new beings; but that in maintaining the
life of those which already exist, He 'worketh hitherto.' They
knew that none could associate himself as did Jesus with this
world-sustaining energy of God, who was not himself God.
They saw clearly that no one could cite God's example of an
uninterrupted energy in nature and providence as a reason for
setting aside God's positive law, without also and thereby claiming to be Divine. . . . Our Lord claims a right to break the

Sabbath, because God's ever active Providence is not suspended on that day. Our Lord thus places both His Will and His Power on the level of the power and Will of the Father. . . . He claims distinctly to be Lord of nature, and thus to be equal with the Father in point of operative energy. He makes the same assertion in saying that 'whatsoever things the Father doeth, those things the Son also doeth in like manner' (ver. 19). To narrow down these words so as to make them only refer to Christ's imitation of the moral nature of God, is to take a liberty with the text for which it affords no warrant ; it is to make void the plain meaning of Scripture by a sceptical tradition. Our Lord simply and directly asserts that the works of the Father, without any restriction, are, both as to their nature and mode of production, the works of the Son " (pp. 179-181).

How much may be hidden in a little ! what stupendous conclusions in a few exceedingly vague and ambiguous words ! The commentary of Mr Liddon proves, at least, that the obligation of extracting Orthodox dogma from Scripture alone, develops both audacity and productive ingenuity. The simple, consistent, almost obvious explanation of Christ's language is neglected, and artificial, misguiding assumptions constructed to fit the dogma to be defended, are inserted at nearly every step. Our Lord did *not* " set aside God's positive law ; " He did *not* break the Sabbath, and He claimed no right to break it ; He broke only the Pharisaical and Rabbinical rules respecting it ; (see some pertinent observations on this point, in Smith's *Dictionary of the Bible ;* Art. Sabbath). Does Mr Liddon believe Christ's act of healing to have been a real violation of either the letter or spirit of the Fourth Commandment rightly understood ? and if he does not, what becomes of his argument ? The arbitrarily restrictive rules which Rabbis had appended to the Commandment, were quite separable from the Commandment itself. Our Lord does *not* " cite God's example of an uninterrupted energy in nature and providence as a reason " for His own conduct. He far more naturally, and probably, identifies His own acting with the acting of the Father by Whose might He performed His miracles. The Father wrought, and therefore He, being the Father's obedient Servant and Organ, wrought in resulting unison.

When we fix our attention solely on the Gospel narrative, and on the materials the Gospel furnishes to shape our judgment, the perversity of Mr Liddon's exposition becomes increasingly apparent. The Evangelist does not ascribe the hatred of the Jews, to the notion that our Lord associated Himself on terms of complete parity, with "the world-sustaining energy of God;" but, to the fact of His having, in their estimation, ' not only broken the Sabbath, but said also that God was His own Father, making Himself *equal with*' or, as the term may also mean, ' *like to* God.' It is not within the province of exposition to give disproportionate, or exclusive, predominance to aspects which the Canonical Writer does not put forward. The precise offence lay in the presumed arrogation of a peculiar Sonship, of which the association in working was an indication, and this offence was exaggerated into the blasphemy of challenging equality with God. The Jews malevolently caught at, and misrepresented, Christ's words. The Evangelist does not endorse their construction, either as to the breach of the Sabbath, or the nature of the Sonship, and in his record generally, he assuredly does not depict them as being the best, or at all unbiassed, judges of our Saviour's meaning. They often misunderstood and perverted His sayings, and malignantly blamed His actions (John vii. 20, 23; viii. 48; ix. 16; x. 19, 20, 33). And in the very passage from which Mr Liddon argues, Jesus Himself, with pointed emphasis, denies that His accusers had rightly apprehended His assertion of Sonship, when they saw in it, or pretended to see, an assumption of actual equality with, or near resemblance to, the Almighty One. "The Son can do nothing of Himself, save what He seeth the Father doing; for whatever things He doeth, these also doeth the Son in like manner. For the Father loveth the Son, and sheweth Him all things which Himself doeth; and He will show Him greater works than these, that ye may marvel" (verses 19 and 20; compare verse 30). As regards one point, this language is lucid enough. It is difficult to imagine what terms could signify more plainly, that the Sonship of Jesus was not of a kind to equalize Him with *the Only God* (verse 44). He acts by the Father's instruction, and at the Father's instigation. His action waits upon the Father's Will. He can do nothing from Himself; He originates nothing; He derives unceasingly, leading and knowledge from the Father, Who is His Teacher and Example. ' He does what He sees the Father doing, and the Father loves Him, and shows Him all things, &c.' The single feature which this phraseology throws distinctly out, is just that which corrects the Jews' mistake. Whatever undescribed, and indescribable, privileges of near communion and instrumental agency the Son may possess, there is between Him and the Father a vast difference; a difference which puts equality completely out of the question. Transpose the names Father and Son, and in the opinion of every sane mind, the Father's Godhead will be clearly denied. We cannot eliminate the relation of receptiveness, imitation, dependence, and comparative inability, even though we should arbitrarily distend the *whatsoever things* and *all things*, beyond the sphere of the works in which Christ was engaged on earth, and which the Father wrought through Him.

Elucidated by our Lord's own revelations, which Mr Liddon conceives to have been with such singular authenticity preserved in the Fourth Gospel ; His announcement, *My father worketh hitherto, and I work*, is, at the utmost, simply a statement that He was the Father's privileged Associate and Instrument ; that the Father was working in Him, and with Him, prompting, directing, and empowering, His deeds. "The Father Who dwelleth in me, He doeth the works. As the Father hath commanded me, so I do" (xiv. 10, 31)). "My judgment is just, because I seek not mine own will, but the Will of Him Who sent Me. I am come down from heaven, not to do mine own will, but the Will of Him Who sent Me" (v. 30 ; vi. 38). These expressions accord with the immediate context of the announcement, *My Father worketh*, &c., and leave an expositor without excuse when he tells us, the spiteful, carping Jews, ' were not mistaken as to our Lord's meaning.' The sense manifestly is, that Jesus was the Father's willing and obedient, as well as chosen and favoured, Organ : He spoke not His own words, and did not His own works, but always acted in virtue of the Father's Might, and revealed the Father's Mind and Will. In everything, the Father wrought; and therefore the Son, "Whom the Father had sanctified, and sent into the world" (x. 36), wrought correspondingly.

I have bestowed what will perhaps seem to some readers an unnecessary amount of attention on a very poor argument, but John v. 17 is just one of those texts which feeble but pretentious Biblical Orthodoxy loves to isolate, and fill with preconceptions. It is subjected to exacting stress, and loaded with the largest significance its terms could possibly, under the most favourable circumstances, be made to carry, while the context, and the numerous other passages which shed a bright light upon its meaning, are either quite ignored, or, with painstaking ingenuity, explained away. The concurring voices of many previous expositors are, doubtless, with Mr Liddon, but constitute only a slight palliation of his conduct, in wresting Scripture with such a violent hand. The time has gone by for parrot-repetitions of other men's opinions on the doctrine of our Lord's Divinity. We must either cease to make acceptance of the doctrine a condition of communion, or we must put the doctrine on its true basis. We must either interpret the Bible honestly beneath the beams of devoutly inquisitive reason, comparing Scripture with Scripture, or, we must make the decisions and authority of the Church Universal our starting-point and standard. Without impugning Mr Liddon's conscientious integrity, I cannot help thinking he would have appeared morally to greater advantage, if he had shown himself mentally more blind, but he saw quite well the obstacles besetting his way, and made the following attempt to reconcile the language of his cherished Evangelical document with Orthodox tradition :—

" Certainly our Lord insists very carefully upon the truth that the power which He wielded was derived originally from the Father. It is often difficult to say whether He is speaking, as Man, of the honour of Union with Deity, and of the graces which flowed from Deity, conferred upon His Manhood ; or whether, as the Everlasting Son, He is describing those natural and eternal Gifts which are inherent in His Godhead, and which He receives from the Father, the Fountain or Source of Deity, not as a matter of grace or favour, but in virtue of His Eternal Generation. As God, ' the Son can do nothing of Himself,' and this, not from lack of Power, but because His Being is inseparable from That of the Father. It is true of Christ as God in one sense—it is true of Him as Man in another—that, ' as the Father hath life in Himself, so hath He given to the Son to have life in Himself.' But neither is an absolute harmony of the works of Christ with the Mind and Will of the Father, nor a derivation of the Divine Nature of Christ Itself from the Being of the Father by an unbegun and unending Generation, destructive of the force of our Lord's representation of His operative energy as being on a par with that of the Father. For, our Lord's real sense is made plain by His subsequent statement that the 'Father hath committed all judgment unto the Son ; that all should honour the Son even as they honour the Father.' (v. 22, 23). This claim is indeed no more than He had already advanced, in bidding His followers trust Him and love Him " (p. 181).

Many theologians, sincere believers in Christ's Deity, have explained the words, *I and my Father are one* (John x. 30), of union in purpose and working, not of oneness in Substance, and identity in Nature. Neander gave up the text for the uses of controversial advocacy, when he wrote ; " We understand by the *oneness* here spoken of, the oneness of Christ with the Father in will and works, in virtue of which His work is the work of the

Father ; but this was founded on the consciousness of His original and essential oneness with the Father, as is clear (?) from His testimonies in other places as to His relations to God. In and of itself the language of Christ contained nothing that might not have been said from the standpoint of the Jewish idea of the Messiah. But the hostile spirits gladly seized the occasion to accuse Him of blasphemy, and preparations were made to stone Him " (*Life of Christ*). But Mr Liddon resolutely commits himself to an interpretation from which orthodox men of keener discernment, or feebler faith, have deliberately retired.

" Our Lord reveals His absolute Oneness of Essence with the Father. . . . He insists upon the blessedness of His true followers. With Him they are secure ; no power in earth or in heaven could ' pluck them out of His hand ' (ver. 28). A second reason for the blessedness of His sheep follows : ' My Father which gave them Me is a Greater Power than all :* and no man is able to pluck them out of My Father's Hand ' (ver. 29). In these words our Lord repeats His previous assurance of the security of His sheep, but He gives a different reason for it. He had represented them as ' in His own Hand.' He now represents them as in the Hand of the Almighty Father. How does He consolidate these two reasons which together assure His ' sheep ' of their security ? By distinctly asserting His own oneness with the Father : ' I and my Father are One Thing.' Now what kind of unity is that which the context obliges us to see in this solemn statement ? Is it such a unity as that which our Lord desired for His followers in His intercessory prayer—a unity of spiritual communion, of reciprocal love, of common participation in an imparted, heaven-sent Nature ? (as in St. John xvii. 11, 22, 23). Is it a unity of design and co-operation, such as that which, in varying degrees, is shared by all true workers for God ? (1 Cor. iii. 8). How would either of these lower unities sustain the full sense of the context, which represents the Hand of the Son as one with the Hand—that is, with the Love and Power—of the Father, securing to the souls of men an effectual preservation from eternal ruin ? A unity like this must be a *dynamic* unity, as distinct from any mere moral and intellectual union, such as might exist in a real sense between a creature and its God. Deny this dynamic unity, and you destroy the internal connection of the passage. Admit this dynamic unity, and you admit, by necessary implication, a unity

---

* Against a very heavy balance of MSS. testimony, Mr Liddon arbitrarily puts the adjective *greater* in the neuter. The Vulgate supports him, but the true reading is, pretty certainly, the masculine.

of Essence. The Power of the Son, which shields the redeemed
from the foes of their salvation, is the very Power of the Father ;
and this identity of Power is itself the outflow and the manifestation of a Oneness of Nature" (pp. 182-184).

As usual, the text, and immediately preceding context, are
cleverly, but palpably and grossly distorted. Jesus is not made
to say, that no one *can*, but, that no one *will*, pluck His sheep
out of His hand. The ground of this predicted security is then
stated ; " My Father Who gave them to Me is greater than all,"
&c. No one will pluck them out of Christ's hand, because they
are His Father's gift, and His Father being greater than all, (' a
stupid truism ' again ?), no one *is able* to pluck them out of His
Father's hand. In relation to their safety, He and His Father
are, in effect, one. To be by gift of the Father in Christ's hand
is to be in the Father's hand. The climax of security is the
Father's Almightiness. But if Christ is Omnipotent God, as
truly as the Father is, the reference to the Father does not
heighten the assurance of safe-keeping ; the Father's guardianship
adds no protection, and the Father's giving is a merely formal
and superficial, if not quite an unintelligible, consignment.

Surely the employment of the neuter numeral—in literal English, *one thing*—tells rather against than for Mr Liddon's object.
If the masculine or feminine form had been employed, there
would have been, so far, better reason for our surmising Essential
Oneness to have been predicated. With the masculine, it might
have been urged that *God* was the noun in agreement ; with the
feminine, that *nature* should be supplied. And, more than all,
the text would then have been dissociated from those other texts
which now so conclusively help to fix its meaning. The neuter
numeral is used in John xvii. 11, 21–23, where Jesus prays that
the disciples " may be *one thing*, as He and the Father are *one
thing*." It is used likewise, in 1 Cor. iii. 8 ; " He that planteth
and He that watereth are *one thing*." The unity between the
Father and the Son must, moreover, upon any tenable explication,
be of a kind not at variance with the declared facts, that the
Father Who sent Jesus Christ is *the Only True God ;* is *greater
than the Son;* and, that *the Son can do nothing of Himself.* But
a mind of thorough ecclesiastical culture is, perhaps, competent
to bend these enigmatical declarations into agreement with the
profoundly precise significance embodied in the neuter gender of
a numeral.

Some observations, in the course of which Professor Norton
refers to John x. 30, are very judicious, and capable of general

application in the exposition of the Fourth Gospel, if exposition is to be conducted on reasonable principles.

" Even where there is no peculiar boldness or strength of expression in the original, we are liable to be deceived by a want of analogy to our modes of speech. Figures and turns of expression familiar in one language are strange in another ; and an expression to which we are not accustomed strikes us with more force, and seems more significant, than one in common use, of which the meaning is in fact the same. We are very liable to mistake the purport of words which appear under an aspect unknown or infrequent in our native tongue. The declaration, *I and My Father are one*, may seem to us at first sight almost too bold for a human being to use concerning God, merely because we are not accustomed to this expression in grave discourse. But in familiar conversation, no one would misunderstand me, if, while transacting some business as the agent of a friend, I should say, *I and my friend are one ;* meaning, that I am fully empowered to act as his representative " (*Statement of Reasons, &c.*, Section 7).

Professor Stuart arguing for the Deity of Christ, against Channing, wrote (*Third Letter*)—

" You will expect me, perhaps, to adduce John x. 30, *I and my Father are one.* It is a clear case (?) that the Jews here seem to have understood Christ as claiming equality with God, or rather claiming to be God. (See verse 33.) But I am not satisfied that the manner in which they often expounded His words is a sure guide for our interpretation of them at the present time. The malignant disposition which they frequently displayed may well lead us to suspect that they would, if possible, put such a construction on His words as would subject Him to the imputation of blasphemy, or rebellion against the Roman government. I would expound the words of Christ, therefore, independently of any construction which His embittered enemies put upon them. And in the present case, it seems to me that the meaning of, *I and my Father are one*, is simply, I and my Father are united in counsel, design, and power."

Union in power does not, of course, denote identity of power, or possession of equal energy and might, but co-operative union for a common end. Identity of power (qualitative and quantitative) with God, must, in strictness, imply identity of Nature.

To the authority of the Jews as interpreters of Christ's sayings, Mr Liddon attaches a high value. He repeats the well-worn adage, so pertinently rebuking the Arians—'The Jews understood what the Arians do not understand.' He knows, and presumes the author of the Fourth Gospel to have known, how greatly malice sharpens the moral and intellectual perceptions. The moral disposition of the Jews accounts for the superior keenness of their intelligence, as compared with that of the Apostles and disciples. "They understood our Lord to assume Divine honours, and proceeded to execute the capital sentence decreed against blasphemy by the Mosaic law. His words gave them a fair ground for saying that, ' being Man, He made Himself God ' (ver. 33)."

Now, the reply of Jesus (ver. 36), to all appearance, testifies the imputation of blasphemy did not rest specifically on His claiming unity with God, but (as in an instance already discussed) on His calling God in some special sense His Father. The Jews' misconception, real or feigned, of the saying *I and My Father are one*, was, therefore, as it would seem, less gross than Mr Liddon's, and he cannot be sure he is sustained by their reputable alliance. But the answer ascribed to Jesus, if it was not studiedly evasive and diplomatic, excludes the blunders both of His ancient adversaries and His modern expositor. He referred to the Originator and Cause of the good works He had shown—they were *from* (ἐκ) *the Father*—and He asked, for which of these works the Jews menaced Him (ver. 32). They answered ' for a good work we stone thee not, but for blasphemy, *and because thou, being a man, makest thyself a god*' (Θεὸς without the Article. Observe the use of the Article with Θεὸς in the immediate context, and compare its use in v. 18). The sense would perhaps be more accurately conveyed to an English ear, by, *because thou, being human, makest thyself Superhuman* or *Divine*. Certainly the Jews did not mean that Jesus affirmed Himself to be individually, in His own person, the Almighty One. They did not, even with their stimulated insight, detect His saying to be in effect ; ' I am Jehovah, the God of Israel.' Such depth of penetration was a stage in the unfolding of Christian discernment. "Jesus answered them, Is it not written in your law, *I said ye are gods ?* If he called them gods unto whom the word of God came (and the Scripture cannot be made void), say ye of Him, whom the Father sanctified and sent unto the world, Thou blasphemest ; because I said, I am a Son of God ?" *

* As a rule in the Fourth Gospel, Jesus when naming Himself *Son*, and *Son of God*, uses the Article ; in x. 36 He does not, and I translate accordingly. If *Son of God* was a familiar and recognised Messianic title, the absence of the

Psalm lxxxii. has in verse 1, *God judgeth among gods;* in verse 6, *I said ye are gods, and all of you sons of the Most High* (comp. Luke i. 32). The Septuagint Version, of course, marks the distinction between *the God* and *gods,* by prefixing and omitting the Article. The reasoning, such as it is, in connection with the quotation ascribed to our Lord, seemingly turns upon the fact that *gods* are synonymous with *sons of the Most High,* and that the words cited would inevitably recall to Jewish minds the more apposite words left uncited. If unjust judges could be called *gods* and *sons of the Highest,* He whom the Father had consecrated and sent, could not justly incur the imputation of blasphemy by calling Himself *a son of God.* The reasoning implies that Christ would not have blasphemed had He called Himself θεός, since in official dignity and mission He was superior to those who were in Scripture called θεοί. He did not, however, employ that title, but the humbler and more customary designation, *son of God,* which could then only be equivalent to θεός, when, as in the instance quoted, the appellation was applied in some lower, relative, representative sense. By assuming Jesus to be Very God, we surrender the right to criticise any words which we hold to be really His, but if, being truly God, He could use the language quoted, in order to evade the charge of claiming to be what He truly was, then clearly, the Divine standard of truthfulness is among the mysteries of the Divine Nature, and is no pattern or standard for mankind. Taking for granted Mr Liddon's two suppositions—(1.) that Jesus in asserting His oneness with the Father, intended to reveal His own Deity ; (2.) that the Jews penetrated His meaning, and accordingly accused Him of identifying Himself with the Nature of the Almighty;—His expostulation, judged by the rules of human reason and morality, would be mere guileful evasion and deceit, because it carries every semblance of repudiating an imputation which, upon the suppositions above stated, was in all main points perfectly legitimate and true. No honest and moderately intelligent man deducing from Scripture only, would, I think, venture to affirm, our Lord's reply was calculated to suggest to His hearers the sense ; " I am indeed God, and do not, therefore, blaspheme when I announce my Unity in Nature with the Father."

But Mr Liddon's entire argument, apart from its other falla-

Article would make no practical difference, unless the context supplied reasons for supposing that the omission was designed to indicate a distinction in sense.

cies, appears to me to rest on the substitution of a fiction of his
own for the specific reproach urged by the Jews, who, according
to the terms of their accusation, and of our Lord's answer,
censured Him because He, being, as they considered, merely human
(compare John vii. 27), claimed to be Superhuman, by claiming
to be, in some peculiar sense, *Son of God.*   Good declamation is
wasted in the sentences :—

" Who then shall anticipate the horror of His soul or the fire
of His words, when He is once made aware of the terrible misap-
prehension to which His language has given rise in the minds
around Him ?   ' Thou, being a man, makest Thyself God ?'   The
charge was literally true ; being human, He did make Himself
God.   Christians believe He only ' made' Himself That which
He is.   But if He is not God, where does He make any adequate
repudiation of a construction of His words so utterly derogatory
to the great Creator, so necessarily abhorrent to a good man's
thought ?" (p. 199).

It would be far more to the purpose to ask ; What conceivable
relevance is there in the citation from the language of the
eighty-second Psalm, if our Lord's relation to the Father was not
only nearer and more elevated in degree than, but utterly
different in kind from, that of the theocratic chiefs of ancient
Israel?   Things absolutely diverse in kind are not mutually
illustrative, except in the hands of a bad reasoner, or a cunning
verbal trickster.   Here again Mr Liddon, unhappily for his own
reputation, shows himself to be not altogether blind ; " Our
Lord's quotation justified His language only, and not His full
meaning, which, upon gaining the ear of the people, He again
proceeded to assert."   The imagined re-assertion is in the remaining clauses of Christ's vindication of Himself from the
reproach of blasphemy ; " If I do not 'the works of My Father,
believe Me not.   But if I do them, though ye believe not Me,
believe the works ; that ye may know and understand, that *the
Father is in Me, and I in Him*" (x. 37, 38).   The concluding
words are, to Mr Liddon's mind, " expressive of our Lord's shar-
ing not merely a dynamical, but an essential Unity with the
Father."   But, presuming the words to have the force Mr Liddon
awards to them, will he explain the reciprocal indwelling of
Christ and His disciples, as enunciated in John vi. 56 ; xiv. 20 ;
xv. 4 ; xvii. 21, 23, 26 ; and give some valid reason for subject-
ing phrases of one and the same cast, to totally different interpretations ?

Like a skilful strategist, Mr Liddon gives the boldest front to arguments of more than ordinary weakness. In treating the words, *Before Abraham was, I am* (John viii. 58), he says :—

"In these tremendous words, the Speaker institutes a double contrast, in respect both of the duration and of the mode of His existence, between Himself and the great ancestor of Israel. *Before Abraham was born.* Abraham, then, had come into existence at some given point of time. Abraham did not exist until his parents gave him birth. But, *I am.* Here is simple existence, with no note of beginning or end. Our Lord says not, 'Before Abraham was, I was,' but, 'I am.' He claims pre-existence indeed, but He does not merely claim pre-existence; He unveils a consciousness of Eternal Being. He speaks as One on Whom time has no effect, and for Whom it has no meaning. He is the *I AM* of ancient Israel; He knows no past, as He knows no future; He is unbeginning, unending Being; He is the eternal ' Now.' This is the plain sense of His language, and perhaps the most instructive commentary upon its force is to be found in the violent expedients to which Humanitarian writers have been driven in order to evade it" (pp. 187, 188).

This exposition is the product of a prejudiced imagination, and on every ground, grammatical and other, is not what the guidance of Scripture alone suggests. Before it can be fairly imposed, the doctrine it conveys should be so settled and determined as to invest with probability a merely possible sense. As regards the grammar, the present tense of the verb substantive is often, in the Fourth Gospel and elsewhere in the Sacred Writings, equivalent to the past ; for examples, see Greek, in John v. 13, 15 ; vi. 24, 64 ; xii. 9 ; xiv. 9 ; xv. 27 ; xx. 14 ; xxi. 4, 12 ; Acts ix. 26, (comp. Sept. Psalm lxxxix. 2 ; Jer. i. 5). Winer makes the saying, " Before Abraham was, I am," an illustration of his remark : " Sometimes a Past Tense is included in the Present, when, for instance, a verb expresses a state which commenced at an earlier period, but still continues—a state in its whole duration."—(*Gram. New Test.*, Sec. xl. 2). The rendering, *Before Abraham was* (or *was born*), *I was*, is therefore not merely permissible, but so highly probable, that weighty objections are required to exclude it. Jesus claimed pre-existence, either actual, or, in the Mind and purposes of God. But actual pre-existence, even before the world was (xvii. 5), is not necessarily the Everlasting, Uncaused, existence of Deity; and its assertion, taken alone, cannot mount higher than the Apocalyptic title, *the beginning of the creation of God* (Rev. iii. 14).

The Gospel 'according to John,' must, I conceive, be admitted both to affirm and imply Christ's veritable pre-existence, and, therefore, I have no inclination to argue that anything less than really antecedent Being is the more probable sense of John viii. 58.* But pre-existence need not, as Mr Liddon concedes, imply true Divinity; and the attempt to establish, from rational and Scriptural considerations, that the words in question mean more than pre-existence, must, in any hands, be a ridiculous failure.

For connecting Christ's saying with Exod. iii. 14, there is absolutely no justification whatever. The Hebrew title in that passage is either, *I am What I am;* or, *I will be What I will be :* " say unto the children of Israel, *I Am*, or, *I Will Be*, hath sent," &c. The Septuagint Version, and the Vulgate, render; "*I am He Who is. . . . He Who is* hath sent, &c. Now, the distinctive force and significance of the title are certainly not in the fragment *I am*, but either in the whole title, or, in the portion, *He Who is.* The supposition that Jesus appropriated, or was understood, even by the Jews, to appropriate, a most sacred and peculiar designation of the Self-existent Immutable God, is too arbitrary and improbable to merit examination. Take *I am* as a designation of the Almighty One, equivalent to Jehovah, and the saying of Jesus ceases to be a proposition :—" Before Abraham was, *Jehovah.*" It is perfectly futile to contend, Christ's words had the same force as if He had said, *I am Who I am ;* or, *I am He Who is. I am* is far too common and indispensable a form of language to be a name or appellation, and, when more than a bare statement of existence, must be supplemented into a proposition, as the context suggests. And the whole connection of the passage demonstrates that, if more was intended than the bare affirmation of existence anterior to Abraham, it was the avowal of Messiahship.

Beginning at verse 12, we learn that the self-assertions of Jesus respecting His own office, relation to God, and mission from Above, elicited from the sceptical Jews the inquiry : " Who

* I do not forget how facts and events designed and pre-ordained by the Almighty, are frequently described in Scripture as though they had actually existed previously to their realization. Not to mention examples from the Old Testament, see Rom. iv. 16, 17 ; Eph. i. 3, 4 ; 2 Tim. i. 9 ; Tit. i. 2 ; Rev. xiii. 8. Language of this type is characteristically Hebraistic, and Professor Norton (*Statement of Reasons, &c.,* Third Edition, p. 283) illustrates its use by instances from Rabbinical sources ; but I cannot doubt that the writer of the latest Gospel teaches Christ's pre-existence. It seems to me as unreasonable to deny he teaches Christ's pre-existence, as it is unreasonable to assert he teaches Christ's Godhead.

art thou ?   And Jesus said unto them : Even what I said unto you from the beginning ;" or, according to a preferable translation, " Altogether what I say unto you."   (I am entirely what in my discourses I profess to be.   *Winer*, Sec. liv. 1.)   Our Lord then went on to say, that ' He did nothing of Himself, but was instructed and sent by the Father, and had the Father's presence with Him, because He did always those things which pleased the Father ' (ver. 25-30).   He reproached His enemies (ver. 40) with *seeking to kill Him, a man who had spoken to them the truth, which He had heard from God ;* and He met their boast that God was their Father with the reasoning, " If God were your Father, ye would love Me, for I came forth, and am come from God, neither came I of myself, but He sent Me " (ver. 42).   Having upbraided the Jews with diabolical parentage and diabolical deeds, He disclaimed a counter charge of having a devil, and said, " I honour my Father, and ye do dishonour Me.   But I seek not my own glory ; there is One that seeketh and judgeth. Verily, verily, I say unto you, if a man keep my saying he shall never see death" (ver. 49, 51).   This made the Jews renew their abuse : " Now we know that thou hast a devil.   Abraham died, and the prophets ; and thou sayest if a man keep my saying he shall never taste death.   Art thou greater than our father Abraham, who died ? and the prophets died ; whom makest thou thyself ?"   According to the Evangelist, Jesus answered, " If I glorify Myself, my glory is nothing ; it is my Father that glorifieth me, of Whom ye say, He is our God : and ye have not known Him ; but I know Him ; and if I should say, I know Him not, I shall be a liar like unto you ; but I know Him, and keep His saying.   Your father Abraham rejoiced that he should see my day ; and he saw it, and was glad.   The Jews, therefore, said unto Him, Thou art not yet fifty years old, and hast thou seen Abraham ?   Jesus said unto them, Verily, verily, I say unto you, before Abraham was born, *I am*," or, amending the translation, since the verb substantive is coupled with the mention of past time, " before Abraham was born, *I was*" (ver. 52-58). Now, only in our Lord's character of Messiah, could Abraham, by faith, have ' seen His day,' and this fact, together with the whole scope of the context, obliges us, if we regard Christ's assertion as a partially expressed proposition, to see in it a declaration of Messiahship.   I do not dwell on the virtual negations of Godhead with which the context must be admitted to abound, unless it was dictated by an inspiration of concealment and perplexity paving the way for the subsequent and higher revealing functions of the Church. The identical expression, *I am*, occurs in this very same eighth chapter, and in other places of the Fourth Gospel, in a manner which alone is sufficient to evince the absurdly untenable nature of the interpretation Mr Liddon endeavours to enforce. "If ye believe not that *I am*, ye shall die in your sins" (ver. 24). "When ye have lifted up the Son of Man, then shall ye know that *I am*" (ver. 28). "Jesus said unto her, *I am*, who speak unto you" (iv. 26). "And he saith unto them, *I am;* be not afraid" (vi. 20). "I tell you before it come to pass, that, when it is come to pass, ye may believe that *I am*" (xiii. 19). "Whom seek ye? They answered Him, Jesus of Nazareth. Jesus saith unto them, *I am*. As soon then as He said unto them, *I am*, they went backward and fell to the ground. He asked them, therefore, again, Whom seek ye? And they said, Jesus of Nazareth, Jesus answered, I told you that *I am*" (xviii. 4-8). In all these instances, the supplementary idea requisite to complete the sense, is unmistakably indicated by the context. But if *I am* is to be understood as a most sacred and yet familiar Divine title, then according to Mark xiii. 6, and Luke xxi. 8, the false Christs were to claim Deity; a blind man also who had been healed, used dangerously ambiguous language when he said, *I am* (John ix 9.; comp. Sept. Isa. xlvii. 8, 10).

When these considerations are duly weighed, "the plain sense of Christ's language" is seen to be either the simple assertion of pre-Abrahamic existence, or, the avowal of Messiahship. The conjecture of an intention to announce Eternal, Self-existent Being, is, if rationally measured by Scripture evidence, wildly unwarranted and improbable.

CHAPTER X.

Supposed Evidence that the Sanhedrim condemned Christ for claiming to be God.—The Title *Son of God* never, in Jewish estimation, equivalent to *God*, or more than a Messianic designation.—Force of the Exclamation attributed to the Apostle Thomas when he was convinced of Christ's Resurrection.—The Argument from certain sayings in the Synoptical Gospels assumed to be closely similar to sayings found in the 'Gospel according to John.'—Baseless, reprehensible, and irreverent character of the Dilemma, 'If Jesus Christ is not God, He is not morally good.'—Language ascribed to Christ Himself, is, plainly and often, not rationally reconcilable with the Dogma of His Godhead.

WITH his accustomed hardihood, Mr Liddon affirms; "Nothing is more certain than that, whatever was the dominant motive that prompted our Lord's apprehension, the Sanhedrin condemned Him because He claimed Divinity. The members of the court stated this before Pilate, 'We have a law, and by our law He ought to die, because He made Himself the Son of God' (St John xix. 7). Their language would have been meaningless if they had understood by the 'Son of God' nothing more than the ethical or theocratic Sonship of their own ancient kings and saints. If the Jews held Christ to be a false Messiah, a false prophet, a blasphemer, it was because He claimed literal Divinity. True, the Messiah was to have been Divine. But the Jews had secularized the Messianic promises; and the Sanhedrin held Jesus Christ to be worthy of death under the terms of the Mosaic law, as expressed in Leviticus and Deuteronomy (Lev. xxiv. 16 ; Deut. xiii. 5)." [For the very doubtful appropriateness of these references, consult the passages themselves.] "After the witnesses had delivered their various and inconsistent testimonies, the high priest arose and said, 'I adjure Thee by the living God, that Thou tell us whether Thou be the Christ, the Son of God. Jesus saith unto him, Thou hast said ; nevertheless, I say unto you, Hereafter shall ye see the Son of Man sitting on the right hand of power, and coming in the clouds of heaven. Then the high priest rent his clothes, saying, He hath spoken blasphemy' (St Matt. xxvi. 63–65). The blasphemy did not consist either in the assumption of the title Son of Man, or in the claim to be

Messiah, or even, excepting indirectly, in that which by the terms of Daniel's prophecy was involved in Messiahship, namely, the commission to judge the world. It was the further claim to be the Son of God, not in any moral or theocratic, but in the natural sense, at which the high priest and his coadjutors professed to be so deeply shocked. The Jews felt, as our Lord intended, that the Son of Man in Daniel's prophecy could not but be Divine; they knew what he meant by appropriating such words as applicable to Himself" (pp. 190, 191).

Here, again, there are traces that Mr Liddon sees the difficulty, which by a clever exercise of his talent for special pleadership he endeavours to disguise. In what acceptation could the Jews have felt that the Son of Man, as described in Dan. vii. 13, 14, was Divine? He is not put on an equality with the Ancient of Days; there is no particle of excuse for identifying Him with the Most High; and there is nowhere any approach to evidence that in Jewish estimation either *Son of Man*, or *Son of God*, meant *God* in the full, true, proper sense of the term, as applied by the Jews to Jehovah, the Sole Personal Object of their faith and worship. What is "the natural sense" of the term *Son* in relation to God? and, where in the Canon of Scripture is there any shadow of warrant for understanding the term to denote a relation different in kind from that of *produced* intelligent Beings, either celestial or human? Will Mr Liddon deny the strictest Monotheism to have been the fundamental basis of Jewish conceptions of the Divine Entity, and if he will not, what sort of Co-eternal, Co-equal, Consubstantial, and yet distinctly Personal Sonship, does he hold to be—I do not say familiarly, but possibly—associable with a scrupulously jealous faith in One God? The chief priests and rulers may have thought Christ to be guilty of blasphemy when He hinted at, or alleged, the possession of Sonship in an antecedent celestial nature, because such an allegation involved high claims to deference and authority as the Ambassador and Representative of God. Such claims would appear to them impious intrusions into the sphere of the Divine government, and, therefore, derogatory to the Divine honour, but there is no pretext for supposing even the blundering spite attributed to Jews, to have been so blundering as to charge Jesus with arrogating to Himself identity with the Eternal One.

Mr Liddon, in common with many controversialists on his side, indulges in the conjecture that the inquiry, "tell us whether thou be the Christ, the Son of God" (Matt. xxvi. 63), does not intimate that in the opinion of the high priest, *the Christ* was *the*

Son of God. He presumes the titles to be distinct, and our Lord to have claimed them both in their separate meanings. The word *and*, which ought to have stood between the titles, is unfortunately missing, but the requirements of Orthodox argument show us how to correct a clause which has no various readings. In his reply (ver. 64, and Mark xiv. 62), Jesus takes the undoubtedly Messianic appellation, *Son of Man*, which, combined with the form of the imputation in John xix. 7, implies that *Son of Man* and *Son of God* were both recognised Messianic designations. The record in Luke xxii. 69, 70, is varied, and the announcement; ' the Son of Man will be seated on the right hand of the power of God,' at once evokes from the whole assembled council the demand, ' Art thou then the Son of God ?' plainly suggesting that *Son of God* was, in the opinion of the Sanhedrim, a Messianic title.

From Matt. xxvii. 54, we learn how, " when the centurion, and they that were with him watching Jesus, saw the earthquake, and those things that were done, they feared greatly, saying, Truly this was the Son of God." Are we to suppose them to have meant that Jesus was the Messiah, or, that He was God ? By St Mark's narrative (xv. 39) the saying is ascribed to the centurion alone, and he is made to say explicitly, "truly *this Man* was the Son of God," a form of speech which may be a recognition of Messiahship, but is hardly a recognition of Deity. St Luke's narrative (xxiii. 47) makes the centurion say, " certainly this man was righteous." It is to be regretted the circumstances of the case forbid the application of the ordinary process for reconciling differences, and will not permit us to maintain all the inspired accounts to be *verbatim* accurate, the centurion and those with him having spoken once, and the centurion alone twice.

The derisive taunts of the passers-by, and of the mocking priests and scribes, are related by the three Synoptists with a general, but by no means minute, agreement (Matt. xxvii. 40-43 ; Mark xv. 29-32 ; Luke xxiii. 35-37). The asserters of verbal inspiration, no doubt, have harmonizing expedients capable of eliminating all appearance of discrepancy in details, but, assuming the verbal exactness of St Matthew's record, there is an utter absence of indication that *Son of God* was equivalent to *God*, or other than a Messianic description.

I may add ; the Fourth Gospel—Mr Liddon's paramount authority when obscurities are to be illuminated—to some extent witnesses the Jews had not so "secularized the Messianic promises," as to popularize the notion that Christ was *not* to be

Superhuman. " We know this man whence he is ; but when the Christ cometh, no man knoweth whence He is " (John vii. 27), are words which can hardly point to the place of Christ's birth (comp. vers. 41, 42). The aim of the Gospel, as stated in the concluding words of the twentieth chapter, is to create the belief " that Jesus is *the Christ, the Son of God,*" where the discriminative *and* is again wanting. See also, John xi. 27, with which read verse 22.

In seeking to ascertain what was, in Christ's own earthly lifetime, the full meaning of the phrase *Son of God,* as descriptive of Him, we cannot overlook that confession of St Peter's, which was, according to the First Gospel, though not according to the others, made in the words :—*Thou art the Christ, the Son of the Living God* (Matt. xvi. 16 ; comp. Mark viii. 29 ; Luke ix. 20 ; John vi. 69, with correct reading). Mr Liddon assumes the verbal fidelity of St Matthew's single record, and argues :—

" If St Peter had intended only to repeat another and a practically equivalent title of the Messiah, he would not have equalled the earlier confession of a Nathanael (John i. 49), or have surpassed the subsequent admission of a Caiaphas (Matt. xxvi. 63). If we are to construe his language thus, it is altogether impossible to conceive why ' flesh and blood ' could not have ' revealed ' to him so obvious and trivial an inference from his previous knowledge, or why either the Apostle or his confession should have been solemnly designated as the selected Rock on which the Redeemer would build His imperishable Church " (p. 11.) But difficulties too formidable to be ignored, without moral discredit, lie in the way of this bold assumption. Not only are the words, *Son of the Living God,* no part of St Peter's confession as reported by three Evangelists, but the one Evangelist who does report them, makes them, to all appearance, a practical equivalent, or at most an explanatory extension, of Messiah's name. The confession is not " the Christ *and* the Son." The significance introduced by separating the designations is entirely the achievement of interpretation. Our Lord Himself, by the plain tenor of the narrative, saw in Peter's words an acknowledgment of Messiahship, and charged His disciples that they should tell no one He was *the Christ* (Matt. xvi. 20 ; comp. Mark viii. 30 ; Luke ix. 21). The Fourth Gospel, it must be conceded, makes the knowledge of His Messiahship familiar, and relates how He had Himself, from the very commencement of His ministry, proclaimed in the freest way His Messianic character.

There is, in fact, a glaring and irremovable discrepancy on this topic, between the last written and the earlier Gospels, and to utilize any feature of this discrepancy, in the elucidation of Peter's confession, is a remarkable stroke of expository daring and skill. But if St Peter, in making the solemn, profoundly significant, and heaven-inspired reply, which only one Evangelist has correctly transmitted, meant all that Mr Liddon imagines, how are we to explain the circumstance, that neither he nor any of " the other disciples in whose name he replied," ever exhibited the awe-struck veneration of men who knew the Master whose companions they were, to be Very God, the Almighty Father's Equal, in human form? Where is there, in the recorded conduct of Apostles and disciples, a single trace of the effect which the strong suspicion, not to say the faith, that Jesus Christ was indeed the Eternal God, must inevitably have produced? That His first followers loved and revered their Great Master, believing Him to have been sent by God, and to have God with Him, will not be disputed, but that they believed Him to be Himself God, is a conclusion which the Evangelical Histories absolutely refuse to yield.

Surveying the facts to which I have referred, it is, I think, quite manifestly a gratuitous and untenable opinion, that the Jews employed, or supposed our Lord to have employed, the title *Son of God*, to signify " literal Divinity," that is, possession of the One Eternal, Uncreated, Omnipotent Nature. And if Caiaphas, and his fellow priests and rulers, had employed it in this sense, in what respect would Peter's confession have 'surpassed their admission?' In his Fourth Lecture, Mr Liddon contends that, members of the Sanhedrim saw what he conceives to have been the full sense of the designation *Son of God*, and condemned Christ for claiming to be Divine (*i.e.*, God) ; but, in his First Lecture, he refers to the language of Caiaphas (Matt. xxvi. 63), as of more circumscribed meaning than Peter's confession. Is there not inconsistency here?

The exclamation ascribed to Thomas ; *My Lord, and my God* (John xx. 28), Mr Liddon (Lect. vii.) calls *an adoring confession,* and pre-eminently *the language of adoration.* If he concludes Thomas to have been convinced Jesus was the Lord God Himself, and to have expressed the conviction, he defies every inference which the context suggests. The evidence offered to Thomas was not evidence that Jesus was God, but, that Jesus had risen from the grave. The fact which the faith of the previously unconvinced Apostle recognized, was the fact of Christ's

Resurrection.   Does that fact prove Christ to be God ?   Our Lord accepted the acknowledgment in strict relation to the circumstances out of which it grew, and pronounced a blessing, not on those who without having seen His wounded body believe He is the Immortal God, but on those who without having seen, believe He rose again from the dead.   If after His Resurrection, or, at any period of their intercourse with our Lord on earth, all, or any, of His Apostles entertained the persuasion they were associating with their God and Creator, their state of mind must have imprinted deeply corresponding marks upon their conduct. But, beyond dispute, such marks are totally wanting, and against the absence of them, the isolated phraseology of an excited exclamation cannot for one moment be rationally set.

If *the Absolute Good* and *the Absolute Truth*, are comprehensive descriptions of Godhead, then, it is an error to fancy descriptions synonymous with them are applied to Christ in the Fourth Gospel ; and a double misrepresentation to say, as Mr Liddon does, in his Fifth Lecture ; " When we weigh the language of the first three Evangelists, it will be found that Christ is represented by it as the Absolute Good and the Absolute Truth not less distinctly than in St John."   To support this misrepresentation we have some choice specimens of exposition.   " It is on this account that He is exhibited as in conflict, not with subordinate or accidental forms of evil, but with the evil principle itself, with the Prince of Evil.   ' I beheld Satan as lightning fallen from heaven' (St Luke x. 18).   The temptation by Satan (St Matt. iv. 1-11).   ' If I cast out devils by the Spirit of God,' &c. (St Matt. xii. 27-29).   'The field is the world ; the good seed are the children of the kingdom, but the tares are the children of the wicked one,' &c. (xiii. 38, 39)" (p. 251).

Read the passages referred to, as they stand in the Gospels, and the ridiculous folly of connecting them, even indirectly, with claims to Godhead, or inferences of Godhead, is palpable.   If Mr Liddon was so disinterested as to have no respect for his own intellectual reputation, when he devoted himself to the occupation of defending from untenable grounds the Church's faith, he might have respected his audience.   But he goes on, in the same strain ; " And, as the Absolute Good, Christ tests the moral worth or worthlessness of men by their acceptance or rejection, not of His doctrine, but of His Person.   It is St Matthew who records such sentences as the following: ' Be not ye called Rabbi ; for One is your Master, even Christ' (xxiii. 8) ; ' He that loveth father or mother more than Me is not worthy of Me' (x. 37 ;)

' Whosoever shall confess Me before men, him will I confess also before My Father' (x. 32 ; St Luke xii. 8) ; 'Come unto Me, all ye that labour, and I will give you rest ; Take My yoke upon you, and learn of Me' (xi. 28, 29). In St Matthew, then, Christ speaks as One Who knows Himself to be a universal and infallible Teacher in spiritual things ; Who demands submission of all men, and at whatever cost or sacrifice ; Who offers to mankind those deepest consolations which are sought from all others in vain. Nor is it otherwise with St Luke and St Mark " (p. 252).

Differences of reading are here of little moment, but Mr Liddon must be aware, the probably true reading in the first of the texts he quotes, is, " Be not ye called Rabbi ; for One is your Teacher ($\delta\iota\delta\acute{a}\sigma\varkappa\alpha\lambda o\varsigma$)." The name *Christ* is not mentioned, and our Lord went on consecutively, " And all ye are brethren. And call none your father upon the earth ; for One is your Father, the Heavenly. Neither be ye called leaders ;* for one is your Leader, the Christ." The highest title, and the supreme honour, are reserved for the Father in heaven. The disciples are forbidden to be like the self-exalting Scribes and Pharisees, in appropriating names of authority and distinction ; and, in matters of religion and conscience, they are forbidden to recognize any right to childlike, implicit obedience, except the right of God. The appellation they are forbidden to give, is manifestly, in its spiritual aspect, of higher import than the customary preceptorial appellations they are forbidden to accept ; and I am at a loss to understand why Mr Liddon should have referred to the passage, unless he hoped to catch the ear with a semblance of argument unfit for the mind to investigate.

Matt. x. 32 and 37 are, of course, to be studied with their contexts. They demand confession of Christ, and self-denying submission to Him, as the God-sent Messenger and Instructor, and they stand in a connection which clearly points to One greater and more exalted than Christ—even the Father in heaven Who sent Him. Our Lord enforces the duty of receiving those whom He sends, by the statement ; " He that receiveth you, receiveth Me, and he that receiveth Me, receiveth Him Who sent Me " (ver. 40), where He either identifies His messengers with Himself in the same way in which He identifies Himself with the Father, or He implies that, as He is superior to His messengers, so the Father by Whom He was sent is superior to Him.

* The term used may be *Guide, Leader,* or, *Teacher.* To mark the difference from the other term (ver. 8), I give the more radical and literal meaning.

Q

No other interpretation is possible, unless we are able to bring in, from extraneous sources, clear light and fixed conclusions.

In making a joint reference to Luke xii. 8, did Mr Liddon fail to notice, how the confession on the part of the Son of Man is there said to be *before the angels of God,* instead of, as in Matthew, *before my Father Who is in Heaven?*

In studying Matthew xi. 28, 29, the surroundings of the passage must again be our guide. Perhaps it is enough, to add the clause Mr Liddon omits ; *because I am meek and lowly in heart;* and to·ask, with relation to whom this meekness and humility existed. If they existed towards God, then, it is difficult to see how the text in which they are adduced as reasons for taking Christ's yoke and learning of Him, can at all help to bring into view His Personal Godhead. Are not the words *learn of Me,* &c., explanatory of the preceding invitation and promise, and indicative of one whose standing is that of Instructor and Example, not that of Omnipotent Sovereign and Benefactor ? Only by an intellect rarely gifted, or peculiarly conformed, can the passage be perceived to involve claims of Deity.

"If the title of Divinity is more explicitly put forward in St John, the rights which imply it are insisted on in words recorded by the earlier Evangelists. The Synoptists represent our Lord, Who is the object of Christian faith no less than the Founder of Christianity, as designing the whole world for the field of His conquests (St Matt. xxviii. 19 ; St Mark xvi. 15 ; St Luke xxiv. 47 ; comp. St Matt. xiii. 32, 38, 41 ; xxiv. 14), and as claiming the submission of every individual human soul. All are to be brought to discipleship. Only then will the judgment come, when the Gospel has been announced to the whole circle of the nations (St Matt. xxiv. 14). Christ, the Good and the Truth Incarnate, must reign throughout all time (St Luke xxii. 69). He knows, according to the Synoptists no less than St John, that He is a perfect and final Revelation of God. He is the Centre-point of the history and of the hopes of man. None shall advance beyond Him ; the pretension to surpass Him is but the symptom of disastrous error and reaction (St Matt. xxiv. 23-26, &c.)" (pp. 252, 253).

That Jesus, conscious of His own mission from God, and of the adaptation to the needs of Humanity, of the few but pregnant spiritual and ethical precepts which He promulgated, may have looked forward to the universal spreading of His religion, is, doubtless, what might be expected ; but the texts to which Mr Liddon refers are not, I think, sufficient to prove that our Lord either explicitly announced the universal diffusion of Christianity, or enjoined His disciples to preach to all the nations of the earth. The whole context around Matt. xxiv. 14, on which Mr Liddon relies, goes to show that, *the end* there, was not a final judgment, but a very proximate event ; and the phrase employed for *world* is really only commensurate with the inhabited parts known to the Jews—at most, the Roman Empire ; and yet, the promulgation of the Gospel in this comparatively narrow sphere, is said to be *for a witness to all the nations.* The preaching of the Gospel *among all the nations* (Luke xxiv. 47) is not, therefore, language altogether conclusive as to definite designs, and express injunctions to make the whole globe the field of Christianity. But I have already touched upon this subject, and need not repeat reasons, more particularly as its bearing upon the theme of Mr Liddon's Lectures is very indirect. The universality of Christ's religion, if it were at this moment absolutely universal, would not aid in proving His Deity, unless the dogma of His Deity were demonstrably an integral portion of His religion.

Before deducing copiously and exactingly from Matt. xxviii. 19, any Protestant controversialist is bound to recognize, and endeavour to remove, the discrepancy which exists—(1.) between that passage and the sentiments and conduct of the Apostles relative to the admission of the Gentiles into the Christian Church (see Acts x. and xi.) ; and, (2.) between that passage and every other notice of the formula for Christian Baptism which is found in the New Testament. The arguments I have already advanced on this point, are merely the expression of ordinary fairness and common sense. They are too obvious and inevitable not to have been well known to Mr Liddon, and until they are met, it is worse than useless to talk of, " self-intrusion into the sphere of Divinity," and to tell us ; Jesus " deliberately inserts His own Name into the sacramental formula ; He inserts it between that of the Father and that of the Spirit." Bapti-m " into the Name of the Father, and of the Son, and of the Holy Ghost," was the common practice of the Church early in the second century, so far as the scanty evidence we possess reveals her practice, but by every rule of reasonable interpretation, the Acts of the Apostles and the Epistles attest Baptism to have been, at the first, administered with another and a simpler formula. Words of solemn command and instruction, uttered by the risen Jesus Himself, would not be forgotten or disobeyed, and therefore, only one conclusion remains ; the words are not really His, though found in every known MS. and Version of the First Gospel.

It is pretty certain St Matthew's Gospel was originally written in the Hebrew dialect. In being transferred to Greek, the document may have received additions, and for such additions, the endings of sections and discourses would present the most favourable points. The exact date of the present Greek Gospel cannot be determined ; neither the extent of its correspondence with, nor deviation from, the lost Hebrew original. We ought not causelessly to suspect modifications or enlargement, but the circumstance that the Canonical Matthew is a translation, renders modifications and additions to some extent highly probable, and in them the candid investigator will believe he has the most rational explanation of discrepancies. Dr Davidson considers ; " The baptismal formula, and some other passages, prevent the critic from putting the Canonical Gospel before A.D. 100." Neander, who, in his *Life of Christ,* surrendered nothing which could with any sort of prudence or plausibility be retained, evidently had very grave doubts respecting the accuracy of Matt. xxviii. 19, and practically admits the text to be unauthentic, though he wraps his meaning in a verbal haze, and, after the manner of an Orthodox Protestant in difficulties, shuns straightforwardness.

But if the text were undoubtedly genuine, it would not necessarily be an announcement of a Trinity of Persons, Co-eternal and Co-equal. The doctrine of the Trinity in Unity would, indeed, be a fair exposition, provided that unfathomable paradox were so stated elsewhere in the New Testament, as to intimate its having had a place in the professed faith of the early believers. Without this sustaining statement, the reasonable expositor of Scripture will not think himself warranted to see in the words, " Name of the Father, and of the Son, and of the Holy Ghost," the metaphysical mystery whose verbal expression the Church subsequently incorporated with the Faith. And, assuming the words to have proceeded from Christ Himself, and to have been from the first apprehended in the maturer Church's sense, there could have been little reserve about the triformal and trinominal composition of the Infinite Substance, and the silence (not to mention the virtual negations) of the Acts and Epistles, become more than ever an insoluble enigma to the Protestant. A theory of the Self-existent Being, which the Baptismal formula was generally understood to communicate, was assuredly no reserved topic.

There are, however, other singularly delicate and subtle, if not persuasive, tokens, that the Synoptical Gospels furnish implications of Christ's Deity. "Equally with St John they represent Him as claiming to be not merely the Teacher but the Object of His religion. He insists on faith in His own Person (St Matt. xvi. 16, 17). . . . If Christ is the Logos in St John, in these Gospels He is the *Sophia* (Wisdom). (St Luke vii. 35 ; St Matt. xi. 19 ; *Wisdom was justified of all her children ;* and apparently, St Luke xi. 49, where *the Wisdom of God* corresponds to *I* in St Matt. xxiii. 34). Thus He ascribes to Himself the exclusive knowledge of the Highest. No statement in St John really goes beyond the terms in which, according to two Synoptists, He claims to know and to be known of the Father. 'No man knoweth the Son but the Father, neither knoweth any man the Father save the Son, and he to whomsoever the Son will reveal Him' (St Matt. xi. 27 ; St Luke x. 22). Here then is a reciprocal relationship of equality : the Son Alone has a true knowledge of the Father ; the Son is Himself such, that the Father Alone understands Him" (p. 251).

The witness to Christ's insistance "on faith in His own Person," and, to His identification with *the Wisdom of God,* may be left uncriticized. The remaining testimony is far from unimpeachable. Does Mr Liddon suppose the Son's knowledge of the Father, is of that unique and incommunicable sort which presumes the possession of Godhead? and if he does, will he explain what is meant by the words, *he to whomsoever the Son will reveal Him?* If Christ could impart the knowledge to men, it was within the grasp of created capacity, and may be identical with the knowledge referred to in the saying ; " Father, this is life eternal, that they may know Thee the Only True God, and Jesus Christ whom Thou hast sent " (John xvii. 3 ; comp. *Ye have known the Father : knoweth God.*—1 John ii. 13 ; iv. 7). The Son is known by His true disciples : " I know my sheep, and *am known of mine* " (John x. 14) ; *we know Him* (1 John ii. 3). And St Paul looked onward to a day, when he *should know as also he was known* (1 Cor. xiii. 12).

Christians, then, are capable, through Divine gift and illumination, of a knowledge of God and Christ. Mr Liddon's selected texts testify, the Father can be revealed to men, and if the Father can be known in the sense of the texts, even a theologian will not dispute that the Son can be known equally. The " reciprocal relationship of equality " is not, therefore, equality in the incommunicable attributes of Godhead. The unbelieving Jews were not participators in the knowledge of the Father, and their persecuting virulence is ascribed by Jesus to their ignorance of the Father and Himself. "These things will they do unto you, because they know not Him Who sent Me ; because they have not known the Father, nor Me" (John xv. 21 ; xvi. 3). The difference between the outside world and the enlightened circle of Christ's disciples is displayed in the words : " O Righteous Father, the world knew Thee not ; but I knew Thee, and these knew that Thou didst send Me. And I made known unto them Thy Name, and will make it known ; that the love wherewith Thou lovest Me may be in them, and I in them" (xvii. 25, 26).

The connection, both in St Matthew and St Luke, of the statement from which Mr Liddon deduces, is the reverse of suggestive that there is between the Father and the Son, "a reciprocal relationship of equality." Our Lord's words are prefaced by an expression of devout thankfulness for the Father's action, and by a recognition of the Father's absolute sovereignty : " I thank Thee, O Father, Lord of heaven and earth, because Thou hast hid these things from the wise and prudent, and hast revealed them unto babes. Even so, Father ; for thus it seemed good in Thy sight." And does the saying : *All things are delivered unto Me by my Father*, accord with the idea of Co-equal Deity in the Recipient ? Straining the word *all*, in order to enlarge the capacity of the Recipient, cannot efface the recipiency, which is in itself inconsistent with Godhead. And the adjective *all* is very freely used in Scripture when its meaning is manifestly circumscribed, or, at the utmost, restricted to what pertains to the Christian dispensation. To take a few examples from the Fourth Gospel only : "*All things* which I have heard from my Father, I have made known unto you" (xv. 15). Are we to conclude that everything which the Second of the Co-equal Persons "in the Three Who yet are One," heard from the First, is here declared to have been communicated to the Apostles ? (See also iii. 26 ; iv. 25, 29, 39 ; xiv. 26.)

But further indications, full of significance in Mr Liddon's estimation, are producible from the Synoptical documents :—

"In these Gospels, moreover, Christ ascribes to Himself, sanctity ; He even places Himself above the holiest thing in ancient Israel. 'I say unto you, that in this place is a greater thing than the temple' (Matt. xii. 6). He and His people are greater than the greatest in the old covenant (Matt. xi. 11 ; xii. 41, 42 ; xxi. 33-42 ; Luke vii. 28). He scruples not to proclaim His consciousness of having fulfilled His mission. He asserts that all power is committed to Him both on earth and in heaven

(Matt. xi. 27 ; xxviii. 18; Luke x. 22).   All nations are to be made disciples of His religion (Matt. xxviii. 19)."

Is not every sincere Christian, to say nothing of God's chosen and exceptionally qualified Messenger, Servant, and Son, more truly a temple of God, greater and more holy, than the consecrated fabric of wood and stone at Jerusalem ?   May not the least in the kingdom of heaven be greater than John the Baptist, and Jesus Himself greater than Jonah, or Solomon, without entailing the inference, ' Jesus is God ?'   The avowed consciousness of having fulfilled His mission, implies, in a very inexplicable manner, Christ's consciousness of parity with the Father Who gave Him His mission (John xvii. 4 ; iv. 34 ; v. 36 ; comp. the proximately Divine consciousness of St Paul, 2 Tim. iv. 7, 8).

If it were not a very serious matter for men to reason falsely from Scripture, and to build the Church's dogmatic faith on thoroughly insecure foundations, Mr Liddon's argument from the Gospels, and more especially from the former three, would be simply amusing.   But, in his fervid zeal and blind confidence, he stakes everything on the soundness of palpably invalid reasonings and expository inferences.   If the sayings recorded in the Gospels do not implicate and reveal what Mr Liddon is persuaded they implicate and reveal, then, our Lord is not morally good ; He is neither sincere, nor unselfish, nor humble.   This fearful alternative, presented in terms of passionately appealing rhetoric, is no doubt sufficient to terrify the great majority of minds, warped as they are by education, into the belief that the faith of the Church respecting Christ's Person can be rationally deduced from Scripture.   A very potent temporary weapon of Protestant Orthodoxy, is this presentation of an alternative which shocks sacred prepossessions, and enlists the pious emotions against the duty of inquiry.   Its employment is, indeed, calculated to awaken intellectual suspicion, but theological controversialists know that when a widely prevailing belief is to be sustained, intellect may be disregarded, provided the emotions can be roused into active play.   When reason is discovered to be inadequate to dogmatic exigencies, what course is open to the Protestant champions of ecclesiastical truth, but to stem investigation by presenting an alternative so alarming, that ' devout and earnest (?) thought cannot falter for a moment in the agony of its suspense.'

Beneath all Mr Liddon's declamation there lurks, as I have already had occasion to notice, the supremely false assumption, that the rank of Christ is, according to Scripture, either mere

Manhood, or, absolute Godhead. His argument is powerless against the really Scriptural position, that Christ fills in the scale of Being a place not perfectly defined, but certainly above man,* and as certainly beneath God. With what unscrupulous vehemence he urges the abandonment of all love and reverence for Jesus, if Jesus is not confessed to have proclaimed or implied His own veritable Deity, may be gathered from the following sentence :—"If Christ is God as well as Man, His language falls into its place, and all is intelligible; but if you deny His Divinity, you must conclude that some of the most precious sayings in the Gospel are but the outbreak of a preposterous self-laudation ; they might well seem to breathe the very spirit of another Lucifer" (p. 196).

Undiscriminating attachment to every portion of an inherited system which has been elaborated and fortified through genera-tions of devoted reception, is too natural to be very discreditable. The deep and sound convictions which respond to the intuitions, and satisfy the cravings of man's religious nature, are strong enough to carry a vast weight of speculative lumber, and impart to feeble indefensible theories some measure of warmth and vitality.   It is, therefore, to be expected that, when times of in-tellectual sifting come, the clergy should be impelled by other forces than those of merely selfish interest, to display a blindly obstinate conservatism in defence of the very questionable accre-tions with which doctrines not at variance with reason, have been encompassed and overlaid. A dread lest beliefs having a permanent and independent basis in man's nature, should be disturbed, makes the Protestant clerical mind refuse to surrender time-honoured tra-ditions, which never could bear reason's scrutiny, and which, if not guaranteed by revelation from God through the Church, re-present only decaying moods and phases of human thought and sentiment. But mental apathy and moral cowardice, though they affect most injuriously Protestant adhesion to primary spiritual truths, are very different from the alarm-cries of profes-

---

* I mean, of course, if every statement of Scripture is accepted in its natural rational meaning, with unquestioning acquiescence. The Christ of an uncritical Biblical Protestantism is an Arian, superhuman Christ. The Christ of a critical Protestantism is a merely human, but extraordinarily endowed Christ. For the Catholic Christ there is, without the admission of the Church's revealing inspiration and authority, no logical basis anywhere.

Apart from free criticism, Arian and Orthodox expounders of texts, are both stronger in attack than in defence, but their contests do not result in a dead-lock, the decided advantage, if not the complete victory, being neces-sarily with the Arians. Before rational criticism neither Arianism nor Orthodoxy will stand.

sional controversy, and the outbursts of emasculated bigotry, deliberately invoking terror, and formally staking precious verities on the continued acceptance of precarious opinions. The servants of the God of Truth, and the ministers of the Anointed King in Truth's Kingdom, do not let their light shine, and certainly do not advance their Master's glory, when in angry effeminate desperation they brandish in men's faces the alternative, ' You must take the whole of our system, or, let all religion go.' Consent won by fear against intelligence, is too speedily and terribly avenged to be worth winning. Yet we saw Dignitaries of the Anglican Church promptly sink to this degraded style of argument, when an adventurous Prelate published his persuasion, that the Pentateuch is by no means unmixed truth, and Moses not its sole author; and now we see Mr Liddon demean himself to imperil all loving veneration for Christ, all faith in Christ's precepts, example, inspiration, and mission from the Father, by frantically waving the ugly scarecrow,—' if Jesus be not infinitely Divine, He must be almost Satanic.'

I have now shown by copious reference to Scripture, and more particularly to the Fourth Gospel, that Christ's claims did not rise to the height Mr Liddon imagines. They were distinctly, and studiously (unless we isolate and inflate at pleasure a few little patches of vague and metaphorical diction), below the appropriation of Deity, or the assertion of equality with the Father. Mr Liddon's dilemma cannot be formally retorted, because the suppositions, that Christ is God, and, that His words have been handed down with unerring correctness, lift His sayings above all criticism and the application of any moral standard; but, if the rules of human veracity and sincerity could be applied, Christ would be convicted of untruthfulness, and a cruelly misleading phraseology, when, knowing Himself to be God, and knowing also that faith in His Godhead was to be a vital necessity, He, without elucidating and guarding explanations, expressed Himself as follows :—

" Why callest thou Me good? None is good except One, that is, God " (Mark x. 18 ; Luke xviii. 19).

" The Spirit of the Lord is upon Me, because He hath anointed Me," &c. (Luke iv. 18, 19 ; comp. Matt. xii. 18).

" Of that day or that hour knoweth no one, neither the angels in heaven, nor the Son, but the Father " (Mark xiii. 32 ; comp. Matt. xxiv. 36, and Acts i. 7).

" To sit on my right hand, and on my left, is not mine to give, except to those for whom it has been prepared by my Father " (Matt. xx. 23 ; Mark x. 40).

" Thinkest thou that I cannot now pray to my Father, and He will furnish Me with more than twelve legions of Angels ? " (Matt. xxvi. 53).

" My Father, if it be possible, let this cup pass from Me ; nevertheless not as I will, but as Thou wilt " (Matt. xxvi. 39, 42 ; Mark xiv. 34-36 ; Luke xxii. 42).

" My God, my God, why hast Thou forsaken Me " (Matt. xxvii. 46 ; Mark xv. 34).

" Father, into Thy hands I commend my spirit " (Luke xxiii. 46).

The dogma inculcated by Mr Liddon, pronounces the soul and spirit of Jesus to have been inextricably taken into a Personal Form of the Divine Nature, Very God, possessing in their entirety the attributes of Deity.   But upon this hypothesis, the language just cited is not only mysterious and inexplicable, it is also, in the highest degree, artificial, histrionic, and misguiding.   What must it have been understood to express and imply, by those who heard it, more particularly if, in their minds, there already existed, or were in the progress of dogmatic revelation soon to be sown, the seeds of faith in Christ's veritable Godhead ?

" Simon, Simon, behold Satan hath sought to have ye, that he might sift ye as wheat ; but I have prayed for thee, that thy faith fail not " (Luke xxii. 31, 32).

" Verily, verily, I say unto you, the Son can do nothing of Himself, except what He seeth the Father doing.   I can of mine own self do nothing," &c. (John v. 19, 30).   " I do nothing of Myself ; but as my Father hath taught Me, I speak these things " (viii. 28).   But I have already referred sufficiently to some of the multitude of utterances in the Fourth Gospel, which, if accepted as veracious and intelligible statements, afford the strongest inferential evidence against the supposition of Christ's Deity.   I will now confine myself to sayings of a very direct and explicit nature ; they could not, indeed, be more direct and explicit, unless they had been pointed, formal, negations of Christ's true Godhead.

" *The Only God.*" " That they may know *Thee* (*Father*), *the Only True God,* and Jesus Christ whom Thou hast sent " (v. 44 ; xvii. 3).

" My Father is greater than I " (xiv. 28).

" Go to my brethren, and say unto them : I ascend unto my Father and your Father, and my God and your God " (xx. 17).

Tried by the rules of human morality, these sayings are conspicuously untruthful, insincere, and deceptive, if Jesus knew Himself to be the Father's Equal, Essentially and truly God ; and if further, He designed His own utterances should be ingredients in the revelation of His Nature.   But if He knew Himself not to be God, these sayings are, in their natural sense, and with their inevitable suggestions, simple, intelligible, and honest.   The former of the pair of alternatives which really issue from the evidence, is exactly the reverse of that ('the conscious and culpable insincerity of Jesus if he is *not* God') on which Mr Liddon insists. He assures his readers with reference to his own fancied *reductiones ad horribile* ; " Certainly we cannot create such alternatives by any process of dialetical manufacture, if they do not already exist."   He has, with laborious ingenuity, striven to effect what he pronounces to be impossible.   But as he himself reminds us, " If such alternatives are not matters of fact, they can easily be convicted of inaccuracy " (p. 203).

Looking solely to " the language which Christ actually used about Himself," and taking it as their sufficient guide, Protestants have, in reason and candour, no choice left but to deny that He is God.   By the light of reasonably interpreted Scripture, no apostrophe can be further from the truth than that with which Mr Liddon concludes his Fourth Lecture :—

" Eternal Jesus ! it is Thyself Who hast thus bidden us either despise Thee or worship Thee.   Thou wouldst have us despise Thee as our fellow-man, if we will not worship Thee as our God."

By the light of ecclesiastical revelation the case is, I admit, changed : words acquire new meanings, Scripture is transformed, and rational significance is banished.

CHAPTER XI.

Examination of the Scripture testimony adduced in support of the proposition;
"from the earliest age of Christianity, Jesus Christ has been adored
as God."—The terms which precisely and definitely describe the worship and service due to the Supreme Being, are never connected with
the Name of Christ.—Detailed investigation of the feeble and forced
pretexts on which Mr Liddon relies.—Meaning of the expressions, *to
call upon the Lord*, and, *upon the Name of the Lord*.—Dying petitions
of St Stephen.—Words of frequent use, and specific, restricted application, denoting prayers and vows to the Almighty, are never used of
petitions addressed to Christ.—The prayer at the election of the
Apostle Matthias, was offered to our God and Father, not to our Lord
Jesus Christ.—Argument from the prayer of the disciple Ananias, and
from the first prayers of St Paul, examined.—Supposed recognition,
in St Paul's Epistles, of prayer to Jesus Christ, including the Apostle's
entreaty to be freed from 'the thorn in the flesh.'—Strained and erroneous constructions of passages in St John's First Epistle, and in the
Apocalypse.—Brief summary of the evidence that Christ was *not* wor-
shipped as God.—A glance at some arguments from the earlier Fathers.
—Frequency of devotional addresses to our Lord Jesus Christ in the
Anglican Book of Common Prayer.—Remarks on the action of the
Clergy, and on the use of Family Prayers, and Hymns, wherein Jesus
Christ is studiously equalized with the Father, in the language of
supplication and praise.

Mr Liddon's failure in his attempt to prove that, "from the
earliest age of Christianity, Jesus Christ has been adored as God,"
is no fault of his.   The task to which he applied himself was beyond the powers of any special pleadership, however talented.
The worship of Christ as God, is nowhere enjoined in Scripture,
while the worship of *the God and Father of our Lord Jesus
Christ* is enjoined, and shown by clear and plentiful evidence to
have been the habitual practice of the Apostles and first disciples.
About the general and prescribed Scripture rule with regard to
prayer and thanksgiving, there can be no dispute.   The worship of Jesus must, as its Protestant advocates well know, be
based upon presumed implications, and indirect teachings, and
upon instances which carry on the face of them discriminative
and exceptional circumstances.   The precepts of Jesus Himself,
perspicuously and unequivocally set the Father before us as the

only Object of strictly religious homage. The teaching and example of the Apostles, so far as Scripture recounts them, repeat, and are conformed to, the Great Master's precepts. From a mass of testimony, I select a few texts: Matt. vi. 6-15; vii. 11; Luke xi. 1, 2, 13; Mark xi. 25; John iv. 21-24; xv. 16; xvi. 23, 24, 26; Acts iv. 24-30; Rom. i. 8-10; xv. 5, 6, 30; 1 Cor. i. 4; Eph. i. 16, 17; iii. 14; v. 20; Phil. i. 3-6; iv. 6; Col. i. 3; 1 Thess. i. 2; 2 Thess. i. 3, 11, 12.

When we lay aside foregone conclusions, and look steadily at the subject, we can scarcely escape perceiving how the existence of exhortations and directions to render to the Almighty Father the tribute of prayer and praise, and the lack of directions and exhortations to render the like tribute to our Lord Jesus Christ, constitute a very serious obstacle to the reception of Mr Liddon's *dictum;* "The adoration of Jesus is as ancient as Christianity. Jesus has been ever adored on the score of His Divine Personality, of Which this tribute of adoration is not merely a legitimate but a necessary acknowledgment" (p. 364). The worship of Christ on the ground of His Essential Deity, and, with "that adoration which is due to the Most High God, and to Him Alone," would be, both to Jewish and Gentile converts, a peculiar and difficult feature in their newly-adopted faith. Very little encouragement or counsel would be needed to impress the duty of praying to, and praising, *the one God and Father of all*, but most explicit and repeated encouragement and counsel would seem to have been necessary, in order to develop and direct, 'that worship of Christ's Person, that tide of adoration,' which is imagined to have 'burst upwards from the heart of His Church' immediately after His Ascension. Without expressed guidance and pointed admonition, it is simply inconceivable that the adoration of Christ, "on the score of His Divine Personality," could have been, as Mr Liddon opines, "the universal practice of Christians;" "in the judgment of Christians an imperious Christian duty;" "rooted in the doctrine and practice of the Apostles, and handed down to succeeding ages as an integral and recognized element of the spiritual life of the Church."

I am fully conscious, dearth of Scriptural mandate is not, from the Catholic point of view, an effective argument against paying to Christ the honours of supreme worship. The section of Apostolic teaching which related to the adoration of Christ, may, owing to its intimate connection with the revelation of His Deity, have been withheld from the written documents, and committed to the less exposed channel of the Church's oral tradition. The witness to the Divine adoration of Jesus, would indeed appear naturally to follow the witness to His absolute Divinity; and how jealously the presiding inspiration of the Canonical penmen restrained and veiled that witness, we have already seen. But, upon the primary Protestant hypothesis, that the Bible alone yields sufficient rules of faith and practice, the circumstance of our being taught and counselled to offer supplications and thanksgivings to God our Heavenly Father, and not taught and counselled to offer them to our Lord Jesus Christ, is a very formidable barrier against the proposition which Mr Liddon so ardently affirms. The evidence is, undeniably, in a vastly inverse proportion to the rational demand. The New Testament rule of worship is copious and lucid where new light was little called for; it is most meagre and indistinct where full and precise statement was indispensable.

In common with all expositors who undertake to find in Scripture intimations of Christ's having been the Object of supreme religious worship, Mr Liddon is compelled to fabricate negative testimony, by assuming the point he was bound to prove. He remarks, " never was the adoration of Jesus protested against in the Church as a novelty, derogatory to the honour and claims of God," forgetting, apparently, that the absence of prohibition and protest in the New Testament, has for him no auxiliary bearing, unless the New Testament contains proof of his positions ; " The early Christian Church approached Christ's Glorious Person with that very tribute of prayer, of self-prostration, of self-surrender, by which all serious Theists, whether Christian or non-Christian, are accustomed to express their felt relationship as creatures to the Almighty Creator. . . . The Church simply adored God ; and she adored Jesus Christ, as believing Him to be God " (p. 360). " The historical fact before us is, that from the earliest age of Christianity, Jesus Christ has been adored as God."

The negative evidence, so far as it has weight, is measured more equitably, when we see in it a token that Divine adoration was *not* paid to Jesus. Assuming the Canonical records to comprise a moderately complete exhibition of prominent facts, it is significant that no charges of idolatry and misdirected worship were laid against the first Christians by their Jewish adversaries, more particularly since the Fourth Gospel (as understood by Mr Liddon) attests the Jews to have suspected and accused Christ of claiming to be the Almighty One. The question whether ' the unlettered multitudes of the Church so acted and spoke as to imply a belief that Jesus Christ is actually God,' was a question likely to be very keenly scrutinized by Priests, and

Scribes, and Pharisees ; and unless proof to the contrary is forth-coming, the natural inference from Jewish silence is,—Christians did not, by adoring Jesus Christ as God, afford a pretext for the charge of idolatry. The 'heresy' which St Paul confessed, was not, that in the matter of worship he had in any degree put Jesus of Nazareth in the place of *the God of his fathers* (Acts xxiv. 14 ; comp. iii. 13).

And what proof is Mr Liddon able to construct, that the adoration of Christ is coeval with the Church? He begins with a totally unapt disquisition on the difference between admiration and adoration. No one who is willing to accept and abide by the statements of the New Testament, can suppose, "the early Christian Church contented herself with 'admiring' Jesus Christ." According to the representations in the New Testament, He was venerated with a veneration distinct from that paid to angels or men, and distinct also from that paid to God. He was reverenced and honoured as one who held a heavenly commission, was fur-nished with heavenly gifts, and filled an altogether peculiar place and office between the Most High God our Father, and the great human family whom the Father's love was seeking to elevate and save. To descant on the difference between admiration and adoration, serves no purpose, except that of diverting the reader's attention to a false issue. What Mr Liddon's case requires, is Scriptural proof of the position, Jesus was worshipped because He was apprehended to be verily God. If the proof is not producible in the shape of direct assertions of His Godhead, and injunctions to worship Him as God, it may be produced in the shape of evidence, that the homage rendered Him was of such a nature as to be incom-prehensible on any other ground than His veritable Deity. And, for the production of proof in the latter shape, a primary neces-sity is refutation of the opinion, that His claims and qualifica-tions as an exalted Spiritual Being, who is in a special sense the Messenger, Servant, and Son of the Highest, are adequate to explain the veneration and service of which He was the Object. But Mr Liddon entirely fails to furnish this necessary refutation. As usual, he shirks the real question, leaving out of the calcula-tion the singular Messianic functions and endowments, and stat-ing his argument as though it were enough to show, that the pro-found reverence accorded to Jesus was more than only a good man, or an Angel, would have received.

Some of the texts adduced to vindicate the worship of Christ, have been already examined in conjunction with other portions of Mr Liddon's reasonings. I shall try to avoid needless repetition, but repetition to some extent is unavoidable.

As a sample of adoration, Rev. i. 17 is cited.   " 'When I saw Him,' says St John, speaking of Jesus in His glory, 'I fell at His feet as dead.'   That was something more than admiration, even the most enthusiastic; it was an act in which self had no part; it was an act of adoration."   It looks far more like the effect of sudden and overpowering alarm and awe, and as such, seems to have been dealt with by the glorified Son of Man, in the vision : " He laid His right hand upon me, saying, Fear not: I am the first, and the last, and the living (one), and I was dead, and behold, I am living for evermore."   That the writer of the Apocalypse did not consider Jesus Christ to be the Lord God Almighty, is abundantly clear from the language of verses 1, 5, and 6, of the first chapter.

The reverential respect paid to Christ while upon earth, Mr Liddon conceives to have been, at least in some instances, Divine worship.

" During the days of His early life our Lord was surrounded by acts of homage, ranging, as it might seem, so far as the intentions of those who offered them were concerned, from the wonted forms of Eastern courtesy up to the most direct and conscious acts of Divine worship. . . . It may be that in some of these instances the 'worship' paid to Jesus did not express more than a profound reverence.   Sometimes He was worshipped as a Superhuman Person, wielding superhuman powers ; sometimes He was worshipped by those who instinctively felt His moral majesty, which forced them, they knew not how, upon their knees.   But if He had been only a 'good man,' He must have checked such worship.   He had Himself re-affirmed the foundation-law of the religion of Israel : ' Thou shalt worship the Lord thy God, and Him only shalt thou serve ' (Matt. iv. 10).   Yet He never hints that danger lurked in this prostration of hearts and wills before Himself ; He welcomes, by a tacit approval, this profound homage of which He is the Object " (pp. 364-366).

Now, there are in the New Testament certain words of not infrequent occurrence (σέβεσθαι ; λατρεύειν ; λατρεία), which express with precision and definiteness the worship and service due to the Supreme Being.   These words are never found in connection with the Name of Christ.   Will Mr Liddon explain that fact ? If these words had been used to describe the homage and service done to Christ there would have been, so far, reason for surmising some perception of His Deity to have dwelt in the minds of His first disciples, though, even then, the absence, during His earthly lifetime, of all other traces of the state of mind and feeling which must have been engendered by belief in His Deity, would have been a serious difficulty. But the terms used to describe the homage and service He received, are such only as are often employed to express relations and obligations of respect and service between man and man. The same terms are, doubtless, employed also, as many other common terms are, to express the relations in which we stand to God, and the duties we owe to Him, but when so employed, they acquire, from the known attributes of the Almighty, a peculiar and intensified meaning. The claims of the Most High upon the affections, the homage, the obedience, of His rationally intelligent creatures, are at once, so singular and supreme, that ordinary language is transfigured by association with His Holy Name and the duties owing to Him. The supposition that the customary Eastern usages of kneeling and prostration, with which our Lord was frequently approached during His mortal lifetime, were ever 'direct and conscious Divine worship,' is purely arbitrary and unfounded. There can be no doubt genuflexion and prostrate obeisance were acts of reverential salutation and suppliant respect, not unusual on the part of inferiors to men of superior rank ; and the verb προσκυνεῖν, by which the homage or ' worship ' paid to Christ is denoted, is assuredly not limited to the expression of Divine worship (see Matt. xviii. 26 ; Mark xv. 19 ; Acts x. 25 ; and Septuagint, Gen. xxiii. 7, 12 ; xlii. 6 : Exod. xviii. 7 ; 1 Sam. xxiv. 8 ; 1 Kings i. 23, comp. xviii. 7 ; Dan. ii. 46). *To worship,* in the modern religious and restricted use, is not its equivalent, except in its application to the Almighty, when, of course, the application affixes the highest and utmost meaning the verb will bear.

Mr Liddon admits that, in the intentions of those who offered them, the acts of homage, and the ' language of devotion,' by which our Lord was surrounded, had a very wide range, and unequal significance, and he can supply no fragment of indication, that in a single instance, the manifestations of respect and deference from which he argues, were incited by the knowledge, or the suspicion, that Jesus was the Supreme Being. The instances of " the worship of Jesus during His earthly life," which he has flung together, simply fill his space, without aiding his argument. He 'freely concedes,' many of the prostrations by which the worship was expressed, did not involve the payment of Divine honours; but, in reply to Channing's insistence on "the indifference of the Jews to the frequent prostrations of men before Christ," urges : "That the Jews suspected the intention to honour Christ's Divinity in none of them, would not prove that none of them were designed to honour It. The Jews were not present at the confession of St Thomas after the Resurrection; but there is no reasonable room for questioning either the devotional purpose or the theological force of the Apostle's exclamation, *My Lord and My God."* Men's ideas of 'reasonable room' in theology, vary with their prejudices and controversial aims, but there would seem to be the least possible room for assuming the doubting Thomas, who was invited to accept proofs of Christ's Resurrection, to have passed over in a moment to the conviction that the Being who had been crucified, and raised from the dead, was the Lord God Almighty. The devotional purpose, is on a par with the theological force, of the exclamation ascribed to the Apostle.

Mr Liddon says : " Apparently Mary of Magdala, in her deep devotion, had motioned to embrace His feet in the garden, when Jesus bade her *Touch Me not."* The deep devotion is more apparent in the commentary than in the Evangelist's recital. "Jesus saith unto her, Mary. She turned herself, and saith unto Him, Rabboni, which is to say, Teacher. Jesus saith unto her, Touch me not ; for I am not yet ascended to my Father ; but go to my brethren and say unto them, I ascend unto my Father and your Father, and my God and your God" (St John xx. 16, 17).

Mr Liddon cites the conduct of the eleven disciples who "met our Lord by appointment on a mountain in Galilee, and ' when they saw Him,' as it would seem, in their joy and fear, 'they worshipped Him.' If 'some doubted,' the worship offered by the rest may be presumed to have been a very deliberate act (St Matthew xxviii. 17)." What does Mr Liddon consider to have been the subject of their doubt ; the Resurrection, or, the Deity of Jesus ? If the former, there is no pretext for converting the demonstrations of reverence and obeisance made by any of the eleven, into acts of deliberate religious adoration.

" When the Ascending Jesus was being borne upwards into Heaven, the disciples, as if thanking Him for His great glory, worshipped Him ; and then 'returned to Jerusalem with great joy ' (St Luke xxiv. 51, 52)." Does not fair exposition demand that verses fifty-two and fifty-three, which together form one sentence, should not be put asunder; " And were continually in the temple praising and blessing God." The narrative, when reasonably and honestly read, may well suggest, they thanked God for Christ's great glory, but cannot suggest, they thanked

Christ Himself. Their worship was not a rendering of honours belonging to God, but a showing forth of the veneration and awe which the character of Jesus, and the marvellous events of His Resurrection and Ascension, naturally inspired. The thanksgivings in the temple were worship in the strictest, highest sense.

When we are told, the man born blind accompanied his confession of faith in the Son of God "by an undoubted act of adoration" (St John ix. 35-38), we are led to ask, whether the title *Son of God* was a recognized synonym for *God*, or for the post-canonical designation *God the Son*. If it was not, the blind man's reverent homage has no proper place in Mr Liddon's argument. If the man did not worship Jesus under the persuasion that Jesus was indeed God, his "worship" was not adoration of God.

It seems scarcely credible, but Mr Liddon actually inquires—"Did not the dying thief offer at least a true inward worship to Jesus Crucified, along with the words, 'Lord, remember me when Thou comest into Thy kingdom?' (St Luke xxiii. 42)."

The difference is not very material in relation to the point under discussion, but the true reading most probably is—"Jesus, remember me when thou comest in thy kingdom." In the verse next preceding, the repentant robber is reported to have said respecting Jesus, "This (man) hath done nothing amiss." But *man* is not supplied in the original, and perhaps the ecclesiastically irradiated instinct which detects the latent harmonies of the written and unwritten Word, may have taught Mr Liddon, *God* is the noun in the agreement. At any rate, if the penitent malefactor had not attained to the conception that the human vesture of a Self-existent and Deathless Person was expiring by His side, his "true inward worship" was not worship offered to Jesus as God.

In truth, no assertion can less endure rational scrutiny than the assertion that any of the acts of homage which Christ received during His earthly lifetime were "most direct and conscious acts of Divine worship." They could not possibly have been so, unless the men and women from whom they proceeded, believed Christ to be in very deed God. It is, I know, a rash thing to set bounds to the eccentricities of pious Protestant exposition, but I doubt whether an interpreter of established sanity could be found, with the capacity for discovering in the pages of the Gospel narratives, tokens our Lord was apprehended to be God by any of His earthly friends and followers.

Inferences from the circumstance of Christ's not having checked the worship with which He was often approached, can have no validity, apart from the assumptions that such worship was either intentionally offered to Him as God, or was, in its own nature, and by the light of customary practice, beyond what any Being less than God could lawfully receive. But both these assumptions are unwarranted. When Mr Liddon writes about "the prostration of hearts and wills before Christ," he uses language which may correctly convey his own impressions, but which certainly exceeds the Evangelical statements.

In "the foundation law of the religion of Israel—*Thou shalt worship the Lord thy God, and Him only shalt thou serve*," quoted Matt. iv. 8-10, and in the fuller account, Luke iv. 5-8, the exclusive restriction is with *the service*, which is expressed by a word consecrated to God, and never applied to Christ. This *service* includes *worship* in the highest sense, and following modern English usage, the closer translation of the injunction would be, " Thou shalt bow down to (or do homage to), the Lord Thy God, and Him only shalt thou worship." Satan is not, in the story, represented as having asked for *latreia*, but for *proskunesis*. It is indisputable that, as an external form of homage, *proskunesis* was comparatively common, and if not intentionally directed to the Almighty, was not, in the estimation of a Jew, Divine worship. Our Lord's answer is a refusal of any kind of homage to Satan. *Proskunesis* is due to God, and to God alone, *latreia* must be paid. Thus, the phraseology of the text is, when exactly weighed, rather against, than for, Mr Liddon, because it tends to illustrate the distinction between terms which severally express an outward homage customarily rendered to superiors, and the devout service due to God alone. I confess myself quite unable to see the relevance of a reference to our Lord's re-affirmation of ' the foundation law of the religion of Israel.' The ancient Israelites certainly did not understand their law to prohibit bowing down before superiors in office and station : and, how can the refusal of *proskunesis*, which the Tempter sought to obtain by a lie, be at all suggestive that Jesus, the authorized Messenger and chosen Servant of God, was bound to repudiate *proskunesis*, if He were not in very truth God ?

So far as we have means of judging, the language which Christ is made to employ as a quotation, is not a repetition of the precise words written in Deut. vi. 13 ; (comp. x. 20). The Hebrew is, *Thou shalt fear the Lord thy God, and serve Him*, and with this, the better (the Vatican) MS. of the Septuagint Version agrees, in all but the introduction of *only*.* The quotation is, however, sufficiently near to the sense of what is written, and is illustrated by the Second Commandment. The verbal divergence would not be worth notice, if the force of a particular word were not in question.

Recurring again to a passage which has already been discussed, and shown to afford no ground for such violently comprehensive deductions (John v. 23), Mr Liddon characteristically writes; " He claims all the varied homage which the sons of men, in their want and fulness, in their joy and sorrow, may rightfully and profitably pay to the Eternal Father; all men are to *honour the Son even as they honour the Father*" (p. 367).

When we have left the Gospels, and the incidents of Christ's earthly life, we find only one passage, seemingly an adaptation of language taken from Psalm xcvii. 7, in which even the lower and unrestricted term for homage or worship is applied to Christ. On that passage (Heb. i. 6), Mr Liddon comments: "Apostles believed that when the First-begotten was brought into the inhabited world, the angels of heaven were bidden to worship Him." The exceeding dignity and endowments with which the Almighty Father enriched ' the Son of His love,' no doubt induced Apostles to believe that the Son was looked upon with humbly venerating regard by the angelic host: but if the First-born Son were the Everlasting God robed in our nature, it is difficult to conceive what sense or necessity there could have been in bidding the Angels worship Him. Was the Eternal Personal Logos, Who possessed every attribute of Deity, at any period subsequent to the creation of the Angels, not an Object of angelic worship? The reasonable inferences from the expressions to which Mr Liddon points, are adverse to his doctrine. If Apostles entertained the belief which he ascribes to them, and along with it, a belief in the Self-existent, Infinite, Deity of Jesus, then, their understandings must have been either peculiarly constituted, or dominated by an inspiration of a very remarkable kind.

Mr Liddon sedulously insists that prayer to Jesus was a settled practice among the first generation of Christians, and discovers intimations, satisfactory to his own mind, of our Lord's having, while upon earth, prepared for, and in effect, encouraged such prayer.

" He seems to invite prayer to Himself, even for the highest

---

* Mr Turpie, in a collection of facts and materials, entitled, *The Old Testament in the New*, says; " The reading of the Alexandrine MS. appears to have been changed to agree with the New Testament."

spiritual blessings, in such words as those which He addressed
to the woman of Samaria : 'If thou knewest the gift of God, and
Who it is that saith unto thee, Give me to drink ; thou wouldest
have asked of Him, and he would have given thee living water'
(St John iv. 10).   He predicts indeed a time when the spiritual
curiosity of His disciples would be satisfied in the joy of perfectly
possessing Him ; but He nowhere hints that He would Himself
cease to receive their prayers (St John xvi. 20-22)."

To be taught by Christ—"to hear His word, and believe on
Him who sent Him" (John v. 24), was, doubtless, to receive the
highest spiritual blessings ; and there is no reason to suppose that
by "living water," He meant more than that knowledge of truth
which is the means to nourish and develop spiritual life.   The
woman of Samaria did ask for the living water (ver. 15), and the
answer to her request was instruction as to the nature of true
worship ; a declaration that the Object of worship, the Father
and God, is a Spirit ; and, an announcement that Jesus is the
Messiah (verses 21-26).   Indefinite phrases which admit the intrusion of Mr Liddon's dogmatic beliefs, may seem to him to
sanction those beliefs, but unbiassed minds will discern in the
narrative of the conversation at Jacob's Well, no invitation to address to Christ the devotional dependence and service of prayer;
and will identify the living water with "the sanctifying truth"
(John xvii. 17); " the cleansing word " (xv. 3); " the word which
was not Christ's own, but the Father's Who sent Him" (xiv. 24) ;
" the doctrine of God" (vii. 17).   Would not the accustomed
methods of ecclesiastical, as distinguished from rational, interpretation, stimulate us to perceive in the language to the Sama-
ritan woman, *the gift of God, and who it is, &c.*, an oblique and
veiled annunciation of Deity ?   Jesus seems to identify *the gift
of God* with His own gift ; therefore, Jesus is God.   This more
capacious form of deduction includes Mr Liddon's.

In referring to John xvi. 23, Mr Liddon says—"Here the Greek"
(translated in our Version *ye shall ask*), " clearly means *question*."
The Greek verb may bear, but does not *clearly* bear, the meaning Mr Liddon approves.   It has precisely the same ambiguity
which belongs to the English verb *to ask*, and sometimes denotes
interrogation and inquiry, sometimes request and entreaty.   In
the ' Gospel according to John,' the places where it occurs in
the sense of *request* are rather more frequent than the places
where it occurs in the sense of *question* (see iv. 31, 40, 47 ; xii.
21 ; xiv. 16 ; xvi. 26; xvii. 9, 15, 20; and xix. 38, with which
compare Matt. xxvii. 58).   The instance about which Mr Liddon's

verdict is so decided, is doubtful. In xvi. 5, 19, 30, *questioning* is indicated, but in verse 26, *requesting*. The different verbs rendered, *ask* and *pray*, are, in verse 26, so far synonymous that both denote *requesting;* and the same is perhaps the case in verse 23, where both are rendered *ask* (compare 1 John v. 16).*

I may be mistaken, but, as I understand Mr Liddon's exposition, the words, *in that day ye shall ask Me nothing*, do not relate to the period between our Lord's Resurrection and Ascension, to

* In his *Synonyms of the New Testament*, Archbishop Trench has an article on these verbs. He writes: "It is very noteworthy, and witnesses for the singular accuracy in the employment of words, and in the record of that employment, which prevails throughout the New Testament, that our Lord never uses αἰτεῖν or αἰτεῖσθαι of Himself, in respect of that which He seeks on behalf of His disciples from God ; for His is not the *petition* of the creature to the Creator, but the *request* of the Son to the Father. The consciousness of His equal dignity, of His potent and prevailing intercession, speaks out in this, that often as He asks, or declares that He will ask, anything of the Father, it is always ἐρωτῶ, ἐρωτήσω, an asking, that is, as upon equal terms (John xiv. 16 ; xvi. 26 ; xvii. 9, 15, 20). . . . It will follow that ἐρωτᾶν, being thus proper for Christ, inasmuch as it has authority in it, is not proper for us ; and in no single instance is it used in the New Testament to express the prayer of man to God, of the creature to the Creator."

Now, about the general accuracy of the distinction on which the Archbishop insists, there can be no dispute, but the point in debate is New Testament usage, and more particularly that of the Fourth Gospel, where, it should be observed, the more customary, appropriate, and exact words for prayer do not occur. The term which the Archbishop conceives ' to have authority in it,' and to denote ' asking as upon equal terms,' denotes solicitation, begging, the humble request of an inferior to a superior, in Mark vii. 26 ; Luke iv. 38 ; John iv. 40, 47 ; xix. 38 ; 1 John v. 16 (comp. Ps. cxxii. 6). On comparing the parallel places in the Evangelists, it will be seen that three of them in narrating the solicitation of Joseph for the body of Jesus use one, and the fourth (John xix. 38) the other, of the two verbs, between which the Archbishop so elaborately discriminates. Whatever, therefore, may be argued on general grounds against the fitness of the term ἐρωτᾶν to express petitioning, we cannot deny that, in the hands of the New Testament writers, it sometimes covers prayerful petitioning, and is especially likely to do so in passages of the last Evangelist, because in the phraseology of supplication his vocabulary is peculiarly narrow, and has the remarkable feature of being without words for prayer which are at once both common and precise.

With regard to "the singular accuracy in the employment of words," &c., on which Archbishop Trench dilates, our Lord himself uses a supplicatory verb in stating that he had prayed for Peter (Luke xxii. 32) ; and in Matt. xix. 13, the Evangelist describes the ' request of the Son ' on behalf of others, by a term which is confined to the devotional entreaties ' of the creature to the Creator,' and is also constantly employed to describe the prayers offered by Jesus to the Father (see Matt. xiv. 23 ; xxvi. 36, 39, 42, 44, and parallels in Mark and Luke : Mark i. 35 ; vi. 46 ; Luke iii. 21 ; v. 16 ; vi. 12 ; ix. 18, 28, 29 ; xi. 1). The earlier Evangelists, and the author of the Epistle to the Hebrews (v. 7), appear to have thought Christ's prayers for Himself the prayers of a man to God ; and since Christ had no proper human personality, an expository argument which turns on a nice verbal distinction between His requests on behalf of Himself, and His requests on behalf of His disciples, pertains to that lofty and obscure region into which only minds ecclesiastically illuminated can venture.

which the promises, *again a little while and ye shall see Me* (ver.
16), and, *I will see you again* (ver. 22), seem naturally to point;
but to the period when His visible bodily presence would be entirely withdrawn.   Jesus, therefore, will be concluded to have
meant that, when His disciples *could* no longer put questions
to Him, they *would* no longer put questions.   But if our Lord
spoke only of the indulgence of an inquisitive spiritual curiosity
while He was visibly present, what connection has His saying
with prayer to Him?   If He is supposed to have meant that,
after the Holy Ghost should have become their Teacher, the
Apostles were no longer to seek instruction from Himself, there
is, of course, no distinct prohibition of asking in every sense; but
to argue, " He nowhere hints that He would Himself cease to
receive their prayers," is transparently sophistical, since no proof
is discoverable of His ever having been addressed in prayer,
or ever having enjoined the offering of devotional petitions to
Himself.   The remainder of the passage from which Mr Liddon
quotes, undoubtedly enjoins prayer to the Father, in the Name of
Christ (compare Matt. xviii. 19, 20).

From the fact of Christians being described (Acts ix. 14, 21;
1 Cor. i. 2) as "those who call upon the Name of Jesus Christ,"
Mr Liddon unfalteringly makes the largest inferences.   He
could not be more confident, if the verb translated *to call upon*,
were so perfectly definite and circumscribed as to admit no
other meaning than *to pray*.   But the term ἐπικαλεῖσθαι, on
which he builds, is unquestionably loose and ambiguous.
When the reference is to the Eternal Father, the phrases, *to call
upon the Lord*, and *upon the Name of the Lord*, may signify
not only openly proclaimed trust and allegiance, but prayer
in the strictest sense.   Numerous instances in the Septuagint
attest this.   The few examples of New Testament usage in conjunction with the Name of God, do not so specifically as Mr Liddon fancies, signify prayer.   Even the quotation from Joel, in
Acts ii. 21; Rom. x. 13 (comp. Pss. lxxix. 6; lxxx. 18; Jer.
x. 25), may indicate summarily the acknowledged general
standing and relation of God's servants, rather than the one
particular practice, prayer.   *Calling upon God*, may be a brief
equivalent for undisguised and habitual service of God, the
public confession of being His, obeying and worshipping Him;
prayer would be involved and implied, but not prominently, and
still less exclusively, specified.   Dean Alford (*Revised Version*)
construes 1 Pet. i. 17, *if ye call upon as your Father, Him, &c.*,
a construction which may be disputed, but is probably right,

and has, at least, the merit of carrying over the ambiguity of the Greek into the English.

But whatever may be the exact force of the expressions, *to call upon*, and *to call upon the Name of*, when the reference is to our God and Father, they need not when the reference is not to Him have the same force. No one will pretend the verb is by usage confined to prayer, or capable of only one sense. It is used of appealing to Cæsar, where the appeal is plainly not devotional petitioning (Acts xxv. 11, 12, 21, 25; xxvi. 32; xxviii. 19). St Paul employs it (2 Cor. i. 23), in the imprecation, *I call God for a witness upon my soul.* In the passive, it denotes the being surnamed (Acts i. 23; iv. 36; x. 5, 18, 32; xi. 13; xii. 12, 25; Heb. xi. 16, comp. Acts xv. 17; James ii. 7). This passive use, in connection with persons and things belonging and dedicated to the Almighty—*called by the Name of Jehovah*—might be abundantly illustrated from the Septuagint, and tends to show that those who *called upon the Name of the Lord* were often, not pointedly suppliants, but persons *upon whom God's Name was called*, that is, who proclaimed their fealty to God, and were notoriously His servants.

The alleged practice of prayer to Jesus requires, therefore, to be substantiated by some better evidence than is supplied by the phrases on which Mr Liddon is compelled to rely. The 'calling upon the Name of Jesus Christ,' which specially distinguished Christians, was not, upon any reasonable estimate of the evidence, praying to Christ as to God, but, professing faith in Him, owning Him to be Leader, Master, Messiah; confessing Him before men; baptizing into His Name; working miracles in His Name; and, according to His own directions, asking the Father in His Name. The prominence Christ's followers gave to His Name as that of their Lord and Head in the Kingdom God was establishing through Him, was a calling His Name upon themselves, and caused them to be designated Christians, or, to have His Name 'called upon' them.

Mr Liddon says: "It cannot be doubted that in Acts xxii. 16; 2 Tim. ii. 22, the *Lord* Who is addressed is our Lord Jesus Christ." In the former of these texts, *the calling on His* (*i.e.*, Christ's) *Name* is joined with Baptism, and more probably denotes profession of Christian faith and discipleship, than prayer to Jesus. The context (ver. 14), certainly does not put Jesus *the Just* (comp. Matt. xxvii. 19; Luke xxiii. 47; Acts iii. 14; vii. 52) on a level with *the God of our fathers*, and, in relating what took place during his trance (verses 17-21), St Paul betrays no consciousness of having beheld and conversed with, One Who was in Essential Nature and dignity on a level with *the Blessed and Only Potentate, Whom never man saw nor can see.*

In 2 Tim. ii. 22, *call on* may differ little, if at all, in sense, from *name the Name of* (ver. 19), and may stand for 'acknowledge and serve,' rather than *pray to :* the details of the acknowledgment and service depending on the position and claims of the Being designated. Jesus is probably *the Lord* referred to, and 'them that call on Him' are probably identical with the Lord's servants (ver. 24), but there is room for doubt, because in verse 19, the true reading is, *let every one that nameth the Name of the Lord, &c.*, and if in that verse, the writer intended to quote from the Old Testament (see Numb. xvi. 5 ; Nahum i. 7 ; Ps. xcvii. 10), *the Lord* will be *Jehovah.* The best, though far from a conclusive argument for the opinion that Jesus is designated (ver. 22), is the likelihood that *servant of the Lord* (ver. 24) means *servant of Christ.*

But it is contended ; the true force of the expression *call upon* " is illustrated by the dying prayer of St Stephen, whom his murderers stoned" while he was '*praying*, and saying, Lord Jesus, receive my spirit.' The Name, *God*, is, I need scarcely remark, not in the original, and its introduction into the Anglican Version was unwarranted. The former of Stephen's invocations (Acts vii. 59, 60) was, according to the narrative, indubitably directed to Christ, the latter not indubitably. The account is too condensed and undetailed to sanction positive conclusions. There may have been an interval between the dying martyr's petitions. If the first petition was uttered—either at the commencement of the stoning, or during the preparations for the stoning, or when the mob 'ran upon him and cast him out of the city,'—and the second, just before the moment of death, the supposition that the second petition was directed to God, the Father, is the more probable. But if the petitions followed each other in quick succession, there will be a probability both were addressed to Christ, and the change of posture, *he kneeled down* (assuming that to have been a voluntary act), and the difference between the appellations, *Lord Jesus*, and *Lord*, will not justify inferences.

Mr Liddon, therefore, travels beyond the firm ground of the record, in the incautious confidence of his assertions,—" The words which were addressed by Jesus to the Father (Luke xxiii. 34, 46), are by St Stephen addressed to Jesus. To Jesus Stephen turns in that moment of supreme agony ; to Jesus he prays for pardon on his murderers ; to Jesus, as to the King of the world of spirits, he commends his parting soul." To the objection that Stephen's words were ' only an ejaculation forced from him in the extremity of his anguish, and that, as such, they are highly unfitted to be made the premiss of a theological inference,' Mr Liddon replies :—

"The question is, whether the earliest apostolical Church did or did not pray to Jesus Christ. And St Stephen's dying prayer is strictly to the point. An ' ejaculation' may show more clearly than any set formal prayer the ordinary currents of devotional thought and feeling ; an ejaculation is more instinctive, more spontaneous, and therefore a truer index of a man's real mind, than a prayer which has been used for years. And how could the martyr's cry to Jesus have been the product of a ' thoughtless impulse ?' Dying men do not cling to devotional fancies or to precarious opinions ; the soul in its last agony instinctively falls back upon its deepest certainties." After drawing attention to the faith and inspiration (Acts vi. 5 ; vii. 55), official position, and almost apostolic rank, of Stephen, Mr Liddon proceeds : " Is it urged that St Stephen's prayer was offered under the exceptional circumstance of a vision of Christ vouchsafed in mercy to His dying servant ? But it does not enter into the definition of prayer or worship that it must of necessity be addressed to an invisible Person. And the vision of Jesus standing at the right hand of God may have differed in the degree of sensible clearness, but in its general nature it did not differ, from that sight upon which the eye of every dying Christian has rested from the beginning. St Stephen would not have prayed to Jesus Christ *then*, if he had never prayed to Him before ; the vision of Jesus would not have tempted him to innovate upon the devotional law of his life ; the sight of Jesus would have only carried him in thought upwards to the Father, if the Father alone had been the Object of the Church's earliest adoration. St Stephen would never have prayed to Jesus if he had been taught that such prayer was hostile to the supreme prerogatives of God ; and the Apostles, as monotheists, must have taught him thus, unless they had believed that Jesus is God, Who with the Father is worshipped and glorified " (pp. 369, 370).

The argument is put with all the dexterity of accomplished special pleadership, and also with the suppression, misrepresentation, and unfairness which attaches to mere advocacy of foregone conclusions. Granting, what cannot be proved, that the last words of Stephen were directed to Christ, it is not true they are equivalent to the words addressed by the crucified Jesus to the Father. Stephen asks that the guilt of their crime may not be imputed to, or laid to the charge of, his murderers. The term he is recorded to have used is employed in a metaphorical and unusual sense, and is not, in this sense, found elsewhere in the New Testament. It is quite distinct from the term which, in Luke xxiii. 34, signifies forgiving; and before we can determine its precise force in a petition to Christ, we must have ascertained the relation in which Christ stands to God, the Sole ultimate Judge, and Source of pardon. Theologians, pledged to engraft ecclesiastical dogmas upon Scripture language, may experience insuperable difficulty in withstanding the temptation to construct from a single dubious word, but unshackled minds will not, in the absence of corroborating testimony, be content on the strength of one ambiguous expression, to believe Christ is put on a level with God as the Pardoner of sin. If we assume the prayer to have been directed to Christ, and assume further, its designed purport to have been : " When Thou as Judge of all, weighest their actions in Thy balance, do not place this sin in the scale against them," there still remains the stubborn fact that rational interpretation imperatively demands the supposition of Stephen's having shared the persuasion of the Apostles who held Jesus to be, in the functions of judgment, subordinate, representative, and delegated—*ordained of God to be the Judge, &c.—a Man by whom God will judge the world in righteousness,* in His appointed day (Acts x. 42 ; xvii. 31).

The artificial and forced character of the reasoning whereby Mr Liddon labours to establish the palpable fallacy, that circumstances undeniably marvellous and exceptional, would lead to no exceptional results, and divert in no degree the current of religious thought and emotion, hardly calls for exposure. A vision of the Divine glory, and of Jesus standing on the right hand of that glory, was, we may fairly presume, calculated to give Jesus a very realized prominence in the martyr's mind. The ' deepest certainties,' on which such a vision would impel the soul to fall back, would be the certainties of Christ's exaltation, Messiahship, and possession of dignity and power bestowed by God.

Mr Liddon tacitly assumes that Stephen's petition, being addressed to Christ, must have been addressed to Him as God, and then, from the petition itself, he infers ' Christ is God.' But, if we search for ' indices of Stephen's real mind,' in the discourse which issued in his martyrdom, we do not find any trace of his esteeming Christ to be God. On the contrary, his words clearly bespeak his conviction that Christ was inferior to God. We cannot doubt he had an eye to Jesus, in quoting the saying of Moses, " A prophet shall God raise up unto you from among your brethren, as He raised up me" (Acts vii. 37 ; comp. iii. 22), and we may well doubt whether he understood the saying to foretell a Personal Incarnation of the One Uncreated Nature. He was content to speak of Jesus as the Just or Righteous (Man), whom the Jews had betrayed and murdered (ver. 52), and the statement which, to his enemies, had the sound of blasphemy, was very far indeed removed from an affirmation of Christ's Godhead. That vision which, "in its general nature did not differ from the sight upon which the eye of every dying Christian has rested from the beginning," *was the Son of Man standing on the right hand of God.* Beneath the revealing light of ecclesiastical inspiration this may mean ; Co-eternal and Co-equal God standing on the right hand of the One God ; but beneath the light of reason it has a less profound significance. Stephen appears to have beheld a brightness which indicated the Divine Presence, and, by the side of that brightness, the glorified Man Christ Jesus in an attitude evincing readiness to succour and receive His servant, perchance, to punish His servant's destroyers. If the spiritual senses of a dying Christian were opened to perceive ministering spirits around him, he might, I think, quite innocently, and without any " innovation upon the devotional law of his life," say to them, *receive my spirit ;* for, he would address them as God's messengers, and with a meaning distinct from that which he would put into his words, if he were appealing to God in prayer. And if he were expiring under the hands of wicked violence, and believed that those ministering spirits, who were ready to receive him, were able also to inflict vengeance on his murderers, he might, without conscious or unconscious " hostility to the supreme prerogatives of God," deprecate such vengeance, in the benevolent entreaty, *lay not this sin to their charge.* The numerous members of the older branches of the Church Universal, are as strict Monotheists as Mr Liddon himself is, or, as he supposes the Apostles to have been, and yet they fail to discern in the invocation of glorified Beings an invasion of the Divine rights. The historically manifested consciousness of the Church (more particularly since her clearer apprehension of the mystery Mr Liddon defends) has steadily contradicted the idea that Christian Monotheism restricts all venerating homage, and prayerful invocation, to God. Orthodox Anglicans should remember obvious facts, before pronouncing what " the Apostles, as Monotheists, must have taught."

Mr Liddon argues ; " It does not enter into the definition of prayer or worship that it should be addressed to an invisible Person," intending, of course, prayer or worship such as is due to God.   Now, before this remark can have the smallest weight, proof must have been given that God is ever other than an invisible Person.   The truer shape of the proposition is ; petitions and homage offered to a visible Being are to be distinguished from prayer and worship offered to God, unless there is independent and adequate testimony the visible Being is God.

The fact that, the verb *to call upon* is accompanied, in the story of Stephen's death, by explanatory adjuncts proving it to have been in that instance connected with prayer, is certainly no sufficient evidence for its usual connection.   Stephen named the Name of, or invoked Christ, " and said" what were words of prayer ; but, *calling upon the Name of the Lord Jesus Christ,* might have introduced language of a different kind, as, profession of faith, avowal of attachment and discipleship.   The use of a vague term, indisputably open to several varieties of meaning, is ridiculously inadequate testimony for an alleged universal, and specially characteristic, devotional practice.

An Orthodox Christian, educated to believe, and officially pledged to maintain a particular doctrine, is perhaps literally unable to see what militates against his own positions, and therefore, Mr Liddon may be excused for not having noticed a fact which demolishes his cunningly woven theories about Apostolic prayers to Jesus Glorified. Προσεύχεσθαι, προσευχή, δέησις, εὔχεσθαι, εὐχή, are, in the New Testament, words of specific and restricted application, denoting prayers and vows to the Almighty.   The Lord Jesus is, in no single instance, the Person to Whom the devotions indicated by these words are directed.   The use of the three former, to express prayers to God, is exceedingly frequent. If the Christians of Apostolic days were in the habit of praying to Christ as God ; if petitions addressed to Him were an element in their united and their individual worship, how comes it to pass their petitions are never described by the accustomed, familiar, and specially appropriated terms? Why does no Canonical Writer furnish an example of the application of properly precatory terms, with reference to a form of Christian devotion supposed to be prevalent and distinctive ?

The verb δεῖσθαι is used of prayer to God, but not limited to that use, being sometimes employed of earnest requests made by one man to another.   It occurs of prayer to God ten or eleven times, and among them of Christ's own prayer to the Almighty for the spiritual preservation of Simon Peter (Luke xxii. 32).

It describes requests made to our Lord while He was upon earth (Luke v. 12 ; viii. 28, 38 ; ix. 38), and likewise requests made to His disciples (Luke ix. 40 ; see also Acts viii. 34 ; xxi. 39 ; 2 Cor. x. 2 ; Gal. iv. 12, and other texts), but it describes no requests made to our Lord in Heaven.

These facts explain, and, from the Protestant advocates' point of view, palliate the vapouring expository efforts which have been so often concentrated upon the phrase, *to call upon the Name of the Lord Jesus.* The most *must* be made of that phrase. The weak side must be covered in some fashion, and with the multitude of sympathizing readers, a pliant verb and bold assertions will pass muster undetected.

In the first eight chapters of the Acts of the Apostles, the simple title *Lord* very rarely betokens Christ, but it might betoken Him, and there is a case in which Orthodox exigencies demand that it should be understood to do so. When Matthias was elected to the Apostleship, prayer (described by the proper and most frequent term) was made to the Almighty (Acts i. 24, comp. iv. 29, 30). Mr Liddon, encouraged by some previous commentators, has been able to write deliberately as follows :— " It would seem more than probable that the prayer offered by the assembled Apostles at the election of St Matthias, was addressed to Jesus Glorified " (p. 368). The particular epithet *Heart-knower*, by which the Most High is described, is found only in one other place in the New Testament, viz., Acts xv. 8, where it is, beyond doubt, applied to God (comp. Luke xvi. 15). There is no shadow of reason for asserting it has not the same application in Acts i. 24. To assume it there refers to the Lord Jesus, is to frame a conjecture utterly devoid of probability.

But Mr Liddon contends ; " The selection of the twelve Apostles is always ascribed to Jesus Christ (Acts i. 2 ; Luke vi. 13 ; John vi. 70 ; xiii. 18 ; xv. 16, 19) ;" and though " St Paul was indeed accustomed to trace up his apostleship to the Eternal Father as the ultimate Source of all authority (Gal. i. 15 ; 2 Cor. i. 1 ; Eph. i. 1 ; 2 Tim. i. 1), yet this is not inconsistent with the fact that Jesus Christ chose and sent each and all of the Apostles." Certainly, it is not inconsistent with the fact that Jesus Christ was, while upon earth, God's visible Instrument and Organ in the choosing and sending, but it is unfavourable to the supposition that Jesus Christ when no longer upon earth, was, not only on God's behalf, but independently, the Selector and Authorizer. In Acts xv. 7, Peter says; " From ancient days God made choice among us, that the Gentiles by my mouth should hear the word of the Gospel, and believe :" a saying on which Mr Liddon remarks, "that *God* can have no reference to our Lord is an assumption. Moreover, St Peter is clearly referring, not to his original call to the Apostolate, but to his being directed to evangelize the Gentiles." To the Church Catholic the whole mystery of the Trinity is, of course, latent in the denomination *God*. "One God, the Father ; and, one Lord, Jesus Christ," may, for a Church inspired so to understand, be the inspired mode of intimating the One God, and the One Lord, to be each Personally, and in the full sense *God*, and nevertheless both together *One God*. With this I have nothing to do, but in the estimate of reason, the ever recurring distinctive and separating appellations of God and Christ, and the reservation from Christ of the title *God*, which is so many hundred times applied to the Almighty Father, are revelations that God and Christ are not both comprised in the One Uncreated Nature, and that, therefore, in the lack of clear evidence to the contrary, the Protestant investigator of Scripture 'assumes' nothing by holding that, in Acts xv. 7, the denomination *God* "can have no reference to our Lord." Unless the expression, *from ancient days*, is transformed by exposition, the reference will be to an election preceding and determining St Peter's call by Christ to the Apostolate. And if Christ did, as Mr Liddon believes, give the command ascribed to Him in Matt. xxviii. 19 ; the direction to evangelize the Gentiles, proceeded from Him as much as the selection of the twelve Apostles. Are we to imagine that, when His solemn parting command was forgotten, our Lord, acting not in His distinct Personality, but in the Unity of the Father, made choice of Peter, and issued fresh injunctions ?

"The epithet *Heart-knower*, and still more the word *Lord*, are," we are informed, "equally applicable to the Father and to Jesus Christ. For the former see John i. 50 ; ii. 25 : vi. 64 ; xxi. 17. It was natural that the Apostles should thus apply to Jesus Christ to fill up the vacant chair, unless they had believed Him to be out of the reach of prayer, or incapable of helping them." The texts referred to, are quite insufficient for the end for which they are cited. Our Lord's acquaintance with the human heart, and profound insight into human purposes and character must, since they are not specifically attributed to inherent Deity, be regarded as imparted gifts, flowing from the anointing and presence of God's Spirit. Peter knew what was in the heart of Ananias and Sapphira (Acts v. 2-9), but the circumstance would not warrant the application to him of the designation, *Knower of hearts.* However, mere assertion that a rare epithet is 'equally applicable' to two Beings, when it is only known to have been applied to One of them, is not worth attention.* The assumption of the point to be proved, is very manifest in the sentence, "It was natural that," &c.

Mr Liddon's comments on Acts ix. 13, 14, are perhaps more original than convincing :—

"The reply of Ananias, to whom Jesus appeared in a vision, and desired him to go to the newly-converted Saul of Tarsus, is an instance of that species of prayer in which the soul trustfully converses with God, even to the verge of argument and remonstrance, while yet it is controlled by the deepest sense of God's awful greatness : 'Lord, I have heard by many of this man, how much evil he hath done to Thy saints at Jerusalem : and here he hath authority from the chief priests to bind all that call on Thy Name.' . . . Ananias' remonstrance is a prayer; it is a spiritual colloquy; it is a form of prayer which implies daily, hourly familiarity with its Object; it is the language of a soul habituated to constant communion with Jesus. It shows very remarkably how completely Jesus occupies the whole field of vision in the soul of His servant. The 'saints' whom Saul of Tarsus has persecuted at Jerusalem, are the 'saints,' it is not said of God, but of Jesus ; the Name which is called upon by those whom Saul had authority to bind at Damascus, is the Name of Jesus. Ananias does not glance at One higher than Jesus, as if Jesus were lower than God; Jesus is to Ananias his God, the Recipient of his worship, and yet the Friend before Whom he can plead the secret thoughts of his heart with earnestness and freedom" (p. 370).

Is then the sight of God, or the hearing of God's voice, in a vision, so ordinary and simple an experience, as to encourage a reverent familiarity, and to put the soul of the worshipper at ease ? To most minds the trustfulness and freedom, "even to the verge of argument and remonstrance," will irresistibly suggest that Ananias did *not* apprehend the Object of his vision to be the Eternal God. What tokens are there of "the deepest sense of God's awful greatness ?" Where is there, in the account, the faintest shadow of an indication, " Jesus was to Ananias his God, the Recipient of his worship ?" The narrative tells of neither prayer nor worship, but of an exceptional state, and of some

* Dr Bloomfield thought the epithet 'equally applicable' to Christ, but recorded the acknowledgment ; "Certainly the appellation is not unfrequent in the Old Testament, Josephus, and Philo, as applied to *God the Father.*"

abnormal communication with the inner senses through a dream or trance. The complete occupation of the field of spiritual vision, in the colloquy with the glorified Jesus, is, perhaps, better evidence that the field was finite, or the soul's faculties awakened only so far as to attend to the Object presented, than that the Object was Infinite, sufficing to engage and satisfy all capacities for devotion.

The 'conspicuousness' of St Paul's "devotion to the Adorable Person of our Lord," furnishes Mr Liddon with materials for a number of rhetorical, indiscriminating, and exaggerating statements :—

"At the very moment of his conversion, Saul of Tarsus surrendered himself by a prayer to Christ, as to the lawful Lord of his being: 'Lord,' he cried, 'what wilt Thou have me to do?' (Acts ix. 6). And when afterwards in the temple our Lord bade St Paul, 'Make haste and get thee quickly out of Jerusalem,' we find the Apostle, like Ananias, unfolding to Jesus his secret thoughts, his fears, his regrets, his confessions ; laying them out before Him, and waiting for an answer from Jesus in the secret chambers of his soul (Acts xxii. 19, 20) " (p. 371).

There is something stronger than a probability the words by which Saul of Tarsus is supposed to have "surrendered himself," &c., were never spoken. They are in the Vulgate Version, but are wanting not only in the three most ancient MSS., the Sinaitic, the Vatican, and the Alexandrine, but in the Greek MSS. generally. Dean Alford says of them : " They are without any authority whatever from the Greek MSS." They may have been based upon Acts xxii. 10 ; xxvi. 14 ; passages which for Mr Liddon's purpose are not parallel. But, assuming for the moment, Paul did, trembling and astonished cry, 'Lord, what wilt Thou have me to do?' are we to assume also, that by *Lord*, he meant *Lord God*, or, that if he had not believed Christ to be God, he must have said, 'Lord, wilt Thou tell me what God would have me to do?'

The expostulation during the trance, or ecstasy in the temple (Acts xxii. 17-21), does not, either in form or matter, excuse Mr Liddon's inflated commentary, and, if we exactingly draw inferences, the unawed and outspoken unfolding of the entranced Christian's thoughts suggests that his soul was *not* conscious of beholding, and conversing with, the Everlasting God. The purpose of his pleading, after Jesus had told him the Jews at Jerusalem would not receive his testimony, was to show there were strong reasons why they ought, and in his opinion were likely, to receive it. Is this remonstrance, and preference for one's own judgment, at all natural, when the soul's inward senses are opened to direct and conscious intercourse with the Almighty?

But Mr Liddon has brought to the study of Scripture a penetrating discernment conducting him to the persuasion thus expressed,—

"St Paul constantly uses language which shows that he habitually thought of Jesus as of Divine Providence in a Human Form, watching over, befriending, consoling, guiding, providing for him and his, with Infinite foresight and power, but also with the tenderness of a human sympathy. In this sense, Jesus is placed on a level with the Father in St Paul's two earliest Epistles. 'Now God Himself and our Father, and our Lord Jesus Christ, direct our way unto you' (1 Thess. iii. 11). 'Now our Lord Jesus Christ Himself, and God, even our Father, Which hath loved us, and hath given us everlasting consolation and good hope through grace, comfort your hearts, and stablish you in every good word and work' (2 Thess. ii. 16, 17). Thus Jesus is associated with the Father, in one instance, as directing the outward movements of the Apostle's life, in another as building up the inward life of the recent converts to Christianity. In other devotional expressions, the Name of Jesus stands alone. 'I trust in the Lord Jesus,' so the Apostle writes to the Philippians, 'to send Timotheus shortly unto you' (Phil. ii. 19). 'I thank Christ Jesus our Lord,' so he assures St Timothy, 'Who hath given me power, for that He counted me faithful, putting me into the ministry' (1 Tim. i. 12). Is not this the natural language of a soul which is constantly engaged in communion with Jesus, whether it be the communion of praise or the communion of prayer? Jesus is to St Paul, not a deceased teacher or philanthropist, who has simply done his great work and then left it as a legacy to the world; He is God, ever living and ever present, the Giver of temporal and of spiritual blessings, the Guide and Friend of man, both in man's outward and in his inward life" (pp. 371, 372).

Whether the tone and diction of the Epistles to the Thessalonians are in any degree calculated to suggest or encourage the fancy of St Paul's having, in one or two expressions, which may by total isolation become ambiguous, purposed to place Jesus on a level with the Father, can readily be determined by readers of those Epistles. The personal distinction between God and Christ is everywhere clearly and prominently presented, and God is the

Christian's God and Father, the Source of the Christian's election, the Object of the Christian's prayers and thanksgivings. The conversion of the heathen to Apostolic Christianity was a turning from idols "to serve the Living and True God, and to wait for His Son from the heavens, even Jesus whom He raised from the dead" (1 Thess. i. 9, 10).

The first of the passages which Mr Liddon cites, and in which the Apostle sets forth the earnest and pious desire of his heart, is prefaced by a reference to his thanksgiving and fervent prayer to God, and followed by the expression of a hope that the Thessalonians' hearts may be established unblamable in holiness, *before our God and Father, at the coming of our Lord Jesus with all his saints.* There can, I should imagine, be no doubt, even in the most ecclesiastically tutored mind, that *our God* (ver. 9), is synonymous with *our God and Father* (ver. 11 and 13), and, therefore, does not include the personally separate Son, *our Lord Jesus.*

The text quoted from the Second Epistle to the Thessalonians, stands in a passage where the Apostle declares his obligation to give thanks to God always, for His election of the Thessalonians, and His calling of them by the Gospel, to the obtaining of the glory of our Lord Jesus Christ.

If St Paul had conceived Jesus Christ to be on a level with the Father, and included with Him in one and the same Divine Nature, it seems impossible he should have so habitually and sharply discriminated Them from each other. There is no evidence St Paul was a man of slovenly, unsystematic mind, or was afraid to face and proclaim the results and conclusions which his faith involved. If he was really enlightened to believe and know that Jesus is, in virtue of Very Godhead, the Father's Equal, his language in every Epistle singly, and in all taken together, cannot be rationally explained when severed from the hypothesis of his being the Mouthpiece of an inspiration whose fruits are to be judged by no received rules of human intelligence.

The argument—the Name of Christ is mentioned conjointly with the Name of the Father, in references to the bestowal of spiritual guidance, and strength, and comfort—has no cogency, unless proof is forthcoming that Jesus and the Father are in the same sense, kind, and degree, the sources of spiritual guidance, and strength, and comfort. The truer and solely Scriptural point of view is, that God imparts blessings by and through Christ. That the exalted Jesus, as the Messiah, the Head of the Church, and the Recipient of vast and peculiar gifts from the Almighty Father, is the Channel of grace, and the secondary and subordinate Dispenser of blessings, was unquestionably a portion of the Apostolic Faith, and amply accounts for sundry forms of expression which the Bampton Lectures misinterpret; while it does not contravene the mass of direct statements and clear implications which attest Christ's inferiority and exteriority to the Unoriginated, Incorruptible Essence. The Apostle, who could cheer and exhort his converts with the assurance, *ye are Christ's; the Head of every man is Christ,* would, doubtless, believe in Christ's loving care and ability to afford gracious assistances; but, in the expressions which his belief instigated, he would not intend to bring the *one Lord* to the level of the *One God,* and would not forget that *Christ is God's;* that *God is the Head of Christ* (1 Cor. iii. 23; xi. 3); and that *the God and Father of our Lord Jesus Christ,* is *the Father of mercies and God of all comfort* (2 Cor. i. 3).

The Apostle's benedictory salutations, &c., "Grace be unto you, and peace, from God our Father, and the Lord Jesus Christ" (1 Cor. i. 3), "The grace of our Lord Jesus Christ be with you all" (Rom. xvi. 24), and the like, are *not* "indirect prayers offered to Christ that His blessing might be vouchsafed to the Churches which the Apostle is addressing," unless prayer is the same thing as kind commendations, benevolent wishes, and pious aspirations. A believer in angelic ministrations and guardianship, would not indirectly pray to Angels, if he said, "May angelic care be with you, may the holy Angels guard you." Since all things and events are within the scope, and subject to the sway, of the Divine wisdom and power, every expression of hope and desire with respect to the bestowal of good gifts might be called an 'indirect prayer' to God, but could not be called prayer in the strict and proper sense. If the gifts were contemplated as flowing from, or through, a secondary and intermediate Giver, it would be simply absurd to say that kindly-expressed hopes, wishes, and commendations, were prayers to him, proving him to be the Object of truly religious supplication.

Before adducing the texts quoted in the last paragraph, Mr Liddon should have studied the contexts. The very next words after the text from the first Corinthian Epistle, are, "I thank my God always concerning you, for the grace of God which was given you in Christ Jesus;" and the next sentence (ver. 9), is, "God is faithful, by Whom ye were called into the fellowship of His Son, Jesus Christ our Lord."

The text from the Roman Epistle should have been referred, xvi. 20; verse 24 not being found in either of the three great Manuscripts. Verse 20 is immediately preceded by an announcement; "The God of peace will bruise Satan under your feet shortly;" and followed (ver. 25–27), by a doxology of rather involved and incoherent construction (see Winer, *Grammar of N. T.* Sec. lxiii. 1): "To Him that is able to stablish you according to my Gospel, and the preaching of Jesus Christ, ... to *the Only wise God*, to Whom, through Jesus Christ, be the glory for ever."

A theologian must be suffering grievously from scarcity of materials, when he endeavours to build reasoning on such phrases as, *in the Lord Jesus; in the Lord; in Christ.* If my readers will consult a few of the many examples in which those phrases occur, they will see how much out of place are minute doctrinal deductions. Mr Liddon borrows the following commentary on Phil. ii. 19, from Bishop Ellicott :—" *I hope in the Lord Jesus to send Timothy shortly.* This hope was *in the Lord Jesus* ; it rested and centred in Him ; it arose from no *extraneous* feelings or expectations, and so would doubtless be fulfilled."

St Paul's avowal of gratitude to Christ (1 Tim. i. 12), is no 'devotional expression' of religious adoration, implying Jesus to be God, and equally with the Father the primary Fountain of spiritual endowments and energy. It is a simple expression of thankfulness for his call to the Apostleship, and for the strength which had, through Christ, been imparted to him. The original of *I thank*, is not the verb εὐχαριστεῖν, which is in the New Testament almost exclusively appropriated to the sacred purpose of thanking God—(Luke xvii. 16 ; Rom. xvi. 4; being the only exceptions in between thirty and forty texts)—but a phrase which is not frequent, and is not in itself devotional (Luke xvii. 9), though it is used with reference to God in 2 Tim. i. 3. If devout thanksgivings were continually ascending to the Glorified Jesus, how is it that Mr Liddon can adduce only a single imperfect instance, from the whole range of the Acts and Epistles? And again, how is it that, in the same wide field, the consecrated term εὐχαριστεῖν is never applied to Christ? And yet again, how is it that, the Pauline phrase *thanks be to God*—χάρις τῷ Θεῷ (Rom. vi. 17 ; vii. 25, probably ; 1 Cor. xv. 57 ; 2 Cor. ii. 14 ; viii. 16 ; ix. 15) has nowhere one parallel *thanks be to Christ ?* Have these facts no weight, and are honest men who profess to learn from the New Testament, at liberty to ignore them?

Mr Liddon might, moreover, have gathered the precariousness of the conjecture, Christ was "to St Paul, God ever living," &c., from the context of 1 Tim. i. 12. In verse 11, the Apostle names "the Gospel of the glory of the Blessed God," where *the*

Blessed God is not Jesus Christ; and in verse 17, he writes: "Unto the King of the Ages, the Immortal, the Invisible, the Only God, be honour and glory for ever and ever;" where, again, *the Only God* is not Jesus Christ.

What is meant by coupling with Christ's "Infinite foresight and power, the tenderness also of a human sympathy ?" The Incarnation of Deity can scarcely be imagined to have augmented God's tender love, and capacity of feeling with, and for, His creatures. Our Maker does not acquire a better knowledge whereof we are made, and come to understand more thoroughly the work of His own Hands, by enveloping One of His Own Divine Persons in the raiment of an Impersonal Humanity. Is not God's Nature, inasmuch as It is the fountain and sustenance of ours, the One conceivable Nature Which can perfectly sympathise with our infirmities, and can learn nothing about us by the assumption of our flesh and blood ? A created Being, not one of ourselves, or even an Arian Christ, such as the Fourth Gospel, when not ecclesiastically expounded, so distinctly yields, might attain complete sympathy with us by entering our ranks; but Incarnation could not add to our Creator's Omniscience, or extend His loving tenderness. The Personal and absolutely Divine Word cannot have furnished Himself with one additional or enlarged sympathetic qualification, by becoming Incarnate. If the undiminished Attributes of Deity did not deprive His experience of veritable human reality, still, His experience could not have enhanced His perfect comprehension of His rational and sensitive creatures.

Rom. x. 9-13 is a passage which we are asked to accept as proof of St Paul's having believed Christ to be God, and consequently, the Object of prayer :—

" In point of fact, the Apostle has not left us in doubt as to his faith or his practice in this respect. ' If,' he asserts, ' thou shalt confess with thy mouth the Lord Jesus, and shalt believe in thine heart that God hath raised Him from the dead, thou shalt be saved. For with the heart man believeth unto righteousness, and with the mouth confession is made to salvation. For the Scripture saith, Whosoever believeth on Him shall not be ashamed. For there is no difference between the Jew and the Greek; for the Same is Lord over all, rich unto all that call upon Him. For whosoever shall call upon the Name of the Lord shall be saved.' The Prophet Joel had used these last words of prayer to the Lord Jehovah. St Paul, as the whole context shows beyond reasonable doubt, understands them of prayer to Jesus" (p. 372).

I have already shown that the context does anything rather than remove " reasonable doubt" St Paul understood the prophet's words in the sense Mr Liddon asserts ; but I may add a few remarks here. The alteration in the translation, " the Same *is* Lord of all," is probably not an improvement. At any rate, it is a matter of opinion, arbitrary, on no ground provable, and of no consequence in the interpretation of the passage, " God Who raised Christ from the dead" (ver. 9), being the more probable Object of the faith and the invocation in verses 11 and 12. In Acts ii. 21, we meet with the same quotation from Joel, where, if the original sense of the prophet's words is departed from, and *the Lord* designates Christ, and Christ is God, ecclesiastical exposition becomes eminently requisite in the next sentence, " Jesus of Nazareth, *a man* proved by God unto you by miracles, and wonders, and signs, which God did by Him ;" and again, in ver. 36, " God hath made this same Jesus whom ye crucified both Lord and Christ." If it should be said, as the present Bishop of Lincoln, Dr Wordsworth, does say (*Smith's Bible Dictionary*, Article, *Son of God*), '*Lord* equals *Jehovah*,' then we have the portentous disclosure, that the Self-existent, Eternal One, has made a Being Who expired upon the cross, Self-existent and Eternal. To soften this startling revelation, by explaining the making of Jesus into *Jehovah*, to signify merely the giving Him the Name Jehovah, is to abandon its witness to Christ's Deity, for to bear the Name, is not the same thing as to possess the Nature, of Jehovah.

If *calling upon the Name of the Lord*, is understood of Jesus, in Rom. x. 13, then that form of expression, which has been shown not necessarily and specifically to indicate prayer, may be synonymous with *confessing with the mouth the Lord Jesus* (ver. 9). The probably true reading in verse 17, is, *the report is through the word of Christ;* but before we draw upon this circumstance for inferences favourable to Mr Liddon's exposition, we should study, in the certainly true reading of Col. iii. 16, 17, a description of the devotional effects which *the word of Christ* ought to produce. " Let the word of Christ dwell in you richly ; in all wisdom teaching and admonishing each other with psalms, hymns, spiritual songs, in grace singing in your hearts *to God.* And everything whatsoever ye do in word or in deed, do all in the Name of the Lord Jesus, *giving thanks to God, the Father*, through Him." The denomination, *Lord of all*, being used in Gal. iv. 1, can hardly be reckoned among the consecrated and exclusive titles of God.

In the particular case we are discussing, there is no proof, and no preponderance of likelihood, "St Paul applies to Jesus the language which the prophets had used of the Lord Jehovah;" and if he had so applied it, no convincing testimony for the Apostle's belief in Christ's Godhead would be involved. The great characteristic of Christ's disciples in the Apostolic Church, was, that they did in every way supplicate, acknowledge, and praise their God and Father. To believe in, confess, and call upon the Name of, Jesus Christ Whom God had sent, was included in the Christian worship of God, not because Christ was held to be God, but because the very position and offices of Christ were understood to be those of Example, Leader, Lord, and Head, in the family of God's worshippers. From the Apostolic standpoint, the disciples of Jesus were, in virtue of their discipleship, most emphatically and distinctively the servants and children of God. I speak, of course, only upon the basis of a reasonable interpretation of Scripture, and under correction from ecclesiastical light. Ecclesiastical interpretation may teach, and upon Catholic as opposed to Protestant principles, may teach rightly, there is a Divinely-devised and irrefragable argument for Christ's Deity contained in the fact, that a prophet used certain language concerning Jehovah; that St Peter (Acts ii. 21) quoted the prophet's language, to all appearance in its original application, and that St Paul afterwards quoted it, in a passage sufficiently obscure and ambiguous to leave room for doubt whether his designed reference was to Jehovah, or to Christ.

Mr Liddon inquires; "What shall we say of St Paul's entreaties that he might be freed from the mysterious and humiliating infirmity which he terms his 'thorn in the flesh?' He tells us that three times he besought the Lord Jesus Christ that it might depart from him, and that in mercy his prayer was refused (2 Cor. xii. 8, 9). Are we to imagine that that prayer to Jesus was an isolated act in St Paul's spiritual life? Does any such religious act stand alone in the spiritual history of an earnest and moderately consistent man?" (p. 373).

From the particular term, παρακαλεῖν, by which St Paul describes his petition, no argument can be drawn for the petition's having been prayer to God. That term is never by the Apostle used of requests to the Almighty, but it repeatedly occurs of entreaties and exhortations addressed to the brethren. In the Gospels it frequently describes petitions made to Christ while He was upon earth; but it is, in the entire New Testament, only once used of prayer to God, in the words, 'Thinkest thou that I cannot now pray to my Father, and He will furnish Me with more than twelve legions of Angels?" (Matt. xxvi. 53).

Dean Stanley, on 2 Cor. xii. 8, says of the verb of entreaty used by St. Paul : "This is often applied to Christ in the Gospels, and implies that personal communication which the Apostle always presupposes in his language concerning Him."

But the petition cannot be fairly disjoined from the exceptional circumstances, the 'visions and revelations of the Lord,' with which it is, in the Apostle's narrative, associated. From verse 9, we learn there was some sort of sensible, unusual communication. The answer given to St Paul was, in its degree, a revelation, and the account leads us to suppose, Christ appeared and spoke. So far as our knowledge of the Apostle's spiritual history extends, we have no warrant for 'imagining that that prayer to Jesus' was other than an 'isolated act,' or at any rate, an act attached to conditions foreign to ordinary experience, and therefore, no guide to us, unless in our cases the conditions should be repeated. I do not doubt that all persons who believe in Christ's exaltation, and His mission from God, would, if they were to behold and hear Him, either in their normal, or in an entranced state, address petitions to Him. They would do so, whether they held or repudiated the doctrine of the Church Catholic respecting His Person. Exceptional experiences, such as those of Stephen, Ananias, and St Paul, naturally produced exceptional results. These saints of the primitive Church, did not appeal to Christ as to the Invisible and Omnipresent God, but, as to a Being marvellously disclosed to, and communicating with, the inner senses of their souls. The visions and colloquies vouchsafed to St Paul (see Acts ix. 27 ; xviii. 9 ; xxii. 18 ; xxiii. 11 ; 2 Cor. xii. 1-9), would have had a practically incontrollable tendency to make prayer to Jesus the Apostle's habitual practice, if he had held Jesus to be Omnipotent and Omniscient Deity. He would himself continually have prayed to Christ, and would have enjoined prayer to Christ, as among the foremost and most profitable of Christian duties. But if we know anything about his life, teaching, and devotional habits (and the reasonable supposition is, the Acts and Epistles tell us the prominent features), he did nothing of the kind. We may, therefore, fairly infer, his views of his exalted Master's Nature caused him (times of ecstasy and revelation apart), to abstain from offering prayers to our Lord, and to abstain from encouraging or directing others to offer them. "An earnest and moderately consistent man," convinced of Christ's Godhead, and enjoying the intercourse with Christ, with which St Paul was favoured, must have shown his earnestness and consistency by practices and injunctions which the known history and extant writings of St Paul totally fail to exhibit. The attempt to deduce Christ's Godhead from St Paul's ' worship' of Christ, is an impolitic blunder, because it at once, and necessarily, fixes the attention on facts most adverse to the deduction. The Apostle had special individual inducements to render, and prescribe, the adoration which, in Mr Liddon's opinion, he would on general grounds of doctrine feel to be due. But while there is superabundant testimony he himself adored, and taught others to adore, the Unseen Father, with the tributes of prayer and praise, there is no testimony he adored, or counselled the adoration of, the Unseen Christ.

Mr Liddon reverts again to a portion of the much-discussed passage in the second chapter of the Epistle to the Philippians, for the purpose of asserting that, in verses 9 and 10, " Apostles declared Jesus, when His day of humiliation and suffering had ended, to have been so highly exalted that the Name which He had borne on earth, and which is the symbol of His Humanity, was now the very atmosphere and nutriment of all the upward torrents of prayer which rise from the moral world beneath His throne ; that as the God-Man he was worshipped by Angels, by men, and by the spirits of the dead. The practice of the Apostles did but illustrate their faith ; and the prayers offered to Jesus by His servants on earth were believed to be but a reflection of that worship which is offered to Him by the Church of heaven " (p. 374).

That the Name bestowed upon Christ was "the Name He had borne on earth," is not less manifest than many other things which are stated in the Lectures I am reviewing, but at the same time is very far from being really manifest. The wording of the text, certainly, leaves the impression that the giving of "the Name which is above every name," was concurrent with the exceeding exaltation Christ Jesus received from God, and therefore posterior to the "day of humiliation and suffering." Mr Liddon strengthens himself by quoting Dean Alford :—

" The general aim of the passage is the *exaltation of Jesus.* The *to the glory of God the Father,* below, is no deduction from this, but rather an additional reason why we should carry on the exaltation of Jesus *until this new particular is introduced.* This would lead us to infer that the universal prayer is to be *to* Jesus. And this view is confirmed by the next clause, where every tongue is to confess that Jesus Christ is *Lord,* when we remember the common expression, *to call upon the Name of the Lord*, for prayer" (Rom. x. 12 ; 1 Cor. i. 2 ; 2 Tim. ii. 22).

The worth of the references, in connection with the statement, "*to call upon the Name of the Lord*, is a common New Testament expression for prayer," my readers are in a position to estimate. No man could write with more clearness than Dean Alford, when he was not engaged upon the task of elucidating Catholic dogma by the exposition of intractable texts ; but I am greatly mistaken, if he was thinking or writing clearly, when he affirmed that the words, *to the glory of God, the Father* (ver. 11), are no deduction from the exaltation of Jesus. Take the bending of the knee in the Name of Jesus, and the confession of the Lordship of Jesus, in what sense we will, the glory of God, the Father, is the supreme and ultimate aim and end ; and if this does not deduct from the exaltation of Jesus, it at least implies that the exaltation did not, in the Apostle's thought, reach the height of Co-equal Godhead. If, in the Sacred Writer's estimation, Jesus and God were distinct Beings, so decidedly on different levels, that the one could be ' exceedingly exalted' by the Other, there is, of course, no deduction from the exaltation, but rather a guarantee and continuation of it, in the " new particular introduced ;" but if the writer judged Jesus to be in Nature the Eternal Father's Equal, his language is among those products of revealing inspiration which are wholly inscrutable to reason.

I may remark,—the Dean's Revised Version of Phil. ii. 6,— "deemed not His equality with God a thing to grasp at," will not pass with unprejudiced scholars, however it may deceive the body of English readers, whom the Dean was bound with scrupulous fairness to enlighten. *Equality with*, is a translation too doubtful ever to be given without an intimation of its doubtfulness ; and for the intrusion of the pronoun *His*, there was no authority but the Dean's own conviction, which he might have stated and defended, but had no right to foist upon the public, under the guise of literal rendering.* An expositor's opinion of the Apostle's meaning may be very valuable in its proper place, but

---

* While referring to Dean Alford's Revision, which is in so many points a real improvement, I may notice two glaring faults. He retains in St Matthew's Gospel, the inaccurate and misleading phrase, "end of the world ;" and in Rom. ix. 5, gives no hint that the rendering, " Christ, Who is God over all, blessed for ever," is only one of two translations equally admissible on grammatical grounds. The preponderance of evidence, on all other grounds (excepting, of course, the Church's final dogmatic authority) is so heavily against the punctuation applied, and the rendering given, in the Authorized Version, that a Reviser, whatever his private opinion may be,

that place is not a translation supposed to be as closely literal as the different idioms of different languages will permit.   Orthodox Protestant scholars have an instinctive, and almost insuperable reluctance to acquaint English readers with the ambiguities involved in the construction and language of Rom. ix. 5 ; Phil. ii. 5–11.   But however natural this reluctance may be, the translator's duty should be performed with conscientious equity, and in the few instances of phrases with a controversial bearing, where two renderings are, on merely philological grounds, equally probable, both should be given.   Fear lest the majority of readers should, when thrown on the contexts, and on the general teaching of Scripture, arrive at what the translator judges to be a wrong conclusion, is no sufficient palliation for making a Sacred Writer definitely say one thing, when it is quite as likely he meant another.

The treatment which the Philippian passage has long received, is a discredit to commentators.   Every Greek scholar knows quite well, that the far more general and fundamental sense of the word translated *form*, is, outward semblance, shape, fashion, appearance ; and from this sense, the meaning of the very difficult and figurative expression, *form of God*, should be derived ; yet, because *form* may, in the refinement of philosophical diction, possibly signify, 'aggregate of the qualities,' 'specific character,' it is boldly declared to be, in the Apostle's statement, tantamount to *essence, nature, possession of distinctive attributes.* It is used in only one other instance in the New Testament (Mark xvi. 12), where the expression, *He appeared in another form*, does not mean in another *essence* or *nature* (comp. Septuagint ; Job iv. 16 : Isa. xliv. 13 ; Dan. v. 6, 9, 10 ; vii. 28 ; also Wisdom xviii. 1).   The cognate and derivate words occurring in

ought, in Christian truthfulness and honesty, to apprise English readers of the ambiguity of the text.

Another, though in comparison trivial, blemish of the Dean's work, is that, in every instance except one, he translates Greek which is, word for word, *the God and Father of us*, by, *God and our Father*.   The sense is undoubtedly that which he has in the exceptional instance (Phil. iv. 20) given, *Our God and Father*.   The phrase, *the God and Father of our Lord Jesus Christ*, he always construes literally and correctly ; yet, in Rev. i. 6, he declines to substitute, *unto His God and Father*, for the less faithful rendering, *unto God and His Father*.

The English reader should consult, along with Alford's Revised Version, Sharpe's well-known translation from Griesbach's Text.   These together will put him in possession of the true sense of the Original.   If he adds 'Tischendorf's English Testament, with various readings from the three most celebrated Manuscripts,' he will have every aid of real importance, as regards translation and Text.   The three volumes I have named, may all be purchased for five shillings.

the New Testament, do not aid to sustain the conjecture which doctrinal considerations recommend to Orthodox scholars. The similar designation, *image of God*, is protected by its application to man, otherwise subtle theologians would have discerned that, since it cannot relate to external shape, it must imply identity of 'essential qualities' and 'distinctive attributes.'

The phrase assumed to betoken *equality with God*, more probably betokens *likeness to God, the being as God*, and all attempts to make it definite by inserting the particulars, or specifying the extent of resemblance, are mere surmises.* Together with the previous phrase, *form of God*, it indicates, with vague generality, a Godlike condition, but could never be accepted as an allegation of Christ's Godhead, without a strong previous persuasion that Christ is God. Its evidential force, for minds not already persuaded of our Lord's Deity, is rather adverse to the dogma, because the subject of Christ's dignity and exaltation was in the Apostle's thoughts, and, unless checked by inspiration, he may be fairly presumed to have written freely from the depth and fulness of his faith and knowledge. Ambiguity and reserve imply the absence of clear conviction and didactic purpose, and if the stupendous dogma, 'Jesus is the Most High God,' had not been already proclaimed and established among the converts at Philippi, they certainly would never have gathered it from doubtful and dark phraseology. The scope and diction of the Philippian Epistle generally, as I have shown in examining an earlier section of Mr Liddon's Lectures, lend no support to the notion that St Paul believed and taught the Essential Equality of Christ and the Father.

The Fathers of the early Christian centuries, are eminently instructive in their treatment of the passage we have been considering. Handling it with vivacious imagination, penetrating boldness, and untiring pertinacity, they smite with it numerous heresies, and construct from its condensed and comprehensive teachings, impregnable defences for the Church's Faith concerning the Nature and Person of Christ. Bishop Bull, a diligent student of their writings, was truly a partaker of their spirit when he said respecting the seemingly cloudy, metaphorical, and difficult phrases addressed to the converts at Philippi, " This one passage, if it be rightly understood, is sufficient for the refutation of all the Heresies against the Person of our Lord Jesus Christ" (*Def. Nic. Fid.*)

---

* No man with a competent knowledge of Greek, can deny the greater probability that *ἴσα* is used adverbially, in the sense of *as* or *like*.

With laudable self-restraint, Mr Liddon abstains from appealing to the 'less clearly traceable belief in the brief Epistles of St
Peter,' but he hazards the remark ; " Yet 1 Peter iv. 11, is a doxology framed, as it might seem, for common use on earth and in
heaven.   See also 2 Peter iii. 18."   In the former of these texts,
the doxology is, in all probability, directed to God, " Whom the
Apostle would have to be glorified in all things through Jesus
Christ," but the wording is ambiguous, a circumstance which
begets absolute confidence in a Christian controversialist.

What is less conspicuous in St Peter is, however, " especially
observable in St John.   St John is speaking of the Son of God,
when he exclaims, ' This is the confidence that we have in Him,
that, if we ask anything according to His Will, He heareth us :
and if we know that He heareth us, we know that we have the
petitions that we desired of Him' (1 John v. 13–15).   The
natural construction of this passage seems to oblige us to refer
of Him, and *His Will*, to the Son of God (ver. 13).   The passage
1 John iii. 21, 22, does not forbid this ; it only shows how fully,
in St John's mind, the honour and prerogatives of the Son are
those of the Father" (p. 374).

A man who has no theory to serve will perceive that we cannot
insist on construing the pronoun with reference to the last antecedent title, *Son of God.*   Verses 12 and 13 are parenthetical,
and the confidence spoken of in verse 14 is, by the more natural
construction, confidence towards God, of Whom it had been
affirmed in verse 11, " God gave to us eternal life, and this life
is in His Son."   Macknight rightly paraphrases ; " This is the
boldness which we have with the Father, through our believing
on His Son," &c.   The passage (iii. 21, 22), which unquestionably relates to the Father, is in its phraseology parallel and illustrative, and enhances the contextually strong probability that in
v. 14, 15, the reference is to God.

With a curious disregard for the plain sense of the very texts
which he quotes,—unless, indeed, his object is to infer, in the
teeth of the Apostle's language, the Godhead of *the Lamb*,—Mr
Liddon brings forward the Apocalyptic vision of " the adoration
Above, where the wounded Humanity of our Lord is throned in
the highest heavens" (Rev. v. 6–14).   The Lamb slain and
glorified, is first declared to be " worthy to receive the power,
and riches, and wisdom, and strength, and honour, and glory,
and blessing " (ver. 12), and then, every creature joins in saying,
" Blessing, and honour, and glory, and power be unto Him that
sitteth upon the throne, and unto the Lamb, for ever and ever."

This "hymn of the whole visible creation," Mr Liddon introduces with the liberally imaginative statement : "All created life, whether it wills or not, lives for Christ's as for the Father's glory." But the chapter from which Mr Liddon's argument is drawn, does not in the smallest degree betray an intention to equalize Christ with God. The Lamb is clearly distinguished from God. He is called "the Lion which is of the tribe of Judah, the Root of David" (ver. 5) ; and is pronounced to be "worthy to take the Book, and to open the seals thereof; because He was slain, and did redeem to God by His blood, out of every kindred, and tongue, and people, and nation ; and did make them unto our God a kingdom and priests." The adoration, so far, is most palpably not to Jesus as God, but to Jesus as Redeemer; and in verse 13, there is, as I have before observed, no trace of identity, or unity of nature, and a very manifest separation of persons, between *Him that sitteth upon the throne* and *the Lamb.* To show "how the Redeemed Church on earth bears her part in this universal chorus of praise," Mr Liddon cites Rev. i. 5, 6 : "Unto Him That loveth us, and washed us from our sins in His blood, and made us a kingdom and priests unto His God and Father ; to Him be the glory, and the dominion, for ever and ever. Amen ;"—words, be it remembered, which follow immediately after the description ; "Jesus Christ, the faithful Witness, the First-born of the dead, and the Ruler of the kings of the earth." It is possible the writer may, in the ascription of glory, have had Christ's *God and Father* in view, but grammatical construction refers the clause to Christ.

The feelings of those who deny, from the Protestant ground of reasonably interpreted Scripture, the dogma which Mr Liddon upholds, may, I should imagine, be here expressed in his own language : "You will not, my brethren, mistake the force and meaning of this representation of the adoration of the Lamb in the Apocalypse. . . . . You cannot doubt for one moment Who is meant by 'the Lamb,' or what is the character of the worship that is so solemnly offered to Him" (p. 376).

When we are admonished that,—"To adore Christ's Deity while carefully refusing to adore His Manhood, would be to forget that His Manhood is for ever joined to His Divine and Eternal Person, Which is the real Object of our adoration"—we are tempted to ask how it is that, in the Apocalypse, Christ never receives the appellation *God*, to which "His Divine and Eternal

Person" entitles Him ?   Why is the title of Deity so jealously restricted to the Almighty Father ?   A writer with no stronger incentive than a cherished speculative suspicion that Christ was, in His Personal Being, a Form of the Self-existent Nature, could scarcely refrain from sometimes calling Him *God*, especially if He were desirous to extol Christ, and depict Christ's highest dignity.

What intimations the New Testament affords of a worship of Jesus entailing the inference, ' Jesus is in Essential Nature the Most High God,' my readers can now judge.   If the decision of the Church is authoritative and binding, then, any intimations, however ambiguous, and however scanty, are enough, and no evidence to the contrary can have weight, but if the appeal is to Holy Scripture as a document of rational proof, the assertion, ' Jesus was worshipped with the adoration due to God ' is thoroughly baseless.

Mr Liddon rightly contends that the homage paid to Jesus, " cannot be accounted for, and so set aside, as being part of an undiscriminating cultus of heavenly or superhuman beings in general.   Such a cultus finds no place in the New Testament, except when it, or something very much resembling it, is expressly discountenanced " (Acts x. 25 ; xiv. 13-15; Col. ii. 18 ; Rev. xxii. 8, 9).   But this statement, though true, is not to the point, because, in the view of the Canonical Writers, Jesus did not rank among heavenly or superhuman Beings in general, but held peculiar, unshared, position and office between God and man. The tributes of affection, reverence, and homage, paid to Him, are attached to the qualifications with which God has enriched Him ; to the pre-eminent place to which God has exalted Him, and the glorious dignity which God has bestowed upon Him. If numerous and perspicuous announcements are not forcibly put aside ; if constant implications of a very direct kind are not refused a hearing ; if every rule of rational exposition is not reversed ; the claims of Jesus all flow, not from intrinsic and independent attributes of Self-existent Essence, but, from the originating Will and Energy of an Omnipotent Producer ; from what God has made Him to be ; and from what He has become in virtue of derived powers, a Divine Mission, and the abiding, imparted, presence of His God and Father.   And while this guiding fact stands out conspicuously in the pages of the New Testament, " the worship of Jesus," were it much more than the meagre scantily displayed thing it is, could not possibly imply His Godhead or raise Him to a level with the Supreme One,

T

Whose beloved and glorified Offspring, Servant, and Ambassador, He is.   There is no need for the clearly drawn "distinction between a primary and a secondary worship," on the absence of which Mr Liddon builds.   The honours rendered to the glorified Redeemer and Head of the Church, are not rendered to Him as God, nor as one of a class of superhuman Beings, and still less as a rival of God, but, as one whom God has made worthy of honour.

Viewing the subject from the Scriptural as distinguished from the Ecclesiastical standing-point, Mr Liddon appears to me to exaggerate, colour, and misrepresent, the New Testament indications of the homage accorded to Jesus.   He chooses to ignore altogether the distinctly specified grounds of conferred office, qualification, and dominion, which explain that homage, and then, he sophistically handles the English term "worship," as though it were a fair equivalent for all the Greek terms, and were definite enough to exclude all gradations of lower and higher, whenever the gradation is not formally mentioned.   The worship of respect, reverence, humble request, and gratitude, is, unquestionably, denoted in the New Testament by several words differing from each other in range and force, the stronger, more restricted, and more sacred of which, are never found in conjunction with the Name of the Ascended Jesus, yet, Mr Liddon could permit himself to pen and publish the sentence : "Worship is claimed for, and is given to, God alone ; and if Jesus is worshipped, this is simply because Jesus is God" (p. 378).

With Patristic arguments for "the worship of Jesus Christ," I am not concerned.   I will only remark that, in estimating their value, the exact question at issue must not be lost sight of, viz., whether Christ was worshipped under the persuasion of His being truly, and in the full sense, God—in Essence, Nature, and Attributes, the Uncreated, Almighty Father's Equal.   From the first Epistle of Clement, the earliest of the authentic writings ascribed to the Subapostolic, or, as they are sometimes called, the Apostolic Fathers, no testimony conducive to Mr Liddon's dogma can be cited, and its absence agrees with the opinion that the dogma was progressively revealed through the Church, and not through the preaching and writings of the Evangelists and Apostles.   The exceedingly uncertain authorship, and certainly corrupted text, of the Ignatian Epistles, condemns such language as : "Even before the end of the first century, St Ignatius bids the Roman Christians 'put up supplications to Christ' on his behalf, that he might attain the distinction of martyrdom."

"The Epistle of St Polycarp to the Philippians" does not, either in the introductory benediction, or the twelfth chapter, teach or imply, that Christ is God, or, as an Object of worship, on a par with God. The date of Polycarp's Epistle is towards the middle of the second century; the date of the story of his martyrdom, which successive transcribers have probably garnished, is, of course, somewhat later.

The writings of "St Justin" (about A.D. 150) are when impartially examined, seen to be strikingly deficient in the dogmatic insight, and accurate definition, which distinguish the teaching of the maturer Church concerning the Nature, Person, and worship of Jesus Christ.

In the Authorized Services of the Church of England, devotional addresses to our Lord Jesus Christ are very frequent. Mr Liddon reckons the number of them to exceed eighty, of which the Litany, a Service of peculiar form,* contains more than half, while the numerous Collects, the most precious of the Church's prayers, contain only three. On the whole, there can be no question, the Church of England, in common with the older branches of the Church Catholic, has advanced greatly beyond merely Scriptural practice and proportion, in her public religious services. She has hitherto borne her part in the grand work of diffusing and inculcating the plenary Ecclesiastical Revelation in which Holy Scripture is but a subordinate factor. She has inherited, and holds fast, more than Scripture, and is therefore, a living portion of that organized and inspired Body, whose duty, in relation to Scripture, has been to bring forth what is secreted, to complete what is imperfect, and in so doing, to suppress and nullify some conclusions delusively apprehensible by reason and common sense. At the present time, through the harmonious action of a majority of her Priests, the Church of England fulfils her task, in maintaining a well-developed dogmatic faith, of which the most ancient extant Creed (*The Apostles'*) is no sufficient presentation. The wants which the Bible does not meet, and the faith which the Bible does not establish, are met and

* "The Litany is one of the parts of the Prayer Book which has its origin in a time neither primitive nor reformed. . . . Its form is very peculiar, and the explanation is to be sought in the occasion of its first introduction. The usual mode of addressing our prayers, both in the Scriptures and in the Prayer Book, is to God, our Father, through Jesus Christ. This is the form of the Lord's Prayer, after which manner we are all taught to pray. . . . This was the general mode of prayer throughout the early ages of the Church. Even those earlier forms of prayer which are most like the Litany, are, for the first three hundred years of the Church, always addressed direct to God the Father."—Dean Stanley on the Litany : *Good Words, July* 1868.

established, not merely by the Nicene and Athanasian Creeds, and by forms for public prayer, but also by hymns, and forms for private prayer. The heretical interpretations of devout but erring common sense, are answered, not by investigation and reasoning, but by multiplied repetitions, in the most sacred and influential associations, of the doctrine or practice whose Scripturalness is challenged. Convinced that uninquiring habit is the safest road in theological belief, the Clergy confirm their lay brethren in the faith of Christ's Godhead, by the selection, and congregational use, of hymns in which Jesus is, with studied distinctness, and systematic frequency, declared to be internal to the One Divine Nature, and equalized with the Father in expressions of supplication and praise. Forms for family prayer, likewise, compiled and recommended by the Clergy, address Jesus as God, in the language of highest adoration. These methods engrain the Church's doctrine, while they help to shape and feed the adoring instinct of which the One God is the proper Object. Mr Liddon rightly observes ; " Hymnody actively educates, while it partially satisfies, the instinct of worship ; " and there can be no fair objection against making it, and the words of our household worship, vehicles for fixing and propagating the persuasion that Christ is God, provided only the persuasion is rested on Ecclesiastical, and not on solely Scriptural, revelation. But there is a very palpable inconsistency between the Protestant position, that Holy Scripture is the sole sufficient and Divine Rule of Faith and Practice, and the use of prayers and hymns, whose sentiments and diction are either utterly devoid of Scriptural sanction, or quite out of Scriptural proportion.

Men who decline to see revelation outside the Canonical pages, seem to be overtaken by a retributive intellectual blindness, when they take in hand to promulgate the Deity of Jesus. If we confess that the Incarnate God still speaks through His Church, no less certainly than He speaks through the written Gospels, we can, without inconsistency, accept in Christian forms of prayer and praise, modification, enlargement, and completion of the temporary and imperfect model given in the Lord's Prayer, and the introductory direction, *After this manner, pray ye.* Our Divine Master's utterances in His living Church, are not shaped and restrained by His voice in the Evangelical histories. There is no need that the one should be, to the ear of reason, consonant with the other. Upon His first disciples He laid the injunction ; "when ye pray, say *Our Father.*" His praying followers in the nearer ages, He, by means of His Church, teaches to address

Himself, as often and as devoutly as they address the Father, if
not more often and more devoutly!   To His first disciples He
is reported to have said, "I am the Way, and the Truth, and the
Life, no man cometh unto the Father, but through Me;" to His
disciples of later date, He, by means of His Church, says, 'I
am the Goal; no nature and attributes excel mine; look
to me as your God, the rightful and sufficing Object of your
devotions.'   The earlier instruction survives only as a slightly
flavouring ingredient amid the more recently vouchsafed knowledge.   Revelation is a perpetually unrolling scroll; identity is
not lost, but growth is constant, and new particulars and adjust-
ments are superadded.   Together with unbroken continuity,
there is marvellous development.   The Old Testament, the New,
and, explanatory, complementary, and superior to both, the
Church,—such is the outline and proportion in the series of
messages sent from Heaven for the guidance of Christian worship.   The variations and progress impressively proclaim an
abiding presence of the Incarnate God, and the high prerogatives with which that presence clothes His Organ, the Church.
A trustful unparleying faith, likewise, is invigorated by well-
sustained exercise; and the All-Wise Source of our Intelligence,
affords larger latitude for ennobling virtue, in the self-denying
repression of His dangerous intellectual gifts.   From the Protestant point of view, the expansion and divergence of Christian
worship into its present shape, may appear dissonant and shame-
ful; but from the Catholic, it is harmoniously suggestive and
sublime.

The fact is very observable, that the customary prayers to
Jesus are not directed to Him in the character and office of
High Priest, Advocate, and Intercessor, which a few passages of
Scripture assign Him, but in the character of Almighty God.
To entreat Him to intercede with God, would be making one
Personal God intercede with another, and, in other respects,
would not suit Orthodox ideas, or correspond with Ecclesiastical
definitions of Christ's perfect Deity.

CHAPTER XII.

Texts which imply or assert Limitation of Knowledge in Christ.—There is
nothing to prompt or justify Mr Liddon's forced explanations.—Asserted illuminative power of the dogma of Christ's Deity, in relation
to the Atonement.—Examination of an attempt to meet the objection
that the dogma detracts from the value of Christ's Life as an ethical
model for Mankind.—The dogma cannot be shown to be morally
fruitful in giving intensity to Christian virtues, and is not calculated
to promote the devotion of the heart to God.

In his last Lecture, Mr Liddon explains and guards, from his
point of view, the statement (St Luke ii. 52), *Jesus increased in
wisdom and stature.* He approaches the subject with modest
diffidence, his own previous theories making a plain text difficult
and obscure.

"We can scarcely doubt," he concedes, "that an intellectual
development of some kind in Christ's human soul is indicated.
This development, it is implied, corresponded to the growth of
His bodily frame. The progress in wisdom was real and not
merely apparent, just as the growth of Christ's Human Body
was a real growth. . . . . . But, on the other hand, St Luke had
previously spoken of the Child Jesus as *being filled with wisdom*
(ii. 40); and St John (i. 14) teaches that, as the Word Incarnate,
Jesus was actually *full of truth.* St John means not only that
our Lord was veracious, but that He was fully in possession of
the objective truth" (p. 456).

Now every Protestant of Orthodox faith, and perhaps many
Catholics, will be quite confident that St Luke, before he wrote
his Gospel, had apprehended the mystery of our Lord's Being,
and saw in Jesus, God Incarnate. St Luke had, as his preface
assures us, taken some trouble to search out the facts of a history
about which many had taken in hand to furnish accounts. He
may, therefore, be presumed to have written with knowledge,
accuracy, and consistency; and, particularly, with a thoughtful
regard to the grand mystery which must necessarily, wherever it
is believed, dominate and mould all unrestrained didactic expression. The question then simply is, whether a writer would be
likely, if he held Jesus to be the Infinite God robed in human

flesh, to say of Him, that He *increased in wisdom and stature, and in favour with God and man ?*   Would not his conceptions and his words arrange themselves around, and take their form from, his knowledge of the Divine Personal Being of Jesus ?   Assuming Jesus to be a Divine Person, Consubstantial with the Omniscient God, is it reverent, judicious, or even intelligible to declare, He *increased in wisdom, and in favour with God ?*   The same sort of difficulty attends verse 40, of which, as of verse 52, Mr Liddon quotes (perhaps not inadvertently) only a fragment, " The child grew, and waxed strong, being filled with wisdom ; and the grace (or favour) of God was upon Him."*   The argument may be urged ; the Evangelist Luke (taking for granted his Gospel has not been interpolated) taught the miraculous conception of Jesus, and nevertheless, in a loose unguarded way, wrote of *the parents of Jesus* (ii. 27, 41, 43), and of *His father and His mother* (ver. 33 ; comp. ver. 48) ; but this argument does not render adequately probable, incautiousness of description regarding internal qualities, and relations to God.

In deducing from St John i. 14, it is as well, though it may not be convenient, to remember that the Evangelist's words are *full of grace and truth.*   Were the grace and truth inherent, or imparted ?

The difference between a miraculous paternity of Christ in the Virgin's womb, through the agency of the Holy Ghost, and the assumption of our nature by the Personal Logos, Who is in the full sense God, must strike every one who compares the opening statements of the First and Third, with the prologue of the Fourth Gospel.   To suppose the difference amounts to radical discrepancy in the representations of our Lord's Person, may be, in Mr Liddon's judgment, a " vulgar rationalistic expedient ;" but the question is ; can inquiring reason and common-sense suppose anything else, unless the Holy Ghost was Personally the Logos, not only creating the germs of His Own Humanity, but dwelling Personally in the Virgin during some months of her pregnancy ? And even upon this latter supposition, we sorely miss in the Evangelists, the discriminating perception and lucid definition with which younger sons of the Church exhibit the inner Economy of the Infinite, Uncreated Essence.

Mr Liddon enters into a learned and very laboured, but per-

* *In spirit* is wanting in the Sinaitic and Vatican MSS.   Dean Alford translates the present participle, *becoming filled.*   In the other verses quoted from Luke ii., I follow the Sinaitic and Vatican readings, with which the Vulgate Version agrees.

plexed and hesitating discussion of the avowal recited in St
Mark xiii. 32 : " Of that day or hour knoweth none, no not the
Angels in heaven, neither the Son, but the Father." In the
parallel passage (St Matt. xxiv. 36), the received Text is in substantial accordance, confining the knowledge of the Father alone ;
but the Sinaitic and Vatican Texts have the words, *neither the
Son.* Great Fathers of the Church, Western and Eastern, are
appealed to, who, if not unanimous in the details of their exposition, concur, as might be anticipated, in the opinion that, whatever Christ's words may mean, they can mean nothing at variance
with the hypothesis of His Deity. That hypothesis fills, in the
minds of Orthodox Commentators in all ages, the place of a prior
and regulative conclusion. A potent solvent of the tremendous
difficulty involved in this confession of ignorance, is, of course,
found in contemplating our Lord's Human Nature apart from
His Deity. In the Human knowledge of the Incarnate Son, the
possible existence of limits is admitted ; or, we may accept the
admirably acute suggestion that, for the sake of His disciples,
and to rebuke their forwardness, Jesus refrained from gazing at
secrets which, owing to His Deity, were necessarily within the
ken of his mental vision ; or, we may learn from " what appears
to be" the mind of St Cyril of Alexandria, " that our Lord did
know as God, but in His love He assumed all that belongs to
real manhood, and, therefore, actual limitation of knowledge "
(p. 461).

The recorded words of Christ contain nothing to prompt or
justify these forced and illusory explanations. In comparing the
Church's doctrine with the language of Scripture, we must always
remember that our Lord's Personal Being is seated in His Divine
Nature, not in the Manhood which has, by the bonds of an indissoluble union, been ' taken into God.' The Church's standpoint
does not permit the supposition of His speaking as a human
Person ; and, moreover, the form of the passage under examination, does not at all encourage the notion that, by *the Son,* Jesus
meant the *Son of Man,* rather than *the Son of God.* The singular
and exclusive character of the Father's knowledge is brought into
prominence by the affirming it to be unparticipated not only by
the Angels in heaven, but even by the Son of the Father. On
every ground, therefore, consistent Ecclesiastical interpretation is
pledged to understand by *the Son,* Christ in His Superhuman
Person. Since the human sphere of Christ's existence is not in
reality separable from the Superhuman, reverence forbids us to
shun the direct sense of His words by interposing the hypothesis

of separability. Jesus, Whom the Church reveals to be God Incarnate, is made in the Gospel to declare there is a subject as to
which He is ignorant; that is the simple fact for the consideration of all who do not question the truthfulness of the record.
Mr Liddon fairly states the invincible objection to the assumption, Christ 'knew as God, but was ignorant as Man.'

"Does not this conjunction of 'knowledge' and 'ignorance'
in one Person, and with respect to a single subject, dissolve the
unity of the God-man? Is not this intellectual dualism inconsistent with any conception we can form of a single personality?"
He replies by noticing the very wide scope of the objection, and
asks, "Is it not equally valid against other and undisputed contrasts between the Divine and Human Natures of the Incarnate
Son? For example, as God, Christ is omnipresent; as Man, He
is present at a particular point in space. . . . . Let me then ask
whether this co-existence of ignorance and knowledge, with respect
to a single subject in a single personality, is more mysterious
than a co-existence of absolute blessedness and intense suffering?
. . . . . If as He knelt in Gethsemane, Jesus was in one sphere
of existence All-blessed, and in another 'sore amazed, very
heavy, sorrowful even unto death;' might He not with equal
truth be in the one Omniscient, and in the other subject to
limitations of knowledge? The difficulty is common to all the
contrasts of the Divine Incarnation" (p. 463).

The dogma Mr Liddon defends, no doubt, involves all these
astounding contrasts, but they do not alleviate each other; for
even in the regions of theology the magnitude and variety of
the difficulties which a particular doctrine involves, do not illustrate the truth of that doctrine. These contrasts are all, upon
rational principles, so many motives to mistrust, and to searchingly re-examine the foundations of the doctrine itself.

A number of fanciful pleadings, the offshoots of assumptions,
and the reflexes of foregone conclusion, are urged in Mr Liddon's
final Lecture. I need do very little more than enumerate them,
since they belong to the outskirts of the controversy. 'Christ's
Person is the measure of His Passion. His Deity illuminates
His Passion, and explains Apostolical language respecting the
efficacy of His death.' Then again, 'His Divinity explains and
justifies the power of the Christian Sacraments, as actual chan-
nels of supernatural grace.' His Godhead warrants the grace
of Sacraments; Faith in It forbids their depreciation. "In view
of our Lord's Divinity, we cannot treat as so much profitless and
vapid metaphor, the weighty sentences which Apostles have

traced around the Font and the Altar, any more than we can deal thus lightly with the precious hopes and promises that are graven by the Divine Spirit upon the Cross. The Divinity of Christ warrants the realities of Sacramental grace as truly as it warrants the cleansing virtue of the Atoning Blood."

Now, before we allege the Deity of Jesus to be "the measure of His passion," and, to "warrant the cleansing virtue of the Atoning Blood," we must be prepared with ideas of Atonement much more lucid and definite than any the Scriptures furnish. The sacrificial language applied in the New Testament to the sufferings and death of Jesus, is very varied, generally figurative, and not always consistent. There is nothing in it to denote that its writers were endeavouring to express with guarded accuracy, the effective relation of our Lord's death to the Mind and purposes of God, or, that they were doing more than freely employing the coarse and imperfect religious phraseology of their age and country. Neither the Canonical Writings, nor the Creeds, make a particular conception of the nature and efficacy of Christ's death an article of Christian Faith. General statements that our Lord's Incarnation and sufferings were *for*, *on account of*, or, *for the sake of*, us men and our salvation, impose no precise theory, and the earliest of the Three Creeds does not contain even these. Vicarious punishment; judicial substitution; satisfaction to Divine justice; imputed sin and righteousness; and the like, are ideas which owe their prominence and definiteness to a comparatively recent theology. Calvinistic and Evangelical divines, to whom the judicial interior of the Almighty Mind is so familiar, would be scandalized at the latitudinarian and undecided opinions of numerous Fathers, on the redemptive meaning and propitiatory power of Christ's sufferings. Archbishop Anselm, in the eleventh century, was the first who unfolded formally, and consolidated the theory which, with slight modifications (mostly for the worse), is a treasured property of Orthodox Protestants. The basis of the theory is, that in the death of Jesus satisfaction or payment was made to the Almighty, and not, as many preceding Fathers had surmised, to the Devil, the Humanity of Jesus enabling Him to take up, and His Godhead enabling Him to discharge, the tremendous debt due from offending creatures to their Omniscient and Omnipotent Creator. The scheme, through all its variations, has been drawn out upon legal lines, but has never failed to outrage fundamental principles of justice. The human mind is quite incompetent to understand how guilt and merit are transferable, though experience attests their mighty and far-extending fruits and influences. Analogy throws no ray of light on vicarious *punishment*, though it abundantly illustrates vicarious *sufferings*—not only involuntary endurances on the part of the innocent, occasioned by the transgressions of the guilty, but also endurances deliberately incurred with a view to succour and save the guilty. Self-sacrifice, the willing bearing, at all costs, of another's burden, is, doubtless, the strongest proof of love, and the surest channel of beneficence; but we cannot, without changing God into something lower than our own likeness, imagine Him to be capable of punishing the guiltless *instead of* the guilty, or, of exacting judicial satisfaction and payment for men's moral delinquencies, from *penal endurances* in One Who was morally unblemished. By imaginations of this nature, God's perfections are doubly disparaged. Unwillingness to forgive freely, and willingness to be mollified by undeserved sufferings, are both ascribed to Him. But we may be sure our Heavenly Father sees us as we verily are, with a vision on which forms of forensic procedure and commercial bargaining have no effect, and if we heartily love and revere Him, we shall stipulate for very explicit, unmistakeable revelation, before we believe that any features of His dealings with us are repugnant to the intelligence and moral sense which are His implanted gifts.

When a preacher with the qualifications of talent and culture presupposed in the office of Bampton Lecturer, talks of "the cleansing virtue of the Atoning Blood," he knows he is using words of exceeding vagueness, though their Scriptural cadence may please the ear of a mentally apathetic Protestantism, which loves customary sound better than ascertainable sense. Atonement may consist in the reconciliation of man to God, and ' the cleansing virtue ' may be exercised exclusively in the region of human consciousness, and not at all in God's judicial estimate of human deserts. But however this may be, in lieu of perfunctory deductions from figures of speech, Mr Liddon should have shown the existence of a necessary connection between the Coequal Deity of Jesus, and His death as an expiatory oblation to the First Person of the Godhead, on account of the original and actual sins of mankind. Perhaps the hypothesis of such a connection involves intellectual or moral absurdity, and will not bear examination. Duns Scotus, one of the profoundest masters in scholastic theology, ' rejected altogether the notion of a necessary Divine infinity in Christ's piacular merits, declaring that the scheme of redemption might have been equally accomplished by the death of an angel or a righteous man.'*   At the end of the eighteenth century an Anglican prelate, Bishop Watson, stated a similar opinion in his Charges.

We are admonished how, " depreciation of the Sacraments has often been followed by depreciation of our Lord's Eternal Person. True, there have been and are, earnest believers in our Lord's Divinity who deny the realities of Sacramental grace. But experience appears to show that their position may be only a transitional one. History illustrates the tendency to Humanitarian declension, even in cases where sacramental belief, although imperfect, has been far nearer to the truth than in the bare naturalism of Zwingli " (p. 483).

This admonition to so-called Evangelical Protestants is, I think, perfectly just and well-founded. The Church's system hangs together, and her central dogma is endangered when divorced from pretensions, and teachings, which are at once its products and its preservatives. But if the dogma had a sound and sufficient Scriptural foundation, it would be able in Protestant Churches to stand alone, and would also be powerful enough to call back and confirm subordinate and related Sacramental tenets, instead of tottering whenever these tenets are for a time withdrawn.

Mr Liddon insists : " It is belief in the Divinity of our Lord which has enriched human life with moral virtues, such as civilised paganism could scarcely have appreciated, and which it certainly could not have created. The fruitfulness of this great doctrine in the sphere of morals will be more immediately apparent, if we consider one or two samples of its productiveness " (p. 488). The examples he selects are the graces of purity, humility, and charity, these being all, according to his judgment, stimulated, deepened, and enlarged, by faith in Christ's Divinity.

But he could not despise, and endeavours to meet, the objection that to insist on Christ's Godhead is to detract from the value of His life as an ethical model for mankind. An impersonal Humanity, appropriated and swayed by Omnipotent and All-perfect Personal Deity, obviously stands apart from and above

* I borrow the information respecting Duns Scotus, from the Dissertation on *Atonement and Satisfaction*, one of the numerous Essays which enrich Professor Jowett's Commentary on some of St Paul's Epistles. In the interests of theology, it is to be regretted that the Commentary is not at present easily procurable.

Mr H. N. Oxenham's History of the *Catholic Doctrine of the Atonement* is a most useful compendium. For the aggravation, if not for the existence, of some stumbling-blocks attaching to theories of Atonement, Protestantism is peculiarly responsible.

all ranges of our human attainment, being *in kind* unlike ourselves. Its actings are not properly human actings, and its
exciting motive power can never be ours. The Catholic Christ is
not truly the brother of men, but is dissociated from them by
differences radical, intrinsic, irremovable. He is Very God,
manifesting Himself through the organism of our nature, not a
human person, crowned in moral manhood by the illuminating
sanctifying presence of God. His life is the Divine perfection
exemplified in some suggestive features, not human perfection
wrought out through an auxiliary imparted strength accessible to
men. He is not a Leader far in advance, but verily on our own
line. He is not a specimen of what we may become. No gradual
elevation, no acquirements of indefinitely prolonged progress, can
so transmute the conditions and possibilities of our Being as to
exalt us to the level of our Incarnate God in the inward reality
of a single moral attribute. The disciple can never be as the
Master. His pattern, however much it may quicken our aspirations, and raise and irradiate our consciences, is light shining
from another sphere, and cannot practically be more than an
illustrated edition of the precepts by which He Himself and His
Apostle St Paul, exhort us to be imitators of God (Matt. v. 48 ;
Luke vi. 36 ; Eph. v. 1). The illustration, whatever may be its
value, is not thoroughly imitable, kindred example, stimulating
our energies, and satisfying our necessities, by showing what is
possible to man.

If example has its greatest efficacy when the imitated and the
imitators are not dissevered by ineffaceable distinctions of nature
and capacity, the Catholic doctrine respecting Christ's Person
cannot enhance the fruitfulness of the pattern His life supplies.
Mr Liddon perceives the difficulties these considerations inter-
pose, and, in seeking to evade them, falls into language which
would be more consistent if he held Jesus to be truly a man
whom the indwelling of God's Spirit had enriched and purified,
and ' filled with all the fulness of God.'

" Nor are Christ's Human perfections other than human ; they
are not, after the manner of Divine attributes, out of our reach ;
they are not designed only to remind us of what human nature
should, but cannot, be. We can approximate to them, even indefinitely. That in our present state of imperfection we should
reproduce them in their fulness is indeed impossible ; but it is
certain that a close imitation of Jesus of Nazareth is at once our
duty and our privilege, for God has ' predestinated us to be conformed ' by that which we do, not less than by that which we

endure, to the Human Image of His Blessed Son, 'that He might be the first-born among many brethren' (Rom. viii. 29)" (p. 486.)

How can the inspiring presence of God, inhabiting human persons, "approximate even indefinitely" to the production of results which flow from the investiture of God Himself with an impersonal humanity? The capacities of our nature woven around, informed, and actuated by the Person of Deity, are lifted into an unattainable region, and conditioned in a manner which precludes the reality of human brotherhood. In company with Mr Liddon's dogma, St Paul's description of our Lord as the *First-born* (πρωτότοκος) *among many brethren*, becomes artificial, inaccurate, and merely verbal. None other has been, or can be, born in the same way, encompassed by the same conditions, equipt with the same powers. Without human personality there can be no veritable human fraternity, whatever there may be of beneficial light, attraction, and fellowship. Mr Liddon grants that, " Certainly the Divine attributes of Jesus are beyond our imitation ; we can but adore a boundless Intelligence or a resistless Will." Yet, in the composition of the God-man, does not the Divinity of the central, energizing Person make every human faculty, in action and effect, Divine ? A passage which I have already cited (see Chapter viii.) quite consistently affirms, " in point of fact God, Incarnate in Christ, willed each volition of Christ's Human Will."

But it is contended—"The power of imitating Jesus, comes from Jesus through His Spirit, His Grace, His Presence. Now, as in St Paul's day, ' Jesus Christ is in us Christians, except we be reprobates' (2 Cor. xiii. 5). The ' power that worketh in us ' is no mere memory of a distant past ; it is not natural force of feeling, nor the strength with which self-discipline may brace the will. It is a living, energizing, transforming influence, inseparable from the presence of ' a quickening Spirit' (1 Cor. xv. 45), such as is in very deed our Glorified Lord. If Christ bids us follow Him, it is because He Himself is the enabling principle of our obedience. If He would have us be like unto Himself, this is because He is willing by His indwelling Presence to reproduce His likeness within us. . . . If the Christ Whom we imitate be truly human, the Christ Who thus creates and fertilizes moral power within us must be Divine" (p. 487).

The thought which underlies this language is very enigmatical. Does Mr Liddon believe there is a Personal presence of the Incarnate Christ in Christians, distinguishable from the sanctifying presence of the Holy Spirit? or, does he suppose the Manhood of Christ adds to the resources, or facilitates the entrance, of God's Spirit in His actual contact with the human spirits He touches and inspires?   Jesus Christ is *in us, lives in us,* and is *formed in us,* through the operation of the Spirit of Him Who raised up Jesus from the dead (Rom. viii. 9–11 ; Gal. ii. 20 ; iv. 19).   He is said to be *in us,* and we in the full realized sense *in Him,* when we are sincerely His followers, coming unto the Father by Him, and being shaped by the Spirit's influence after the pattern of His righteousness.   No one dreams of distorting the continually-recurring phrase, *in Christ,* into metaphysical mysticism, and it is worse than nonsensical to twist the infrequent, indeterminate expression, *Christ in you* (which may mean *among you*) into an announcement of His Personal indwelling, and a subsidiary evidence of His Divinity.   According to Eph. iii. 20, the power that worketh in us, is a power exercised by " the Father, from Whom the whole family in heaven and earth is named."   The close context of 2 Cor. xiii. 5 reminds us that ' Christ was crucified through weakness, but lives by the power of God,' and that St Paul, though weak in (with) Christ, expected to be alive with Him, by the same power.   This does not harmonize with the speculation, ' Christ is God, and His Personal indwelling the source of spiritual strength.'   Notwithstanding the pressure of Ecclesiastical commentary, attentive readers will be led by the surrounding language, strongly to suspect that, *the quickening spirit* (1 Cor. xv. 45) is not the Incarnate Christ, but the *spiritual body,* which is, in the order of nature and grace, a chief constituent in Humanity.   When the more authentic reading, *the second man is from heaven,* is restored in verse 47 (comp. *our house which is from heaven,* 2 Cor. v. 2), all certainty that *the last Adam* is a designation of Christ, vanishes.   Though our Lord is by St Paul contrasted with Adam, He is nowhere in Scripture called Adam, but to make St Paul call Him so, creates the choicest material for dogmatic theorists—a vague and elastic phrase.

In unfolding his views of the relation of Christ's Godhead to the grace of purity, Mr Liddon literalizes figurative phraseology, in order to ascribe to St Paul, a conception of some ineffable conjunction and incorporation with our Lord's Humanity,—" a doctrine of Christ's Sacramental union with His people, which is the veriest fable, unless the indwelling Christ be truly God." Jesus Christ, we are told, " folded our human nature around His Eternal Person ; He made it His own ; He made it a power which could quicken and restore us.   And then, by the gift of His

Spirit, and by sacramental joints and bands, He bound us to it (Col. ii. 19); He bound us through it to Himself; nay, He robed us in it; by it He entered into us, and made our members His own. Henceforth, then, the tabernacle of God is with men (Rev. xxi. 3)" (p. 490).

Language of this complexion, attributing Omnipresence, special pervasive spiritual efficaciousness, and nutritive power, to Christ's Manhood, is common with writers of the strictly Ecclesiastical school, and may not be altogether devoid of significance, for those whose faith joyfully accepts paradoxes at the hands of a revealing Church. But, from the reasonable point of view, the language has the fault of being undecipherable. It may always be reduced to a nullity by the simple demand for explanation. The attempt to present distinctly the ideas it pretends to express, displays its utter emptiness. The texts to which reference is made, do not contain the notion that Christ's Humanity is in-fused into individual souls as a life-giving and refreshing force. The Body of which Christ is the Head, and Christians are members, is the Church,—the great ' company of all faithful people,' —not Christ's human body. The clause (Eph. v. 30) which is commonly supposed to make the curious statement; we are "mem-bers of His flesh and His bones," is wanting in the three great ancient MSS., and is almost indubitably a spurious addition; yet, Mr Liddon (p. 482) invites us to listen in it, "to Christ's Apostle proclaiming," &c.

He also cites 1 Cor. vi. 15, "Know ye not that your bodies are members of Christ? Shall I then take the members of Christ, and make them members of an harlot? God forbid." The in-corporation with Christ here alluded to, is membership in His Church. The preceding context (verses 13 and 14) tells us; " the body is for the Lord, and the Lord for the body. And God both raised the Lord, and will also raise up us by His power." The succeeding context (verses 17 and 19), tells us; "he who is joined unto the Lord is one spirit;" and pronounces explicitly what the true spiritual indwelling is,—not an inconceivable, indescribable residence or impartation of Christ's Humanity,—but the presence of the Holy Spirit Which our Heavenly Father gives : " Know ye not that your body is the temple of the Holy Ghost Which is in you, Which ye have from God?"

Reason, diligently searching Scripture, can assuredly discover no intimation of an inhabiting presence of the Incarnate Christ, which can be differentiated from the presence of the Unincarnate Spirit of God. Without explanation, and proof from Scripture, the notion of Sacramental union with Christ's Humanity is no basis for the deduction,—" He did that which He could only do as being in truth the Almighty God." But Mr Liddon rightly speaks of this topic as being " in a sphere so inaccessible to the measurements of natural reason, so absolutely controlled by the great axioms of faith." I do not dispute these ' great axioms;' but what is their parentage—are they Scriptural or Ecclesiastical ?

The humility and love exhibited in the life and Self-sacrifice of Jesus Christ, are, doubtless, powerful incentives to the cultivation of like virtues in Christ's followers, both because they find a responsive witness in our hearts and consciences, and because they are believed to be the fruits of a special and abundant measure of Divine inspiration residing in One Who was truly a sharer of our nature. They are grand displays in man, of qualities which God bestows and approves, and they mightily evoke and expand our better feelings, and ' fertilize the moral soil of human life.' But when we cease to see in their exhibitor the real brotherhood of human personality, their power as examples of human graces, if it escapes diminution, can be in no degree increased. Probably, few Christians pursue the train of thought which meditation on the idea of Christ's Infinite Personality could not fail to suggest. If the seat of His Personal Being was Absolute Deity, He must, at every stage of His life on earth, have ' known the end from the beginning,' and, by a Divine foresight of results, have been incapable of that faith, trust, and resignation, which, at their greatest strength, are less than knowledge, and, through being less, give to human self-sacrifice its chief value. All that He did was done with clear vision of the joy and exaltation which awaited the human portion of His Incarnate Being, since He was Himself ' Very God,' and the elements of Manhood He had drawn around Him, could have no individual personal existence in separation from His Godhead. To talk of lack of knowledge, of intermitted percipience, of a clouded consciousness of the Father's companionship, or, of any of the limitations, intellectual and moral, which afford latitude for faith, and trust, and dependence, is manifestly ·to use words which belie the plainest dictates of the logical understanding.

When our ideas are formed upon the first three Gospels, such representations are not incongruous, because even the Divine indwelling, which secured moral perfection in a miraculously conceived Human Person, might not be necessarily exempt from restriction and remission. But when a Person pre-existent,

U

superhuman, and very highly exalted, though still beneath the Almighty, appears, such representations are incongruous, and, therefore, in the Fourth Gospel, there is scarcely a trace of them. In conformity with the idealism of the Fourth Evangelist, the distinctively human features of inward suffering, and exposure to temptation, which belong to the earlier narratives, are omitted, and their place supplied by experiences more in unison with the metaphysical conception of a Personally pre-existent and glorious Son of God. There are no temporary breaks in the calm and assured anticipation with which Jesus looks through, and beyond, the pre-determined events of what is called His Passion. " He knew that His hour was come that He should depart out of this world unto the Father. He knew that the Father had given all things into His hands, and that He came forth from God, and was going to God" (John xiii. 1, 3). The treachery of the companion who betrayed Him might, for a brief season, trouble His spirit, but when the unfaithful Apostle went out to complete his perfidy, Jesus could exclaim, " Now is the Son of Man glorified, and God is glorified in Him " (ver. 31). His prayer (John xvii.) breathes intimate communion with the Father, unobscured perception, and confident assurance, of approaching glory. In the Synoptists, prophetic prevision, and inspired glimpses of Resurrection and Messianic exaltation, intermingle with the lights and shadows of human faith and fear, resignation and despondency. In the Fourth Gospel, the creaturely emotions and innocent infirmities of humanity, almost wholly disappear, in presence of the Higher Personality whom the earthly tabernacle enshrined. And the delineation furnished by the latest Evangelist becomes a necessity of inexorable logic, when we go forward from his position to the dogma that the Person of Christ was not merely the glorious, pre-existent Son of God's love, but a veritable Form of the Self-existent Essence, possessing every attribute of Almightiness. The perfections of such a Being ' made flesh, and dwelling among us,' may afford an illustrious and inspiriting ensample, but to call them *human* virtues is to describe them with more of laxity than of truth. The holiness and energy of Personal Godhead clothed with impersonal Manhood, are not the springs of sanctity in the greatest saint.

The assent of reflective and unprejudiced minds must, therefore, be withheld from the propositions ; " On the one hand, the doctrine of our Lord's Divinity leaves His humanity altogether intact ; on the other, it enchances the force of His example as a model of the graces of humility and love " (p. 496). With every disposition to affirm the vast influence, and moral fruitfulness, of Christ's example, men may justly demur to the statement ; ' His example is more cogent when regarded as that of Incarnate Deity, than when regarded as that of God-inspired man.'

But this is not all. When the extremity of our Lord's Self-abasement, the magnitude of His Self-sacrifice, and the infinity of the love which that Self-sacrifice discloses, are inferred from the dogma of His Godhead, we are reminded of difficulties with which the superficial pleadings of Orthodoxy quite fail to grapple. The blessedness of Deity is not susceptible of decrease ; and, as we have seen, Mr Liddon himself assumes that in one sphere of existence, Jesus was All-blessed, while in another, He was agonized. The humiliation and Self-sacrifice were, therefore, accomplished in the human sphere ; and even if we pass over the tremendous paradox involved in supposing the impersonal portion of our Lord's complete Being, to have been during any sort of action or endurance, divorced from the Infinite attributes of the Personal, we must yet admit that the Humanity was grasped and directed by the Deity, with a perfect foresight of all future events. And the foreseen consequences of briefly transient Self-humiliation and suffering, were, to the human side of Christ's existence, the loftiest exaltation and everlasting felicity. If, according to Mr Liddon's assumption, the two Natures, though united in a single Person, can have diverse fields of experience, then, with the inaugmentable bliss of Deity, has been joined a perfectly beatified Humanity. And this gainful consummation was reached through processes, wherein the Manhood was unceasingly steered and controlled by a Divine Person, incapable of the ignorance, the misgivings, the trusting reliance, and the hope, which impart depth and reality to human self-sacrifice in its relations to God and man.

Mr Liddon rightly declares ; " The warmth of the spirit of love varies with the felt greatness of the sacrifice which expresses it, and which is its life." And, he reveals the strength of very sincere prepossession, when he adds, " Therefore, the love of the Divine Christ is infinite. ' He loved me,' says an Apostle, ' and gave Himself for me ' (Gal. ii. 20). The ' Self ' which He gave for man was none other than the Infinite God : the reality of Christ's Godhead is the truth which can alone measure the greatness of His love " (p. 495).

The infinite perfections of the Most High are not, indeed, incompatible with love, for love is their chief ingredient, but they are, by all rational conception, incompatible with the experiences which constitute human self-sacrifice. The composition of the Orthodox Christ reduces His Sacrifice of Self to a *minimum*. When Mr Liddon argues ; ' Christians have measured the love of Jesus Christ as man measures all love, by observing the degree in which it involves the gift of self : the Self which Christ gave was none other than the Infinite God,'—he seems hovering on the verge of the silly verbal quibble, 'everything done by an Infinite Being is infinite.'

The reasoning of the most plausible rhetorician, in support of the assertion that, Christian virtues are in some specific sense effects of faith in Christ's Deity, cannot be otherwise than unsatisfactory, and will have no weight with men who believe the Lord Jesus Christ to have been produced and sent by the *One God and Father, the Only True God.* Our Lord's precepts, and our Lord's example, have, on valid grounds of reason as well as moral feeling, great power, if He is acknowledged to be the elect Revealer of the Divine character and purposes ; the Messenger and Image of the *Blessed and Only Potentate, the Invisible God.* If in the Man Christ Jesus, men behold the light and glory of a moral manifestation of God, the mirror on which the brightness of the Father's glory falls, then, the teaching and the pattern which Christ has left us will not be deficient in force and fruitfulness. The idea that He is Personally the Infinite God, may seem to add force and intensity to His example, but it will do so, only by causing us to transfer a portion of our highest devotional affections from the Father. The sum total of emotional religious energy will not be increased, but differently distributed, and disorganizing germs of intellectual confusion will be implanted.

Dissentients from the Church's dogma, would, from their point of view, make short work of the argument, that love to God is enlarged by the doctrine Mr Liddon advocates. They would declare, the heart's supreme love and worship are divided and impoverished, when the One Infinitely Perfect and Absorbing Object is verbally split up into two or more mysterious Subsistences, each Personally God, and yet together only One God. They would aver, the Church is but too surely a loser in the depth and constancy of spiritual, truthful worship, when her faith, trust, love, and devotional service, are as much, and in the same sense, given to the Begotten and Incarnate Son, as to the Unbegotten and Infinite Father.

And, they would reply to Mr Liddon's inquiry—" What is the fountain head of the many blessed and practical results of Christian civilization and Christian charity, but the truth of His Divinity, Who has kindled man into charity by giving Himself for man ?"—by recounting results of a widely different kind, which háve been most intimately associated with the manifested life of the Christian Church. There are very prominent facts in the Church's history, which certainly do not point to the conclusion that, the vital power of Christianity in the production of Christian graces, has been promoted by the Church's unflagging insistence on the particular dogma which is Mr Liddon's theme. The tendency to arrogate a tyrannous dominion over men's faith and consciences, has been nowhere more rank and vigorous, than in the Sacerdotal Hierarchy by whom the tenet of Christ's Deity has been most jealously proclaimed and fostered. Meekness, humbleness of mind, "the bearing of a little child (St Matt. xviii. 3), that true note of predestined nobility in the Kingdom of Heaven," have never been, from the fourth century to the nineteenth, distinguishing virtues of Orthodox Ecclesiastics—the dauntless champions of the dogmatic Faith. Neither has Christlike charity been remarkably displayed in conjunction with a scrupulous holding of Nicene and Athanasian definitions. Ferocious cruelty, unsurpassed in the annals of heathenism ; unpitying, savage, deliberate atrocities, were long and largely perpetrated with the sanction, and mostly at the instigation, of the Church's Hierarchy, in the name of that religion which inscribed Christ's Godhead on its banner. And the sentiments which gave birth to the horrors of individual torturings and wholesale butcheries, were not subjugated by "the moral results of Calvary, which are what they are, because Christ is God." They were not abated or banished, because Christian faith deduced lessons of love from "the charity of the Redeemer, which is infinite because the Redeemer is Divine," but, because the experienced failure of fiendish barbarity to extirpate heresy, induced prudent hesitation, and won a hearing for the voice of natural tenderness, and the general teachings of Christian brotherhood and compassion : and even now, so far as modern civilization permits it to emerge, the persecuting spirit is seen to cling to earnest faith in Christ's Deity; and suspicion is never so keen-scented, denunciation never so bitter, opposition never so relentless, resentment never so fierce, as when the delicate, fragile, and incomprehensible definitions, by which the Church depicts the internal relations, constitution, and economical distribution of the Uncreated Nature, are imagined to be traversed. Our Lord's saying, ' I came not to send peace, but a sword : I came to set men at variance,' referred to the resistance which Christianity would provoke among Jews and heathens; but believers in His Deity have laboured with no small amount of success, to make the saying intensely applicable to the demeanour of Christians towards each other.

"The Divinity of God's Own Son, freely given for us sinners to suffer and to die, is the very heart of our Christian faith. It cannot be denied without tearing out the vitals of a living Christianity" (p. 497). This dashing statement will have no more weight with thinkers, than the baseless assertion—"Apostles, differing in much besides, were made one by faith in Christ's Divinity, and in the truths which are bound up with it"—will have with candid searchers of the New Testament Scriptures. The statement may indeed be true, if by "a living Christianity," is meant the system of dogmas wrapt by the Church Catholic around the essential truths which Christ and His Apostles taught ; but if, by a living Christianity, is meant the faith which works by love to God, and love to our neighbour, we cannot easily understand how the doctrine of Christ's Deity increases its efficacy. Which of the great leading conceptions, demanded by the religious sentiments, hangs upon the theory that Jesus Christ, as well as our Heavenly Father, is Almighty God ? Do God's existence, and His care for man ? Does a future life, attended with recompenses corresponding to real deservings and character ? Does our Maker's Fatherly compassion, and willingness to forgive the transgressions of His erring and repentant creatures? Is not belief in One Personal God and Father sufficient to kindle the brightest flames of morally intelligent affection, and to quicken, and raise to the highest pitch, every pious emotion ? Is not the conciousness of Our Father's near and dear Presence—that which feeds the heart with the strongest motives to holiness,—that which takes a mighty hold on the emotional side of our nature, and is ratified and reinforced by the intellectual ? The introduction of a second, Personally distinct Form of Godhead, neither facilitates, nor deepens, the play of the indispensable spiritual forces—dependence, love, trust, conviction of sin, and a sense of the need for pardoning and assisting grace. Loving trust in an infinitely Wise, Holy, and Kind Father,—the Father Whom Jesus and His Apostles proclaim,—is the prime inward spring of Christian holiness; and from this trust, the dogma of Christ's Co-equal Deity, is in theory calculated to detract, by producing in our minds the partition of endearing Attributes, and thereby dimming the lustre of the Father's Moral

Glory. If we try to understand our words, and realize our conceptions, the notion of a Plurality of Persons in the Divine Nature, becomes either an unprofitable and disconcerting repetition of One and the same God, or a presentation of more Gods than One, with claims more or less diverse. Submissive, unquestioning reliance on authority is necessary, to shelter the notion from the blight of rational inferences decidedly adverse to real and fundamental Monotheism.

CHAPTER XIII.

The doctrine defended by Mr Liddon is, wholly and necessarily, outside
the sphere of reason.—Even the explicit statements of the Creeds
cannot be rationally harmonized, and are fitted for a blindly confiding,
rather than a reflective and intelligent reception.—Utter insufficiency
of the supposed Scriptural testimony for Christ's Godhead ; and re-
capitulation of the adverse testimony.—Mistaken impressions kept up
by false statements in Commentaries, Sermons, &c.—The Church's
teaching cannot be fully appropriated without an acknowledgment
of the Church's paramount authority.—This fact appears to have
been at times forgotten even by great Fathers in the Church.—Necessity for an explicitly speaking Supreme Tribunal.—The inevitable
outcome of Protestant principle.—Conclusion.

I HAVE now examined in detail the strength of Mr Liddon's
argument from Scripture, and trust I may have enabled my
readers duly to estimate the worth of the reasonings on which he
relies. To me, those reasonings appear to be sometimes absurd,
often really, however unconsciously, sophistical, and always insufficient. The whole structure of the Lectures, so far as they
are an appeal of reason to Holy Scripture (and all exposition
not avowedly based on the Church's supreme authority must be
such an appeal), rests upon untenable ground, and exposes to
inevitable capture the citadel of Ecclesiastical Faith. Whenever
the primary doctrine of God's Unity is maintained, the doctrine of Christ's Deity is outside the sphere of reason, and, if
true, is emphatically and solely a disclosure of Revelation. The
terms in which the doctrines are conjointly stated, become, by a
hard necessity, either meaningless, or irrational and conflicting.
This fact does not, for any large class of minds, attest the Deity
of Christ to be revealed from Above ; but it, at least, attests the
proclamation of His Deity to be addressed to trustful, unquestioning faith. How imperative is the need for intellectual abey-
ance and submission, may be seen in the circumstance, that even
the Creeds wherein the Church most explicitly sets forth her
teaching, are not reasonably reconcilable with each other. If
the Athanasian Symbol conveys the Church's riper wisdom, and
more thorough analysis of the One Infinite Self-subsisting Nature,
then, that drawn up by the Councils of Nice and Constantinople

is manifestly defective, if not absolutely heretical. The Symbol of Nice and Constantinople presents to our faith One God, the Father Almighty, and, in addition, a Begotten God of the Self-same Substance,—Very God, of or from Very God. Clearly, therefore, in the conception which the Church's words compel, if the Father is God, and the Son is God, there are two Gods. The Father is, as the Father Almighty, One God; and the Son—Whose eternity is dubiously predicated in the clause, *begotten before all the ages*, is a second God. There is no intimation that *One God* means One Indivisible Self-existing Essence, within Which are enfolded different Persons, Who severally have One Divinity, equal Glory, and Co-eternal Majesty.

The phrases *Begotten*, and *Only-begotten*, are robbed of all cognizable import, when we are bound to reconcile them with the Son's possession of unabridged everlasting Deity. With the concession of derivation in any actual sense, the distinctive quality of true Godhead, Self-existence, vanishes, and a gulf of severance, impassable by rational thought, yawns between the derived glory of the Son, and the underived Majesty of the Father. And in another particular, the Nicene Creed itself, if it has not the escort of a despotic Commentary, must be confessed, in spite of its definitions, to imply with clearness the Son's inferiority. The creation of all visible and invisible things is attributed to the One God, the Father Almighty. The organizing action of the *Only-begotten Son, through,* or, *by means of Whom, all things were made*, must therefore have been instrumental and deputed. He was not the Co-equal Partner, but the Agent of the One God, for, if the Son created by His own inherent might, the Omnipotent Father was not the Maker of all things. The language of the Creed, as regards creation, cannot be harmonized without an acknowledgment of the Son's subordination, servitorship, and mere agency. The affirmation, *Very God from Very God*, is quite inadequate rationally to annul this fatal implication of vast inferiority, unless we introduce direct antagonism to the Creed's opening clause, and also cut down to nothing the meaning of the 'Generation' which took place *before all the ages*. Nor are the renowned and sagacious words, *of the same Substance with the Father*, competent, from a philosophical point of view, to the task for which they were devised. Since things visible and invisible come forth from the One Fountain of Unoriginated Being, are they not all *of one Substance with the Father?* They may manifest Him, and exist by His presence and energy, in differing modes and degrees, but of what other Substance than His, can they be ? Where is there any other Substance ? To devout and reflective minds, one inscrutable feature in the mystery of the Self-existent Creator, is the union of universally-diffused, upholding Presence with personal attributes. An adoring and philosophical faith combines Pantheism with a belief in a Personal God. The combination is confessedly paradoxical, but it follows the direction given by lines of rational indication, and does not contravene reason, though its ultimate statement is not within reason's boundary. In propositions relating to the Divine Nature we can scarcely hope to attain certitude, or to avoid paradox, but we ought to avoid baseless, discordant, fanciful specifications. When we have forsaken the ground of Ecclesiastical authority, we act more reverently in confessing our ignorance, than in contradicting ourselves, and uttering sounds without sense. Piously-inquisitive thought uninstructed by infallible revelation, will find no pretext for conceiving the Divine Nature to consist of three Persons, Each of Whom is by Himself God, and Who, nevertheless, are together only One God ; but will discern inducements of great probability for the faith that, in the Universe the Divine Substance is diffused and displayed, while nevertheless, the One God has a Personal Subsistence and Attributes apart from the Universe. Protestant Monotheism, retaining the consecrated metaphor of dogmatic theology, has declared by the pen of one of its ablest representatives : " For the God of the Trinity must be substituted the one God, above and within the world, filling the immensity of time and space with the inexhaustible riches of His power, whose eternal Word is the Universe—the revelation of His thoughts, the expression of His wisdom " (Réville, *On the Deity of Christ.*)

The Church's insight was deeper at the date of the Athanasian, than at the date of the Nicene Creed, and she beheld more vividly the imminent peril of dividing the Substance in the intricate process of distinguishing the Persons ; but owing to the imperfection of human language, her ability of expression could not keep pace with her inspired penetration, and so, in her last analysis of God, there is, for mere reason, inconsistency, whatever nutriment there may be for humble faith. Through the Symbol called Athanasian, the Church asserts concerning the Father, the Son, and the Holy Ghost, that each Person must be acknowledged to be, by Himself, both God and Lord, Uncreated, Infinite, Eternal, Almighty, and yet They are not three Uncreated, Infinite, Eternal, and Almighty Beings, but One Almighty. To the intellect, this phraseology is either totally unintelligible or flatly self-contradictory. If *Person* signifies anything, *One* is meaningless ; if the Unity of God is held fast, *Person* loses all significance. Sameness of Nature there may be in different individuals, but Oneness of Being is singleness of Person. If both the Unity and the separate Personality are roundly affirmed, the affirmation can evoke nothing but conceptions diametrically opposed, and mutually exclusive. Manifestation, pervasion, indwelling, and influence locally concentrated or universally diffused, differ widely from multiplied Personality.

Assuming Eternity, and Independent Unoriginated Existence, to be inalienable Attributes of God, the Creed of Nicæa and Constantinople either falls short in defining Christ's Godhead, or is ditheistic. The Athanasian Creed, unless its definitions of the Divine Nature are wholly shorn of sense, is self-contradictory. To the vision of Ecclesiastical credence, both Creeds may be perfectly harmonious, and both lofty achievements of illuminated wisdom, but I speak from the inferior ground of merely rational inspection. The Creed known as *the Apostles'*, though it has but slender claims to Apostolic parentage, yet exhibits, in relation to God and the Lord Jesus Christ, a confession that satisfied the demands of Ante-Nicene times, but no reasonable exposition can make it cover the dogma of Christ's Deity. The Anglican Church, indeed (see *Catechism*), teaches us to learn from it faith in *God the Son*, and in *God the Holy Ghost*, but she does so, only by making it mean what it does not say, thus honouring the Creed with the mode of interpretation applied to inspired writings. Men are sometimes told to take the Creed as their compass in the study of the Bible ; but when this sage advice is given, we must expect the inquiry, ‘which Creed ? ’ for, in delineating Christ's Person, the three Creeds carry us to very different lengths, and do not run in precisely the same direction.

The Bible and the Creeds are thoroughly dissimilar in composition, yet the principle of rational interpretation is almost as dangerous in its application to the one as to the other. The notion, that formulas offered to Christian faith are at the same time offered to the intelligence of Christians, is in its very nature, disintegrating, and subversive of Orthodoxy. In secular and temporal concerns, truth requires that words should closely correspond to thoughts, but in the higher concerns of religion and eternity, this correspondence should not be looked for, and we walk more humbly and securely in the traditional tracks, when we portray the Adorable, Uncreated Nature, by language into which consistent thoughts cannot be put. The subject is, doubtless, impenetrably mysterious, and the human intellect quite unable adequately to comprehend the Form of Self-existent Being; but this inability, while it forbids the un-inspired intellect to frame definitions, does not forbid the examination of definitions, since they must be to some extent the fruits of the intellect's exercise, and, if not examples of human error, are instances of Divine condescension employing the very imperfect machinery of human parlance and capacity. From whatever source, therefore, the Church's knowledge proceeds, if she cannot intelligibly express the revelation entrusted to her keeping, her demand must be for reliance upon herself, for a confiding and blindly-acquiescent, as distinguished from a reflective and intelligent, acceptance of her tenets.

The Creeds, though they declare the Church's judgment, do nothing towards unriddling the co-existence of Essential Unity and Personal Plurality. The paradox remains unsolved, because Plurality of Personal Being is the negation of Unity, and Unity the negation of Plurality. If reason be permitted to enter the field, one-half of the Church's definition falls immediately. The analogies to which zealous faith and inflexible prejudice have had recourse,—the tripartite nature of man, body, soul, and spirit,—the triple energies of the human mind, intelligence, love, and will, and the threefold qualities of the Sun, its substance, light, and heat, are obviously pointless. The conjunction of differing parts, powers, affections, and efficiencies, in one complex Being, bears no true illustrative analogy to the concomitance of distinct, co-equal, and severally complete Persons in One Substance.

Definitions external to the Canon of Scripture have not tended to assist in bringing the subject within the apprehension of reason. And, the detailed investigation of Mr Liddon's argument has impressed upon my mind a reluctant persuasion, that Scripture clearly proclaims the Almighty to be, in the intelligible, exclusive sense, One Individual Personal Being. The mode of His Existence, and the exercise of His Omnipotent, Omnipresent Energy, are beyond the grasp of finite understandings; but absolute Personal Unity is the conception of His Nature which reason approves, and the only conception which the Bible, reasonably interpreted, sets forth. The supposed Scriptural evidence for Christ's Godhead crumbles vexingly away as the meaning of text after text is explored. Scarcely a single fragment wears a respectable look, and the whole fabric is miserably weak, and without cohesion.

The plain fact is,—with regard to that doctrine of Christ's

Person which the two later of the three Creeds embody, the Bible has been more talked about than really consulted. The conscientious effort to reach the original meaning and occupy the Sacred Writers' point of view, the calm and unbiassed investigation demanded by Protestant principle, have been very rarely bestowed upon the Book which Orthodox Protestants so vauntingly declare to be the Divine Code of their Faith. Nicene and Athanasian theologies have been taken for granted, and, after a fashion illustrated, not searchingly weighed and examined by the balance and the light which the venerated Volume supplies ; and so, the majority of Protestants have gone on repeating the dogma of a plurality of Persons in the One Godhead, contentedly ignorant that, rational investigation demonstrates the dogma to have been always outside and beyond Scripture—outside and beyond the Old Testament Canon, and again, outside and beyond the New. I do not deny, that God may, in His own way, have revealed the dogma, but I do deny He has revealed it in a way which their fundamental principle enables Protestants to recognize.

The Old Testament furnishes nothing to set over against its own repeated, explicit, and emphatic annunciations that God is One Being ; and only by neglecting contexts, forgetting original senses, and ignoring obvious characteristics of Eastern thought and diction, can even a semblance of exposition be constructed for the detention of minds trained from childhood to believe, and not to inquire. In the New Testament, the Great Speaker, Who is in the Church's preaching Very God veiled in Humanity, gives no hint of His own boundless Uncreated Greatness. He claims, indeed, intimate communion with, and mission from, the Father—*His Father and our Father, His God and our God*, Whom He also names *the Only God*, and, *the Only True God*, but He never approaches an affirmation that He is internal to the Self-subsisting Nature, and, by independent necessity of Being, the Father's Co-equal Partner. His language is always that of filial dependence, filial love ; and the highest Self-assertions attributed to Him, rise no higher than announcements of might and gifts, office and dignity, bestowed by the Father. That He designed any words of His own to reveal His possession of Godhead, or to identify Himself with the One perfectly Good God Whom He enjoins us to love with all our heart, and soul, and strength, is a conjecture which, to the unaided eye of reason, must appear violently arbitrary and improbable. If we argue from inferences suggested by His words, we are confronted, at every page, with natural and direct implications adverse to the

Church's dogma, while the whole pleading in favour of the dogma, reposes upon unnatural and forced deductions, and senses, not read *in*, but *into*, a few expressions whose ambiguity invites theological manipulation.

And the Evangelical historians, when speaking in their own persons, show no perception that the Teacher sent from God, Who is the subject of their narratives, is God, or God's Equal. The metaphysically speculative introduction to the Fourth Gospel, does not identify *the Word* and *the God* with Whom the Word was; and, by saying, the Word was *in the beginning*, does not adequately affirm the Word's Eternity. The Greek, although it twice asserts the presence of the *Logos* with *the God*, does not assert the *Logos* was *the God;* and the wording of verses 1 and 2 strongly favours, if it does not quite establish, the surmise that, in ascribing Divinity to the *Logos*, the Article was designedly omitted, to mark a distinction in sense. The whole tenor of the last Gospel moreover (unless inspiration destroys consistency), is at variance with the supposition of a purpose on the writer's part, to put God and Jesus Christ in the same rank. Jesus is pre-existent, superhuman, highly exalted, and in most near and privileged fellowship with the Father, but is always distinctly dependent upon and beneath the Father; and we are rationally bound to conclude, the Evangelist's conception of Christ was in easy unison with the testimony which He makes Christ Himself bear respecting the Father's superior greatness and exclusive Deity.

The authors of the Acts of the Apostles, the Epistles, and the Apocalypse, can, by no variations of intelligent or equitable interpretation, be made to put Jesus, the Son Whom God has raised and glorified, on a parity with God in Nature and underived Majesty. The tone of each document singly, and the force of all combined, forbid the idea that, in the writers' thoughts, Jesus occupied the place of Almighty God. Rom. ix. 5; Tit. ii. 13; 1 John v. 20, are not, by grammatical necessity, descriptions of Christ, and, by every guide but ambiguity of construction, are shown to be descriptions of the One God, our Father. The clamorous adherence to a possible, but demonstrably improbable, application of the debated expressions in these texts, betrays the desperate straits into which Orthodox Protestant exposition has fallen.

But not only is there, throughout the New Testament, an absence of indications which we are by the rules of rational evidence bound to expect, not only do the men who are presumed to have been entrusted with a new and most momentous revelation, withhold that revelation, but they also employ language which must, to Monotheists in every age, be charged with obstructive and hostile suggestions. In fearlessness, earnestness, and intellectual grasp, St Paul was not a whit behind the chiefest Apostle, and yet, while he constantly employs the Name *God*, he never once gives the Name to Jesus Christ, but distinguishes Him from God, in sentences of pointed precision, capable of carrying but one meaning to minds not filled with undoubting assurance that Jesus Christ is God. He lays down as axioms of the Faith; *there is no God but One;* to Christians, *there is One God, the Father*, and *one Lord Jesus Christ;* there is *one Lord*, one faith, one baptism, *One God and Father of all;* there is *One God*, and *one Mediator* between God and men, *the man Christ Jesus.* He calls God, *the Only God; the Only Wise God; the Blessed and Only Potentate; the God and Father of our Lord Jesus Christ.* If in inspired, no less than in uninspired men, the mouth speaks from the abundance of the heart; if language has any intrinsic connection with opinions and thoughts, St Paul knew no God but the One Almighty Father, *the God of our Lord Jesus Christ, the Father of Glory.* Against his witness for the real Personal Unity of God, it is vain to erect the sham testimony composed of exorbitant deductions from isolated, vague, and opaque phrases. At the bar of human intelligence, no writer can be held to imply through the merely possible, or less probable, meanings of obscure, or ambiguous, or metaphorical statements, opinions which he never explicitly avows, and seems explicitly to exclude. Even in the Philippian and Colossian Epistles (assuming their present Text to be in every clause Apostolic), there is a studied avoidance of the open straightforward method of calling Christ *God*, and an attribution to Him of gifts, glory, and official exaltation from God, which persuasively intimate, that when Jesus had been magnified to the utmost verge of Apostolic conception, God was in the height above, and God in unapproachable Sovereignty beyond.

The Volume which Mr Liddon so suicidally makes his repertory of proofs, presents its two most prominent figures, our Lord Himself, and St Paul, both plainly inculcating, that the Father is *the Only True God, the One God, the Only God.* And the Father is, incontrovertibly, a Personal Being, not a Divine Nature embracing a Plurality of Persons, each of Whom is God. When to this truth is joined the admitted fact of the Son's Personal distinctness from the Father, the conclusion is irresistibly brought out,—the Son is not Personally *the One Only True God*, and is, therefore, either a second God of a lower grade, or, not God at all. Arianism testifies how the minds of multitudes in the early Church did not shrink from the former of these alternatives, which, to Christians of modern days, appears to be more verbally than really distinguishable from the latter. The intellectual difficulties of the Arian Christ are not greater than those of the Christ of Catholic Christendom, but they are a favourite topic with Orthodox Protestants, and are eagerly assaulted with Rationalistic weapons, whose use against Orthodoxy is vehemently cried down.

In some largely circulated editions of the Bible (*Bagster's*) long lists of texts are given, wherein Christ is imagined to be called *God*. Most of these are utilized by Mr Liddon, and have in the preceding pages been investigated. Corrected readings in a few instances, and, in general, the contexts, and the exercise of common sense, disperse the laboured blunders concocted for the edification of credulous Protestants, who exult in possessing an all-sufficient Written Rule, by which they do *not* test their inherited beliefs. Ecclesiastical authority originating doctrines of faith is repudiated, but a selection of Ecclesiastical traditions, labelled ' Bible-teachings,' and illogically patched on to Scripture in Commentaries and Sermons, passes muster undetected, through willing ears and prepossessed minds.

Besides the quotation from Psalm xlv. (Heb. i. 8, 9), the New Testament contains only two texts in which Christ is denominated *God*—namely, John i. 1 ; xx. 28, all other asserted instances being either mistaken applications or erroneous readings.* The former of these texts has been discussed in the preceding pages; and the adequacy of its obscure phraseology to sustain an elaborate pile of doctrine, may be safely left to the judgment of all candid men acquainted with Greek. As to the exclamation of Thomas when convinced of our Lord's Resurrection, theologians who will build a doctrine upon that, are not likely to see the unsoundness of their foundation. Rational exposition will ungrudgingly leave them the text for what it is worth, and afford them the opportunity of performing exegetical feats in arguing

---

* The reading, *only begotten God*, for, *only begotten Son* (John i. 18), is too decidedly unsuited to the sentence in which it stands, to be probable, but it has very respectable external evidence. Theologians who turn that reading to account are bound to show how the specific difference between *begotten* and *unbegotten*, is compatible with the Self-existence and Eternity inseparable from true Godhead. Generated Self-existence, and Eternity with a starting-point, are curious ideas.

from a couple of words against inferences and statements with which the New Testament teems.

Attempts have been made to appropriate the Church's teaching, without any frank, honest recognition of the Church's paramount authority as the Divinely-commissioned Teacher of truth. The mere witness of the Church to an asserted sense of Scripture, has been held to establish that sense, and to guarantee Apostolicity of doctrine ; but no mere witness can establish an unreasonable interpretation of documents which lie open to reason's inspection, and the doctrine of Christ's Deity is, besides, very far from possessing a full and unbroken historical attestation. The century after the departure of the Apostles is an undepicted and undepictable time. Its literature has almost entirely perished, and nothing survives duly to represent its features. Writers, the most nearly subsequent, throw no true light on its details, crises, and disputes ; for, in Ecclesiastical history, "first among general facts, is the ignorance of the third and fourth centuries respecting the first, and earlier half of the second." And this destitution in necessary evidence, is not all the difficulty with which students are confronted who refuse to take for granted the Church's revealing office and Divinely-insured freedom from error in Articles of Faith. The Arianism of the fourth century was very widely spread, and invoked both Scriptural and post-Scriptural testimony. The language of the Ante-Nicene Fathers is often such as no sensible, well-informed, Orthodox man of later days could have permitted himself to use. The necessity which Bishop Bull experienced of adding much commentary and explanation in order to show how the right meaning was contained in the language of the Fathers whom he cites, has been the occasion of frequent remark.

The statements of a learned and moderate Roman Catholic theologian (Mr H. N. Oxenham) very pertinently exhibit the strict truth in relation to this aspect of our subject : —

"We must not imagine that the principle of development applies only to the less fundamental doctrines of Christianity. It is most conspicuously illustrated in the case of those two supreme verities on which all the rest depend—the Trinity, and the Incarnation. We are reminded of this as regards the former doctrine, by two of the greatest names respectively in Anglican and in Catholic theology—Petavius, the Jesuit, and Bishop Bull. The *Defensio Fidei Nicænæ* has won for its author a deservedly high reputation, and is quoted respectfully by eminent Catholic divines ; but in his controversy with Petavius, though he may have the better of the argument in some detailed instances, he has certainly failed to make out his case as a whole. All impartial judges on either side, are now agreed that Petavius is right as to the heterodox language, implying often heterodox notions, about the Holy Trinity, which many Ante-Nicene writers use. The fact that, in an elaborate treatise on the Holy Ghost, written expressly against heretics, St Basil studiously refrains from giving Him the Name of God (which was first done by the Council of Alexandria in 363) would alone indicate this. So again, Justin Martyr speaks of the Son as inferior to the Father, in His Divine Nature. . . . Many Fathers, both Greek and Latin, in arguing with the Arians, treat the unity of Persons in the Holy Trinity as specific rather than numerical. Cudworth (*Intellectual System*) not only says this with especial, though not exclusive, reference to Cyril of Alexandria, Gregory Nyssen, Anastasius, Maximus the Martyr, and John of Damascus, but roundly accuses them of teaching a ' Trinity no other than a kind of tritheism,' while he charges several others with denying a co-equality of Persons" (*Catholic Doctrine of the Atonement*, Introduction, 2d ed., pp. 23–25).

Mr Oxenham sustains these statements by quotations from Dr Newman's Anglican work, *The Arians of the Fourth Century;* from the late Professor Blunt's Lectures on the *Right Use of the Fathers;* and from Dean Merivale's Lectures on the *Conversion of the Northern Nations.* The writer last named, speaking of the Trinitarian dogma in the age of the Apologists, says: " The time was not yet ripe for its full and consistent exposition. . . . The discrimination of the Persons of the Godhead was as yet unsteady and fluctuating." Mr Oxenham, and the concurring authors whom he quotes, while they do not attempt to conceal the frequently halting, inadequate, doubtful, or more than doubtful, language of the earlier Fathers, are individually satisfied, that the Nicene dogma is ' the legitimate outcome of Ante-Nicene theology as a whole.'

Mr Liddon declares: " Undoubtedly, it should be frankly granted that some of the Ante-Nicene writers do at times employ terms which, judged by a Nicene standard, must be pronounced unsatisfactory." But he follows up this declaration with the plea: " In truth, these Ante-Nicene Fathers were feeling their way, not towards the substance of the faith, which they possessed in its fulness, but towards that intellectual mastery both of its relationship to outer forms of thought, and of its own internal harmonies and system, which is obviously a perfectly distinct gift from the simple possession of the faith itself. As Christians, they possessed the faith itself. The faith, delivered once for all, had been given to the Church in its completeness by the Apostles" (p. 420).

This pleading is not sufficiently to the point. Language which falls below the Nicene definitions, suggests that its authors did not entertain as a necessary article of faith, that view of the Divine Nature which the later Church put forth with authority, and confirmed by universal acceptance. The difficulty involved is the same in kind, though not for the Protestant so formidable in degree, as that which the Sacred Scriptures furnish. The dogma of Christ's Deity, however perplexing when contested and weighed, admits and incites most simple and unmistakable statement, when thoroughly believed. Its very mystery causes the sincere believer to be clear and unflinching in its avowal. Yet, in the literary remains of the earlier Christian times, the more nearly we approach the century after our Lord's resurrection, the more loose and defective, not to say palpably erroneous, do the statements regarding Christ's relation to the Everlasting Godhead become, Justin Martyr's Logos-doctrine does not mount to the level of the Church's requirements, and the sub-apostolic Fathers who preceded Justin, do not make use of the indispensable metaphysical conception which, in varying forms, appears in Plato, Philo, and the Fourth Gospel. Non-heretical theology, for the first hundred years following the day of Pentecost, did not go beyond the Synoptical Gospels, on the topic of Christ's Person. No fact in the history of opinion is more clearly provable, than that the Orthodox dogma was a growth, developed amid controversy, and fixed in the face of strong opposition. If it had an existence in Apostolic days and teachings, it was only as a seed, the smallest of all seeds, invisible to eyes not specially invigorated to discern it. The Catholic believer may rejoice in the full assurance of an unquestioning faith, that the dogma was, through Divine instruction, from the very first, germinally and potentially present in the Church; but the critic who discards the assumption of the Church's immunity from error, will trace the real roots of the dogma in the treatises of Philo, and the philosophy of Plato.

The most able of the Fathers, in their anxiety to argue from Scripture, at times weaken their position, and seem but imperfectly to apprehend the sovereignty and magnitude of the Church's mission. The extensive prevalence of equivocation, jealousy, turbulence, violence, and persecution, in the theological strifes of the fourth century, clouded the spiritual glory of Ecclesiastical movements, and, perhaps, the fact that Imperial favour had much to do with the alternating preponderance of wrestling factions, predisposed minds to seek too cravingly, an adequate Scriptural base for the minutely definite formulas which sprang from a newer inspiration. A highly-nurtured and keenly-sensitive faith was needed to recognize the Divine guidance, and to catch the accents of Heaven-descended, revealing wisdom, amid the din and turmoil of excited disputants, some of whom, according to the testimony of the historian Socrates (writing at the middle of the fifth century), were proved by their letters to have been troubled about the term *homoöusion—of the same Essence,*—and to have contended for the faith in the dark, with no intelligent comprehension of the propositions before them (Socrates, *Eccl. Hist.*, Bk. i. 23).

The Church of the period when the confession concerning Christ's Person was settled, was not resplendent in morals and intellect. Measured by the conduct of its members, it bore few outward prints of sanctity, and was blurred with many stains of ignorance, credulity, profligacy, impiety, and blindly-savage contentiousness. The short-sighted and derogatory estimate of Episcopal Conventions, avowed by Gregory of Nazianzum, was excusable. He could not look along the stream as we do, and admire the wonderful unanimity of Ecclesiastical adherence to a dogma which transcends consistent expression,—an unanimity conspicuous through ages broadly stamped with intellectual suppression, political enormities, and moral corruption. There is, therefore, no cause for astonishment, if the combatants, and near spectators of the fray, occasionally failed rightly to perceive and appreciate the Church's living voice, inspiration, and supremacy. From Episcopal Conclaves themselves, uncertain and discordant sounds issued. Councils held in the fourth century, between those of Nicæa and Constantinople, set forth Creeds purposely eluding the Nicene faith, and among them one assembled at Ariminum (Rimini), A.D. 359, consisting of more than four hundred Bishops (the number at Nicæa was about three hundred), naturally had an appearance of weight.

The late Dean Goode, in the second volume of his large and learned work, *The Divine Rule of Faith and Practice* (p. 130), cites from St Augustine a striking passage, in which the ill-judged and virtually destructive reasoning of Protestants, is anticipated. The Dean writes; "Nay, even in the highest points, not only is Catholic consent incapable of proof, but the partial consent ad-

duced is met by counter-statements, pleading an opposing witness
of equal authority.

For instance, take the case of Arian, Nestorian, or Pelagian
errors. Arius, as we have seen, appealed to Antiquity as in his
favour, and not only were there several dissentients to the decision
come to at Nice, but not long after, at another Council composed
of nearly twice as many Bishops, *the opposite doctrine was maintained.* Can we appeal, then, to the decision of the Nicene
Council as infallible, as binding the conscience to belief, as
authoritative? Augustine knew better than to do so. When
disputing with Maximinus the Arian, what is his language?
"But now," he says, (*i.e.*, while arguing this question), "neither
ought I to bring forward the Nicene Council, nor you that of
Ariminum, as if we could thus settle the question. Neither am
I bound by the authority of the one, nor you by the authority of
the other. We must argue the matter point with point, cause
with cause, reason with reason, *by authorities of Scripture*, witnesses not belonging to any party, but common to both. Was
not this, then, to make Scripture the *Judge* of the controversy?"

This much at least is plain; without a Tribunal of appeal,
authoritative and unambiguous in its sentence, the controversy
over Christ's Deity will be a wasting one for Orthodoxy.
Whether the Bible or the Church is assumed to be the Divinely-
commissioned Legislator and Judge, two things are absolutely
necessary, the legislative and judicial authority must be unques-
tioned, the laws and decisions clearly stated. If either of these
things is wanting, the storms of theological dissension will continue, except in so far as they give place to contemptuous indifference. Make Holy Scripture the sole standard, clothe every
sentence, word, and syllable, in the mantle of infallible inspiration,
and what is gained for Orthodox Protestantism, if the sense of
Scripture is too latent, or too equivocally expressed, for reason's
recognition? If disputes are to be ended in favour of Orthodoxy,
an interpreting voice is needed, whose prerogative will be magnified in the same proportion as Scripture is exalted. Make Holy
Scripture subordinate, and subsidiary to the Church, in the scheme
of revealing Instrumentality, and then, however intrinsically
mysterious the doctrine, there will be no cause to complain of
inadequate statement, while the assumption of unerring guidance
may be as reasonably made on behalf of the Church, as on behalf
of the Bible. But if, in compliance with the fundamental axiom
of Protestantism, the Church is dethroned from both revealing
and interpreting supremacy, the doctrine in aid of which Mr

Liddon has contended, will vanish from the Creed of Protestants. Not being the plain, ascertainable meaning of the Sacred Writers, and not having been entrusted to any other Divinely-appointed Channel, it will be classed among seemingly kindred examples of human error. The history of mankind notifies a tendency to exalt and Deify not only personified ideals, but also the Founders and Renovators of religious faiths.   In the absence of clearly pronounced, ordaining Revelation, the dogma of our Lord's Divinity is sure to be measured from the basis of this tendency, and so measured, the figure of Jesus as He appears in the three first Gospels, would be judged to have grown under the progressive action of hallowing imagination, into His figure as conceived by the fourth Evangelist, and that again, after a struggle with Monotheistic tradition and instinct, to have been expanded into Coessential Godhead, nominally One with the Father, to allay the alarms of Monotheism,—Personally a Being distinct from the Father, to satisfy the old Polytheistic propensity which had always bribed speculation to dilute the sublime truth that, ' the Only True God, the One God and Father, is a Spirit, an Invisible King of the ages, Whom never man saw, nor can see.'

Thoughtful believers in the Deity of Jesus Christ, cannot be grounded and settled in their faith, without the conception of a revealing Church to whose guardianship Christian doctrine has for all time been committed, and through whose assenting and formally certifying voice the great stages in the unfolding growth of doctrine have been, from time to time, announced. The incompetence of Protestantism for Orthodox ends, becomes daily more perceptible and more perceived. The conclusion forces itself upon men's minds, that adherence to Protestantism signifies abandonment of Orthodoxy ; adherence to Orthodoxy, abandonment of Protestantism. Those various Protestant communities which, differing in much else, concur in persistently proclaiming the Catholic doctrine of Christ's Person, are surely paving the way for large accessions to the Catholic Church. Intellectual consistency, though temporarily violated, will eventually triumph, and individuals who are unable to renounce the dogma, will, in multiplying numbers, accept along with the dogma, the only foundation on which the dogma can logically rest.

The doctrine most assiduously, though after an injudicious mode, defended by Mr Liddon, has a tendency when made a *sine quâ non*, and clung to as the heart and citadel of Christian Faith, to turn the eyes of the understanding, and attract the heart, towards the beauty of the ancient Organization which our forefathers deserted. This tendency, long dormant, and suspected by few, now exerts itself with accumulating force, as the unnoted impulse of traditionalism, carried away by the Reformed Churches in their revolt, becomes sufficiently relaxed to be the subject of sober and unprejudiced inquiry.

Trinitarian Nonconformists in this country, vauntingly proclaim their attachment to Reformation principles, and especially to the notion, that Holy Scripture reasonably understood, is a supreme and sufficient Rule of Faith; but if they set store by their Protestantism, let them take heed lest the Catholic dogma, faithfully cherished, should entail gravitation towards the duly accredited Catholic Body. English Dissenters, who are steadfast in their Orthodoxy, may learn to see that complete truth is the heritage and ever-enlarging treasure of the Divinely-inhabited Church, and is not, as they once fondly imagined, deducible from Scripture by individual searching and judgment. The more steadily they resist the inducements of Rationalism, and repudiate a form of religion which has no better foundations than faith in God, in conscience, in a future life, and in Christ as God's inspired Servant and Messenger, the more prevailingly will they be drawn to retrace the steps, and forsake the tenets, of their revolutionary ancestors. Startling as the thought of such a transformation may appear, they will probably yet perceive the traditions of the Church to be as precious as, and more revealing than, the Written Word, and will acknowledge Bishops alone to be endowed with the right and the power of announcing and imposing what is pure and legitimate in Christian doctrine.

In the Church of England, Protestant elements are confessedly balanced by elements of an opposite kind, and the recurrence to pre-Reformation principles is, therefore, less obviously necessary than among professors of Puritan Christianity. But though the departure from definite, unmutilated Catholicism has been, among us, less wide and fundamental than among our Nonconforming fellow-countrymen, and has left us, on one side of our Church's teaching, more tenable ground, yet, even within the Anglican Communion, jealously tenacious retention of the grand Ecclesiastical dogma will work towards an eventual restoration of unity, and contribute to heal the Disruption of the sixteenth century, by attracting our fragment into union with the main body of Christendom. It is, indeed, impossible to ponder the historical manifestations and the individual influence of the dogma, without feeling in how great a degree the Deity of Jesus is the sap and fibre of the whole Ecclesiastical system. The methods and details of dogmatic Orthodoxy have been penetrated with it, and unfolded around it by intrinsic connection and natural growth. For all the distinctive doctrinal characteristics of Catholic Christendom, the belief that Jesus Christ is God, appears to be directly or indirectly responsible.

And by this belief, far more than by anything else, Evangelical Churchmanship and Orthodox Protestantism are at the present hour instigated and sustained, in their virulent, but inconsistent and impotent, antagonism towards free religious thought. Modern Evangelicals, whether Churchmen or Nonconformists, are not the true intellectual progeny of the Reformation. The Anglican Reformers, and the Puritans, had valid excuses—which advancing knowledge has deprived of validity—for their adherence to traditional dogma. The questions to which modern criticism has given birth, could have been anticipated by very few in the sixteenth and seventeenth centuries ; and preconceptions, rooted through forty zealously-assenting generations, disguised for a season the fact that, together with a freely-consulted Bible, the pretensions of Rational, as opposed to Ecclesiastical, Monotheism, must be at no distant date urgently revived. The revival was at first within a narrow circle, and expressed itself through arguments too refined and intellectual to kindle popular sympathy ; but in the maxims of the Reformation it found the food of an intense and imperishable life. Indeed, nothing less than the safeguard discarded by the Reformers—authority, imperiously ruling interpretation—could have preserved the doctrine of Christ's Deity intact amid the destructively free handling applied to other portions of the Church's system. Protestant principle commanded the whole dogmatic field, and openly-avowed reserves and exemptions were impossible. The extremest forms of prostration before, and arbitrary assumption about, the Bible, were never imagined to protect the contents of the Bible from diligent searching and reasonable exposition. And, upon the axioms enunciated by the Reformers, no preliminary conceptions respecting the inspiration, the purposes, and the sole supremacy of the Sacred Volume, could eventually escape rational scrutiny, and, if needful, corrective modification.

Two dangers, therefore, threatened the tenet of Christ's actual Personal Deity ; the nearer and more obvious danger springing out of deferential but reasonable interpretation, and the remote and unforeseen danger springing out of unrestrained historical and critical investigation into the origin, authenticity, and general claims and warranty, of the Canonical Books themselves. Both dangers have established their reality, have acquired formidable proportions, and are now menacing with accumulated force and urgency. The tree planted by the Reformation has borne unexpected and unwelcome fruits. The Latitudinarian theory maintained by Jeremy Taylor, Archbishop Tillotson, and others : ' Reason is the judge ; that is, we, who are the persons to be persuaded, must see that we be persuaded reasonably '—is the expression of fundamental Protestantism, and is cruelly adverse to conclusions accepted when faith was capacious and eager, intelligence and morality contracted and slow.

Protestants are not the legitimate, and cannot be the efficient, champions of traditional dogma. Their attempted action in a province not properly theirs, either ends in their gravitation towards the Church-system they repudiate, or wins their consent to the Rationalism they assail. Within the Anglican Establishment, the former of these results has been conspicuous since the avidity displayed by the Evangelicals in the prosecution of two contributors to the memorable volume, *Essays and Reviews.* The temporary coalition with High Churchmen, for the ejection of moderate and cautious exponents of Protestant liberty in thought, has been followed by the arrested growth and rapid decline of the Evangelical Party. Whether this sequence of events is to be viewed as a recompense of reward, or, of punishment, is a point about which opinions will naturally differ. Catholics will recognize a Divine gift and blessing in the reviving perception of the Church's prerogatives ; consistent Protestants will discern a well-merited righteous retribution, in the paralysis of a Party which, in the hour of trial, spurned the offspring of its own principles, and deserted the work God had given it to do. The Protestantism which refuses now to go forward, is, in the judgment of every Liberal thinker, apostate, and doomed to speedy extinction.

And, ' to go forward,' unquestionably means, to relinquish, as conditions of Christian fellowship and brotherhood, the Nicene and Athanasian definitions of the Divine Nature. Intelligible Monotheism, practically exhibited in the exclusive worship with the honours due to Deity, of the ' One God and Father of all,' is the heart and essence of Progressive, as opposed to Conservative, theology. To set forth this issue distinctly, and to expose the mischievously untenable and mentally debasing nature of Orthodox Protestant pretensions to stand upon Scripture reasonably understood, is the best service to Truth that either Liberal or Catholic writers can at the present juncture render.

Between the assertors of Ecclesiastical sovereignty, and the advocates of free inquiry, there are wide and clearly-marked differences of preliminary conception, of method, and of practical teaching. Each lays at the other's door a heavy impeachment. The Catholic reproaches the Theist with leaving men to wander in the mazes of speculation, unchecked and unguided; with abandoning the essentials of Christianity, and shaping the details of education and conduct without regard to God's Revealed Will. The Theist retorts, by pointing to the effects of Catholic teaching, and declaring that Ecclesiastical dogmas have darkened the mind, diminished faith, lowered morality, hampered and twisted the devotional instincts, and stereotyped ideas of God and God's dealings, calculated to retard the soul's progress, and defraud mankind of half the benefits attainable through an undogmatic, simple, and pure Christianity.

These retaliatory accusations contain matter for interminable debate, and, as to their truth or falsehood, I am not called to offer an opinion; but the incapacity of Protestantism, logically and morally, to curtail Christian fellowship by the imposition of Catholic doctrine is, I think, a fact demonstrable to the great majority of honestly-inquiring minds. The particular doctrine so eloquently re-stated in the Bampton Lectures for 1866, may be the grandest and most profitable among Christian verities, but it rests upon the foundation of Church authority, and falls when the support of that authority is withdrawn. In enforced association with Protestantism, it is totally out of place; and whatever advantages may attend it elsewhere, its imposition as an Article of Faith within the Churches of the Reformation, is unwarranted and demoralizing.

SUPPLEMENTARY NOTE.

A PAMPHLET on *The Thirty-nine Articles and the Creeds, By a Country Parson*, has recently come into my hands. It is written with undeniable vigour and acuteness, in the form of conversations, wherein an Archdeacon, a Dean, a Diocesan Chancellor, and a Bishop, are the interlocutors. The following extract illustrates portions of my argument, by showing how next to impossible is explicit statement of Trinitarian dogma in conjunction with the fundamental truth of the Divine Unity. If my readers should think the reasoning unfair or defective, they can exercise their minds in trying to amend it, and will at least reap the benefit of learning to measure more equitably the wisdom and moral rectitude displayed by some Protestant Communities, in enforcing, as an item of necessary belief, a tenet which the thought of a Monotheist cannot grasp, and the vocabulary of a Monotheist cannot, without logical contradiction, be used to express :—

Dean.—I fear that in your reading of our first Article there is a little quibble between God and Godhead, between Θεός, the Living God, and τὸ Θεῖον, the Godhead, the Divine, the generic term of the old philosophers, under which they spoke of one deity or of many, according as they discoursed with the initiated who believed in One, or with the vulgar who believed in many. Let us try to avoid heathenish ambiguity by writing down the shortest propositions, that we may keep them steadily before us. Will you allow me to write down as certain verities the two, *A* and *B*, thus?—

    A. God the Father is the one true God.

    B. The one true God is God the Father.

Archdeacon.—They are both undeniably true.

Dean.—And the two *C*, *D*, thus?—

    C. God the Son is the one true God.

    D. The one true God is God the Son.

Archdeacon.—These are both true, like the former pair.

Dean.—Then if all four be true, the first and the fourth are both true, thus :—

  A. God the Father is the one true God.

  D. The one true God is God the Son.

Are these fairly put together? What follows from them?

Archdeacon.—Of course, by mere logic, that God the Father is God the Son ; but, because I acknowledge the Christian verities in your premisses, I am not responsible for your false conclusion. There is something wrong.

Dean.—The premisses *A*, *D*, are your own, and you logically drew the conclusion. If the premisses are right, there can be nothing wrong, unless the shortest and plainest step that human reason can take from truth to truth is something wrong.

Archdeacon.—Ah ! I see my oversight : your propositions, *B* and *D*, ought both to be—The one true God is God the Father, God the Son, and God the Holy Ghost. That is the Church's full truth.

Dean.—Then call that *E*, and write it under *A*, thus :—

  A. God the Father is the one true God.

  E. The one true God is God the Father, God the Son, and God the Holy Ghost.

These are your premisses—now draw the conclusion.

Archdeacon.—I decline ; I am not bound by your logical methods. I will maintain the Catholic Faith in the Church's perfect language—but not your contradictions.

Dean.—Then I must draw it for you : it follows of necessity that God the Father is God the Father and God the Son and God the Holy Ghost, which is nonsense and impossible, unless God the Son and God the Holy Ghost are either each of them nothing at all, or somehow nothing when taken together. This would make the conclusion into—

  God the Father is God the Father,

which is undeniably true.

Archdeacon.—My dear friend, you and I are both out of our depth in this great mystery. All this was quite familiar to the Nicene Fathers, and belongs to the most profound investigation into the Holy Trinity. It is nothing else than the sublime truth of the περιχώρησις, whereby Each of the Persons is in Each, Each in All, All in Each, and All in All.

Dean.—So *it is* a contradiction, and also *not* a contradiction, but the sublimity and profundity of the περιχώρησις. What is your derivation of that famous word ?

Archdeacon.—Of course from περί, *round about*, and χωρέω, *I move on ;* it is a figurative word, drawn from the mystery of circular motion.

Dean.—As you say, it is a figure in theological science. I can easily show you an illustration. You see this metal disk, moveable on an axis, a gyroscope top of my grandchild's. I put three white wafers on the disk, which you can conceive to symbolize the three Persons of the Trinity. Now, I whirl the disk rapidly round—what do you see?

Archdeacon.—I see one complete circle of white.

Dean.—That is the περιχώρησις„ or, if you prefer it, the ἐνύπαρξις. Don't you agree with me that both these renowned words may be well rendered by the English word *Allroundinallation ?*

Archdeacon.—I have been over hasty in allowing you to write the proposition *E.* The Catholic doctrine is not exactly that, but this : " In Unity of this Godhead there are three Persons—God the Father, God the Son, and God the Holy Ghost.

Dean.—I thought you would get tired of the word God, and recur to the Godhead. It is fatiguing to stand long on one leg, when Nature has given us two. A change is comfortable. So you may stand on the other leg. We will talk a little about the Godhead. But, first, are we quite agreed that the Godhead, the Divine Nature, and the Divine Substance all mean exactly the same Object of thought ?

Archdeacon.—Assuredly they do ; the comparison of the Latin and the English first Article with the Athanasian Creed proves that they have all one and the same meaning.

Dean.—From the second Article, which affirms that "two whole and perfect natures, the Godhead and the Manhood, were joined together in One Person," namely, the Second Person of the Trinity, we are quite sure, are we not? of the proposition *F.* I now write :—

F. The whole Godhead is in God the Son.

Archdeacon.—This *F* is infallibly true.

Dean.—And from the first Article, which affirms that all the Three Persons are in the Unity of the Godhead, are we not quite as certain of this proposition, *G ?*

G. God the Son is in the whole Godhead.
I do not know what you understand by the Godhead, or the whole Godhead, different from " the one Living and true God ;" but I hope *you* know what you mean. All that I ask is your assurance that *F* and *G* are both alike true.

Archdeacon.—I am certain that they are both alike true.

Dean.—If *F* be true, the following must be true :—

H. God the Son is not less than the whole Godhead ;
for, if He were, the whole Godhead could not be in God the Son.
And if *G* be true, this *I* must be true :—

I. God the Son is not greater than the whole Godhead ;
for, if He were, He could not be in the Godhead, as the first
Article affirms Him to be. Are these propositions, *H* and *I*,
quite true ?

Archdeacon.—What right have you to introduce these terms of
quantity, *greater* and *less*, into propositions about the Trinity ?

Dean.—I am only doing what is already done in the Articles
and in the Athanasian Creed. The Church makes propositions
containing *whole*, and *greater*, and *less*, and *equal*, about the Three
Persons.

Archdeacon.—I agree that she does; and I confidently affirm
your two propositions to be true, namely :—

H. God the Son is not less than the whole Godhead.

I. God the Son is not greater than the whole Godhead.
They are the Church's plain teaching; but I am not bound by
the methods of your long-winded logic.

Dean.—I shall not be long, as you will see ; and now you may
stand on both your venerable legs. For from *H* and *I*, whether
you will or no, follows this proposition *J* :—

J. God the Son is verily and truly the whole Godhead ;
for He is neither greater nor less than it.

Archdeacon.—Of course the Church has always taught that
each of the Three Persons has in Himself the whole undivided
Godhead.

Dean.—I ask, are you content with the truth *J*, as I have
deduced it from *H* and *I* ? If it is faulty, show me where.

Archdeacon.—I allow that it is true as it stands, by inevitable
necessity of consequence from *H* and *I*.

Dean.—Look now at the first Article : ' in Unity of this Godhead there be Three Persons, of one Substance, power, and eternity; the Father, the Son, and the Holy Ghost.' I ask you, is
the whole Godhead in any way greater than the Three Persons ?

Archdeacon.—Certainly not.

Dean.—I ask, again, is the whole Godhead in any way less
than the Three Persons ?

Archdeacon.—It cannot possibly be less.

Dean.—Then, it is not in any way unequal to the Three Persons ; wherefore it is equal to them ; and this *K* must be true.

K. The whole Godhead is God the Father, God the Son,
and God the Holy Ghost.

Is this true or not true?

Archdeacon.—Assuredly true.

Dean.—Now we write *J* and *K* together.

> *J.* God the Son is verily and truly the whole Godhead.
>
> *K.* The whole Godhead is God the Father, God the Son, and God the Holy Ghost.

From these follows by the inexorable law of human thought,—

> *L.* God the Son is verily and truly God the Father, God the Son, and God the Holy Ghost;

that is, either God the Father is nothing at all, and God the Holy Ghost is nothing, or else both together they make nothing. Thus the quibble between God and Godhead cannot save you from the absurdities before demonstrated from the propositions *A* and *E*. Of course you will content yourself with the same reply—the περιχώρησις again.

Archdeacon.—And of course you know that reply has been sufficient for the last 1800 years. You have said nothing new—nothing that has not been answered a thousand times.

Dean.—I wish you all the comfort you can have from that popular consideration, and I am exceedingly obliged to you for standing your ground so well. It must be a long time since two men of our age and reading spent as much time on these ancient quibbles with zeros and infinites. I shall keep a little note of our conversation, which will read as something very new; for in truth no man now-a-days ever either condescends to attack, or is required to defend those Athanasian contradictions, so that while thinkers have felt ashamed of such inglorious assaults, many dunces on your side have begun to fancy their positions inexpugnable.

.   .   .   .   .   .

Chancellor.—What dangerous combustibles these old dogmas are! I see no way of escape, unless by moistening the powder with my distinction of personal and substantial. You can go to the Dean, and tell him that you accept the conclusion *L* thus :—

> *L'.* God the Son is substantially God the Father, God the Son, and God the Holy Ghost.

Archdeacon.—Yes, and I shall put in the *verily and truly*, and say this—

> *L''.* God the Son is substantially, verily, and truly God the Father, God the Son, and God the Holy Ghost.

Of course I deny that He is such *personally :* but the Dean cannot say that I deny the logical conclusion *L*, when I declare that I accept it *substantially, verily, and truly.*

Chancellor.—Here comes the Bishop. We must even ask his

Lordship. Let me write the whole argument from *A, B, C, D,* down on a clear page of your pocket-book.

So he wrote it, ending thus—

A. God the Father is the one true God ;

D. The one true God is God the Son ;

Ergo, salvâ Trinitate in Unitate.

P. God the Father is God the Son ; *id est,*

R. God the Father is substantially God the Son, although—

Q. God the Father is not personally God the Son.

·   ·   ·   ·   ·   ·

Bishop.—It is most perilous heresy, or next door to it, to make one Person of the Trinity the subject, and another the predicate, of any negative proposition whatever ; for by so doing you reduce them to finite personalities. I am myself, but I am not either of you two ; the Archdeacon is himself, but he is neither the Bishop nor the Chancellor, who is also himself, and is not either of the other two. This is the way in which we affirm, and it is the only way in which we can affirm, our own limited personalities. If now you say that the Persons of the Trinity are so related really and in Themselves, that the Father can say—I am Myself, but am not You the Son, nor You the Holy Ghost ; that the Son can say—I am Myself, but am not the Father nor the Holy Ghost ; and that the Holy Ghost can say—I am Myself, but I am neither the Father nor the Son—you have three Persons mutually limiting and excluding each other ; that is, three finite persons, and not one of them the Infinite and the Absolute, which the one true God of necessity must be. Thus you undeify the Divine Persons. The same thing may be shown thus :—Suppose a man to pretend that God the Son is not God the Father in Person, then you can reason thus :—

God the Father in Person is the only true God ;

God the Son is not God the Father in Person ;

Ergo, God the Son is not the only true God,

which is absurd and blasphemous, proving the absurdity of the man's pretence in the second premiss ; for the first premiss is infallibly true ; and the absurdity remains if you erase the words " in Person " from the premisses.

Archdeacon.—But surely, my lord, in some sense or other the Son is not the Father, for the Church clearly distinguishes the Three Persons one from the other, in the Catechism, the Creeds, and the Articles.

Bishop.—*Distinguishes* is not the right word. The Church affirms their co-existence, enumerates them and names them ; and she takes care to teach the child to enumerate and to name them. Of difference of existence apart from that inherent in the pure order of Personality, she says not a word, and above all she never writes a *not* between any two of them. "There is one Person of the Father, another of the Son, and another of the Holy Ghost:" this is far from affirming a distinction and difference between any two. On the contrary, "Such as the Father is, such is the Son, and such is the Holy Ghost." They are not *different;* They are *other* by number and by name; nor are They *identical :* They are One *such as* Another, *qualis talis,* in the Latin. If I may be allowed as a Bishop to coin a term of theological science, I should say that the relation between the Persons of the Trinity is neither of identity nor of difference, but of a certain mutual and mystical *qualitality.* But in these profound mysteries it is always safest to employ the exact words of the Creeds; and it is a perilous thing to swerve by a hair'sbreadth from them. Also remember above all that the numerical character is not that of three things; not a Trinity in *triplicity,* but a Trinity in *unity.* I hope I have made this clear to you.

Archdeacon.—As clear, perhaps, as the subject can be made.

Chancellor.—Almost as clear as it was to me when, at six years of age, I learned my Catechism. I could count Them and name Them then, and I can count Them and name Them now; and that exhausts all the conception that I shall ever get of the matter, except that it is a qualitalitive threeness, not at all in threeness, but in oneness.

INDEX

TO

TEXTS SPECIALLY REFERRED TO.

GENESIS.
i. 26 . . 46
iii. 22 . . 46
xi. 7 . . 46
xix. 24 . . 48
xlix. 10 . . 55

EXODUS.
iii. 14 . . 232

NUMBERS.
vi. 23-26 . . 47

DEUTERONOMY.
vi. 4 . . . 47
vi. 13 . . . 260

2 SAMUEL.
vii. 14 . . . 181
vii. 16 . . . 56

PSALMS.
ii. 7, 12 . 56, 112
xvi. 10 . . 137
xlv. 6, 7 . . 57
lxxii. . . 58
lxxxii. 1, 6 . . 229
lxxxix. 26, 27 . 181
cx. i. . . 58

PROVERBS.
viii. 22 . . 51

ISAIAH.
vi. 3 . . . 47
vi. 8 . . . 46
vii. 14 . . . 63
ix. 6 . . . 61
xi. 3 . . . 60

JEREMIAH.
xxiii. 5 . . 62
xxxi. 31-35 . 60

DANIEL.
iii. 25 . . 180
vii. 13, 14 . . 236

HOSEA.
xi. 1 . . . 181

HAGGAI.
ii. 7-9 . 66

ZECHARIAH.
ii. 10-13 . . 65
xii. 10 . . 65
xiii. 7 . . 63

MALACHI.
iii. 1 . . . 66

ST MATTHEW.
i. 23 . . . 63
ii. 15 . . . 181
iv. 8-10 . . 260
v. 22, et seq. . 198
vii. 29. . . 197
ix. 6 . . . 216
x. 32 . . . 241
x. 37 . . 217, 241
x. 40 . . . 75
xi. 27 . . . 245
xi. 28, 29 . . 242
xvi. 16, 17 . 87, 238
xxii. 41-45 . . 58
xxiii. 8-10 . . 241
xxiv. 14 . 77, 243
xxv. 31-46 . 214-216
xxvi. 63, 64 . 237
xxvii. 46 . . 193
xxvii. 54 . . 237
xxviii. 17 . . 258
xxviii. 19, 20 78, 243

ST MARK.
x. 17, 18 . . 195
xi. 12-14 . . 77
xiii. 32 . . 296
xv. 39 . . 237
xvi. 12 . . 285

ST LUKE.
i. 68, 69 . . 159
i. 76 . . . 81
ii. 52 . . . 295
ix. 26 . . . 157
x. 22 . . . 245
xiv. 26 . . 217
xxviii. 18, 19 . 195
xxii. 30 . . 74
xxii. 42, 44 . 193

xxiii. 42 . . 259
xxiii. 47 . . 237
xxiv. 51-53 . . 258

ST JOHN.
i. 1 . 82, 88, 318
i. 18 . . . 320
ii. 19 . . . 136
iii. 34 . . . 84
iv. 10-26 . . 262
iv. 14, 23, 24 . 202
iv. 22 . . . 202
v. 17, 18 . 220-223
v. 21-30 . . 204
v. 23 . . . 205
v. 26, 44 . . 201
vi. 32-63 . . 202
vi. 39 . . . 204
vi. 57 . . . 201
vii. 16, 17 . . 197
viii. 12 . . 200
viii. 12-57 . . 233
viii. 23, 38, 44 . 203
viii. 28, 40 . . 197
viii. 42 . . . 209
viii. 58 . 231-237
ix. 35, 38 . . 254
x. 8 . . . 202
x. 18 . . . 136
x. 28, 29 . . 226
x. 30 . . 224-228
x. 31-36 . . 228
x. 37, 38 . . 230
xi. 25 . . . 204
xii. 49, 50 . . 197
xiv. 1-6 . . 201
xiv. 9, 10 . 219, 220
xiv. 11 . . 33
xiv. 14 . . 203
xiv. 15, 24 . . 207
xiv. 23 . 213, 214
xiv. 26 . . 43
xiv. 28 . 208-210
xv. 1-3 . . 203
xv. 15 . . 198
xvi. 13 . . 126

PAGE

xvi. 20-23 . . 263
xvii. 3 . 211-213
xvii. 22 . . 101
xviii. 36 . . 74
xix. 7 . . 237
xix. 35 . . 43
xx. 17 . 250, 258
xx. 28 239, 258, 320

ACTS.

i. 2 . . . 86
i. 24. . . 271
ii. 21. . . 280
ii. 24 . . 137
ii. 33 . . 138
iii. 15 . . 134
iii. 16 . . 139
iii. 21 . . 137
iv. 9-12 . . 139
vii. 37 . . 269
vii. 59, 60 . 266-270
ix. 6 . . 274
ix. 13, 14 . . 273
ix. 14, 21 . . 264
x. 36 . . 138
x. 42 . . 268
xv. 7 . . 272
xv. 28 . . 157
xvii. 18-31 . . 150
xvii. 31 . . 268
xx. 18-36 . . 150
xx. 28 . . 151
xxii. 16. . . 265
xxii. 17-21 . . 274

ROMANS.

iii. 30 . . 175
viii. 29 . . 302
ix. 5 . . 93-98
x. 9-13 . . 280
x. 13 . 158, 264
xi. 36 . 107, 170
xvi. 25-27 . . 175

1 CORINTHIANS.

i. 2 . . 264
i. 30 . . 164
i. 31 . . 158
ii. 8 . . 131
ii. 11 . . 33
iii. 23 . . 175
vi. 15 . . 304
viii. 4-6 . . 169
x. 16 . . 161

PAGE

xi. 3 . . 175
xi. 27-29 . . 161
xii. 3 . . 126
xv. 28 . . 174
xv. 45 . . 303
xvi. 23, 24 . . 156

2 CORINTHIANS.

i. 3 . . 175
xi. 31 . . 175
xii. 8, 9 . . 282
xiii. 5 . . 303
xiii. 14 . . 156

GALATIANS.

i. 1 . . 156
i. 15, 16 . . 152
iii. 20 . . 175
iv. 14 . . 176

EPHESIANS.

i. 3, 6, 13 . . 162
i. 17 . . 175
ii. 18 . . 162
iii. 6 . . 162
iv. 6 . . 171
v. 22-24 . . 176
v. 30. . . 304

PHILIPPIANS.

ii. 6-11 99-102, 163, 284
ii. 19 . . 278
iv. 13 . . 103

COLOSSIANS.

i. 15-17 . 103 *sq.* 170
i. 18, 19 . 108, 109
ii. 3 . . 163
ii. 9 . 109, 110

1 THESSALONIANS.

iii. 11 . . 276

2 THESSALONIANS.

ii. 16, 17 . . 276

1 TIMOTHY.

i. 12 . . 278
i. 17 . . 173
ii. 5, 6 . . 172
iii. 16 . 157, 172
v. 21 . . 157
vi. 15, 16 . . 173

2 TIMOTHY.

ii. 22 . . 266

PAGE

TITUS.

ii. 13 . 92

HEBREWS.

i. 2 . . 114
i. 3 . 113, 114
i. 5 . 112, 181
i. 6 . 114, 261
i. 8, 9 . 57, 111
i. 10-12 . 115
ii. 18 . 115
iv. 15 . . 115
v. 7 . . 115
vii. 3 . . 116
vii. 26 . . 192
xii. 23, 24 . . 157

ST JAMES.

i. 21 . . 127
ii. 1 . . 131
iv. 12 . . 129

1 ST PETER.

i. 7, 8 . . 142
i. 11 . . 141
i. 12 . . 142
i. 23 . . 143
ii. 22, 23 . . 193
iii. 21, 22 . . 144
iv. 11 . 144, 287

2 ST PETER.

i. 1 . . 93, 144
i. 3, 4 . . 145
iii. 18 . . 146

1 ST JOHN.

v. 13-15 . . 287
v. 20 . . 90

ST JUDE.

4 . . 147
25 . . 148

REVELATION.

i. 5, 6 . . 288
i. 17 . 120, 256
ii. 8 . . 120
iii. 1 . . 121
iii. 5 . . 157
iii. 12 . . 122
iii. 14 . . 120
v. 5-13 . 123, 287
xix. 12-16 . . 121
xix. 16 . . 122
xxii. 21 . . 122

INDEX

TO

QUOTATIONS AND SOME PRINCIPAL TOPICS.

PAGE

Alford, Dean ; *How to study the New Testament* . . . 162
——, —— ; quoted by Mr Liddon 283
——, —— ; his *Revised Version*, remarks upon . . . 284
Ante-Nicene Fathers, the doubtful language of 321
Apocalypse, Christology of the 119–124
Athenæum, on the Ignatian Epistles 36
Atonement, certain assumptions respecting . . 13, 298, 299
Baptismal Formula, what the Apostolic ? . . . 79, 243
Basilides, was he cognizant of the Gospel 'according to St John' . 37
Bloomfield, Dr S. T. ; *Notes on the Greek Testament* . 78, 170, 273
——, —— ; *Lexicon to Greek Testament* 206
Bull, Bishop ; *Defensio Fidei Nicænæ* 286
Christian Charity ; how related to the Dogma of Christ's Deity . 309
Conybeare and Howson ; *Life and Epistles of St Paul* . 54, 113
Councils, the discordant voices of 324
Creeds ; the Three ; differences of, &c. . . . 312–315
Davidson, Dr S. ; *Introduction to the Old Testament* 46, 51, 59, 64, 66, 137
——, —— ; *Introduction to the New Testament* . 38, 80, 84, 121, 122, 244
——, —— ; Articles in *The Theological Review* 41, 48, 50, 69, 70, 122, 137
De Bunsen, Ernest ; *Hidden Wisdom of Christ* . . . 35, 42
Donaldson, Dr James ; *Critical History of Christian Doctrine, &c.* 38, 83
Ellicott, Bishop, quoted by Mr Liddon 92, 278
Ewald, Professor, quoted by Mr Liddon 39
——, —— ; his *Life of Christ* 136
First-born, the Title considered 105
Form of God, meaning of the expression . . . 101, 285, 286
Fourth Gospel, authorship of the 36–44, 184
——, —— ; Justin Martyr's knowledge of the . . . 38
Fuerst ; *Hebrew Lexicon,* 47, 64, 65
God, how often is Jesus so called ? 320
God the Son, not a Scriptural Title 177
Goode, Dean ; *Divine Rule of Faith, &c.* 325
Gospels, the ; their Origin and Purity . . . 34, 181, 244
Hebrews, the Epistle to the, Christology of . . 112–117

                                                             PAGE

Hengstenberg; *On the Apocalypse* 119

Human perfections ; can they co-exist with Personal Godhead?   301–306

Image of God, the Title considered . . . 103, 104, 286

Jesus Christ; Catholic Dogma respecting His Person, 30, 31, 194. Difficulties attaching to the Dogma, 32–34, 86, 102, 106, 184–187, 192–194, 313–315. His exceptional Mission, Offices, &c., explain the Scriptural language concerning Him, 155, 160, 217. His own plainest sayings, when not Ecclesiastically interpreted, adverse to the conception of His Deity, 249, 250.

Jowett, Professor; *Commentary on St Paul* . . 96, 164, 300

——, ——; *Essay on Interpretation* . . . 6, 29

Leeser, Isaac; *Translation of the Old Testament* . . . 62, 65

Macknight, Dr James; *On the Epistles* . . . 99, 287

Mill, John Stuart 27

Muller Max, Professor ; *Semitic Monotheism* . . . 46

Muratori, the Canon of 39

Neander; *Life of Christ* 136, 216, 224, 244

Norton, Andrews ; *Statement of Reasons, &c.* . 227, 232

Only-begotten, force of the designation 186

Oxenham, H. N. ; *Catholic Doctrine of the Atonement* . 321

Perowne, J. J. S., *On the Psalms* . . . 57, 67, 137

Philo Judæus, his relation to the Fourth Gospel . . 53

Prologue, The, of the Fourth Gospel . . . 81–86, 88

Prophecy, Messianic, the Three Stages of . . . 55–66

Pusey, Professor, cited by Mr Liddon . . . 64

Rabbinical Messianic Doctrine 68–70, 122

Religious faith and emotion, how far dependent on the Doctrine of Christ's Deity ? 310

Resurrection of Christ, ascribed to the Father's power . . 135

Réville, Albert ; *History of the Dogma of the Deity of Jesus Christ*

                                              14, 18, 314

Rowland, David ; *The Apostolic Origin of the Fourth Gospel* . 38

Schenkel, Dr D. ; *Sketch of the Character of Jesus* . . 41, 202

Schöttgen ; Canon Westcott's estimate of . . . 69

Scrivener's, F. H.; *Collation of the Codex Sinaiticus, &c.* . 145

Self-sacrifice minimized by the possession of Personal Deity   307, 308

Septuagint Version, Article on the; *Smith's Dictionary of the Bible*   61

Socrates, the Historian 324

Son of God, the Title considered 184–187

St James's Epistle, Christology of 127–133

St Jude's Epistle, Christology of 147, 148

St Paul's Discourses and Epistles, Christology of . . 150–179

St Peter's Sermons and Epistles, Christology of . . 133–146

St Paul, his Witness to the Divine Unity . . 168–179

PAGE

Stanley, Dean ; *Commentary on the Epistles to the Corinthians*   98, 282

——, —— ; *On the Litany* 291

Stuart, Moses, Professor ; *On Future Punishment* . . . 114

——, —— ; *Letters to Channing* 110, 219, 227

Summary of Philonian *Logos-epithets ;* from Dr Pye Smith . 54

Sympathy of the Divine Nature, not susceptible of Increase through Incarnation 279

Tayler, J. J. ; *On the Fourth Gospel* 38, 41

Texts, a few in the Epistles supposed expressly to assert, or clearly to imply, the Deity of Jesus Christ 89–114

Theophanies, the, in the Old Testament 48–50

Trench, Archbishop, Remarks of his on New Testament Words   138, 263

Westcott, B. F. ; *History of the Canon of the New Testament* . 39

——, —— ; *Introduction to the Study of the Gospels* . 40, 43, 69, 122

Winer, G. B. ; *Grammar of the New Testament Diction* 82, 83, 91, 93, 95, 171, 219, 231

Wisdom, in the Apocryphal Books 52

Word, or *Logos,* the Title discussed . . 81–84, 183–185

Wordsworth, Christopher, Bishop of Lincoln . . 98, 112, 280

Worship of Jesus Christ as God ; how deducible from Scripture ? 256–290